P9-AOJ-685

South of Heaven

a novel by

Patti Frye Meredith

MINT HILL BOOKS
MAIN STREET RAG PUBLISHING COMPANY
CHARLOTTE, NORTH CAROLINA

Library of Congress Control Number: 2021952853

ISBN: 978-1-59948-905-6

Produced in the United States of America

Mint Hill Books
Main Street Rag Publishing Company
PO Box 690100
Charlotte, NC 28227
www.MainStreetRag.com

To Lee

Fern

Time lingered more than passed in the Sandhills of North Carolina, where no ancient mountains or ocean tides marked the days. The Sandhills lay low, midway between. Flat land where, in summer, acres of lank-leafed tobacco flourished in spite of its fall from grace.

A venetian blind sagged over the front window of the *Citizen-Times*. Fern McQueen was careful with the tattered pull. Every morning she expected the string to unravel in her hand.

Across the way on the courthouse lawn, her son sat on a granite bench tucked beneath a white oak, a memorial to her husband, Mac, missing in action since the Vietnam War. Dean visited the bench most mornings before clocking in at Frank's Garage. "We talk, Mama," he said. "In my head." Fern had tried to dissuade her son from telling people about these "talks," knowing it only brought about more pity from the town of Carthage. But Dean was Dean. Her boy had no secrets.

Fern had never held out hope Mac would be found alive. She'd known he was gone, maybe even before the earnest men in stiff uniforms said *missing in action*. That was twenty-six years ago.

A woman whose husband had been lost on the same mission as Mac recently sent Fern a letter claiming to know about an excavation site in Laos. She said news would be coming soon. Fern had gotten other letters through the years from groups asking her to sign petitions, join their efforts. She never had. Fern believed Mac going missing was a misery dealt by the hand of God. A misery she'd brought upon herself. She'd thrown all the letters away.

With the dogwoods declaring spring, tired Christmas lights still dangled from worn cords along the flat roofline of

Moore County's sandstone courthouse. The lights remained year-round, being too much trouble to take down and put back up. Surely the strands had been replaced, but in Fern's mind, they were the same ones that glowed red and green years ago on that snowy December night that changed everything.

It was as if every way she turned, a monument stood to all she could not undo.

Fern stepped back from the window so as not to be seen by other early risers making their way to work. She knew plenty in town thought her standoffish, but she was mostly only wary of attention.

She fiddled with the tortoiseshell clip slipping from her hair. Forty-six was too old for a ponytail. Too old for hair that fell halfway down her back. But Fern had never gotten around to cutting it. Premature gray sneaked through the black like an omen. Soon she would wind her hair in a bun, declare herself a crone, and be done with it.

She settled into her unsteady chair that was more apt to tilt than swivel. She felt a strain in her wrist when she typed at her shiny new IBM computer, reminding her that despite the idle nature of time, change could come. She'd refused the sleek metal furniture sent over from the home office in Southern Pines. "Come on, lady, get with it. It's 1998," the delivery man had said.

"I'm not trading solid wood for that," she'd told him.

Her new boss, a boy nearly half her age and a recent graduate of the University of North Carolina, had instigated the upgrade. The Carthage bureau for the *Citizen-Times* was a two-person operation, and his side of the room reminded Fern of a spaceship cockpit with that chrome-legged desk and black mesh chair she wouldn't trust. Her great-grandfather had built this building across from the courthouse for a dry goods store, and to her relief, the pine floors, tin-tile ceiling, and what she couldn't help but believe was the scent of her grandmother's rosewater perfume overcame Robert Clayton Yarborough II's vision for the future.

Fern lit a Salem Light. Robert was an occasional smoker, and without discussion they had struck a bargain to break company rules. Another of his positive qualities was he rarely showed up before ten o'clock, giving Fern plenty of uninterrupted thinking time. She'd been worried when her old boss retired, but Robert had turned out to be fairly entertaining. She'd never seen anyone get so excited over a school board meeting, even though he had yet to remember exactly when and where the meetings were held. "Job security," she told her best friend, Carol Ann. "He may have a high-priced diploma, but I've got sense enough to use a calendar."

She found her daily e-mail from Thompson Funeral Home to get a start on the obituaries. Eileen Robinson. Good riddance. Eileen had been one of her daddy's high school girlfriends and hadn't liked it one bit when he eloped with Matilda Moore from Red Springs. Fern suspected Eileen had made it her mission to spread the worst gossip about her parents, not that either of them ever missed a chance to cause a scene.

Now gossip sold newspapers. Even the front page of the *Citizen-Times* featured a picture of President Clinton and that pretty intern. Stories about the President's alleged affairs printed in black and white on the front page rattled Fern. That kind of mess had been going on since the beginning of time. How come reporters wanted to talk about it all of a sudden? Robert maintained revealing the scandal "broke new ground for freedom of speech and ushered in a new era of accountability."

She'd asked him if he was familiar with the *National Enquirer*.

"We're talking about the truth, Fern," he'd said. "Everybody knows he's a hound dog. I can't believe you're defending him."

It wasn't the hound dog she was defending. She pitied the girl, her dalliance in twenty-four-point font for all to see. Fern recognized innocence in her young starstruck brown eyes. Innocence and need. A cruel combination. Fern knew how a young mistake could mark a life.

The bell over the front door jangled and a broad-shouldered man in a light gray suit stepped inside. His smile made it seem like they already shared a joke. "Too early?"

Fern covered her ashtray with yesterday's paper. No need to flaunt a bad habit. "A little, but come on in." She believed in dressing for comfort, and it wasn't like her to judge, but she thought the man's suit would benefit from a steam iron.

He reached out a hand when she came from behind her desk. "Roy Puckett, pastor at New Hope Methodist."

She'd seen him at his mailbox. "Fern McQueen. I live across the road from you." To her way of thinking, preachers were all a bunch of hypocrites, but Roy Puckett's round innocent face and curly brown hair hindered her cynical side.

"Barrett House. I read the historical marker." His accent confirmed the church's claim he came from Charleston. A widower with a young daughter, the press release said. Fern lived with her eighty-year-old aunt, and there was a time Belle would have insisted on carrying her new neighbors a cake, but with her aunt's mind slipping, those days were gone.

As tall as he was, Fern stood eye-to-eye with the preacher. "My sister Leona says if we don't paint soon the preservation people are going to take back their sign."

"Looks fine to me. I don't care to see the old places all shined up. It's unnatural." He held out an envelope. "My Faith Corner column. You probably prefer what I believe they call a floppy disc, but I'm having trouble with my computer." He looked up at the ceiling, then back to her. "It's not entirely the computer's fault. Truth is, I'm still in the dark ages."

"You'll be right at home around here," Fern said. "I feel lucky not to get these things on stone slabs."

He didn't hesitate to laugh, and she was grateful. "We rotate through all the denominations. The Presbyterians are coming up. I'll slip yours in next Friday's paper."

"Thanks," Roy said. "The deacons weren't too happy I missed the deadline."

"You're new. Folks need to cut you some slack," Fern said. "Of course, that's not what church people are known for."

Roy's eyebrows shot up and a hot flash crept across Fern's chest. "Sorry," she said, flapping the neck of her blouse. "I didn't mean any disrespect. All my people are buried at New Hope. My family used to be members until my aunt riled them up with her politics. Come to think of it, I guess the riling went both ways." Fern let out a nervous laugh, pulled a Kleenex from her pocket and dabbed sweat from her upper lip. "It was a mutual riling."

"Oh, that's the best kind," the preacher said, nodding. "Nothing like a good old mutual riling among church folks."

It took Fern a second to realize he was joking. She laughed.

"Sorry," he said. "But here's the thing. You've got to give the church another chance because if I can't even talk my neighbor into a pew, the congregation's going to think they got a dud."

"I'll think about it." Fern gave him a big smile to balance her lie.

"Good," Roy said. "Maybe we can rile them up together."

"Oh, I guarantee it," Fern said.

He checked his watch. "I better run. I have a deacons' meeting, and a conference with my daughter's teacher before that. You know Mildred Blevins?"

"Oh, yes." Fern followed him to the door. "Mildred must be a hundred years old. They can't make her retire."

"Well, she's threatened to if Hannah doesn't shape up."

Despite his chuckle, Fern sensed worry. "How old is your daughter?"

"Twelve going on twenty," he said.

"Bring her over for a visit. My Aunt Belle taught for years. She prefers rowdy children."

"I will. Thank you." He reached to open the door.

"Belle has the beginnings of Alzheimer's," Fern said, "but she has more good days than bad."

Roy turned around. "I'm sorry. It's a mean disease." He went for the door a second time.

"She quit teaching to homeschool my son, Dean, when he got expelled. In third grade."

Roy cocked his head. "Expelled?"

"He was a nervous child. He's doing fine now. Works down at Frank's Garage. He lives with us."

"Well, that's good," Roy said. He stood stone still.

Fern, embarrassed by her sudden revelations, saw he was waiting to see if she had more to confess. "You'd better get to your meeting."

This time Roy reached for the door just as it swung open.

Carol Ann gave him the once over. "Well, good morning."

Best friends since church kindergarten, Fern and Carol Ann gave credence to the platitude *opposites attract*. Carol Ann didn't wear a thing that wasn't fitted to her five-foot-four-inch frame. Tight skirts and blouses dealt with her excess curves the best they could. And while Fern wrapped her long graying hair in a loose twist that never quite stayed put, Carol Ann kept her cropped blonde 'do in a swirl of highlights and lowlights. While Carol Ann fought age tooth and nail with cosmetic dentistry and weekly manicures, Fern claimed pleasure in not giving a damn. "If I had those cheek bones, I'd be queen of a small country," Carol Ann would say.

"Carol Ann Kelley, meet Roy Puckett, the new minister at New Hope." Fern emphasized *minister*.

Carol Ann's gold bracelets rattled as she held out a hand to Roy. "Don't run off. I bet she didn't even offer you a cup of coffee."

"I better go," he said. "I'll be late getting to the deacons meeting, and you know how church people are." He winked at Fern. "Nice meeting you both."

They watched him pass by the front window.

"Did that preacher just wink at you?" Carol Ann said.

Fern tossed Roy's envelope on her desk, yanked the clip from her hot head of hair and let it fall around her shoulders. Carol Ann followed Fern into the kitchenette, heels tapping across the wood floor. Fern knew her friend expected coffee with two Sweet'N Lows, ASAP. Fern thought Carol Ann's name ought to be ASAP.

"He's just being friendly. You know how they act when they're trying to get you to church. He sure did get me talking, though. And laughing. Not sure what that was about. Must be some new preacher trick."

"Bet he's fun in the sack," Carol Ann said. "Big men always are."

"Is that all you think about?"

"When I'm not thinking about commission checks." Carol Ann found her favorite mug, the one stamped with her real estate company's logo.

Fern scooped Folgers into a filter.

"I still think you ought to see a head doctor," Carol Ann said. "Celibacy has thrown you straight into early menopause."

"Yeah, but don't the hot flashes make my cheeks rosy?"

She waited for a laugh, but Carol Ann bit her lower lip, a sign of serious news.

"What have you done now?" Fern folded her arms. Between husbands, her friend was inclined to get into some real fixes with well-off retirees who flocked to the Sandhills for golf. Fern was about to reprise her speech about the pitfalls of married men.

Carol Ann leaned against the counter. "Guess who I saw at the country club?"

"Who?" Fern couldn't help but be curious about Carol Ann's latest downfall.

"Doyle Blue."

Fern steadied herself.

"He's left his daddy-in-law's construction business in Charlotte and moved back here to start his own company. He and Martha are getting a divorce and he's living in his parent's old place." Carol Ann lifted the pot and poured all that was ready into her mug. The still-dripping coffee sizzled and spat on the hot burner. "He ordered tonic with lime, so you know he's on the wagon. And, yes, he asked about you. I told him you were running the *Citizen-Times* and hadn't aged a bit."

As the owner of Kelley Real Estate, Carol Ann was a master of exaggeration, but Fern believed her embellishment only shone light on the pitiful truth.

"Maybe it wouldn't hurt if the two of you had a heart-to-heart." Carol Ann took a sip of coffee.

"Doyle Blue's heart. Now there's a quandary." Fern filled her mug.

"I've got to get to the courthouse and pick up an escrow check." Carol Ann looked around for her purse. "Honey, don't fret. Doyle will be back in Charlotte before the gnats get bad. City people forget about summertime in the Sandhills. The humidity alone has cost me a fortune." She pulled out her lipstick and reapplied. "I mean it, don't get all worked up, okay? I just didn't want you to run into him without warning."

"How does he look?"

Carol Ann popped her lips to even out the cherry red. "He looks good. Real good."

"You didn't ..."

"Good Lord, how can you think such a thing? But speaking of, tell Robert I'm sorry I missed him."

"Don't start," Fern said. "You're old enough to be his mother's older sister." Carol Ann's crush on Fern's boy-boss was more than she could handle, and she'd handled her fair share of Carol Ann crushes.

Fern went to the door for one last wave and spotted her son's jeep down at the garage. Did Doyle Blue ever think about Dean?

She tried to get her mind on what she needed to do before Robert came crashing in asking about weekend deadlines, the Sheriff's race, and everything else he ought to already know, but instead, back at her desk, she reached for Roy Puckett's envelope and unfolded the yellow legal pad pages. His careful handwriting reminded her of a child's, one trying very hard to be understood.

Roy's words weren't what she'd expected. He admitted feeling like a failure as a single parent to his twelve-year-old daughter. Fern felt a twinge of guilt. Although she held no nostalgia for the false front of southern hospitality, she should have taken them a meal or at the very least, a plate of cookies. It wouldn't have hurt her to show kindness to a child. She remembered how lost she'd felt when Dean was coming up without a father.

But it was Roy's confession at the end that surprised her the most. He claimed losing his wife to cancer shook his faith.

Well, what do you know? An honest preacher.

Fern was unaccustomed to truth confessed. She handled Carthage's social news. Births and graduations, weddings, and anniversaries. The obits. Milestones polished up to shine. She'd often imagined slipping in the tarnished tales, believing the falls from grace truly marked a life. Who could recall a single thing Adam and Eve did before that apple got picked?

Unwilling to deceive you in any way. She'd never heard of a preacher questioning God and doubted his revelation would go over well with the congregation. He was liable to get run out of town. People professed to admire honesty, but she'd witnessed very little mercy, especially among those who prayed the loudest.

She leaned back into the chair cushion worn to fit her frame. A spindly spider dropped down, suspended in mid-air beside her computer screen. Its body not as big as the head of a straight pin. Fern figured it was a girl spider, being so delicate. She walked over to the edge and stepped off. A thread of silk caught the light. Down she went, and then up she crawled, up and down. When she finally found the floor, her brown body disappeared against the wood.

Fern knew all about dropping into the unknown. How it felt to dangle, crawl, and search for something to hold onto when all you had was the fragile thread you'd spun.

Lies, she thought. The thinnest thread of all.

Leona

L eona hadn't wanted anyone to see the house at Heron Point until she had everything exactly right, but March brought seventy-degree days to the North Carolina coast and her husband insisted on taking his doctor friends down for a golf weekend.

She and Ned had spent over a year driving the two hours to the coast for weekend meetings with their builder. The glass-front contemporary on the intercoastal waterway was nothing like their traditional home in Raleigh. Muted colors and coarse textures blended with the water, sand, and sky. Not one electrical outlet had been left to chance.

With Heron Point, they embraced a minimalist décor to showcase original art collected throughout their marriage. They'd spent whole days sitting in the empty rooms to see how the light changed so each piece would be flawlessly lit.

Leona imagined her Raleigh friends asking who did the interior design and answering, "Ned and I."

Saturday morning, she picked up a painting from the framers. A gift from Ned for her fiftieth birthday. The snow-white egret barely hidden in lush marsh grass had turned out even more striking than Leona expected. She decided to drive straight to the beach, knowing Ned would want to see it. They considered the painting one of their greatest finds. It was close to noon. He and his friends would be at the golf course. She'd leave it without disturbing them.

Ned's car was in the driveway, and Leona assumed he'd ridden with someone else to the country club. At five-feet-five, she struggled to carry the heavy frame up the stairs. Unlocking the front door, she heard music. She met Ned coming down the hall, a martini glass in one hand, an empty bottle of Heineken in the other. Jimmy Buffet blared from the in-wall speakers. The blue silk Brooks Brother's robe she'd given him for Christmas hung open. Thin strands of Ned's comb-over fell across his face. He set the beer bottle and martini glass down and pulled his robe together. A man's voice came from the bedroom. "Go ahead and bring two. I'm parched."

Behind Ned, through the floor-to-ceiling window, sunlight rippled across the water. A heron took flight from the reeds.

The painting slipped to the floor with a crash. Leona's empty hands reached for a cobalt blue vase on the entrance table. She wanted to see Ned's face when their treasure shattered across the tiled foyer. But she couldn't do it. She cradled the vase against her thin chest.

"Why now?" she said, barely able to get the words out.

Ned took the vase from her arms and carefully returned it to the table. "Don't," he said. He brushed the hair from his eyes.

"Come home," she said. She turned away before he could say more and stumbled down the stairs to her car.

Gripping the steering wheel, she drove across the narrow bridge that climbed high above the sound. On ordinary days, the bridge made Leona's palms sweat. Today she trembled. Below, a sailboat crisscrossed the water. She and Ned had talked about getting a boat. She'd imagined sunset rides with the grandchildren. Picnics on the beach.

She felt lightheaded. After everything she'd done. For him. For them. He risked it all for some silly fling. Lots of their friends from Raleigh had houses at Heron Point. What if someone had seen his car? Stopped by for a tour?

Once on the interstate, Leona stayed in the right lane, too shaky to compete with the cars speeding around her. While building Heron Point, she and Ned had been in sync, much like when their daughters were young. She slowed her breathing. She'd throw Ned out. Expose him. Turn their daughters against him. She was thinking like a scorned wife. Something she hadn't been since Doris Holloway laughed in her face over twenty years ago.

She'd been happy when Ned befriended a colleague while finishing up his residency at Duke. Paige was three, Amanda ten months. Michael and Doris Holloway had a son Paige's age. Leona remembered being pleased the couples had so much in common.

They rented a cottage at Wrightsville Beach when both Ned and Michael had a rare weekend off.

After dinner on the first night, the men left to get more beer and stayed gone for so long Leona began to worry. When she said maybe they should call the police, Doris laughed. "You don't know, do you?" She'd had one too many whiskey sours, and Leona was not at all happy about being left alone with this woman who seemed so worldly.

"Don't know what?" Leona asked.

They were outside on the deck. Doris was a silhouette in the moonlight, her long black hair tied back with a white scarf. It was high tide and the waves crashed against the shore, making it difficult to hear. Doris threw her cigarette over the railing. The orange glow fell like a spark. Leona started to warn her about the dry grass below, about how easily it could catch fire.

Doris had reclined on the deck bench and covered her eyes with an arm. "Our husbands. They're lovers."

There in the dark, in the chilling, deafening wind, Leona began to see her life.

She left Doris and made her way inside. Later, when Ned came into the bedroom, she couldn't look at him. In a whisper, she told him what Doris said. She wanted him to be angry, to storm out and tell Doris off, but he sat on the bed and cried.

They left for the long drive home, the girls wrapped in blankets in the backseat, without exchanging a word.

"It won't happen again," he'd said, after they got the children in bed.

Ned stood, staring at the kitchen floor. Leona sat at the table with her back to him. She asked the only question she knew to ask. "Do you love me?"

"Of course I love you," he said. "It's just this thing, Leona. I don't know. Please, don't ask me anything else, okay? I'll deal with it. It's not what you think."

But Leona didn't know what to think. She was twenty-six years old with two small children, estranged from her family, with nowhere to go. Worst of all, Ned was not only her husband, he was her best friend.

They'd started dating when Leona was sixteen, the year her broken family fell completely apart. When Ned went to Duke, Leona went to Meredith College, close by in Raleigh. They appeared to be the perfect couple. No dramatic breakups. No drama at all. She took the fact that Ned wasn't overly sexual as evidence that he was a gentleman. What she'd seen of her parents' drunken passion made her more than content to forgo embarrassing displays. Even after they married, Ned's libido suited her. They wanted children, they had them.

After the night with Doris and Michael in Wilmington, Ned's schedule at the hospital made it easy to avoid more conversation. Leona didn't say a word when he started sleeping in the extra room, claiming he didn't want to wake her when he came in late. She concentrated on the children, on making a home, on being a doctor's wife.

Leona knew Ned loved her. She knew he loved their children. She made what she didn't know unthinkable and never mentioned Michael Holloway again.

As the years went by, she became less naive. She noticed when Ned dressed with care. Spoke too frequently about a colleague. Spent weekends away at conferences she knew didn't exist. She became astute to his affairs, and even though her whole childhood had schooled her in keeping secrets, a desperate Leona dragged Ned from one counselor to another until one called her a complicit wife. "Ned doesn't have a choice about his sexuality," the woman said. "But both of you are choosing to stay in this marriage. Let's talk about that."

Leona and Ned gave the only answer they knew to give. "We want to keep our family together."

In the mid-1980s, AIDS came to light. Leona became afraid for Ned, and for the girls. So afraid, she confronted him. "Are you safe?" she asked. He assured her he was no threat to her or the children and not HIV-positive. But he admitted he was shaken by the disease and afraid of the consequences that being outed as a gay man would have on the new practice he'd established with two other orthopedic surgeons.

Amanda and Paige were teenagers. Ned, always a doting father, became even more involved in their busy lives, driving their soccer teams to tournaments, building sets for high school plays.

Leona lulled herself into believing they were going to make it. She and Ned would never live as man and wife in the traditional sense, but living as a family was enough, more than enough. She didn't miss what she'd never had. When the girls went to college, Leona enrolled at North Carolina State and got a degree in interior design. Decorating became her passion.

The year Ned's mother died, Leona sensed Ned's restlessness and suspected he was seeing someone. One night after too many drinks, he said, "Don't you ever get lonely, Leona? Don't you ever ..."

"What are you talking about?" she said, trying to deflect his question. "Nothing is as important to me as our family."

"And your reputation." He raised his glass. "I'd like to make a toast to Leona Barrett Thomas's impeccable reputation." He laughed. "I've never known anyone, including my mother, who cared more about what other people thought."

Ned never had to worry about what other people thought. His father hadn't died in a one-car crash driving home drunk from an all-night poker game. Ned's mother might have been difficult and controlling, but she certainly hadn't abandoned her family. He thought he knew what it was like for Leona growing up. But he could never understand the fear beneath her steely surface. Yes. She cared what people thought. Leona never wanted to be pitied again, and she'd be damned if her daughters would experience the humiliation she'd felt as a girl. Even now that they were grown with children of their own, Leona steered them toward the lives she wanted them to have.

Last month she'd taken Paige and Amanda to a fundraiser for Senator Jesse Helms. The speakers had a heyday railing against Bill Clinton, each one more incensed than the last by *the immoralities destroying America*. She'd written a check and encouraged her girls to do the same, not because she agreed with everything said by the glad-handing blowhards, but because she wanted Paige and Amanda accepted by the right people. She wanted them to have the security she'd found among people who not only followed the rules but made them.

Ned threatened to compromise them all.

By the time she got back to Raleigh, Leona's anger had turned into resolve. They'd get past this. Ned would come home, apologize, and they'd move on.

But Ned only came home to leave.

She stood in the garage, old arguments lined up on her lips. "What would your mother think about this?" she said.

"Mother's dead, Leona." He brushed past her, clutching an armload of shirts still in dry-cleaner bags. He dipped his head inside the Escalade. For years she'd watched his bald spot spread like oil on water.

"Do I need to remind you what people expect from a surgeon?" Leona fought the urge to straighten the heap of hanging clothes he'd thrown in the backseat, knowing they'd wrinkle, and he'd wear them regardless. "They expect stability."

He shut the car door. Heavy breaths pushed his belly against a too-tight golf shirt. "What about honesty? And do you really think this double life we're living is stable?"

"What double life?" She followed him back into the house. There'd been other times he'd packed a bag, loaded the car, but she'd learned over the years, if she could keep him talking, he'd eventually see that leaving her was impossible.

In the den, he rummaged through the liquor cabinet. "We've been through all this." He stood, holding a bottle of Dewar's. Sweat trickled down his temples.

She blocked the doorway, thin arms crossed against her nervous heart.

"It's not like it used to be," he said. "We don't have to live like this." He looked trapped but determined, Leona thought. She didn't budge. "Listen," he said. "I know we wouldn't have all we have if it wasn't for you. I'm not going to fight you for anything." He nudged past her into the kitchen.

"Where are you going?" she asked. "Where will you live?"

He tore off a paper towel and wiped sweat from his forehead. "I'm not going to lie to you anymore. I'm staying at Steven's."

The young radiologist at the clinic. "Oh, Ned. Is that who … that means everyone in your office knows about your fling."

"For Christ's sake," Ned said. "It's not like that."

"Then tell me what it's like," Leona said.

He leaned back against the counter. "Steven and I are serious."

"Serious," she said, repeating the word like that would help her grasp the meaning.

"We want to make a life together." He paused, clearly expecting a response. Leona remained silent. "I've known I was leaving for a while," he finally said.

"Then why have we spent the past year putting our hearts and souls into Heron Point?" Leona was dumbfounded. "Why did you make me believe …"

"I wanted you to have something you wanted," Ned said.

"My consolation prize," she said. "How generous."

"Come on, Leona," he said.

She could see him getting frustrated trying to explain what she'd never accept.

"Listen, Amanda and Paige need to know the truth," he said.

"That's absolutely ridiculous. Think about the choice you're making."

"It's not a choice, Leona. You know that."

Unless he was talking about orthopedic surgery, Ned had forever made every statement a question. His newfound confidence startled her. She had to buy time until he came to his senses. "Promise me you'll not say a word until we can talk to them together."

"Okay. I promise," he said. "You know, Leona, it's not too late for you to be happy."

"Don't you dare analyze me. *I am happy.*" Her declaration sounded absurd, even to her.

He turned toward the door.

"Do you honestly think if you go through with this you will ever see your grandchildren again?" she said.

He hesitated. She thought she'd found a new argument, one that would stop him, but he shook his head. "The girls won't keep the children from me."

She shrugged. "Maybe not, but their husbands will."

"Stop, Leona. Just stop." Ned turned and faced her. "Think about the example we've set. It's wrong."

"Security? Support? Love? What in the world is wrong with that?"

"Forget it," he said. "You know how to reach me."

After he'd driven away, Leona went into the den and collapsed on the sofa. The example they'd set surrounded her, framed on every shelf. Amanda and Paige as children. Ned holding their tiny hands at the edge of the surf, big grins on their faces. Graduations. Weddings. The girls as new mothers. Ned cuddling adored grandchildren. Family holidays. *Merry Christmas from our family to yours. Our family. Our happy family.* It wasn't a lie. Not all of it.

Leona couldn't summon the strength to move out of the den, where memories protected her from an inconceivable future. She lay in her grief and shock until the phone rang. She prayed for it to be Ned calling to say he'd changed his mind, but it was Helen Hastings. "Can you and Ned get to the gala early Saturday to help price the silent auction?"

Instinct guided Leona to the useful lie. A skill she'd honed as a child to cover for her parents when they were too drunk for piano recitals, ball games, teacher conferences. "Helen, I'm so sorry, I was about to call you. I have to go out of town. My aunt's not doing well, and my sister needs help."

As soon as she said the words, she knew she'd have to make good on them. Leona loathed the thought of Carthage. Her wild-haired sister and delinquent nephew. The aunt she'd never trusted. But she'd do whatever it took to keep the agreement she'd made with herself years ago: to live as if the life she wanted was the life she had.

Ned promised he wouldn't talk to the girls without her. They'd be back from their spring break vacations midweek. She had to get out of Raleigh. Surely with more time to think, he'd change his mind and come home.

Dean

Dean paced from one end of the kitchen to the other. The loose linoleum crackled with each step. He practiced his news in a whisper. *"Mama, I'm twenty-six years old and I need to be my own boss. I'm going to start an emu farm that'll make us all rich."*

The cat clock's tail swung *tick-tock* and plastic paws jumped to eight-thirty. They weren't church people but even on Sunday they didn't dawdle. He heard his mama coming down the steps. When she went to fix her coffee, she'd find a pot made. He needed her to see he wasn't some snot-nosed kid who needed looking after.

She came through the kitchen, her red robe flapping. She yelled into the cordless telephone. "I can't hear you, let me get outside." The back-porch screen door slammed against the frame.

Dean pulled back the window shade. His mama was in the side yard. The cold dew in the high grass had her quick-stepping around the birdbath like a gray-headed witchy woman doing a voodoo dance.

Their new neighbor, the preacher, collecting his Sunday paper from his driveway, took his time walking back to his house. He kept looking over his shoulder. At least the preacher wasn't a Baptist, Dean thought, but even a Methodist wouldn't take to seeing a woman doing a jig in red flannel first thing on Sunday morning. He was liable to show up at the door thumping on his Bible before sundown.

Dean knocked on the window and motioned for his mama to come back in the house, but she just waved her cigarette at him. One of the stray cats Belle fed out by the shed stopped licking its paws to watch.

Aunt Belle tap-tap-tapped her cane into the kitchen. She shuffled up beside Dean. Belle wore flannel pajamas year-round, and from morning to night she carried the old macramé bag she'd made herself years ago. Thick gray bangs curled straight across her forehead about an inch above her round wire-rimmed glasses. His mama called Belle's haircut a Dutch bob.

"Was that Gaston knocking? Is he here to do the yard?" Belle's hearing aids whistled like teakettles.

"Gaston's ten years dead, Aunt Belle."

"Well, he needs to cut back the bamboo," she said, like she hadn't understood a word Dean said.

The doctor had told them to go along with her when her head got sideways. He claimed the truth would only confuse her. But lying didn't make a bit of sense to Dean.

Belle had a thing about the bamboo. Her brother, Dean's granddaddy, had planted the patch that choked the yard and stretched all the way to the piney woods. Belle told Dean all her brother cared about was whiskey, high stakes poker, and fishing the Pee Dee River with a bamboo pole. She said he thought he'd sell fishing poles at the family's store, but there wasn't a soul in Moore County who couldn't stop by the side of most any road and help themselves to all the bamboo they could carry.

Dean took a hacksaw to the stubborn cane every spring. He imagined squeezing through the twenty-foot-high stalks was like being in jungle warfare in Vietnam. His daddy and his Uncle James both served in Vietnam. Dean had asked his uncle, "Is our bamboo like over yonder?"

Uncle James said, "No."

Dean believed the bamboo must be even thicker in Vietnam. So thick it swallowed his daddy up and never spit him out.

When Dean was a boy, he'd get in the bamboo and play soldier. He'd pretend he was on a rescue mission to find his daddy. He imagined walking up on him in a little clearing. "Well, Dean, am I glad to see you," his daddy would say.

The day he'd turned eighteen, Dean put on the camouflage jacket and pants he'd gotten at the Army-Navy Store in Fayetteville. He snuck out of the house knowing if his mama or Aunt Belle figured out what he meant to do, they'd have a fit. He went downtown and stood at attention outside the recruitment office, but when Keith Martin showed up, he said, "Dean, your head's not right for war." He'd never thought much of Keith Martin, but Dean figured his rank gave him the last word.

Dean knew his head wasn't like everybody else's. He'd had trouble as a child. But having his dream so quickly denied had left him adrift and searching for a good long while.

Belle nodded at the TV on the kitchen counter. "Let's see what's on the news."

Dean knew Aunt Belle meant CNN. She thought President Clinton hung the moon, and ever since he did what he did with that young girl, people on TV talked about him every minute. "I don't believe half of what they say," Belle said ten times a day.

His mama warned him not to repeat what he heard up at the garage about the President, but Dean suspected Belle knew all he knew and more. Most days she could tell Dean everything that ever happened in Moore County, North Carolina, the United States, or the whole wide world, even if she couldn't remember who was dead or alive.

She still corrected his grammar like she had back when she was his homeschool teacher. "Dean, ain't is not a word," she'd say. Dean didn't much care for the rules of grammar. He talked like everybody he knew talked. Brandi, his best friend who worked at the Stop 'n Go, said freedom of speech meant a man could say ain't if he dang well pleased.

Belle tapped into the pantry. The rustle of Little Debbie wrappers let Dean know she'd found her breakfast. His mama claimed if it weren't for Little Debbie powdered donuts, Belle would starve.

He changed the channel, poured Belle a cup of coffee and stirred in a big spoonful of sugar and a dollop of half-and-half.

She brought her donuts to the table.

The screen door slammed, and his mama stepped into the kitchen, her eyes wide and wild. "Leona's on her way down here," she said.

"Well, isn't that good," said Belle.

The last time his Aunt Leona came to Carthage, she caught Dean sitting in her brand-new Lexus and had a pure-T fit.

He wasn't doing a thing but checking out the buttons and knobs and such. Being a mechanic meant he had to keep up with the new automobiles, and he'd told her that, but she just kept yelling and got a towel and wiped down the seat and the steering wheel. Afterward, he overheard his mama and her going at it on the back porch.

"He should have been declared mentally incompetent years ago," his aunt said. "I warned James not to leave him this house, but our brother never listened to me."

"Oh, for God's sake, Leona," his mama said. "Dean has more sense than the rest of us put together."

If Leona was on the way to Carthage, Dean was making tracks. He picked up his bowl of Special K and choked down what was left. Telling his mama about his plan would have to wait. He jumped up, grabbed his backpack, and made it halfway to his jeep before she called out.

"Where do you think you're going?" She stood on the front porch, arms crossed.

"I got business up the road."

She tucked her chin. "This better not have anything to do with those crazy birds."

Dean straightened his back and stood as tall as he could. Being shorter than his mama bothered him a great deal. "Emu is the next big thing and I mean to start me a farm and make something of myself like my daddy did." After his careful practice, he'd revealed all in a spurt.

His mama shook her head. "I can't talk about that now. I need you to help me move Belle's quilt pieces off the dining room table and get the porch hosed off. Leona will be here in two hours, and this pine pollen's an inch thick."

Dean threw his backpack in the jeep, "I'll help, but I ain't hanging around."

Belle was famous for the crazy quilts she made from scraps cut all different ways and put together in no particular order. Cataracts and arthritis made it to where she couldn't sew a stitch, but Dean helped her cut the shapes she wanted. His mama kept a piece of muslin on the dining room table where Belle arranged what she called her "puzzle."

His mama lifted the corners of one end of the muslin and Dean took the other. They carried it up to what used to be Belle's sewing room before she got to where she shouldn't climb stairs. Dean didn't waste a minute getting back down and out the door, his mama right behind him. "Pull the hose around here and water those pots of geraniums, then wash everything down," she said. "And don't forget the swing."

"What the hell for?" Dean said. "Aunt Leona's never been one to sit out here. How come you think she'll start today?" He brought a hand up to shade his eyes from the sun. He studied his mama's face. She carried blood from her mother's side, an ornery bunch from Scotland County, and it had gotten to where that ornery blood flared up so quick, she'd just about change color. Sure enough, her face glowed like a winter beet, and her eyes, dark as pools of tar, welled up. Her bottom lip began to quiver. "Hell's bells, Mama, come on now, I'll do it," Dean said.

His mama went back in the house. Dean wrestled the tangled hose out from underneath the head-high azaleas and sprayed the porch. The water ran off the sides thick and yellow as paint.

It had gotten to where Dean never knew what would set his mama off or how long her fits would last. He did know that when she started fanning herself, he needed to steer clear.

He'd told her she ought to listen to Zig Ziglar. That Zig might help her with her state of mind. She'd told him her state of mind wasn't anybody's damn business, especially somebody with a made-up clown name who sounded like he ought to join the circus.

Uncle James had introduced Dean to Zig Ziglar.

After leaving the Army, Dean's uncle had drifted all the way to California. He showed up back in Carthage after being gone from home for nearly thirty years. He had emphysema so bad he needed looking after and said he'd come home to die.

Dean and his uncle became fast friends. He told Uncle James about his dream of being his own boss.

"Your attitude, not your aptitude, determines your altitude," Uncle James had said. "You know who said that?"

Dean shook his head.

"Zig Ziglar."

After he'd been home a couple of weeks, Uncle James bought a used trailer and set it beside the old tobacco barn. Dean's mama said that didn't make a lick of sense, but his uncle claimed he was partial to a trailer. He said he liked having everything he needed about an arm's length away. Dean believed his uncle just wanted to die in peace away from all the fuss and bother his mama and Aunt Belle stirred up. "They'd worry a man to death," his uncle said. "I need my privacy."

Uncle James and Dean would stay up all night listening to people on television talk about how they got rich. When Dean's mama told her brother there was no such thing as easy money, he claimed she lacked vision. And vision, he said, was what Dean needed for his future.

Dean had a rough start. Nothing about school had suited him. He didn't understand what the teachers wanted him to do, or why he had to do it sitting down. The other kids made fun of him, calling him Dumb-Dumb, and worse. The name-calling caused Dean to either throw something or kick someone. When he was in third grade, the principal sent him home for good, claiming Dean "caused a constant disturbance."

Belle quit teaching at the high school and turned the dining room into a classroom with a map of the world pinned to one wall and a blackboard nailed to another. When Dean was thirteen, Belle found him in the backyard taking her car apart and ordered all the books she could find about engine mechanics.

Dean got a fine education, but Uncle James left him with what Zig Ziglar said every successful businessman needed. Uncle James left Dean with a plan.

Last fall, right before his uncle's lungs gave out, they had a summer-like day, and Dean's mama helped Uncle James stretch out in a lawn chair under the pecan tree. Dean was changing the oil in his jeep nearby when Uncle James called out, "Dean, come over here."

His uncle was reading the *News and Observer*, and it wasn't like him to want to talk when he had a paper. Dean went over and took a seat, wiping his hands on his jeans.

"Looky here," Uncle James had said, pointing to a picture of a bird as tall as a man.

"What the hell is that?" Dean asked.

"Says here it's an emu, and pretty soon this is what folks are going to be eating." Uncle James nodded at the picture. "This is how the rich get richer. This fellow lives up around Pittsboro and used to raise beef cows. Now he's got a field full of these emus. He's got money, don't you know, and he's going to get him a damn sight more." Uncle James whistled through the gap in his front teeth like he did all the time. "He's going to be sitting pretty when the boom hits." He shook the paper straight. "God-dog, if I had a dollar or two, I'd fill that tobacco field up with them goddamn skinny-necked birds."

When Dean helped his uncle back to the house for dinner, James swatted Dean with the folded-up newspaper, "Here, keep this, and if you ever get ahead, I want you to buy you some of these birds."

Dean did what his uncle said. He kept the newspaper tucked in the green canvas backpack he got at the Army-Navy store where they sold genuine army supplies.

Uncle James made sure in his will that Barrett House fell to Dean, the oldest son, the fourth generation. Dean didn't give a damn what Aunt Leona said. Uncle James's will was a legal document of the United States of America, it said so in the fine print. James also left Dean his pension and a check from the government for twelve thousand and sixty-two dollars and fifty-five cents. Dean knew every cent was meant for emu.

He had kept the check in a shoebox wrapped in a towel under his bed until his mama made him put it in the bank. She told him to put it in his savings account, but at the teller window he handed the check to Irene Ferguson and said, "I've got a deposit for checking."

Irene pondered the check, "Don't you want to put this in with your savings?"

He let her know right quick that he did not. The next big thing called for ready cash.

The roar of the vacuum cleaner from inside the house signaled to Dean that he had a chance to make a clean getaway.

He finished winding up the hose and headed for his jeep. He had one stop to make before he set out for Pittsboro.

He parked in front of the courthouse across from the newspaper office and walked over to the speckled granite bench. The deep-cut letters on the seat read:

Sergeant Michael Dean "Mac" McQueen
Never forgotten.
MIA

His daddy was proud of the bench. Dean knew that, because ever since he was a boy he'd talked to his daddy. And his daddy talked back. Not out loud, but in Dean's head he heard his daddy clear as could be. He told Dean things like how to swing a bat, how to tell if a carburetor was beyond fixing, or how many peaches it took to make the best homemade ice cream. But his daddy never would talk about where he was. Dean had asked him a thousand times, "Are you dead in heaven or still over there somewhere?" But his daddy never would say.

His mama told him not to tell folks that he and his daddy talked, but when somebody asked how come him to sit so long on the hard bench, Dean told them the truth. He'd never lied in his life. The way things were was the way things were. His mama said people didn't understand, but Dean told her that was their problem, not his.

Some folks beat all, like the ones who came into the garage claiming their tires had been put on wrong, swearing they hadn't run over something. Some folks lied when the truth would be better. His friend, Brandi, didn't cotton to a lie either. She took Dean to the movies over in Southern Pines in her Dodge because she didn't fit good in his jeep. Every Friday night they'd go to Dairy Queen for banana splits and tell each other the truth. Last Friday she'd been the one to start. "Hardee's hamburgers are not the biggest hamburgers in the world." Then Dean said, "Spark plugs for a '93 Chrysler don't cost Mr. Frank ten dollars apiece." They'd keep on until a week's worth of lies got set straight. Having the truth told settled Dean's troubled mind.

Dean stretched out on the granite bench beside the courthouse and made a pillow for his head with folded hands. The chill from the stone ran down his back but the sun warmed his face. He bent his knees and scrunched himself up to fit the slab. He stared up at the white oak, tall as the courthouse. A breeze caused the curled brown leaves to shake like they had a bad case of nerves. Dean had studied the leafy branches all winter long. Other trees went bare but not the old oak. Dean imagined it saying, "Hell with spring, I'm hanging on to what I got." But there wouldn't be room for the dead when the new buds rose. Dean felt bad for the crinkled old things that had stuck it out through winter wind and rain. It didn't seem right to make it through all that just to be pushed to the ground. He closed his eyes and waited for his head to get still. It took quiet for him to hear his daddy's voice.

Hey, son.

Hey Daddy. Aunt Leona's coming down here.

What for?

Beats me.

Don't let her be ugly to you.

I'm staying the hell out of her way.

You going to Pittsboro?

Yep.

Well, it's not easy being a businessman.

I can handle it.

I know you can.

A car horn blew. His daddy stopped talking. The oak leaves scratched against one another. Dean sat up and wiped his nose on his t-shirt sleeve.

The sun had inched higher into the sky and his watch said quarter 'til 10. He rubbed his fingers across his daddy's name like he always did before he left him.

He might pass Aunt Leona on the road, and that was how it ought to be. Him going one way, her going another.

Fern

Fern knew very little about her sister's life. She and Belle had only been invited to Raleigh a handful of times. But Fern knew two things. First, nothing Leona did was without purpose. Her showing up in Carthage was no random act. And second, Leona walked in the front door and every bit of Fern's good sense stepped out back for a cigarette.

Leona's high and mighty airs upended Fern's level head. Without her sister saying a word, Fern awoke to the ratty magazines piled high on the living room floor and Belle's month-old birthday cards cluttering the mantle. With just the sight of Leona's perfectly made-up face, middle-aged Fern became a gangly adolescent with uncombed hair and muddy shoes.

Leona dressed in what Fern called doctor's wife casual. Pressed slacks. A thin belt with a clever gold buckle. Silky ivory blouse. Tasteful flats. Diamond stud earrings just large enough to be noticed. At the last minute, Fern had drug out the ironing board and ironed her best khakis, but no amount of effort could match Leona's easy perfection.

Any other Sunday, Belle, Dean, and Fern would be enjoying BBQ sandwiches from The Pig and watching old favorites on the Classic Movie Channel. But that wouldn't do for Leona. After her sister's call, Fern found a recipe she'd saved from the newspaper and set the dining room table with their mother's blue willow dishes.

"Try this casserole," Fern said when they settled down for lunch. She passed the Pyrex dish to her sister. "The recipe came from the Pinehurst Junior League."

Leona drew back. "So much cheese." She picked beneath the cheddar and Ritz Cracker crust to bring up a flat spoonful of chicken, enough for maybe two good bites.

"Didn't you used to like watermelon rind pickles?" Fern's hand trembled, and she tipped the cut glass pickle plate. The tiny fork bounced onto Grandma Barrett's linen tablecloth splattering dots of bright green food coloring across the table like a constellation.

"Oh, for heaven's sake," Leona barked.

"I'll get a paper towel." Fern slid the chair back and knocked the table with her knees. Leona grabbed hold of her iced tea glass.

Fern brought back a wet paper towel and dabbed at the green spots. They blossomed on the frail linen already marked by past spills and blunders—a visible history of other meals fraught with shaky hands.

Grandma Barrett's china cabinet towered over them like a judgment. As a girl, Fern was drawn to the fragile beauty of her grandmother's porcelain figurines and the china plates trimmed with hand-painted bramble roses, finery Leona had claimed long ago. All that was left on the dusty glass shelves were the blue willow dishes and chipped and cracked odds and ends, like the cat and dog salt and pepper shakers Dean won at the state fair.

She couldn't help but feel conflicted relief when Dean's jeep bounced down the gravel drive. Dean had a tendency to tell Leona all she didn't want to hear.

Fern, on the other hand, told her sister nothing. Not even about Belle's appointment with Doctor McManus. She feared if Leona heard *Alzheimer's*, she'd force Belle into a nursing home. After Carthage Elementary expelled Dean, Leona lectured Fern about how he belonged in what she'd called *a special school*. Fern imagined Leona's life was like the picture-perfect pages of *Southern Living* magazine. No chipped china, no troubled children, and no aunts who set places at the table for the long dead.

"I wish you hadn't gone to so much fuss. I usually have a salad or a fruit plate for lunch," Leona said.

Fern forced a smile and thought how the next time Leona graced her table she'd hand her an apple and a paring knife.

Belle took a bite of pickle. "Tart," she said. Belle had insisted on wearing the soft-pink cardigan sweater Leona had given her for her birthday even though it was not at all her style.

"Have some cornbread," Fern said. Dr. McManus had warned her to expect Belle's appetite to dwindle, but it was heartbreaking to see her stare at the plate as if trying to place its purpose. "You, too, Leona," Fern said. "Have a piece."

Fern believed her sister could stand a bit of lard on her bones. Leona's ivory blouse hung so loose off her shoulders, she looked like a child in grown-up clothes. Leona reminded Fern of the Madame Alexander dolls Mrs. Anderson used to keep in a glass cabinet up at the old drugstore. Fair and fine-featured, silky blonde hair. Leona always had taken time with herself. She'd worn Ponds face cream to bed when she was only sixteen. Now fifty, the lines around her blue eyes and mouth looked as if they'd been drawn with precious care by a light hand.

The sisters did not favor. Some would allow they were two different species altogether. Fern believed Leona had claimed all the fruit from the family tree and none of the thorns. Leona had inherited her delicate features from Grandma Barrett. Fern took from her mother's side and believed her dark eyes and coarse hair made her look like something that crawled straight out of the Dismal Swamp.

Fern felt a hot flash coming on and recalled how storms erupted when hot met cold. Between her fire and Leona's ice, the sisters might concoct their own thunderhead.

"Belle," Fern's voice climbed to a giddy pitch, and she fanned her sweaty face with her napkin, "isn't it nice having Leona with us?" Belle tilted her head like Fern was the most peculiar thing she'd seen in a while, and Fern feared her aunt's mind was afloat, but then she smiled.

"It is," Belle said. She reached a speckled hand over to Leona. "I've wanted to call and thank you for this pretty sweater, but Fern said you were too busy to talk to us."

Fern concentrated on her casserole, fearing Belle might tell Leona what all else she said. Seeing Belle dote on Leona irritated Fern to no end. Leona had been out-and-out hateful when Belle came back home to care for them after their father died and their mother ran off. But Belle was all the time worrying about Leona without ever saying exactly what her worry was. Why in the world would anybody worry about Leona, Fern wanted to know. Leona had everything a woman could want, except the deed to Barrett House. Family tradition held that the house passed to the oldest son, but when their brother James died and the house fell to Dean, Leona threatened to contest the will. She never missed a chance to remind Fern that if Ned hadn't paid for endless repairs, they'd be living under a pile of sticks. But what kept Fern up at night was what would happen to Dean after she was gone. She was determined to leave him with a home no one could take away.

Belle leaned toward Leona. "How come Ned didn't come with you?" This made about the fourth time she'd asked Leona about Ned, even though he hadn't been back to Carthage since his mother died.

Leona took a long drink of tea.

If you're losing patience with her asking the same questions over and over, Fern thought, *stick around, sister. You don't know the half of it.*

"Ned's very busy." Leona put her fork down and turned to Fern. "The front porch floor needs painting. Does Dean understand that's his responsibility?"

Fern braced herself for another lecture about how James didn't have any business leaving Dean the house. "We were just talking about that," Fern lied. "Tell us about Paige and Amanda," she said. "Where did they go for New Year's?"

"Vail, Colorado. Skiing."

"I've read about Vail in *People Magazine*," Fern said. "Carol Ann went somewhere out there. I believe it was Utah because I remember asking her if she saw Donny and Marie Osmond." Fern knew her half-wit jibber-jabber baptized her pure fool, but she'd do anything to steer Leona away from Dean and the house.

Belle piped up. "I wish they'd leave Bill Clinton alone."

Fern was relieved she'd mentioned something timely even if her favorite subject was a scandal.

"He's a disgrace," Leona said.

"I don't believe half of what they say," Belle said, going back to her cornbread. "He's done a lot of good for people."

"Bill Clinton has destroyed the moral fabric of our country," Leona said. "Speaking of morals, has Carol Ann remarried lately?"

"You talked to her at Belle's birthday lunch," Fern said.

A corner of Leona's upper lip rose into a smirk. "That was weeks ago. She could be on number four by now, or is it number five?"

Carol Ann did get married quite a bit, but Fern believed she gave those northern retirees a reason to live when they flocked to Pinehurst to play golf. A reason to live, that is, until they died and left her their considerable estates.

"She's too busy with her new housing development to worry about a man," Fern said, meaning to remind Leona that Carol Ann was, above all else, a successful businesswoman.

"Right," Leona said with a sarcastic twist. "What's it called again? Scotland Yards?"

"Scot's Meadow."

"Just as trite," Leona laughed.

Fern tried to think of something clever to say to defend her best friend, but before she could, Leona cleared her throat. "I'm concerned," she said. "I don't believe Belle should be left alone while you're at work."

Had Leona talked to Dr. McManus? Belle, struggling to get her coffee cup to cooperate with her mouth, didn't appear privy to the conversation.

"Do you really think we should talk about this now?" Fern said.

"All I'm saying is you could use assistance," Leona said.

"So, what are you going to do, move in?" Fern said.

"For a while," Leona said.

Fern choked on her tea.

Leona patted Belle's arm. "Aunt Belle, I've come for an extended visit."

"Well, that's the best news I could hear. Do you think you can stand us?" Belle cackled at her joke, but Fern thought it was a damn good question.

"We'll manage." Leona said.

What did her sister know? Fern felt sure she'd distracted Leona from Belle's dementia. "Belle's not alone," she said. "Not much, anyway, and I'm part-time at the paper now. I told you that."

"Bernice comes right often," Belle said, busy with a slice of stubborn tomato she was trying to cut with a spoon.

"She used to come," Fern said. "That's right, Bernice used to come, and you all had good visits. That was before Bernice died and we went to her funeral. But Dean comes home for lunch most days."

"Oh, for heaven's sake," Leona said. "Dean is certainly not a proper care giver."

Fern expected Leona to call Belle out for bringing Bernice back from the dead, but Leona didn't seem to notice.

"Dean's doing very well," Fern said, "and if you stay down here longer than a minute, which I will believe when I see, you'll have to stop being so hateful to him."

"Why?" Leona clutched her throat. "Because he might attack me like he attacked Paige and Amanda?"

"Oh, for God's sake. He was seven years old."

The commotion of that Christmas day came to Fern's mind in a vivid flash. Leona's girls had gotten into Dean's Matchbox cars and Dean hit Paige so hard with a Baby Tender Love, the doll's head came off, then he kicked Amanda and left a bruise on her leg. That was the last Christmas Day they'd spent as a family.

Leona's nostrils flared. "You should have taken him to a specialist."

Fern had taken Dean to a specialist. One who diagnosed him with Fetal Alcohol Syndrome. That was another thing she'd never told Leona, and she wasn't about to tell her now.

Belle fidgeted in her chair. She stared at Fern as if pleading for her to let go of the secret that had led to so much bitterness.

To pay for Dean's evaluations and therapy, Belle had sold pieces of her mother's antique furniture, silver, and the grandfather clock that had been in the family for generations. Shortly after, Leona came home and saw all that was missing. Accusations flew.

"I have no idea what the two of you have been funding with Grandmother's things," Leona said. "Probably giving it all to Jimmy Carter's useless campaign."

That same day Leona had packed her car full of her grandmother's china and remaining silver, and left for Raleigh.

Belle had wanted to tell her the truth right then and there, but Fern couldn't stand for Leona to know the cause of Dean's trouble. She still couldn't.

"Why don't you mind your own damn business?" Fern said to her sister, a bite of casserole poised on her fork.

Leona and Fern's raised voices inspired a familiar ting-ting-ting. Belle, sitting up school-teacher-straight, tapped her spoon on the side of her glass. "You girls shouldn't talk ugly to one another." She no longer sounded one bit feeble. Her blue eyes, magnified through the thick lenses of her round wire-rimmed glasses, fixed first on Fern, then on Leona. Fern thought Belle might very well be seeing her and Leona as surly teenagers. She knew what was coming and imagined Leona did too.

Belle sighed. "I always wanted a sister."

If they'd heard it once, they'd heard it a million times. That, and how sisters ought to love one other and be glad to have each other. "We won't argue anymore," Fern said. "Let me get the pound cake." She cast a sidelong glance at Leona.

"Yes, I apologize," Leona said. "There's no excuse for bad manners."

Fern made her way to the kitchen. *Bad manners.* The last thing Fern needed was a Leona lecture about manners. She found the strawberry preserves, dessert plates, and new forks. *God help us all if I forget clean forks.* She piled everything on top of the Tupperware cake holder and carried it to the dining room.

"My heavens," Leona said, "did you have to bring everything at once?"

"No. You could have helped me," Fern said, barely above a whisper so Belle wouldn't detect the malice. Fern reached for the knife.

"Where's your server?" Leona said.

Fern stopped mid-slice. "My what?"

"Grandmother's silver cake server?" Leona looked around as if it might float out of thin air.

"Probably at your house," Fern said. "And anyway, I believe I can manage to cut this cake without a silver cake server."

"Suit yourself." Leona folded her hands in her lap.

Fern got cake on the plates, preserves passed around, and cups of coffee poured. She hadn't taken the first bite before Leona started up again.

"It's not just the days that concern me," Leona said. "Fern, I imagine you have an active night life." She smiled ever so slightly. "Carol Ann must keep you in men friends."

Fern slapped her hands on the table. Plates and silverware jumped sideways. "You don't know shit about me."

Belle dropped her forehead on a frail, clenched fist. "Fern," she said, "things come out of your mouth I wouldn't hold in my hand." She scooted her chair back. "I believe I'll go lay down."

Belle cradled the macramé bag she'd kept in her lap during lunch. It held a thick wallet, an old checkbook, a pack of Salem Lights, wads of Kleenex, Juicy Fruit gum, and a Bic lighter. Dr. McManus had explained how Alzheimer's caused people to keep personal belongings close. Belle guarded the bag as if her right mind might be hidden inside.

Leona and Fern trailed close behind, letting Belle take her own good time getting to the back bedroom. Fern helped her onto the narrow bed she'd slept on since coming back home thirty years ago. Fern eased Belle's bag out of her hands and put it on the nightstand where Belle could see it. Then she wrestled the hearing aids from her aunt's ears and laid them on a Kleenex. Belle grabbed Fern's and Leona's wrists with shaky hands. "I'm not going to be around here too many more days. Seeing you two be more loving to one another surely would put my mind at ease."

Fern kissed Belle's warm cheek, soft and thin as parchment. Belle reached up again, this time only for Leona. She pulled her close. "Coming back home was the best thing I ever did. You know why?"

Leona shook her head.

"Because of you children, my family." She closed her eyes. Fern pulled one of Belle's favorite crazy quilts up over her, one crafted from her father's suits and ties. After Belle came home to Carthage, she started making quilts out of timeworn garments left by the dead in chifforobes and cedar chests. She pieced together patches of cloth with no rhyme or reason, like every odd bit was meant to be. She did the same with us, Fern thought. She made a family out of her no-account brother's orphaned children.

Dean

Amile outside of town, the steeple of New Hope Methodist Church cut through the pines. Dean slowed his jeep and dodged the cars parked half on, half off the highway. The new preacher had a full house, and Dean was glad not to be adding to it.

Brandi would want him to park and go in. She had made a nuisance of herself, pestering him to go with her to First Baptist, but he'd never felt the need for religious instruction. He'd told Belle not long ago she ought to go to church, seeing as how she was getting up in age and could die any time. But Belle told him, "The Lord and I are square. Besides, there're folks in heaven I don't care to be around, and folks in hell I'm not done with."

He spotted his family's cemetery plot and thought of his uncle James. Just as he picked up speed, he caught a flash of what looked like a body on the ground between two parked cars. There was nothing behind him, so he backed up and stopped. A girl was hunkered down smoking a cigarette. The preacher's girl. Dean had seen her waiting for the school bus across the road from the house.

"Get out of here," she said.

Meanness didn't fit with her blond curls and lacy dress. Dean didn't know what to make of this ornery child. "You ought not to smoke cigarettes," he said.

"You ought not make little girls talk to you. You're a stranger."

"I ain't no stranger. I'm Dean McQueen. I live right across the road from you. Your daddy's the preacher."

She narrowed her eyes. "You better get out of here, mister, before I scream."

She took another puff like smoking a cigarette crouched between two cars parked on the road was what she ought to be doing. The preacher stood on the steps of the church shaking hands with everybody going in. He was a big man, bigger than any preacher Dean had ever seen.

"What happened to your mama?" Dean said.

"She died, like it's any of your business."

"My daddy's MIA," Dean said.

"What's MIA?"

"Missing in Action. He went missing in the Vietnam War."

The girl stared hard at Dean, and then ground the cigarette out on the pavement. She pulled a piece of Spearmint gum from her sweater pocket.

"Make sure that cigarette's out. You don't want to start a fire," Dean said. "Ain't your daddy going to wonder where you're at?"

"I'm going," she said. "Is he looking?"

"No. Doris Whitlow's got him by the arm. He ain't looking."

She jumped up and scampered behind a pine tree, then wandered pretty as you please back into the churchyard. When she went up the steps, her daddy hugged her. She wiggled away and disappeared into the church.

Little cuss, Dean thought.

Pittsboro was bigger than he remembered, and Dean started to wonder how he was going to find the man in the newspaper. He pulled into Hardee's thinking he'd ask around. The girl behind the counter didn't look like she'd know anything about emu, and sure enough, she did not.

"It's a bird. About so high," Dean raised his hand shoulder high to show her.

"You're messing with me, aren't you?" she said.

The man in line behind Dean shuffled his feet like he wished Dean would move on so he and his wife could order their Sunday lunch. "No, I'm not messing with you. Look here." He showed her the newspaper.

A woman with her black hair crammed in a hairnet came out from the back. She wiped her hands on a paper towel. "You're looking for old man Peavey." She leaned over the counter. "You know where the Ford lot's at?"

"No, I ain't from here."

"Well, you go down to the middle of Main 'til you get to Gentry's Ford. Turn left. Then about five miles out, turn right at the Church of the Nazarene. When the pavement runs out, them birds will be on the hill to your left. Here, I'll draw you a map."

Dean followed the directions and before long his jeep bumped onto loose gravel. His tires spun and dust flew and when he stomped the brakes, the engine stalled. Before he got it cranked back up, he heard what sounded like a giant, hissing snake. A long-necked creature tall as Dean with a little bitty head and great big eyes studied him from behind a six-foot chain-link fence as if pondering its next move. It twitched its skinny neck and poked a pointy beak through the fence, then hissed some more. Its neck alone had to be two feet long. Dean had never seen anything try so hard to get at somebody. But what really spooked him were the bulging eyes with heavy lids that reminded him a little bit of Aunt Leona.

Dean started to shake like he did when his nerves got crossed. He cranked the jeep, but his foot slid off the clutch. The newspaper picture was nothing like the real thing, and he didn't believe he wanted any part of the emu business.

"Whoa now, whoa." A pot-bellied man came trotting down the road from where he'd been stirring up the sandy grass with a riding mower. His straw hat, decked out with feathers, bounced atop his head. He took his hat off and waved it at the bird, "Get on away from here, Bill, you're scaring the boy. He walked over to Dean's jeep. That's an emu, son. A full-blooded Australian emu."

Dean wanted to tell him he knew it was an emu, but the man didn't give him a chance.

"The meat is low in cholesterol. The oil is a known cure for what ails you. Emu birds are the future, son, fixing to take over the pork and beef industry."

"Yes sir, I know," Dean said when the man took a breath. "I read about you in the newspaper, and I come from Carthage to see about getting me some emus, but that one looks pretty mean, and I reckon they're all like that."

"Oh, they ain't mean. A little high strung, but not mean. Not mean a 'tall. You just gotta know how to talk to 'em." He waddled over to the fence where the giant bird rested on one leg. "Ain't that right, Bill?" He smiled back at Dean. "I can tell you one thing. All the damn health nuts up around Raleigh are going crazy for these shit-ass birds." The man put his hat back on, pulled a chew of tobacco from his hip pocket, and fixed a plug. That done, he came back to the jeep and stuck out his hand. "George Peavey, and you are?"

"Dean McQueen."

"Well, Dean, this is your lucky day, boy. I'm of a mind to set you up."

Dean stepped out of the jeep but stayed back from the fence. "Can it fly?"

"No, no, a fellow told me they used to could fly, but when the dinosaurs died off, nothing bothered 'em much and they just got lazy. That's how long they been around," Mr. Peavey said. "Since Adam and the dinosaurs."

Another emu bounced down the hill, legs flopping every which-a-way, and Dean spied more not as tall as Bill moseying around picking at the ground. "How many you got?"

"This here's Bill and up there's Hillary and I got six of their young'uns that ain't but five months old. And over yonder are George and Barbara. They're my oldest pair, and I just sold off their last bunch of chicks."

"How come you to name them like that?"

"My old lady named 'em. She don't have no use for the gov'ment, and she don't have no use for these birds. But looky here," he rolled up his sleeve. "You see that scar? I about cut my arm off trying to take an old limb off a tree that was fixing to fall on the house. My chain saw slipped. I had to have twenty stitches, but I wish you'd look how good it healed up. And you know why?"

Dean shook his head.

"Emu oil. It heals you plum down to the bone. Let me show you around."

Mr. Peavey climbed in Dean's jeep and pointed. "Go that way." Dean drove down a potholed dirt track. "Pull in here," Mr. Peavy said. Dean parked beside a cinder block outbuilding painted up to say *Peavey Farm. Emus Buy-Sell-Trade*. He got a tour of the incubator room, five different pens, and the feeding barn.

"How much does all this cost?" Dean said when they circled back to his jeep.

"Well," Mr. Peavey lifted his feathered hat and scratched at a tuft of gray hair, "it ain't cheap. But you start with just a pair, and in one season, you might have as many as twenty, thirty chicks. Then you trade around and get you another pair, and there you go. You're in the emu business. You ought to have about, oh, I'd say ten thousand to get going."

That was just about every cent Dean had, and he still needed a fence.

The sun dropped behind the trees before he and Mr. Peavey struck a deal. He got Bill and Hillary for two thousand even because Mr. Peavey said he could tell Dean was the right kind of man for emu, and because Dean promised to only use them for breeding.

"I raised them two like pets," Mr. Peavy said. "I'm kind of partial to 'em. Wouldn't want 'em to end up on a dinner plate." He threw in a book called "The Emu Farmer's Handbook." Dean wrote him a check for half.

"I won't charge you but fifty dollars to bring 'em up there," Mr. Peavey said. "You just give me a call when you get your fence ready. My number is on the back of that book."

Dean couldn't help but picture Uncle James smiling from up above. And maybe his daddy was up there smiling too.

Fern

Fern washed and Leona dried. Belle's words and seeing her so frail had drained the piss and vinegar out of both of them, and they worked to the clink and clank of dishes without speaking.

"I'm surprised you aren't down at the beach enjoying your new place," Fern finally said when she could no longer stand her sister's silence.

Leona carried a serving dish into the pantry.

"And what are the girls going to do without you in Raleigh to help with the children?"

"They'll be fine," Leona said, coming back to the sink.

Fern detected a crack in her sister's voice and thought she might be able to get this visit figured out with a few well-placed prods.

Leona folded the drying towel. "I know what you're doing, Fern. Believe me, I will not be here one day longer than I need to be, so stop your inquisition."

Inquisition? Well, there's a five-dollar word. Fern bit her lip.

"Help me get my things out of the car."

In the driveway, Leona took exaggerated steps over the rutted ground while Fern pretended not to notice the straggly, overgrown azalea branches that caught on her sweater and threatened the porch steps.

Tweed suitcases, a bulging hanging bag, and shoeboxes filled every inch of the deep trunk. Fern was about to comment that it looked like Leona was moving in when the preacher's car turned up the driveway.

"Are you expecting company?" Leona asked.

Her question reminded Fern of how little Leona knew about her life.

Roy hopped out grinning. "Hope you don't mind us dropping by. I wanted you to meet my daughter." A gangly girl slid from the passenger side but stayed put behind the open door. "Hannah, this is Miss Fern."

The girl's slouched shoulders and dismissive glance let Fern know the visit had not been her idea.

"Happy to meet you," said Fern. "This is my sister, Leona, down from Raleigh. Leona, Roy just took over the pulpit at New Hope Methodist."

"Our grandmother was a founding member," Leona said, lifting her chin. "I'm sure you've seen her name in the historical records. Elizabeth Townson Barrett."

"The church has a proud history," Roy said, nodding.

Fern raised her eyebrows, signaling to him that she knew good and well he had no idea who Leona was talking about.

Hannah's yellow dress looked a size too small, and Fern longed to straighten the barrettes in her tangled hair. "I hear your teacher, Mrs. Blevins, is still crabby as ever. My aunt Belle taught with her and has some stories I think you'll like." Hannah's face softened and Fern saw how pretty she was.

Roy stepped toward the car. "Looks like you all could use some help."

"That won't be necessary," Leona said, lifting a small travel bag from the trunk. "Fern can manage." She walked up on the porch. "Nice to meet you both. It's good to see the old-fashioned Sunday afternoon church call hasn't been completely forgotten. Getting Fern back in the fold would certainly be a feather in your cap. Please come back when we can be better company."

Fern waited until the front door closed. "Leona's married to a doctor. A surgeon. Mostly knees, I believe."

Roy nodded. "We'll come back another time."

"Please do," she said. "I know that's what people always say, but I mean it. Do come back."

"Your house looks haunted," Hannah said.

"Oh, there're ghosts for sure," Fern said, "but they keep to themselves for the most part. The scariest thing in the house right now just walked through that door." Fern winked.

A slow smile spread across Hannah's face. "Nice to meet you, Miss Fern. Daddy, I'm going home to make a sandwich."

The girl walked across the sandy yard. "Independent," Fern said.

"And blunt," said Roy. "Hannah doesn't have an unexpressed thought."

"Well," said Fern, "like father, like daughter."

Roy laughed. "So, you read my column. You think I'll get run out of town?"

Fern wasn't accustomed to advising members of the clergy and was disinclined to tell him that confessing his struggle with faith would most likely upset the congregation a great deal, but something about the way he looked at her made even a white lie impossible.

"Folks around here like everything on the straight and narrow," she said. "Tobacco rows. Fairways. People. Faith. There'll be talk, I imagine. As for myself, I appreciate the honesty. Tells me you're not a phony."

"Not a phony. Now, that's high praise," he said with a big smile.

Fern laughed. For the first time since Leona's phone call that morning, she felt at ease.

"We'll just leave it alone, then," he said. "I believe it's best if the congregation knows where I'm coming from."

"I'm sorry for your loss," Fern said, immediately regretting the tired sentiment. "You're probably sick of hearing that."

"No. I thank you. Loss feels different over time, but by different I don't mean less. Some days I'm still surprised no one else seems to notice the whole world has changed. It makes people uncomfortable when I talk about her. I get that, but I can't help myself." Roy leaned against his car. "That's your husband's name on the bench outside the courthouse, isn't it?"

"Yes," she said.

"Then you know what I'm talking about."

No one except Dean had mentioned Mac to Fern in a very long time. The complicated truth of how she felt about her loss would shock the preacher.

Roy looked up at the house. "This really is a beautiful place."

"It's the only home I've ever known," Fern said. "My parents moved in with my grandmother after my grandfather died. Guess it's odd these days to stay in one place so long, but that's just how it worked out."

"Nothing wrong with roots," Roy said.

"As long as they don't choke you," Fern said. "Speaking of, I better get this stuff upstairs. Leona isn't used to waiting."

"Enjoy your visit."

The way he said it made her laugh. "Not likely," she said.

Watching his car go down the drive, Fern wondered if Roy was as forthright in the pulpit as he was one-on-one. Maybe she would go one day. Find out for herself. Imagining the looks she'd get at New Hope Methodist took her mind off lugging the bulky hanging bag up the stairs.

Leona stood at the open door to her bedroom with her hand on her throat.

"I haven't been in here for a while," Fern said, pushing around her. Was it possible the neglected room held traces of Spraynet and Shalimar? The scents seemed to mingle with the musty decline. Fern remembered what Hannah said. *Haunted.* She forced a smile. "It's like you never left." Her lie sounded ridiculous.

Leona covered her mouth with a closed fist.

The sisters studied Leona's shrine to the good life she'd willed true—the four-poster spindle bed that Grandma Barrett brought with her from South Carolina as a bride, marble topped nightstands, porcelain lamps painted with red rose bouquets to match the wallpaper. Leona had insisted on the store-bought chenille bedspread. A homemade quilt was never her style.

Fern balanced the hanging bag over the vanity chair and tried to open the front window. Painted shut, it wouldn't budge. She moved to the smaller side windows and finally knocked one loose. Dead flies littered the windowsill and she flicked them aside, behind the curtain, hoping Leona wouldn't see.

"Fresh air will help," Fern said, out of breath from all her banging and tugging. Leona remained at the doorway with her arms crossed. Seeing her sister so disheartened unsettled Fern. "If I'd had more notice, I would have fixed things up a bit." She pointed to where the wallpaper curled like a scroll. "We can get that back up. I've had to glue mine about a hundred times."

"Haven't you ever thought of changing anything?" Leona said.

"No. I mean, the wallpaper's fine, except in some places where it's loose. You picked it out."

Leona took a small step. "Haven't you wanted to freshen it, to update the look?"

"I wouldn't know where to start. And Lord knows you'd have a fit if I was down here changing wallpaper." She threw back the spread. "I'll get these sheets in the wash."

Leona walked to the front window. She brushed off the red velvet cushion of the window seat with a shy hand.

"I haven't cleaned in here in a while," Fern said. "I'll get the vacuum cleaner." She left Leona staring out the grimy window.

As the sisters vacuumed and dusted, Fern remembered how they'd worked as girls to keep the house up. Bernice Walker taught them to use lemon oil on the dark wainscoting in the foyer and the mahogany stair railing. She'd made them keep the floors swept, mopped, and shined. Bernice's mother had worked for Grandma and Grandpa Barrett, and Bernice grew up playing with Belle beneath the pecan trees. Later, when Bernice was in night school, Fern's daddy hired her to help Fern and Leona's mother, Matilda. It was a job nobody in town wanted. Bernice, out of loyalty to Belle, was the only person Matilda couldn't run off. And even after Bernice went to work at the bank, she would stop by occasionally to check on them with an apple cake or, Fern's favorite, a peach pie.

Leona never wanted anyone to know how bad off they were. Not even Bernice. She taught James and Fern to keep people out of their family's business. Leona made sure they showed up for school in clean clothes with their hair combed and their homework done. She forged her parents' names on report cards and made excuses when they missed teacher conferences. Leona, James, and Fern lived in two worlds, the real one and the one Leona created as if they'd been cast in a play.

Leona sprayed Windex on the vanity mirror, and Fern recalled how her sister used to primp and pose. Once, Fern snuck in the room and patted her face with the Coty powder Leona coveted. Leona had laughed seeing her sister's dark skin splotched pale. "Not exactly your shade, Fern," she'd said.

"I'm going to hang your bedspread on the line and let it air out," Fern said.

When she opened the back door, a yellow cat sprinted out from under the steps. She needed to put cat food in the pie pans Belle kept by the shed. Belle's mother had refused to let her have a pet, so as a child, Belle collected strays. Now she believed any cat that showed up at their back door was a descendant of Blackie or Tabby-Cat. Some were friendly, some feral. After what she and Belle referred to as "the summer of love," Fern made it her mission to trap newcomers and take them to the vet to get "fixed."

Fern draped the spread across the sagging clothesline. A rusty thermometer nailed to the porch read seventy-one degrees, and not one cloud marred the Carolina-blue sky. Fern couldn't resist taking a break in the sunshine. She sat in the glider and found her Salem Lights in her sweater pocket. If Leona hadn't shown up, she'd be spending the day with her new John Grisham book. A tangle of forsythia caught by a light breeze swayed against the sunny side of the house, and new-green vines seemed to have grown overnight around the scuppernong arbor. The old house looked best this time of year. Like it was coming, not going.

If Leona had her mind set on owning the house, she'd get it. *Like a dog with a bone.* That's what James said back in the day when Leona set her sights on Ned.

Leona would sit on the window seat like a princess waiting for Ned Thomas's Mustang to pull up the drive. He was her knight in shining armor. People wondered why a pretty girl like Leona would latch onto pudgy little Ned, but Fern knew why.

Leona would come back from Ned's house talking about Mrs. Thomas's cloth napkins and silver candlesticks. She'd go on and on about proper etiquette and how a family ought to have supper in the dining room. But Belle wouldn't have it. It was the sixties. Belle hung a portrait of John F. Kennedy on the wall, and Grandma's fancy dining room became the headquarters for Belle's and Bernice's letter-writing campaigns for everything from integration to voting rights.

"Maybe if you spent more time making a proper home and less time looking for a protest march, you'd find a husband," Leona told Belle.

Fern asked Belle once why she didn't marry. "I never wanted to be anything but what I was," she'd said.

As a child, Fern only knew her aunt through the birthday and Christmas presents that came in the mail. Fern's grandfather had died before she was born, but when Grandma Barrett died, Belle came home for her mother's funeral, after years of living away with no visits home.

Ten-year-old Fern had wandered off at the gravesite, and it was Belle who found her. She'd taken Fern's hand and meandered around the stones, telling her about their kin buried there. Holding hands with an adult was something Fern hadn't done much of. She was shy about it, but liked knowing she was joined by blood to the kind woman who talked to her like she was somebody. It was the memory of that day in the graveyard with Belle that gave Fern the courage to call her three years later.

It was Sheriff Ernie Tate who came to tell them their daddy had crashed his car and died. Leona was sixteen, James was fifteen and Fern had just turned thirteen. It was daybreak on a Sunday morning. Fern woke to banging on the front door. She didn't get up at first, thinking it was her daddy knocking, too drunk to get in the house. He never missed a Saturday night card game at the Elks Club. When the knocking didn't stop, she snuck downstairs and found Sheriff Tate on the porch.

"I need to talk to your mama," he said when Fern opened the door.

Fern knew better than to try and rouse her mother before noon. Matilda's brightest hours were in the evening. She and their daddy drank bourbon and danced to Chubby Checker played on the Magnavox stereo, which had been delivered to the house shortly after Grandma died.

Fern went to Leona's room. "It's Sheriff Tate," she said, shaking her sister awake.

The children were accustomed to seeing the Sheriff at their door. He and their daddy had gone to school together, so while most drunks went straight to the Moore County jail, Spencer Barrett got hand-delivered home. But this time seemed different. Fern had never seen Ernie Tate so solemn.

Leona pulled on her robe and hurried down to where the Sheriff stood with his hat in his hands. James had heard the commotion. He leaned against the stair railing with his arms crossed over his skinny chest. Fern was sure the three of them were a pitiful sight.

"I need to see your mama," the sheriff said to Leona.

Leona had held her chin high and buried her hands in the pockets of her robe, "She's not feeling well this morning."

Fern looked past Sheriff Tate, still expecting her daddy to stumble in.

James went past Ernie. "You need help getting him out of the car?"

Leona cut her eyes at James. He had become more and more unwilling to keep quiet about the plain truth.

"Not today, son." Sheriff Tate puffed out his chest as if that's what his duty required. "Your daddy had an accident." He must have seen by their blank stares that his practiced words didn't register. He was nervous with his news. "A feller found the car still smoking out near Taylor Town. Burned up. The body's done up at the funeral home."

Without a word, Leona turned and climbed the stairs. James got ahead of her, taking the steps two at a time. Fern, paralyzed by all she couldn't comprehend, watched Sheriff Tate leave. He never looked back. His patrol car was pulling out onto the road when Matilda came down the steps screaming, "No! No! No!" She wore a thin white gown stained with coffee. She grabbed for the banister. "Spencer? Spencer? Spencer?" She hollered like his name would bring him about.

Leona followed her into the front room. "Mama, he's not here. Mama, Daddy's dead. Ernie Tate said Daddy's dead." Leona cried, something Fern had never seen and hadn't seen since. Fern cried too. She knew they both were crying more from fear than heartache.

James flew out the front door, his shirttail flapping. He told her later that he'd run all the way to the funeral home. He wanted to see their daddy for himself. But when he got to the white double doors, he lost his nerve.

Meanwhile, their mother had pulled a bottle of Four Roses bourbon from the kitchen cabinet and a juice glass from the shelf. She slumped into a chair. "What are we going to do?" she asked Leona over and over. "How are we going to live?" When the bottle was half gone, Leona helped their mother upstairs and put her to bed.

Fern knew Belle's number was in the red address book by the phone in the front hall. She dialed the number and Belle answered. Leona heard Fern talking to their aunt and hurried down the stairs. She snatched the heavy black receiver out of Fern's hand. Fern thought she might hang it up, but she didn't.

"Aunt Belle, father has been taken from us," she said, resurrecting the stiff dialect passed down to her from Grandma Barrett.

No news travels faster than the news of death. Before long, the preacher's car came up the drive. His wife stood with him on the porch with a dishcloth-covered basket. Leona refused to let them in.

"We are not receiving company," Leona said through the half-opened door. She took the basket of warm ham biscuits and barely thanked them. Fern watched from the top of the stairs. They didn't turn away right at first, just peered through the yellowed sheer curtain that covered the wavy glass, as if they expected someone to come and right young Leona's wrong.

"Well, I never," the preacher's wife had said.

It was as if Leona thought they could pretend their mother wasn't passed out across her bed and their daddy wasn't at the funeral home too burned and broken to be seen.

The one person who wouldn't be cowed by Leona was Bernice Walker. When she drove up, Fern met her in the yard.

Leona came out on the front porch. "We don't need you, Miss Walker. I'm taking care of things."

"You are, are you?" Bernice said. "Well, it's half-past twelve, and Fern's still running around here in a ratty gown, and I'm betting you don't know that your brother is walking the streets uptown, and God knows what your mama's doing in that pigsty of hers. Now come ride with me to get James while Fern gets her clothes on. Belle is on her way, and the good folks you turned away this morning will be coming back to pay their respects. We need to be ready." She'd taken a breath then. "We'll get through this."

When they got back from town with James, Bernice tied an apron around her waist and put them all to work in the kitchen. Leona polished silver, James peeled apples, and Fern kneaded biscuit dough. Bernice sang hymns softly to herself as she washed and dried a stack of plates pulled from Grandma Barrett's sideboard. In hindsight, Fern understood Bernice had meant to comfort them the best she could. When the blue Volkswagen Beetle pulled up behind the house, Bernice dropped her dish towel and ran out the back door. Fern followed, sticky dough still on her fingers.

"Oh, my Lord," Bernice hugged her old friend to her. "Your no-account brother has left you a devil of a mess."

Belle looked tiny in Bernice's arms. When the two parted, Fern stood back, unsure of the diminutive woman with her bowl-cut hair and horn-rimmed glasses. But when her aunt smiled, Fern knew she had rightly remembered her kindness.

Belle was forty-seven when she came back to Carthage in 1965. Her Volkswagen had a peace sign on the back window and a bumper sticker endorsing LBJ for President.

The first thing she did was sit them down at the kitchen table.

"I'm so sorry about your daddy."

Leona sighed and crossed her arms.

"I stopped by the funeral home on the way into town and told Mr. Robbins I'd bring Matilda back up there to choose a casket," Belle said. "If it's okay with you all, I think it's best if we have the wake here at the house."

"I'll choose the casket," Leona said, not hiding her resentment. "Mother isn't able."

Belle nodded. "Well, we'll let her rest. James, will you and Fern help Miss Walker while we're gone? I know this is a hard day, but staying busy will do us all good."

When Belle and Leona got back from the funeral home, Leona dashed upstairs without a word. Belle and Bernice wrestled with the dusty drapes in the front room. The afternoon sunlight exposed what the once elegant room had become. An ashtray overflowed on the red velvet settee. Rings from half-empty glasses marred the cherry end tables. Records and a pair of high heeled shoes littered the floor. It was October and the day carried a chill, but Belle and Bernice pried opened every window they could.

"This house smells like the Five O'Clock Club," Bernice said.

Matilda came down the stairs, her long dark hair disheveled, her face streaked with black Maybelline. "What's this racket down here?"

She stopped dead when she saw Belle. She gathered her green kimono around her, fumbled with the sash like she'd forgotten how to tie a knot, and threw back her head. "Don't come down here thinking you can boss me. Spencer always said you thought you were better than the rest of us."

Hearing her mama go after somebody wasn't new. Fern had heard her cuss out strangers for walking on her side of the street. But Fern had never seen anybody look at her mother like Belle did. Belle wasn't scared. She wasn't even disgusted. It was like she was sorry. Sorry her mama had to be the way she was.

"Fern, come help me in the kitchen," Bernice said.

Fern backed out into the hall, but only far enough to stay out of sight.

"That's the grief talking, Matilda," Belle said. "I'm grieving too. Spencer and I were never close, but he was my brother, and I wish I could have done more to help him. To help all of you. I intend to change that. We'll talk more later, but right now, we've got to get this house in shape. People will be coming this evening, and we need to be ready."

"This is not your house," Matilda said, her words raspy from too many cigarettes. "It belongs to James now. Spencer told me that's how it'd be. He told me a lot of things. I know what you are."

Belle went back to fluffing the chair pillows like they were something precious. "This will be my house until James comes of age."

Fern waited for another outburst, but her mother swung around and stomped upstairs, where she stayed, not even coming down when the funeral home rolled the dark casket into the front room, or to accept pity from the obligated few who showed up to pay their respects that evening. Somehow, with her daddy's dead body in the front room and her mother out of sight, their family seemed almost normal.

When everyone had gone, Fern went to the door of the cramped back bedroom, where she found Belle unpacking. "If this is your house, where will we go?"

"Oh, Fern," Belle said. She sat down on the bed and patted the spread for Fern to join her. "You're going to stay right here. This is your home, honey, and it always will be. I'm going to stay here with you, if that's all right."

"You staying would be fine with me," Fern said, trying to sound as grown up as she could.

The day of the burial, her mother's people came from Red Springs. Her sisters hurried upstairs, where Matilda fell into their arms. Their husbands stayed outside by their old green Chevrolet passing a bottle still in the brown paper sack. The sisters and their men were big-boned and dark-headed like Matilda. One of the sisters smiled at Fern and it scared her. From the back porch, Fern heard the rumble of voices coming from an upstairs window that had been opened despite the cold.

At her daddy's burial, Fern leaned close to her mama under the funeral tent. A cold rain fell. She'd outgrown her coat and only had it wrapped around her shoulders. It did nothing to keep away the chill. The wind blew up and one of the flower stands at the head of the coffin rocked and fell, scattering white carnations across the bare ground. Fern had clung to her mama's arm, knowing somehow she needed to hold Matilda close, keep her still. But after the last amen, Bernice Walker led Fern and James and Leona away to her car. When they got home, the house was full of folks, but their mama wasn't there.

Belle took the children into the kitchen. "Your mother needs rest. She's gone to stay with her sisters."

"For how long?" Leona asked.

When Belle hesitated, James spoke up. "What about you?"

"I'm staying."

Bernice put her arm around Fern. "You all are going to be better off now," she said. "Belle's going to look after you, and I'm going to help her all I can. You're going to be all right, so don't cry over your daddy and mama. Your mama's where she ought to have always been." She paused, then exhaled like her words were red hot on her tongue. "And your daddy too," she said.

Bernice didn't say Spencer Barrett was burning in hell, but Fern knew what she meant.

Fern crept up to her parents' room. The smell of cigarettes lingered. A pile of *Life* magazines covered her daddy's nightstand. A turned-over blue bottle of Evening in Paris and used-up Avon lipsticks littered her mama's mirrored vanity tray. It may have looked unchanged, but the room felt different, like a fever that had long hindered the house had broken. Fern slipped the perfume bottle into her pocket.

After Belle came, Fern couldn't get over the wonder of fresh milk. She drank a quart a day until she saw it would always be there. There were regular mealtimes, help with homework, and Fern could have her best friend, Carol Ann, over to spend the night. Belle put a radio in the kitchen, and it stayed on the Raleigh station all day long. Bernice came often, and there were card games and laughter. "We need a family car," Belle said. She traded her Volkswagen for a green Mercury station wagon.

That was one of the few concessions Aunt Belle made to her new life in Carthage. Leona had recently started dating Ned, and Belle's outspoken liberal attitudes horrified Mrs. Thomas. In Leona's opinion, her aunt managed to make the shaky Barrett family reputation even worse.

When Belle went to court and became their legal guardian, Leona accused her of trying to steal Barrett House from James, the rightful heir. Nothing Belle could say would change her mind, and Leona's bitterness grew.

For so long, Fern believed their family secrets were well kept. She believed no one knew what went on inside their house. But eventually she came to understand that when Spencer Barrett flew his Cadillac off the road, everybody knew he'd been driving home drunk after gambling all night at the Elks Club, and when Matilda got in her sister's old Chevrolet after the funeral, everybody knew she'd left for good.

Leona tilted the truth of their family history. To hear her tell it, their daddy was killed by a drunk driver, which was not exactly a lie. Her excuse for their mama skirted plain fact while also grazing the truth. "Mother was very ill and went back to her family so not to be a burden on her children."

Shortly after the second anniversary of their daddy's death, James and Fern came home from school to find a fresh peach pie cooling on the kitchen counter. Leona was in Raleigh at Meredith College. Belle told them Matilda had died. That she'd been sick, and it was a blessing she was no longer in pain.

For so long, thinking about her parents had felt like a sin as much as lying or stealing. Fern had nightmares about being in that Chevy, squeezed between her mama's loud sisters. She'd never really wanted her mother to come back, had rarely asked about her. Now her mother was dead. Tears finally felt right. She could mourn her mother, maybe even love her.

That night, Fern sat by the Magnavox and tried to picture her parents happy. She pulled out the old records they used to play. Martha and the Vandellas. Chubby Checker. The Drifters.

She remembered standing in the doorway and watching them dance. How her daddy would see Fern and say, "Come on, honey, dance with us." She remembered trying to swing and sway like her mother, but the harder Fern tried, the more her mother shimmied and shook. Soon they'd forget Fern was there, and she'd slip out unnoticed.

Belle said Matilda's funeral had already been, and no one mentioned driving two hours down the road to visit the grave.

Fern stayed out of school the rest of the week, but James went on like nothing had happened. Fern imagined what he kept inside was more than she'd poured out. And Leona, angry with Belle over something Fern couldn't even remember, wasn't speaking to any of them at the time.

Now, James was gone. Belle's mind drifted from one decade to another. And Leona's old blanket spread over the clothesline beat time with the breeze as if trying to free itself. Fern shut her eyes and lifted her face to the sun. The rusty glider slipped back and forth and threatened to slip from its frame. She was in no hurry to get back upstairs to that musty room. Whatever her sister wanted, she would know soon enough.

Leona

L eona had no idea *Wheel of Fortune* ran reruns on Sunday evenings, but Fern and Belle stared at the TV screen like their lives depended on dollars they couldn't win. Leona flipped through a three-year-old *Southern Living* she'd plucked from a pile beside the sofa and made a mental note to add *get rid of old magazines* to her long list of things to do.

Belle and Fern pulled for the underdog, easily identified before the first commercial break. Leona thought it unfair that the bright-eyed teacher from Omaha had fallen so far behind. She was the most skilled puzzle solver, but her last turn left her bankrupt and one peg short of a trip to Wyoming. She'd never overcome that one bad spin, but that was life.

Earlier, when Fern offered leftover casserole for dinner, Leona had opted for a can of Campbell's tomato soup. Now, she was hungry. "Anyone want cake?" she asked, putting down her magazine.

Fern and Belle, captivated by the final puzzle, shook their heads.

The only light in the kitchen came from over the stove. The cake sat on the counter. Leona turned to get a plate from the cabinet. A man sat at the table. Leona screamed.

"God almighty, what's wrong with you?" Dean said.

Leona found the overhead light switch just as Fern rushed in.

"Dean scared the living daylights out of me."

"I'm just sitting here eating." Dean turned to his mother. "I saw her car out front. How come she ain't gone?"

"Dean," Fern said. "Leona's here for a visit."

"How long?" His irritation was obvious.

"I will have you know I can stay as long as I please," Leona said. "It just so happens I've been keeping this house up since before you were born."

"Let me tell you something," Dean pointed his fork at Leona. "We don't need you down here throwing your money around. I'm about to hit it big. I'm starting up an emu farm."

"Emu?" Leona said.

"Honey, why don't you take your supper upstairs?" Fern said.

He pushed away from the table and stood. "I'll be at the trailer 'til she gets the hell out of here."

"Trailer?" Leona said.

Dean swiped his plate from the table and let the back door slam behind him.

"James set a trailer in the tobacco field," Fern said. "He said he needed privacy."

"Can you see it from the road?" Leona asked.

"If you look hard enough, yes," Fern said.

"Oh, my word. That is absolutely the tackiest thing I've ever heard." Leona held on to the back of a chair.

"It's a trailer," Fern said. "There aren't any trailers in Raleigh?"

"Not next door to historic homes." Leona felt faint. She dropped her head and closed her eyes.

"Listen," Fern said. "This house. The land. That trailer. They are all Dean's to do with as he sees fit."

Leona faced her sister. "You know good and well he's not fit to make good decisions."

Belle stood in the kitchen doorway. She rapped her cane on the linoleum. "What's all this commotion in here?"

Leona looked confused, but Fern suspected their raised voices had transported Belle's mind back to her classroom days.

"We're just talking," Fern said, leading her to the table. "It's okay. Let me get you some cake. You want some cake? Leona? Cake?"

"I've lost my appetite," Leona said. She brushed past Belle and grabbed the cordless phone from the front hall table. She'd call Ned. He'd know what to do. Halfway up the stairs, Leona remembered Ned was no longer hers to call. If she dialed his pager and left a message, he'd call her back. He'd listen. But it was his fault she was in this godforsaken mess. Besides, Ned always thought she was too hard on her family.

Ned. Her only confidant in the world. The only person who knew her life. The only person she'd ever trusted.

The heat vents carried sound throughout the house like a furtive intercom. Fern and Belle were still talking in the kitchen. Leona couldn't make out their words, but she could tell by their tone that she was the topic of the conversation. Growing up, Leona stayed aware of her parent's moods by listening to what traveled through the vents. In those days, if laughter changed to shouting, Leona rushed James and Fern into her room to keep them from whatever might erupt. She remembered one night the three of them slipped outside to hide in the shed. They slept in the shed so often, Leona kept blankets in an old army trunk. It was summer. About a year before their father died. She would have been fifteen, James fourteen, and Fern twelve. While Fern and James slept, Leona kept watch. When her father shot a hole through the kitchen wall, she saw the blast before she heard it. Fern and James sat up, startled, wide awake. Leona told them it was nothing. Just the backfire from a passing car. She'd tried to protect them the best she could, not that Fern ever appreciated it. She just thought Leona was bossy and laughed at her behind her back. Leona imagined she still did.

Fern thought Leona wanted Barrett House. She didn't. Not really. But she'd rather have Fern think that was the reason she was back. Anything but the truth.

Leona sat on the sagging bed, the phone still in her hand. How had she ended up here? Yesterday she was trying to decide what to wear to a gala, and tonight she was in Carthage arguing with her sister over a trailer. It was as if her struggles to overcome every hard thing for the last thirty years counted for nothing.

Her nightstand drawer hung crooked, and she had tried to straighten it, but it stuck. She shook the drawer open and rummaged through what was once hers. Old Bic pens, a church bulletin, a monogrammed handkerchief that had been her grandmother's, a gold hoop earring, a tube of Chapstick, copper pennies gone green, two ticket stubs. She didn't have to look to know the ticket stubs were for *Please Don't Eat the Daisies* with Doris Day. The Sunrise Theater. Jack McGregor. The only boy she'd ever kissed besides Ned.

A year older than Leona and Ned, Jack flirted with Leona all through high school, never seeming to mind her rebuffs. Her girlfriends thought she was crazy to turn him down, but Jack was careless. Risky. He let it be known he didn't care about college and meant to stay home and work at his father's Ford dealership. More than anything in the world, Leona wanted out of Carthage. She knew Ned did too.

The summer Leona turned seventeen, Ned was at the beach with his family, and Jack showed up at the house on a Friday night. "Come on," he said. "I know you're Ned's girl, but can't we just go to a movie?" Belle practically pushed her into Jack's car. Even now Leona remembered how her whole body trembled sitting beside Jack in the dark theater. On the drive back to Carthage, with his arm stretched across the seat, his fingertips touching her shoulder, he asked, "You think you and Ned are a sure thing?"

"Yes," she answered. "We're perfect for each other."

Jack laughed. "You've got to be kidding."

Leona pulled away from him.

"Hey, come on, I'm sorry. It's just …" he didn't finish his thought.

When he walked her to the door, he kissed her long and hard before she even thought to resist. "Good luck, Leona," he said, heading down the porch steps.

She trembled now, remembering. The faded ticket stub felt like velvet between her fingers. She could have had another life. But Ned had seemed like a sure thing back then, and a sure thing was all she ever wanted.

Fern

"Did you hear her? Did you hear what she said about the trailer?" Fern knew she sounded like a child but couldn't help herself. She lifted the Tupperware cover off the pound cake. "She turns my mind back-ass-wards."

Belle patted Fern's hand. "Honey, that's just Leona's way. She's got her ideas about things. As I recall, you weren't a bit happy when James set the trailer down there. You were worried sick she'd see it when she came for his funeral."

"I know, but who gives her the right to come in here like the judge and jury."

"Well," Belle said. "Let's try and make her feel at home. Leona seems awfully nervous."

Thankful that Belle sounded clear-headed, Fern brought two hunks of cake to the table on paper napkins. How many nights had the two of them sat like this? Too many to count.

"I need to find out what could happen if she contests the will."

Belle covered Fern's hand with hers, "Look at me. She's hurting. I see it in her eyes. Mama's eyes would get like that, red-rimmed and watery, when she was put out with something. Mostly me. I thought I knew everything back then."

"Legend has it that you broke every rule they had over at the Women's College," Fern said.

"I did," Belle said. "Then I came home and broke all of Mama's. She tried to get my daddy to disown me, but he wouldn't do it. God bless him."

"Grandma was tough, Aunt Belle."

"Oh, she was. But the years have taught me that stubborn can look a whole lot of ways."

Fern laughed and spoke through a mouthful of cake. "Are you trying to tell me something?"

"We've kept too much from your sister," Belle said. "Why not tell her about Dean's trouble."

Fern wadded up her napkin. "Let me sleep on it. We better get to bed. God only knows what she'll have us doing in the morning."

"Take Leona a piece of cake," Belle said. "That's what she came in here for."

Light shone beneath Leona's bedroom door. Fern knocked. "I'm leaving you some cake out here, okay?" She waited, but no answer came.

Fern was not in favor of the hard conversation Belle prescribed. Confessing Dean's diagnosis would lead to recounting every mistake Fern ever made, and she felt sure her sister already had a lengthy list memorized.

Leona never failed to bring up Dean's Christmas tantrum. Shortly after that, he'd thrown a rock during recess and caught a boy right above the eye. It wasn't his first offense at school. When Dean had his fits, he hit. Bit. Kicked. The school shuffled him from first to second grade, but by third, after moving him from one teacher to another until there were no more to try, the principal, Fred Munford, called for Fern to come to the school. He claimed Dean's outbursts were out of control, and if he hurt another child, the school could be sued. Mumford said Dean needed to be tested for psychological problems and claimed his disruptions made it impossible for him to stay at Carthage Elementary.

Fern told him to go straight to hell and stormed out of his office. Dean sat huddled in a hallway chair, swallowed up in his winter coat, his book bag in his lap, his eyes big as quarters. It took all she had not to break down. His fits were like seizures, and after he had one, he'd be worn out. Fern got him by the hand and headed for the door while Fred Munford hollered after them, "I have to let Family Services know about this."

"Will they come get me, Mama?" Dean said, once they were in the car. "Mr. Munford said I ought to be sent off. He said I couldn't come back there, and no school would have me."

Fern cupped his thin face in her hands. "Nobody is sending you anywhere. You've got the best teacher there is at home. Aunt Belle can teach you just fine."

Carol Ann came that evening. The two of them sat on the porch after Dean was asleep.

"I've got to do something," Fern said.

Carol Ann blew out a long sigh. "Belle and I have been waiting a long time to hear you say that. There's a pediatrician in Raleigh. I called up there this afternoon. He works with..." She hesitated.

"Troubled children." Fern wiped her eyes. "Dean got a bad start."

"Honey, that was a hard time. But these people can help him. You know I love that boy. That's why I'm saying you have got to get him some help."

Carol Ann drove Fern and Dean to Raleigh. The doctor's office had a puzzle laid out on a table that kept Dean busy while Fern filled out a thick pile of forms. Alcohol consumption during pregnancy. No box she could check would begin to tell the story.

Before he saw Dean, Dr. Williamson asked to speak to her alone. He was a stocky man with rusty red hair and a beard, only slightly older than Fern. He nodded for her to take a seat while he read over the questionnaire. She studied the books stuck helter-skelter in the bookcase behind his desk. What all did this man know, she wondered. She'd sent him Dean's medical records and the thick file he'd accumulated at school.

"Tell me about your pregnancy?" he said.

Fern told him how Mac went missing while she was pregnant. She told the story without the shadows. Dr. Williamson's expression never changed. When Fern finished her counterfeited tale, all he said was, "I noticed you didn't answer the questions about drugs or alcohol."

It came to her that he didn't give a damn what she'd done or hadn't done. He just needed the facts. She started over. "I drank heavily when I was pregnant. I should've known better, but the truth is, I didn't." She went on to confess she didn't remember much about Dean's first months, except that he never stopped crying. How with every breath it was as if he was trying to tell her the harm she'd done. She told Dr. Williamson she justified Dean's slow development by believing not all babies sat up, or pulled up, or walked at the same time, but in hindsight, she thought Dean's doctor in Carthage had known something was wrong but with her husband missing in Vietnam, he hadn't wanted to add to their worries.

Dr. Williamson took off his glasses and held them up to the light. He pulled a Kleenex from a box and cleaned them. "Are you drinking now?"

"No," she said. "I quit before Dean was a year old when I saw how much he needed me."

"Let me spend some time with him. I'm going to check his balance, coordination, motor skills, and take him downstairs for an eye and hearing test, and an EKG."

Fern and Carol Ann thumbed forward and backward through a pile of National Geographic magazines for two anxious hours before Dr. Williamson called her back into his office. "Mrs. McQueen, there's a relatively new diagnosis we're hearing more about called Fetal Alcohol Syndrome."

Alcohol. She'd always suspected she was the cause.

"There's no definitive test, but Dean's physical features and delayed development are congruent with what I've read." He handed her what looked like pages he'd xeroxed from a textbook. "There are degrees of severity. Dean's case appears mild, and I didn't hear any signs of a heart murmur."

"I did this," she said, unable to say more.

"Mrs. McQueen, no one talked seriously about alcohol consumption when you were pregnant. Beating yourself up isn't going to help Dean. Your son is highly functional. His anxiety can be treated with medication and behavior modification therapy. I asked earlier if you were still drinking because it's important for Dean to live in a stable household. He needs structure and routine. Unfortunately, there probably aren't any special education opportunities in your area, but with treatment, Dean can go back to school."

"No," she said. "I won't have him treated poorly. I have another idea."

The next week, Belle gave notice at the high school. By the time Family Services got around to checking, Dean was officially being homeschooled. The i's were dotted and the t's crossed. Dr. Williamson set up regular appointments with a child psychologist in Southern Pines, and throughout that summer, Belle drove to North Carolina State in Raleigh once a week to get certified in special education.

When Dean turned sixteen, his love of cars drew him to Frank's garage. Frank called Fern. "Your boy has a mechanical mind. Would it be okay for him to work up here?" She told him all she could without naming Dean's affliction. When she was done, he said, "Ain't none of us perfect, Fern. All I know is he can fix cars."

The town of Carthage loved Michael Dean McQueen. He'd do anything for anybody. Help them move, mow their yards, feed their cats and dogs when they went on vacation. Some called him the unofficial mayor of Carthage. Fern knew it was out of love for Dean that the town kept her secret and went along with him when he talked about Mac, his father the war hero.

Fern felt as if she'd struck a bargain with Carthage. She would walk the straight and narrow, and the town would keep her secret.

First Doyle Blue and now Leona coming back put that bargain at risk. She couldn't trust either one of them.

After a restless night imagining all that could go wrong, Fern sat with Belle reading the morning paper as if she wasn't a bit worried about what Leona would say when she came down to breakfast. Dean's jeep was gone, meaning he was having biscuits with Brandi at the Stop 'n Go.

Her sister's footsteps on the stairs made Fern sit up straighter in her chair.

Leona breezed into the kitchen in a long mint-green robe with matching slippers. She reminded Fern of the doctor's wives on General Hospital. "Well, don't you look pretty," Belle said.

"Did you sleep all right?" Fern made her voice light and friendly, hoping last night's fight could be forgotten.

"Not a wink," Leona said. "This house creaks and moans like a ship at sea."

Fern held her tongue, not saying she wished Leona's ship would sail right back to Raleigh. She pushed her chair under the table and slung her pocketbook over her shoulder determined to make a fast exit.

Leona sniffed. "Are you all still smoking? I thought you'd quit."

Belle lifted the newspaper to hide her face.

"We've cut back," Fern said, gathering her car keys. "It's a process."

"I cannot be around cigarette smoke," Leona said. "Or cats. I saw those pie pans outside. I can't believe you are still feeding the stray cat population of Moore County."

Before Fern could remind her sister how much Belle enjoyed her strays, Leona opened the cabinet door. "Where do you keep the Sweet'N Low?"

"I don't keep the Sweet'N Low anywhere," Fern said. "We use old-fashioned sugar. I need to go. I'm behind on a deadline." A fresh lie. There was nothing about the truth that seemed right to tell Leona.

"I thought we'd talk about what needs to be done around here," she said.

Relieved Leona hadn't mentioned Dean or the trailer, Fern pointed to a notepad and pen by the telephone. "Make a list. I'll be back at lunch."

Fern patted Belle's frail shoulder, "See you afterwhile."

Belle lowered the paper. "You pay attention up there today. Learn something."

Hearing the words Belle used to say when they were kids going off to school made Fern's heart skip a beat. She laughed as if Belle had made a joke. "That's right, just like the old days, I'll go learn something." She looked to see if Leona had heard, but she'd gone into the pantry. Fern bent down and whispered. "I'm going to work, Belle, up at the paper, you know, the *Citizen-Times*." Bill Clinton appeared on the television, and Fern pointed. "Who's that?"

"Well, Fern, that's the President," Belle said.

"That's right. President Bill Clinton."

"Yes," Belle said, sure and strong.

Leona burst out of the pantry. "You mean to tell me there's not one package of Sweet'N Low in this entire house?"

"Not a one," Fern said. Belle gazed at the television. Fern hoped the president had charmed her aunt's mind back to 1998. "We prefer the real thing. No substitutions."

At the office, Fern made another pot of coffee to compensate for her sleepless night. She leaned back in her unsteady chair.

"Yoo-hoo," Carol Ann breezed through the door. "Got a closing next door."

"You know, this isn't a diner," Fern said. "You keep showing up, I'm going to start charging you by the cup." She motioned for Carol Ann to follow her to the kitchenette.

"My, my, you're in a foul mood. You might need one of those hormonal patches."

"I'm going to need more than that. Guess who I left at my kitchen table?"

Carol Ann got a look on her face not often seen, one that said she didn't know the answer. Then her eyes got wide. "Not that sweet preacher man."

"No. Leona Blanche Barrett Thomas."

"Get out."

"She says she's worried about Belle and has come down here to help out."

"Bullhocky."

Robert stumbled in the back door. "Hey, look who's here," he said, grinning at Carol Ann. Robert loved Carol Ann because she flirted with him. In Fern's opinion, he was too naive to know Carol Ann was not just kidding around.

"If it isn't the fair prince himself," Carol Ann said, her voice raised to an adolescent key.

Fern pushed herself off the counter. She was in no mood for a Robert—Carol Ann love fest.

"Carol Ann," Fern yelled from her desk. "I need you."

She and Robert came out of the kitchenette. "I'm sorry," she said. "You know this boy drives me crazy. Where were we? Oh yes, Leona's home acting like she gives a damn about

Belle." She sat in the ancient slat-back chair across from Fern's desk. "Well, she's lying because she's never cared one bit about Belle. Could be Ned's finally decided to come out the closet and she's no longer welcome."

"Carol Ann," Fern nodded her head toward Robert.

"Oh, for heaven's sake, Fern. You think Robert doesn't know the ways of the world? I've been telling you for years, Ned Thomas is gay. I don't know why people make such a big deal about it. Why should the man have to live a lie?"

"That's crazy talk. They've been married thirty some years."

"Doesn't matter. Happens all the time. Doesn't it Robert?"

Robert twirled around in his chair. "What?"

Fern spoke up before Carol Ann could explain her theory in more detail. "I think she's here to get evidence against Dean so she can take the house."

"All she'd have to do is get her lawyer to file a contention." Carol Ann threw her head back and studied the pressed tin ceiling like there were answers written on it. "No, I think this is something else. Something big."

Fern started to tell her that Leona throwing them all out on the street was big, but Carol Ann checked her watch. "Got to go. The closing's at ten."

"I'll walk with you," Robert said. "I can't be late for the Board of Elections meeting."

Robert's attempt to sound serious and important made Fern feel a little bit sorry for him. She shook her head, "That's tomorrow night, honey. This morning the county commissioners are voting on the new fire hydrants."

Carol Ann gave Robert her pixie grin with the nose scrunch, "You're still walking my way."

"Is he ever," Fern said under her breath.

"Fern," Carol Ann said. "I say the same for Leona as I said about Doyle. Leave it to the gnats. She'll be gone in no time."

Dean

Dean raised his head out from under the hood of a Toyota Corolla just as Mr. Frank walked in the garage with a tall gray-headed man. They shouted over the high whine of the air hose and a jam box blaring out Kix-106 Country radio. The man said he had a Buick for sale and needed to get it checked out before he put an ad in the paper.

Dean wiped his hands on a grimy towel. "You don't want to do that," he said. "You'll get all kinds of crooks and criminals coming to your house and they'll rob you blind. Take it over to J.B.'s Used Cars. He's out on the highway."

The tall man stared at Dean, then walked over and held out his hand. "Doyle Blue."

Dean backed up. "Grease," he said, holding up his black palms. "You played ball with my daddy, Mac McQueen. I've seen your picture."

"Dean." The man smiled. "How've you been?"

"All right." Doyle Blue stared at him like he might have something on this face. Dean wiped his chin with the back of his hand.

"Doyle," Mr. Frank said, "come on in the office."

Doyle Blue nodded then turned back to Dean, "J.B.'s Used Cars, huh?"

"You don't want no strangers coming to your house. J.B.'s an honest man."

"Thank you, Dean. I'll take your advice."

Dean ended up doing the work on the Buick. Mr. Frank wanted Whitey Whitehead to do it, but Whitey was taking his time on Sissy Murphy's Maverick. He liked the way she came in and talked to him every day. Dean had the Buick finished by the next afternoon.

"Hey, Dean. Is she ready?" Doyle Blue asked, coming in the open garage door.

"Yes sir. I changed out the oil, redone the brake pads, replaced the fluid, and cleaned up around the plugs. Got the tires aligned. You ought not have any trouble getting top dollar. It don't have but 67,426 miles on it, and the interior is good as new." Dean believed a man had a right to know what was done to his car. Mr. Frank came out of his office.

"Sounds like you didn't have to do as much to it as you thought, Frank," Doyle said. "I guess your estimate was a little off."

Whitey yelled over, "Hey, Dean? You tell Frank you're going to be a bird farmer? What do you call 'em? E-moo?"

During the morning break, Whitey had seen Dean studying "The Emu Farmer's Handbook" Mr. Peavey had given him.

Whitey kept on. "Frank, ask Dean how he's going to make his first million." A couple of the other fellows had gathered around, grinning. Whitey liked making Dean the joke, especially late in the day when the work slacked off. Dean felt himself getting the jitters.

Mr. Blue spoke up, "I've heard of emus. You starting a farm, Dean?"

"Yeah. I bought two last Saturday," Dean said. He looked down at the ground and tried to get his head still. "I just got to get the tobacco field fenced in and I'll be ready."

"Them are big old birds," said Whitey.

"He's gonna be riding them things down Main Street," Herman Cox said.

"Yeah, like Super Chicken," Whitey said. Whitey and Herman had the whole shop laughing.

"Sounds interesting," Mr. Blue said. "I tell you what. If you're looking for a partner, let me know. I'm getting my construction business set up, and I'd be happy to help you out with your fence." He pulled out his wallet and gave Dean a card with his name and phone number on it. "Call me and we'll talk." He grabbed Dean's hand and shook it, grease and all, like he and Dean were already partners. Then he turned around to Mr. Frank. "Let's see how much I really owe you."

Dean called Mr. Blue the next morning.

Friday, close to twelve, Dean ducked in the washroom to change into a clean shirt. He didn't want to go up to Mr. Blue's looking a mess. While he was scrubbing his hands with a hard-bristled brush, Whitey came in.

"You got a date?"

"Naw," Dean said.

"How come you're scrubbing the skin off your hands then? That old girl at the Stop 'n Go ain't going to care."

"I ain't going to the Stop 'n Go." Dean knew he was talking about Brandi. Whitey and the rest of them ribbed him about her all the time.

Whitey did his business and came over to the second sink. "You going to the Dairy Bar? If you are, bring me back a shake."

"I ain't going to the Dairy Bar."

Whitey shook his hands and rubbed them through his dirty hair, admiring himself in the mirror. "Then, where in the hell you going?"

Dean grabbed a handful of paper towels and dried his hands. "It ain't none of your business."

Whitey followed him, calling out for all to hear, "Dean's got a nooner."

"I ain't got no nooner."

The other boys sat in the shade at a rickety picnic table smoking and eating their lunch out of paper sacks. They laughed like they always did at Whitey.

"Whitey, you'd better not go to your old lady's for lunch today," one of them said. "You might see that jeep back around her house." That got Whitey going.

Dean headed for Mr. Blue's.

He found the one-story brick building on the road to Pine Bluff. A freshly painted white sign with sky blue block letters spelled out *Blue Construction*. When Dean opened the door, a bell rang, but he didn't see a soul.

Mr. Blue came out of a back office. "Hey, glad you found us." Dean couldn't figure any way to get to him until Mr. Blue pushed open a little half wall that swung like a gate. "I got us some sandwiches and a couple of Cokes. Come on back."

A desk and two chairs sat among cardboard boxes stacked against the walls and knee-high heaps of paper sprouted from every inch of the floor. "I'm still moving in. Have a seat."

"What is all this?" Dean asked, careful not to knock over a paper pile.

"Old contracts, plans, vendor files. I should have gone through it before the move, but I didn't have much time. Listen, I was sorry to hear about your Uncle James."

"It was him who told me about emu farming. He believed it would be the next big thing." Dean settled in his chair and reached into his backpack. He handed Doyle Blue the newspaper story. "I went down to Siler City and found this man here. He sold me two breeders and gave me a book."

Mr. Blue reached under some papers and pulled out a pair of glasses. "It says here you can pay as much as $2,000 for a pair."

"Yes sir. See, Uncle James left me his army pension. We talked a lot about how the way to make money is to be your own boss. Like you. That's how you got your money, ain't it?"

Mr. Blue smiled. "Well, I had some help. Anyway, what I've learned lately is easy come, easy go." He went back to reading. "And you're going to put them down at the tobacco barn?"

"We got three acres, plenty of shade, and there's water run to the barn."

Mr. Blue pointed to one of the lunch bags on his desk. "Go ahead and have your sandwich."

Dean tried to eat without making any noise but couldn't quiet his nervous swallows.

Mr. Blue laid the newspaper down and took off his glasses. "I'll tell you what. If you want, I'll go in with you, be your partner. Looks like you'll need an incubator building along with that fence, and the barn could probably use propping up. I'd like to see this work for you, Dean."

"Are you helping me because you knew my daddy?" Dean's mama said he asked too many questions, but he believed if you didn't ask, you'd never know.

"Mac was the best friend I ever had."

"Mama don't talk about him," Dean said, "and his people have all died or moved off."

Mr. Blue got up and went over to one of the boxes on the floor. He pulled out an eight-by-ten black picture frame and stared at it so long Dean thought he'd forgotten him. "This is Mac and your mama at a baseball game we played up in Asheboro." He handed the picture to Dean. "A state championship. He was a hell of a ball player. We'd just turned seventeen."

Mac had his ball cap turned sideways. A bat hung from one arm, the other held onto a young Fern. They were smiling at each other in a way that made Dean blush.

Mr. Blue went on to tell Dean about the game that day, but Dean didn't hear. He hadn't seen a new picture of his daddy in a long, long time. He had a box of curled-up black-and-whites that he got from Granny McQueen before she passed, and a few from his mama. He had a framed one of his daddy and mama taken right after they got married. They were smiling in that one, but not like this. Dean had never seen his mama's face so soft and easy.

"Can I have this?"

"Sure, and I have some others." Mr. Blue stared Dean dead in the eye. "I think we'll make fine partners."

Dean remembered how Zig Ziglar said it was important to negotiate business deals, not just take the first thing a fellow threw at you, but he trusted Mr. Blue. He'd known his daddy.

"You won't be sorry, Mr. Blue, I promise, you won't be sorry."

Mr. Blue smiled. "Well, it's about time for me to do something I won't be sorry for."

Dean put the pictures of his daddy and mama in his backpack. He couldn't decide whether to go out the office door first or let Mr. Blue, but Mr. Blue motioned for him to go ahead.

"Dean, how about I come by the house Saturday morning. We'll do some measuring. Get this thing going." They walked outside to Dean's jeep.

"We might ought to meet at the barn."

Mr. Blue crossed his arms. "Does your mother know about your plans?"

"No, she don't. She's about half crazy with Aunt Leona around."

"Leona's in Carthage?"

Dean nodded.

"Well, the barn then. Let's meet at 8:30."

Dean stuck out his hand. They shook, man to man.

Two weeks later, Mr. Blue's men had the fence up, and his mama was none the wiser, thanks to a thick range of pine and his aunt keeping the windows shut and the air conditioning cranked down to seventy-five.

"We're missing the last fresh air 'til fall," his mama complained.

In the evenings, Dean slipped into the kitchen to get his supper, then disappeared to the trailer with a plate. He asked his mama every day when Aunt Leona might go home.

"Lord, I wish I knew," she said.

With so much on his mind, Dean had a hard time concentrating at the garage. He came close to letting a car go without tightening the lug nuts on a new set of tires. Withholding his plan wrecked his nerves. He hadn't even told his mama about meeting Mr. Blue. Dean was unaccustomed to secrets, a secret being such close kin to a lie. He'd never kept a thing from his mama, but Aunt Leona hovered about, more than ready to have a fit, and Brandi allowed it was time he got out from under his mama's skirts. "You're a grown man, and I don't care what people say. I don't believe there's a thing wrong with you."

While he waited for the oil pan to empty out of a Ford Escort, his mind drifted to emus. With the fence built, the time had come to call Mr. Peavey and tell him to bring the birds.

He had to tell his mama. There was no way around it. Emus would be hard to hide.

"Dean, telephone!" Mr. Frank yelled. Dean went into the office and Mr. Frank nodded down at the phone. "Sounds like your aunt." Dean turned to go back into the garage, but Mr. Frank grabbed his arm and made him take the call.

"Get home right this minute," Leona said. Dean feared something had happened to Belle. He flew out of the garage and hollered back to Mr. Frank, "Watch that oil pan in yonder."

Dean swung his jeep up the driveway but slowed when he saw Mr. Peavey leaning against a wood slate trailer hooked behind a rusted red pickup truck. Mr. Peavey wore his feathered hat and a pair of dirty overalls that smelled like a barnyard.

"Dean." Leona got up in his face. She reminded him of a speckled banty hen going after the last piece of corn. "This ridiculous man says you owe him a thousand dollars and wants to know where to put these ostrich things."

"For crying out loud," Mr. Peavey said. "Woman, you ain't right. They ain't ostriches, they's emus."

A car door slammed. "What is this all about?" Dean's mama came around the truck. "Leona, why did you call acting like the sky's falling?" An emu poked a pointy beak through the slats and let out a screech. "Good God Almighty," his mama said, jumping back. "What in the world?"

"I told you I was starting me an emu farm," Dean said.

"Oh, Dean." his mama said.

Dean didn't dare look at her.

"And just where do you intend to keep these things?" Leona said.

"Down around the tobacco barn."

"I told you, woman, I told you," Mr. Peavey said, shaking his finger at Leona. He was sweating so badly even the feathers on his hat drooped.

Belle had made her way out of the house. She nudged her cane through the trailer slats, causing the birds to hiss and spit.

"Quit it, old lady," Mr. Peavy said. "You're scaring the pure-T hell out of 'em."

"Dean, you can't keep these things in the barn," his mama said.

Dean pushed his hands into his pockets and kicked at the ground. "I know that. Mr. Blue built us a fence. He's my partner."

"Mr. Blue? Doyle Blue?" Leona asked. "What in heaven's name is he doing in Carthage?"

Little beads of sweat broke out around his mama's mouth, and her left eye twitched. Dean recognized the signs of a forthcoming fit. "When did you talk to Doyle," she asked, "and who's paying for all this?"

Dean stood up as straight as he could. "Mr. Blue came up to the garage with a car he was fixing to sell. We hit it off pretty good, and he told me Daddy was the best friend he ever had." He took a breath. "He's my partner, Mama, and I'm using the money Uncle James left me."

"Oh, my word," said Leona, "you've squandered that money on this?"

Mr. Peavey pushed off the trailer. "A deal is a deal. Him and me shook on it."

Fern stood a head taller than Mr. Peavey. "Listen, I don't know who you are, but there's been a misunderstanding."

Dean's insides rattled. "Ain't no misunderstanding," he said. "Emus are the next big thing, and this is my property." His voice rose. "If I'm ever going to amount to anything, Mama, I got to be my own boss, my own man. You hear me? I'm a grown man."

Belle swung her cane at Mr. Peavey, and he jumped back. "Let them out of there. Let's see what they look like."

Dean motioned to him. "Take a right down at the road and drive up through the field."

Belle shook the handle on Mr. Peavey's truck door. "I believe I'll ride with the bird man." Mr. Peavy helped her settle in the passenger seat.

Dean headed for the backyard. His mama and Leona trailed close behind. His aunt dressed up fancy even when she wasn't going anywhere. Her green sandals matched her flowery dress, but they weren't made for walking. Every time Dean looked back, she was shaking sand out of her shoes.

"Fern? When were you going to tell me about Doyle Blue being in Carthage?" Leona said.

"I'll tell you what I know when we get back to the house."

They got to the path that cut through the pine thicket. "Watch where you step," Dean said. "A blacksnake was sunning in this very spot yesterday."

"What?" Leona said.

"Come on," Fern said. "I won't let it get you." Dean believed he saw his mama smile.

The old tobacco barn looked lost inside the six-foot-high chain-link fence that stretched all the way down to the road. Mr. Blue had helped Dean figure out how to give the emus plenty of room to run. *The Emu Farmer's Handbook* said the birds needed at least a quarter acre. Dean gave them a whole, and made sure they had shade trees, plenty of brush to peck, a drinking trough and another one low enough to kick around in. Mr. Peavy had told him they liked that.

His mama surveyed the scene like she'd walked up on a vicious crime.

"Oh, my heavens," Aunt Leona said, but she wasn't looking at the fence. She was looking at the faded mustard-yellow trailer. Dean had been meaning to straighten up the concrete steps but hadn't gotten around to it. "What was James thinking?" his aunt said.

"Not now, Leona," his mama said. "Please. Not now."

Mr. Peavey's truck bumped up the field. When it shuddered to a stop, Dean helped Belle out of the cab.

"Let's put 'em in the barn," Mr. Peavey yelled. "You better check your fence real good before we turn 'em loose. You don't want to be chasing these things to town."

Dean nodded. "The barn's good."

"Dean, we need to talk about this," his mama said.

"Ain't nothing to talk about." He rubbed the back of his neck. "I've paid Mr. Peavy money, Mama. They're mine."

Mr. Peavey backed the trailer through the gate. He called out to Dean, "I'm going to put some apples in the barn where they can see them. I'll shoo 'em out of the trailer and down the ramp. You be ready to shut the door. And boy, be quick, 'cause they sure are."

Mr. Peavey lowered the trailer ramp. "Git, git, git," he hollered.

But the emus didn't appear to be in any kind of gitting mood. They just hissed and grunted. Finally, one stretched a long, scruffy blue neck out the trailer door. He blinked his heavy eyelids like he was seeing the world for the first time and felt for the ramp with a claw big as a man's hand. He spotted the apples and moseyed into the barn, playing it cool, like he didn't want to appear beholden. The other emu strutted behind him, shaking a puffed-out chest of frilly speckled feathers.

"Why that bird's as tall as I am," Belle said. "With a belly twice as stout."

Dean shut the barn's low half-door. Belle, his mama, and Leona inched closer, taking wary steps as if the birds had fallen from a spaceship instead of walking out of Mr. Peavey's trailer.

The emus kicked at the fresh sawdust, then posed like somebody might take their picture.

"Well, I never," said Belle. "What are their names?"

"Bill and Hillary," said Mr. Peavey.

Belle cackled. The emus twisted their long necks around like she was who they'd come so far to see.

"How do you tell them apart?" Belle wanted to know.

"Bill's feathers are darker," Dean spoke up. He'd been reading the book Mr. Peavey gave him. "And the males aren't as big as the females."

"What do you do with them?" Leona said.

"You raise them," said Dean. "Folks all over the world are eating emu meat, and emu oil cures what ails you."

"That's the craziest thing I've ever heard," Leona said.

"Why, they're too pretty to eat," Belle said.

A Ford Explorer bounced up through the field. When Doyle Blue stepped out, the emus were all but forgotten.

Doyle shut the door of his truck and came through the gate to the barn. "They're here." He flashed a big smile. "Hello Miss Barrett. Leona. Hello, Fern."

"Doyle," Fern said.

Dean expected his mama to be happy to see Mr. Blue, but she didn't seem one bit happy, and Aunt Belle looked like she'd seen a ghost. But Leona spoke up. "What brings you back to Carthage?"

Doyle Blue buried his hands in his pockets like Leona might bite. "I moved back to start a new company," he said. Dean thought Mr. Blue looked important in his khaki pants and ironed shirt. Like Paul Newman, was what the girl who did the books at the garage claimed.

"I see," Leona said. Dean saw his aunt give his mama the evil eye.

Bill and Hillary pranced around and made themselves at home. They bobbed their heads up and down like the goony birds on a stick the carnies sold at the state fair.

"Somebody needs to write me a check," Mr. Peavey said all of a sudden. Dean pulled his checkbook out of his back pocket and followed him to his truck cab.

"Dean, are you sure about this?" His mama came up behind him. It made Dean mad for her talk to him like a kid.

"Yes, ma'am, I am," he said.

"My back hurts," Belle said. "Take me to the house."

Belle turned around and knocked Doyle Blue in the leg with her cane like she was testing to see if he was real. "Belle, you know Mr. Blue, don't you?" Dean said.

"I do," she said.

Mr. Peavey lifted her up into the truck cab and slammed the door. "You've got my number, Dean. Call if you need to. Like I told you, I raised these two like pets. Even kept them in the house when they were chicks. They're friendly, but you know, they can be a little peculiar." He lifted his hat, scratched his head, and nodded toward Leona. "Like all of us, I reckon."

It took right much maneuvering for Mr. Peavy to get his truck and trailer backed out of the gate. When he was on his way, Fern faced Doyle Blue. "We need to talk, but right now I've got to make sure Belle gets in the house."

"Mama?" Dean said, "Mr. Blue told me about him and Daddy playing ball together."

"That's right," his mama said.

"I hear you're working up at the paper," Doyle said. "I'll drop by the office in about an hour if that's all right. We can catch up."

"You do that," she said and walked off with Leona close behind.

Dean waited until his mama and his aunt got to the tree line. "She treats me like a kid. But I ain't."

Mr. Blue laid a hand on Dean's shoulder, and they watched the trees like the women might jump back out of the low, swaying branches. "Well, mamas are like that. I should have gone up there before now and talked to her." He gave Dean's shoulder a friendly shake and smiled. "You know what they say. Sometimes it's better to ask for forgiveness rather than permission."

"Mama ain't much on forgiving."

Doyle Blue let out a sigh. "Can't say that I blame her."

Fern

Fern stretched her long legs in a run-walk meaning to outdistance her sister, but Leona managed an aggressive trot.

"Surely it can't be legal for him to have those birds in the city limits," Leona said.

"You're in Carthage, not Raleigh," Fern said. "We don't set our limits quite so high."

"This is a disgrace." Leona swung her arms like she needed the propulsion, her hands balled in tight fists. "The very idea that you would allow Doyle Blue back in your life is shameful."

Fern stopped and faced her sister. "Today is the first time I've set eyes on him since his mother died."

"I don't believe that," Leona said.

"Believe what you want. That's what you've always done." Fern made one last push to put distance between them.

"I don't recall being wrong," Leona said.

Back at the house, Mr. Peavey had Belle out of the truck cab. He didn't waste time on goodbyes. His truck bounced down the drive, kicking up a cloud of dust.

"Did I just see Doyle Blue down there with Dean?" Belle wanted to know.

"Yes," Fern said. "Leona will explain it. I've got to get back to work."

"Oh, yes. For your rendezvous," Leona said, helping Belle up the porch steps.

Fern wanted to shake Leona. Her, Doyle, the world. She'd made her bed, laid in it. Reaped, sowed. She'd lived every worn-out cliché ever written about sin, and she was damn tired of it. Sweat poured down her back and her heart pounded. She understood Belle's confusion. Had she really just spoken to Doyle Blue?

Back at the office, she leaned her head into the refrigerator freezer to counter a hot flash. When Carol Ann told her Doyle was on the wagon, she should have known what he was up to. She'd downed enough cold coffee in church basements to recognize number eight of the Alcoholics Anonymous twelve-step program. Make amends. Doyle was born self-satisfied. Being a self-righteous convert hell-bent on redemption would suit him just fine. She knew better than most that Doyle was accustomed to getting what he wanted. Now, it appeared, he wanted Dean.

She shut the freezer door and found her cigarettes. She couldn't shake the vision of Dean and Doyle, side by side.

What Dean said was the straight-out truth. There were never two better friends than Doyle and Mac. From the time they were boys, you never saw one without the other. Doyle, blond and blue-eyed. Mac his dark opposite. Both, tall and athletic. Playful as colts. Doyle the thinker, Mac all get-up-and-go.

Doyle's daddy owned filling stations in Carthage and Southern Pines. Mac's family lived hand to mouth with the little his daddy and mama made working at the textile mill in Robbins. But who had a nickel didn't matter. Baseball mattered. During their high school years, if they couldn't play it, they were driving Doyle's Camaro somewhere to watch it. Aside from playing baseball, Mac never strayed too far from Fern, always with Doyle tagging along. Most Friday nights the three of them went to Lottie's, a burger joint with a dance floor, a juke box, and a willingness to turn a blind eye to six-packs of Budweiser being shared in the parking lot. Girls who spent part of the year in Pinehurst with their wealthy families pranced around Lottie's in Pappagallo shoes and monogrammed blouses. The Pinehurst folks left Fern and Mac a little cold, but Doyle liked their showy ways. He met Martha Chapman, a well-proportioned blonde, at Lottie's his senior year.

Doyle would take Martha home from their dates, then he'd come find Mac on Fern's porch. Fern would read them letters from James. Her brother had dropped out of school, joined the Marines, and was serving in Vietnam.

Belle's outspoken stance against the war was no secret in town. Neither was her heartache when James enlisted. "Everybody I know's going," James told his aunt. "I can't let them think I'm chicken-shit."

Mac and Doyle would talk about what a mess the war was. One of them would always say, "It can't last." But it lasted long enough.

Campbell College had offered Mac a baseball scholarship, but Mac's daddy fought in Korea, and his years in uniform were his proudest. To Mr. McQueen, fighting for his country was a badge of honor. As soon as the school year ended, he drafted his son, delivering Mac into the recruiter's hands. Everyone thought enlisted men had a better chance of staying off the front line, but Fern knew from her brother's letters, it didn't matter how a soldier got over there. War was war.

Martha Chapman's daddy drafted Doyle. Mr. Chapman pulled strings to get him into N.C. State and promised him a place in the family's construction company when he graduated.

Belle tried every way in the world to talk Mac out of going. And so did Doyle. He wanted Mac to play ball, to go pro, but where Mac viewed the world as a field that needed plowing, Doyle saw an orchard of low-hanging fruit. The friends were quieter the summer after graduation. Truths too hard to speak filled their heads like an unidentifiable hum. What was not said aloud was Mac would soon be risking his life in a war none of them really understood, while Doyle was set up for fail-safe privilege. That nickel in Doyle's pocket that hadn't mattered before mattered now.

Fern didn't have any idea back then how one thing could lead to another. The world had only been as wide as she could spread her arms, as high as she could reach above her head. When Mac showed up at her door with two gold wedding bands, she didn't think twice.

Fern was barely seventeen, too young to marry in North Carolina without Belle's consent, and she knew better than to ask. Belle had her heart set on Fern going to Elon College. But in South Carolina, the legal age to marry was only sixteen. Doyle drove Fern and Mac to Cheraw a week before Mac reported to Fort Benning, Georgia.

With Doyle as their witness, Fern and Mac stood in the too-bright office of the justice of the peace and vowed to forsake all others.

Belle took the news better than Fern expected. She told Mac he was welcome to stay at the house, much to his mother's dismay.

Mac left for Vietnam after three short months of training. He came home on leave six months later. That first week, he slept all day, sat on the porch, and smoked all night. The second week he was all raw energy. Fern sat with his mama on her porch while Mac and his daddy re-tinned the barn roof.

"I believe the army suits him," his mama told her. "His daddy believes he ought to make a life of it."

That evening, Fern and Mac argued. She told him she wanted him to serve his time and come home. "I don't see coming back here, sitting in a classroom or pumping gas," he'd said. "Trust me, Fern. I'm where I need to be."

Fern finished high school and went to work at Anderson's Drug Store. Mac was on his second tour in Vietnam when Doyle married Martha. Their wedding at the Pinehurst Episcopal Church and the reception at the Carolina Inn reminded Fern of a fairy tale. Martha's daddy sent them to Bermuda on their honeymoon and set them up in an apartment in Raleigh while they finished school. Whenever Doyle came back to Carthage, he'd stop at the drugstore, and Fern would read him her letters from Mac.

Right before Thanksgiving, Mac had a furlough. He said he couldn't get to Carthage but would be in San Diego, California. Doyle paid for Fern to meet him there. Although Fern had never flown and was scared to death, she would have walked across the fifty states to see Mac.

She pretended not to be shocked when he met her at the gate. He was at least twenty pounds lighter, and his eyes were so lifeless she wondered how he still saw through them. In the dingy motel room, they were awkward in ways they'd never been before. She felt shy in his arms.

"I need to go meet a fellow. You stay here," he'd said that very first afternoon.

Fern wouldn't have it and told him so.

Mac borrowed a car from another soldier on furlough and they drove out of town. Fern had never seen the world so flat and brown, not one green thing in sight. The two-story stucco apartment complex rose behind a boarded-up Esso station. Mac checked the piece of paper he pulled from his pocket and stopped in front of a brightly painted planter overrun by weeds. The door of an apartment hung open and a girl came out. Teenagers in Carthage played like they were hippies, but Fern was seeing the real thing. Stringy hair, love beads and filthy bare feet.

"Stay in the car," Mac said.

She didn't argue. Crazy music like something from a horror movie wailed from the windows. The girl went back inside, and Fern could see Mac talking to a stick-thin man wearing blue jeans low on his hips and a leather vest, no shirt. Mac put something wrapped up in foil in his pocket. Seeing him so at ease in that foreign place defied all Fern thought she knew.

On the drive back to the motel, she said, "What'd that man give you?"

"Just something to help me sleep," he said.

"I might try it," she said. "Wherever you're going, I want to go too," she added, not knowing a better way to challenge him, to get him talking about his new life.

Mac pulled into the motel parking lot. "I've got to do what I've got to do. Just trust me, okay?"

Fern had always loved Mac's wild side, how he would try anything. Now she wanted him to be afraid. "You used to think hippie people were crazy," she said.

"I used to think a lot of things. Turns out, the world's not like I thought."

"How is it then? If it's changed, I need to know."

He turned to her. "You don't need to know about any of this, Fernie." Hearing him use her nickname gave her hope that the Mac she knew was still there, beside her. She thought he might reach for her, finally tell her what was on his mind, but he didn't.

Mac spent the four days they were together outside the motel room drinking with the other boys, talking about howitzers and helicopters, near misses and the buddies they'd lost. Fern spent four days trying to decipher the peculiar accents of Mac's new friends and the strange language of war. She sat and smoked with the other wives and wondered if they, too, felt like intruders.

While Mac slept, Fern stroked his back, his arms, his long legs, thigh to ankle. Tight and lean, his body felt like the boy's she'd first explored as a shy teenager. Surely if she could get him back home, they'd get back to who they used to be.

Meanwhile, he swallowed and smoked whatever he could to get to a place where Fern hardly recognized him. It was as if there was nothing real that he could stand.

Their lovemaking left her embarrassed and as alone as she'd ever felt.

"You're killing yourself," she told him the last morning they were together.

"Might as well," he said. "I've killed everything else." It seemed to Fern that it took painful effort for Mac to hold her gaze, but he tried. "Over there, it's nothing but hide and seek, Fern. And I'm it."

Mac had found another sport, Fern thought, but not one she could cheer from the sidelines.

She was home a week when she got a letter Mac had mailed right before they left San Diego. He'd signed up for another tour. He said the military would be his life, their life. *We'll see the world.*

All Fern could see was one year ending and another one just like it beginning. Doyle and Martha were at NC State. Leona had just married Ned. Carol Ann was at Elon College. Fern spent her days at the drugstore making orangeades for giggling teenagers, wondering when her real life would start. But at night, she lay in the dark shrouded in fear. Afraid for the boy she loved, and for her brother, James. Belle tried to shield her from the war news that came on the television, but Fern believed she'd seen the horrors of war firsthand. She was haunted by Mac's dead eyes.

The week before Christmas in '71, the Sandhills had the biggest snow ever recorded. Nickel-size flakes started coming down before daybreak, and by noon every inch of Carthage was smothered in white.

Mr. Anderson, scared he'd lose a dollar, wouldn't close the drugstore, even after the snow got so deep on Main Street the mayor shut the courthouse down. When he told her Mrs. Anderson had called to say their radiators were knocking and going cold and for him to get home, Fern knew what he was going to say before he said it. "Could you stay until at least 3 o'clock, Fern? Would you mind?"

In the early afternoon she had a bunch of red-faced, runny-nosed boys come in who had been all over town pulling the Red Rider sleds their daddies had bought them at the Western Auto Store. Sleds that had been sitting back in the storage room for years. These kids had never in their lives seen more than a dusting of snow, but they'd taken to it like little polar bears. Fern fixed them all hot chocolate with marshmallows, compliments of Anderson's Drug Store. After mopping up the puddles they'd left around the spinning stools of the soda fountain, she stood at the front window and looked straight up at the sky. Flurries darted in all directions like they were lost and couldn't find the ground. She thought she'd have to call Mr. Anderson to get her home when she saw a green Chapman's Construction truck lumbering down the street. The Chapmans were spending Christmas in Pinehurst, and Doyle had been sticking pretty close ever since he'd gotten home for break from NC State. Doyle was the only one she'd told about how bad off Mac was, and even with all she'd said, she hadn't told him everything. She knew Mac would be ashamed for his best friend to know all she'd seen. Doyle came in cussing the cold and Mr. Anderson's stingy soul. He told her to turn out the lights, he'd give her a ride home.

Fern and Doyle went out the back and made their way up the alley. The snow was deep but light and dry, and it fell away without much push. Thick gray clouds hung low, darkening the sky. With no one else in sight, Fern imagined she and Doyle in their own little snow globe.

Doyle jogged ahead of her, made a snowball, and tossed it, hitting her shoulder. She tried to throw one back but couldn't make the snow hold together. She dumped handfuls over his head, and he chased her back to the truck. When she slipped and fell, he gathered her up and held her close. Their laughter echoed against the alley walls. By the time they got inside the truck they were giddy as children. Doyle made fun of Fern's old galoshes that hadn't done a thing but gather snow down around her ankles.

The multicolored Christmas lights strung around the crown of the courthouse had always seemed tacky to Fern, but suddenly they were exotic, like something on a movie screen. She asked Doyle to drive around the square, twice. The heater had finally started blowing hot air, making the windows steam up. Her soggy wool coat smelled like a wet sheep. Doyle pumped the brake at the stoplight.

Fern laughed, caught up in the excitement of seeing Carthage transformed into a snowy wonderland. "Who in the world are you stopping for?"

"You," he said. He pulled her to him and kissed her.

"We're in the middle of town," Fern said. They kissed again. He kept his arm around her and let the brake up. The truck glided effortlessly on the slick road. When he turned in at the high school and stopped at the far end of the empty lot, she never questioned why. Layers were shed until the heat of their skin met. Fern kept her eyes shut, and when Doyle spoke her name, she put a finger to his lips. The indifference Mac had shown her in California was replaced by Doyle's longing. His touch felt as if she was a treasure he had searched the world to find. Neither hesitated, and they were soon silently guiding each other, not in a frantic way, but with sweet purpose. With a sigh, he buried his face in her hair and was still.

Evening had come and a streetlight shone inside the truck. Fern covered herself. "It's nearly dark," she said. "Belle will worry."

They buttoned clothes and pulled on coats. Doyle wiped the foggy window with his sleeve before easing the truck out on the slippery road. Tire chains jingled like sleigh bells. The snow gave way, their tracks the only disturbance in a world quieted by what had fallen. The windshield wipers swiped and smeared delicate flurries before Fern could make out their shapes. Neither said a word until they got to Barrett House.

"I don't think I can make it up the drive," Doyle said. He let the Dodge drift off the road by the mailbox. "I'll walk you up the hill."

Fern shook her head. "No, I'll be all right."

He kissed her. "You don't know how long I've wanted you."

"Don't," Fern said. She stroked his face. "Let's not talk now." When she reached for the door handle, his arm fell from her shoulder. She missed the warmth. In the gray half-light, Doyle's face was both familiar and new. She felt like she ought to say more, but every word that came to mind contradicted the ease she wanted to keep.

"Be careful," he said.

She got out and shut the door. Cold air stiffened her face, and she watched Doyle head back toward town until the falling snow turned his truck into a ghostly thing she wasn't sure had ever been there. She walked up the driveway crunching through the fragile snow, leaving tracks.

On New Year's Eve, Doyle came in the drugstore just before closing and slipped her a note saying where to meet him the next afternoon. Fern didn't think twice. She didn't think at all.

Their affair lasted until early April when Fern came home flushed from stolen hours with Doyle to find two grave army men waiting in the front room. When Fern stopped just outside the door, Belle came and took her gently by the arm. "Honey, Mac's lost. That's all they know."

Since that day, she'd wondered a million times how different things would have been if Carthage had gone through that winter with nary a flake.

Remembering that long-ago girl was like recalling someone Fern used to know but lost touch with. Someone she certainly wouldn't want to have anything to do with now. But that was the girl Doyle knew. That selfish, sinful, thoughtless girl.

Doyle slipped in the door of the *Citizen-Times* so carefully the bell barely rang. Fern's memories had stilled her rage, and it took a moment for her mind to shift to the present. Doyle had a swagger about him even standing still. He stood at the door and didn't wait for her to speak. "Dean said that with Leona home he hadn't had a chance to talk to you, and I thought it was his news to tell."

"His news," Fern said. A shiver ran through her. For years she had imagined coming face to face with Doyle. In daydreams, he begged forgiveness, whisked her away in a romantic fever. In nightmares, he left her in the blinding snow with no coat, no shoes. She'd wake calling his name.

Now he stood before her in the flesh, and she could barely speak. "There's a lot you don't understand." She hated the tremor in her voice.

In his crisp white shirt and shiny loafers, Doyle reminded Fern of the wealthy, confident men Carol Ann went out with from Pinehurst. She felt embarrassed by the shoddy office, by her shoddy self.

"I've kept up, Fern." He took a seat across from her like the chair had been there for him all along.

His cool blue eyes seemed even brighter with his gray hair. The left side of his mouth turned up in a half-smile as if a full one would be too much for the occasion. "You never cut your hair," he said.

She pushed a stray tendril from her face. "After a while you get used to things being a certain way."

Fern searched Doyle's features for the boy she'd known. The sharp angles of his jaw had softened. She recognized the flush of spider veins that too much alcohol wrote across a face, but overall, time had been kind. She doubted he thought the same about her.

"Carol Ann told me you were back," she said.

"She tell you why?" He picked up a pencil and held it like a wand. A gold watch flashed around his wrist. He didn't have the hands of a workingman. He wore his ruby stone class ring from State, but no wedding band, although his flesh showed the pinch where one belonged.

"She told me what you said."

He laughed. "What I told Carol Ann was polite conversation, otherwise known as bullshit. The truth is, Martha finally had enough. My drinking got worse, and to use her words, I was an embarrassment to the family." He tapped the pencil on the edge of the desk. "I got help and managed to quit, but we're getting a divorce. I was asked to leave Chapman Construction." He put the pencil on the desk and leaned back. "But that's not the worst of it. My kids aren't talking to me. Won't even take my calls."

"I'm sorry," Fern said. His confession surprised her. She had expected the half-truths told to Carol Ann, not whole truths delivered straight to her face. She and Doyle had a history of both, half-truths and whole.

"I brought it on myself."

"We usually do," Fern said.

Doyle leaned forward in the chair and rested his crossed arms on the desk. "I have a life coach now, part of my rehabilitation. He's completely changed my way of thinking, opened my eyes. I came back here to start over, you know, to make amends."

Twelve-step talk, Fern thought. "You're living in your parents' place?" she said, meaning to divert the conversation from Doyle Blue's amends.

"I never sold the house after Mama died. It's good to have somewhere to start over, but there's more to it, Fern." He hesitated. "How will it be for you? For me to be back here?"

Fern took time to decide how much truth to put in her answer. She turned away, unsettled by his steely eyes. "It's been a long time," she said. "There's no sense dwelling on what was." She went for a joke, "Why, we're practically grown-ups."

Doyle didn't crack a smile. "I didn't do right."

Fern took in what she recognized as his apology and carefully worded her forgiveness. "Neither one of us deserves any kind of prize." Old shame shuddered inside her, threatening to crumble any pride time had managed to restore. Being alone with Doyle made her feel like she was doing something sinful again.

"I've missed you, Fern. Maybe that sounds crazy after all that happened between us, but I have good memories. You were always straight with me, told me the truth. Maybe that's why I stayed away so long." He leaned back. "But I'm ready for the truth to be told." He smiled like he was about to offer her a gift. "I want Dean to know," he said. "I want to be a father to him."

Even in her wildest imaginings, Fern had never considered this. His words made no sense. "What do you mean be a father to him?"

Doyle didn't even blink. "Dean deserves to know," he said.

"You want to tell my son I'm a liar? Is that what you're saying? You want to tell Dean that I've lied to him for his entire life?" Fern came up out of her chair and walked around to where he sat. "Your kids won't talk to you so now you want Dean?" Her voice rebounded off the ceiling. "My, my. Aren't you proud of yourself? Confession is good for the soul, isn't that what they say? But whose soul? Only yours, Doyle. Not mine. And certainly not Dean's."

Doyle leaned away from her. "Fern, I want to be a father to my son." He threw his hands in the air as if tossing her his troubles. "What's wrong with that? I can't imagine living a lie suits you."

His calm only heightened her temper. "After all these years, you just now started worrying about what suits me?"

"I was a coward." He looked away.

Fern leaned back against the edge of the desk and crossed her arms over her chest. "Dean has problems," she said.

"Like I said, I've kept up." He didn't look away this time.

She heard accusation. Fern could only guess all Doyle's mother had told him.

"I want to help him," Doyle said.

"Setting him up in some kind of boondoggle is no way to help."

Doyle shrugged, "Who's to say emu farming is a boondoggle?"

"Oh, come on."

"I want to be in his life. The boy deserves to know."

Fern pushed off from the desk and went to the window. She jerked the cord and the feeble blind complied as if startled by her lack consideration. "Do you see that bench? Mac's memorial? Dean sits out there and talks to him, talks to a father he's proud of. That's all he has, Doyle, and you'd take that away from him?"

Doyle cradled his forehead and rubbed his eyes with his palms. "But I'm here, Fern. Here. Alive."

"For now," she said. She meant the words to hurt. "We both know how quickly that can change."

Doyle came to the window. "Think about it, that's all I ask."

Fern reached for his arm but stopped herself. "Promise me you won't tell him." She felt an old impatience rise between them.

"I won't tell him until you're ready," Doyle said. "But think about it. Please. It's not too late to make things right." Doyle walked out, letting the heavy door close hard behind him.

For the longest time, Fern stood by the window. What a fool she'd been to think if she only held steady, kept her head down, then the world would kindly step around.

Fern left work and drove around the courthouse. She dreaded Leona's mouthful of questions. Her sister had refused to have anything to do with Fern during those long months she stumbled through pregnancy, mostly drunk. But Ned's mother made sure Leona heard all the gossip. During Leona's obligatory Christmas visit after Dean was born, she didn't hold back. "If Mac makes it home alive, he should kick you and his good friend Doyle Blue to the curb."

In the years since, the sisters had talked around and past each other. Leona, chin up, ready to fight. Fern, stubborn and defiant.

Seeing Doyle again had dislodged the disgrace she'd carried. Fern told herself she hadn't done one new thing to be ashamed of, that her affair with Doyle happened a long time ago, but her head held no sway over her heart.

She found Leona in the kitchen making a pitcher of tea. "Is Belle lying down?"

Leona nodded. "It was all I could do to keep her from going back to the barn."

"Maybe we could charge admission. Get a few goats and start a petting zoo."

Leona's sour expression let Fern know she didn't appreciate the joke. Leona poured two glasses of tea, and Fern took that as her summons to have a seat at the table. "I apologize for getting so upset," Leona said, "but I hope you can see why I would be."

An apology with an out. Shaken by her confrontation with Doyle, Fern didn't have the energy to sidestep straight talk. "As much as you don't want to admit it, that land is Dean's to do with as he pleases. And, right or wrong, James left him his pension."

Leona brushed imaginary crumbs off her placemat. "I thought surely at some point you would have become his legal guardian. And Doyle Blue? For heaven's sake."

Fern reminded herself, again, that she had nothing to hide. "He's back in town because he drank himself out of the Chapman family. He's lost Martha, his job, and from what he says, his kids." Fern sipped her tea. Leona hadn't added a grain of sugar. "Carol Ann told me he was back, but I hadn't seen him until today." She sounded like a teenager caught in a lie. "I had no idea he'd seen Dean."

Leona studied her hands. "You understand it's hard to believe you."

"There's nothing going on between me and Doyle Blue." A trickle of sweat ran down the back of Fern's neck, and she recognized her sister's fake smile.

"That's exactly what you told everyone twenty years ago." Leona sighed. "People don't change."

"You're right about that."

"What do you mean?" Leona said.

"You." Fern's smoldering anger caught fire. "You're just hateful, Leona. A hateful know-it-all, and if you're so ashamed of all of us and so afraid of ruining your precious reputation, what in the hell are you doing down here?"

"I told you. I'm worried about Belle."

"Oh, bullshit." Fear flickered across Leona's face, and Fern pushed on. "You're here to contest James's will. You want this house."

Leona straightened her back against her chair. "That's ridiculous, but you have to admit it should be mine after all the money Ned's sunk into it. Not to mention the thousands of dollars you and Belle squandered on God knows what after you sold Grandma's furniture. And now you've let Dean waste James's pension on those ridiculous birds."

"You're just going to have to take that up with James in the hereafter."

Fern knew one of them ought to stomp out, but the day had drained her of every drop of stomp. Leona appeared just as weary. They were left with nothing but a wobbly table, a pitcher of unsweet tea, and a million ways to piss each other off.

"Listen," Fern said. "I appreciate all you and Ned have done, but Dean needs this house, Leona. It's all he'll ever have."

Leona studied the table like answers might appear in the oak grain. "He does seem better. But I still think you should have gotten him tested."

"He has Fetal Alcohol Syndrome. Because of my drinking," Fern said. "He's been seeing doctors up in Raleigh for years. We sold Grandma's things to pay for all the tests and medication and therapy he needed as a child."

Leona stared at Fern. "Why didn't you tell me?"

"I was ashamed to tell you. I'm ashamed to tell you now."

"Oh, Fern. Didn't Doyle help at all?"

"I told you, today's the first time I've seen Doyle Blue since his mother's funeral. And I sat out of sight, in the back. We never even spoke."

Leona sighed. Fern realized they were both tired of talking without ever saying what needed to be said. "Doyle just got out of some fancy rehab. He's come home to right his wrongs. He wants to tell Dean he's his father."

"Oh, my heavens. That's the most ridiculous thing I've ever heard," Leona said.

Despite her frayed nerves or because of them, Fern laughed. "Thank you. That's exactly what I told him." She got up to get sugar for her tea. "He says Dean deserves to know the truth."

"It would be absolutely ridiculous to put everyone through that," Leona said.

She's on my side, Fern thought. The pressure in her chest eased. "What I'm hoping is, after spending time with him he'll see how much Mac's memory means to Dean. I just don't want Dean hurt. I'll do whatever it takes to keep that from happening." She brought the sugar bowl back to the table. "I know all this is hard for you to understand. You've done so well, Leona. You have a beautiful family, a perfect family."

"I understand," Leona said, cutting her off.

"I mean, you have the kind of family folks are supposed to have."

Leona held up a hand. "Please, listen," she said, her voice shrill.

"I'm serious," Fern said, confused by Leona's reaction.

"I know," Leona said. She took a breath. "You want to protect Dean. Of course you do." She settled in the chair. "I'm sorry. I should have realized that."

Fern couldn't remember a time she'd felt understood by Leona.

"Where's Doyle's office?" Leona said. "He needs to know this isn't his decision to make. I am going to pay that aggravating man-child a visit."

Fern had always admired the lengths her sister would go to avoid a curse word. "I'll handle Doyle," she said. "He promised not to tell Dean unless I agreed."

"Fern," Leona said, tilting her head in a way that made Fern feel ten years old. "You can't leave this to chance. Stop acting so pathetic. You always play the victim. It's exasperating. You've got to stand up for yourself."

"Oh, Leona, don't." Fern closed her eyes and laid her head down on her arms atop the table. How foolish to think she and Leona could have a conversation that didn't end with blame.

"See? Look at you. I am only saying you can't wait for a problem to fix itself. That's not the way life works. You've got to be proactive. Willing to step up and make things be the way you want them to be. You can't just run away." Leona went quiet.

Fern raised her head. "What's wrong?" She pushed back her chair and went to where her sister stood at the kitchen window. The afternoon sun laid bare Leona's paper-thin skin. She had aged. "What's out there?" Fern said.

Leona shook her head. "I won't interfere," she said, "but be careful. I'm beginning to think we don't have any control over our lives at all. I mean, look at Belle. She's always been sharp as a tack, and now I believe she's getting dementia. Yesterday, she asked me out of the blue if I'd seen James. I pretended not to understand and she dropped it."

"Dr. McManus thinks Alzheimer's but won't say for sure." The words rushed from Fern's mouth as if she'd been holding them hostage.

Leona spun around. "How long have you known?"

"Since Bernice died. Not long after the funeral, Belle started saying we needed to go check on her, that Bernice wasn't answering her phone. She hasn't done that for a while, but she still brings Bernice up occasionally as if she's still alive. It breaks my heart to have to tell her over and over that Bernice died. And on any given night, she might set a place for James at the table, and you know how she carries that old macramé bag around? Dr. McManus said that's a sign of Alzheimer's."

"Does Belle know? Does she understand?"

"Yes. And no. We talked about it that day, but she hasn't mentioned it since. We just need to watch her. She has more good days than bad." Fern wasn't about to tell her sister how often Belle got confused. She couldn't shake the fear that Leona would put Belle in a nursing home.

"You should have told me," Leona said.

"I didn't want to worry you." Fern looked away not wanting to say more. A lifetime of sidestepping the truth had taught her it was best to take one small step at a time.

Fern opened the refrigerator door. Seeing an overabundance of berries and yogurt, she went into the pantry.

"Want an oatmeal cookie?" she asked Leona.

"No, thank you," Leona said. "I stay away from junk food."

Really? Fern thought. Is that why the box of Little Debbies she bought day before yesterday was half empty?

God, we are hopeless liars, Fern thought as she ripped open the cellophane.

Leona

In the soft morning light, Leona's childhood room seemed less shabby. She'd been home a month and Ned still refused to listen to reason. He was pushing for her to come to Raleigh so they could have the talk with Paige and Amanda that Leona never meant to have.

She burrowed under the covers. When she came back to Carthage, she'd expected her old mattress to ruin her back. Instead, it made a comforting cocoon, and the sheets felt softer than the Egyptian cotton she paid a fortune for. There was no telling how many times they'd been washed and hung on the line to dry.

Fern's insistence on turning off the air conditioning at night and opening the windows sent Leona into a spin at first, but now she found peace drifting off with the tree frogs and waking with the birds. Although bad memories settled like dust in every corner of Barrett House, there were moments with Belle and Fern—talking about people Leona hadn't thought about in years or helping Belle piece together a quilt— when she felt more at ease than she had in ages.

One morning while watching her aunt manipulate scraps of cloth on the dining room table, Leona asked her, "Where's your sewing kit?" Belle showed her how to pin the pieces into place and stitch a seam along the back of one side. A daisy print became brilliant beside Belle's choice of a green plaid.

"I like ribbons, don't you?" Belle said, reaching in a shoebox. "Let's put this along that seam." Somehow Belle knew Leona needed to keep her hands busy.

Their time together in the dining room among threads and discarded cloth gave Leona a chance to tell Belle she knew why they'd sold Grandma's things all those years ago. "I've wanted to tell you for the longest time," Belle said. "But Fern needed to be ready." She paused, then said, "We ought not keep things from each other. But I guess we have to be ready."

Leona sat up in bed. It was Easter Sunday. Her chest ached when she thought of her grandchildren spending the day with their other grandparents. As comfortable as she'd gotten, she needed to get back to her real life, whatever that might be.

She missed her grandchildren and her daughters terribly. Amanda and Paige sounded more and more curious each time they called and asked about her plans to come home, and Leona knew Fern was suspicious about her indefinite visit. Belle seemed to be the only one who was purely happy she was back at Barrett House.

She heard Fern going down the stairs. Each footstep played a different note on the creaking boards. Water flowed through the pipes, signaling the filling of the coffee pot. The aging house made avoidance impossible. Every time Leona shut a door, it drifted open. The glass doorknobs came off in her hand, and none of the latches stayed put.

Fern came back up the steps in a hurry and pushed Leona's door open. "Are you awake?"

"Barely."

Fern turned on the lamp and handed her the newspaper. "Look."

Leona found her reading glasses.

Ned. On the front page.

Doctor and Radiologist Under Federal Investigation for Medicare Fraud

The North Carolina Attorney General's Office has confirmed that two members of a Raleigh orthopedic clinic are under federal investigation for Medicare fraud. Records have been seized from Oak Park Orthopedics concerning claims authorized by Dr. Ned Thomas, an orthopedic surgeon, and Steven

Carter, a Radiology technician. Both have taken a leave of absence pending the investigation. Clive Baker, attorney for Dr. Thomas, says the FBI can expect his client's full cooperation. No date has been set for a Grand Jury hearing.

"Bring me coffee," Leona said. She pushed out of the bed in search of the upstairs phone. Ned's and Steven's names linked in black and white made her feel faint. How could it be?

Ned didn't answer. She tried his beeper. As soon as she hung up, Amanda called. Then Paige, who was in hysterics. Despite her own panicked heart, Leona assured her daughters there was nothing to worry about. "These things happen," Leona said.

"Mother, do something," Paige said.

Fern brought her coffee, but before she could speak, Leona said, "Don't start with your questions." Despite their newfound harmony, Leona couldn't imagine explaining what the newspaper article might mean.

"Did you call Ned?" Fern asked, ignoring Leona's warning.

"He's not answering. But I need to get home." Leona pulled her hanging bag out of the chifforobe.

Fern sat in the window seat. She picked up the newspaper. "Do you know this man? Steven Carter? Has Ned said anything?"

"I told you, Fern. No questions." Leona wanted to avoid an out-and-out lie. She said what she honestly believed. "This is a mistake. There will be a retraction and a lawsuit. Newspers cannot slander people and get away with it."

"Is Ned going to be arrested? From what this attorney says, it sure sounds like it."

Clive Baker. "I need to make a call," Leona said. Fern didn't budge. "In private."

Fern left, muttering to herself.

Leona dug into her purse and found her address book.

"Ned's here," Clive said. "Out in the guest house. But he's not ready to talk to you. He'll hardly talk to me. Friday was tough."

"What do you mean, tough?" Leona said.

"It doesn't look good." Clive had perfected that southern gentlemanly way of talking suited for bad news. His calm detachment grated on Leona's last nerve. Clive was pompous in ways even she found difficult to stomach.

"I want a lawsuit filed against the *News and Observer* today, do you understand?"

"They're only reporting the facts, Leona."

"Well, the facts are wrong."

Clive interrupted. "Listen. He says he doesn't know anything about it, and I believe him, but to protect your own interest, you need to get up here and stand by him. It could get complicated."

He drew out "complicated" giving the word weight, making it stand for all the words that couldn't be spoken. But Leona, fluent in the language of polite society, understood that Clive was telling her he knew all about Ned and Steven Carter.

"Would it now," Leona said, not liking his tone one bit. Like it was her fault Ned was front-page news. "As our attorney, you should have called me."

"We didn't expect the investigation to hit the news so soon. We were just made aware of it Thursday, and I did encourage Ned to call you."

Leona took a breath she hoped Clive could hear through the phone. "I'm coming home for Paige and Amanda's sake. You understand this nonsense must be contained."

"It's out of my hands, Leona. I need to go. We're having Easter brunch with Janet's mother. I'll have a copy of the charges at ten in the morning, and we'll know more about what we're dealing with. Why don't you meet us at the office?"

Leona had to get her nerve up to ask, "Who will be there?"

"Ned and I," Clive said. "Steven has hired his own counsel. We've got to distance ourselves from him as much as possible."

"Is Ned willing to do that?" she said.

Clive stuttered and stopped, then said, "I got him to move out of Steven's house Friday, so let's hope so."

When Leona finished packing, Fern carried everything to the car without complaint. To Leona's surprise, she didn't ask a single question, but Leona had one. "Did you tell Belle?"

"No, and she's a little fuzzy this morning. I don't expect her to notice that part of the paper is missing."

The sisters walked back to the kitchen where Belle sat with her coffee and donuts. "Belle, I need to go to Raleigh. Ned needs me to help him with some problem at the office."

Belle reached for Leona's hand. "Ned's a good man, and you're good to him. Tell him to get down here to see me, and to bring those girls and their children." Belle pulled herself up and tried her best to stretch past her full height of five-foot-three. "You know you can always come home, don't you? You and Ned both."

It was like Belle knew everything Leona knew plus some she did not. A lump rose in Leona's throat. Belle and Fern walked with her to the front door.

When Leona stepped off the porch, Fern followed. "Let me go with you."

"Heaven's no." Leona said. She realized she'd sounded harsh and took Fern's hand. "Thank you. I appreciate the offer, but I'll be fine."

"Well, be careful, and let us hear when you get home."

Leona's car labored over the bumpy tree roots that snaked across the driveway, roots she'd asked Fern repeatedly to have removed. In the rearview mirror, Fern and Belle looked like people from another era in the too-bright light of Sunday morning, people living more in the past than the present. A choice Leona wished she had.

Fern

Fern hurried to work Monday morning knowing Robert would most certainly forget about the ribbon cutting at the new library if she wasn't there to remind him. When folks told her the crazy questions he asked when covering the news around town, she felt embarrassed for him, but he never failed to strut back into the office clueless and crowing, "This one's going to win an Associated Press Award, Fern, mark my word."

So far, she hadn't needed to dust off the shelves for trophies. Rambling reports about the lack of drainage ditches or how many hogs one could legally raise in the city limits had yet to impress the folks in Raleigh who gave out the prizes.

She never imagined she'd miss Leona hovering about, but she did. Getting Belle settled took longer than Fern remembered.

It was quarter to nine before she got to the *Citizen-Times*, and the back door stood open. She feared they'd had a break-in, but found Robert hunched over his keyboard, fingers flying.

"Fern!" He jumped up. "Spill it."

"When did you start getting to work on time?" She freed her crusty coffee mug from beneath a pile of mail on her desk. "Spill what?"

"The goods, woman. The dirt. Is the doctor a crook? What do you know about the other guy?" He waved the *News and Observer* in the air and slapped it with the back of his hand. "Is this why your sister came home?"

The same questions had kept Fern awake half the night.

"I don't know any more than you do," she said, leaning over his computer, trying to decipher the words on his screen. "But I'm betting the *News and Observer* will print a retraction and write my sister a great big check." She wasn't about to share her suspicions with Robert.

He sat back in his chair and twirled around to type. "Carthage native under Federal investigation plans lawsuit. Is that what you're saying? They deny the allegations?"

Fern headed for the coffee pot. "I'm not saying a thing, and you better delete that mess about a lawsuit." The kitchenette countertop looked like Robert had tossed coffee grounds in the air in hopes the filter would catch enough to brew a pot.

"This is a hot story, and you know it," Robert said from the doorway. "Everybody in town's going to be talking about it."

Fern didn't doubt Ned's trouble would cause a stir. "Didn't they teach you anything at that university about sticking to the facts? All you're doing is snooping and guessing. Besides, this is not the kind of story you were hired to write. If Jack Whitaker wants the *Times* to cover it, they'll decide that in Southern Pines."

He ignored her reprimand and bent his face to hers. "Are you wearing make-up?"

She backed away. "A little, maybe." Knowing she could run into Doyle Blue at any time had led her to use the Estée Lauder Leona left behind. She hated the idea of Doyle feeling sorry for poor old Fern.

"What's up? You've stopped wearing sweatshirts and granny pants." He raised a mocking eyebrow. "Is there a story here?"

"You're just in everybody's business today, aren't you?"

Drying her coffee mug, she noticed the stack of advertising contracts she'd given Robert to take to the home office last Friday. She wasn't surprised. He'd let Fern know he believed having anything to do with ad sales corrupted his journalistic integrity.

"I better get these over to accounting," she said, shaking them in his face. "Ted at the Sears store will have a fit if we don't get his spring sale in Sunday's paper." Fern opened the cabinet for a go-cup and finagled the pot out from under the drip like she hated for Carol Ann to do.

Robert crossed his arms. "So, when Carol Ann was here, she insinuated that your brother-in-law is gay."

Fern laughed out loud. "Insinuated? Do you mean when Carol Ann was in there shooting the bull? You need to get your mind on the ceremony for the new library that starts in about five minutes."

"Today? Damn it."

Fern left Robert looking for his file.

An overcast sky promised a spring shower, and a whipping wind threatened to blow the contracts in her hand to kingdom come. Her purse strap slid off her shoulder causing her go-cup to tilt. Coffee splattered down the leg of her slacks. She was cursing the coffee when Roy Puckett came around the corner.

"I was on my way to see you," he said.

"I have to go to Southern Pines, but I'll be back shortly."

"Mind if I ride along? I'm having trouble deciding which way to go with my next column."

"Roy, plenty of people at the church are better suited to help you. I've never had one good answer to any question."

He laughed. "I don't believe that, and besides, most folks are afraid if they say something I don't like, I'll take their name right off Saint Peter's list. You let me know from our very first meeting you aren't going to tell me just what I want to hear."

"Suit yourself," she said, motioning to her car.

Roy worked his wide shoulders into the Honda.

"Run the seat back and give yourself some room," she said, leaning over to point. "There's a button right down there." She looked up in time to see Rosa Jones walk by, acting as if she hadn't seen Fern in the preacher's lap.

"Thought you might come to church yesterday," he said, adjusting the seat.

"It's hypocritical to only show up for Easter and Christmas, don't you think?" She smiled and fumbled with her key. "That said, I bet you had a crowd."

He chuckled, letting her know he got the dig. "Better than I expected, and I had a good response to my column. Thanks for giving me the courage to say what was on my mind. Some are calling me Doubting Roy, but it's freed up a few to talk to me about their own struggles."

Fern circled the courthouse and turned onto the road to Southern Pines. "Back when I was going to New Hope,

Reverend Perry didn't care much for struggles. You were either a sinner or a saint." When she was pregnant with Dean, the rumors, not untrue, caused her to be shunned by church folks she'd known all her life.

"I've heard a lot about Reverend Perry," Roy said. "Maybe the congregation is trying to tell me I need to buck up and be the kind of church leader they expect."

"Walk amongst us, preacher. You lost your wife. Surely they understand you're still healing."

He stared out the window. "Cathy's death made me question all I ever believed, but God never promised a trouble-free world."

"No, but Sunday School sure did," Fern said. "Jesus healed the sick. Calmed the storm. He even raised Lazarus from the dead." Her boldness surprised her, and she wished she could take the words back. What was it about Roy Puckett that loosened her tongue, made her feel like she could speak her mind?

Roy turned to her the best he could in the tight seat. "I let Hannah believe her prayers would be answered and her mother would heal. Now she doesn't trust a word I say."

What does a heathen say to a fallen angel? Fern swallowed hard, remembering her own prayers. *Please make Mama and Daddy well.* "I lost my parents when I was Hannah's age. Daddy died in a car accident, and Mama went on to drink herself to death." A horn blew and a beat-up pickup sped around them. Fern had slowed down to forty in a fifty-five mile-per-hour stretch.

"I'm sorry," Roy said. "That must have been frightening to lose them both."

"Belle came," Fern said. "She saved us. But I can tell you, children blame themselves when their prayers aren't answered. They think they're not good enough for God."

"Not good enough for God," Roy said. "That would explain why Hannah's 'acting out,' to use the school's words." Roy was quiet for a moment, then said, "Cathy suffered two miscarriages before we adopted Hannah. I know we all love our children, but I can't tell you the joy Cathy and I felt when we brought Hannah home. The joy and the fear." He laughed. "If it hadn't been for good friends who told us we were doing it all wrong, we probably would have just held her until she outgrew our laps. We finally did let her sleep in her own bed, but saying we were overprotective doesn't begin to describe." Roy stared out the car window. "I let Hannah down. I don't blame her for pulling away. Doris Whitlow caught her smoking outside the choir room Wednesday night. Now she's picking Hannah up at school to stay with her in the afternoons."

"I went to school with Doris," Fern said. "She's always been a fixer. When Mac went missing, she put together a letter-writing campaign like she thought that would stop the war and bring the soldiers home."

"I'm sorry. I've been going on and on about myself," Roy said. "You've suffered so much loss."

"That all happened a long time ago," Fern said. A tobacco barn, rusted tin collapsed into weathered wood covered in kudzu vines, sat in a barren field. Fern found it hard to believe Doris or someone hadn't filled Roy in about her past.

"Why don't you let Hannah stay with us after school? She'd be good company for Belle and close to home."

"I was hoping you'd say that," Roy said.

A winding shortcut into Southern Pines led them down Broad Street with its crepe myrtle esplanade. Fern parked across from the train depot. "See that drug store over there?" she said. "They make the best milkshakes you've ever had in your life. I'll take a large chocolate." After all the sad talk, Roy's smile brought relief.

He extracted himself from the car. "One chocolate milkshake coming up."

On the way home, Fern told Roy about Leona going back to Raleigh, and her worry that Dean would be disappointed by the emu business.

"Dean fancies himself an entrepreneur," she said. Longleaf pines on both sides of the road swayed in the wind, tempting the rain to break free from dark clouds. "He has learning disabilities," she said. The formality sounded false on her tongue, but where would frank confession begin and end? "I worry emu farming won't turn out like he wants it to."

"It's impossible to protect our children from all harm, and impossible not to feel inadequate when we don't," Roy said.

"Yes," Fern said. She pulled in front of the *Citizen-Times*. "Roy. When you told Hannah her prayers would be answered, you weren't lying. You were hoping. You can't blame yourself for that." She opened her car door and stepped out. They met on the sidewalk.

"Thank you," he said. "Being back in the pulpit has slammed me right up against everything I've tried to avoid since Cathy died. I believe I know what the next column needs to say. I'll have it to you shortly."

Thunder clapped. Storm or not, Fern wasn't done talking to Roy Puckett. She wished she could think of something to say, something to make him linger. The way he shifted from one foot to the other made it seem like he wasn't done talking to her either. Being with Roy made her feel like the person she wanted to be. They dawdled like a couple of kids back from a first date, too shy for a goodnight kiss. "Guess we'd best not tempt the lightning," she said.

"Or have people say we don't have sense enough to get out of the rain." He looked up at the sky. "You know, for someone who doesn't give two shakes for church people, it seems like you've done right much thinking along religious lines."

"Well, as a child you sing *Jesus Loves Me*, then you spend the rest of your life wondering how that can possibly be true."

He laughed. "As we used to say at seminary, that'll preach! Why am I trying to write a column? Just print that." He jogged to his car as heavy drops of rain bounced off the sidewalk.

The next morning, she found an envelope beneath the office door.

Faith's Corner
By Pastor Roy Puckett
New Hope Methodist Church

I'm a single parent to a twelve-year-old girl. Three out of five days, my daughter is late for school. The chances of her arriving without lunch money are about the same. Homework? Let's just say we're working on it.

Last week I met with her teacher who wasted no time telling me my parenting skills left much to be desired. "Young man," she said, "as a preacher you should be setting a better example." Aside from my joy at being called a young man, her words hit pretty hard.

The title "Preacher" comes with high expectations, which has made me think about the expectations we have for our Heavenly Father.

During my wife's illness, I became overwhelmed. So much so that I failed to prepare my young daughter for her mother's death. Two years later, she still struggles to reconcile her heartbreak with a loving God.

A friend reminded me the Bible stories we teach our children are mostly about the miracles. Jesus heals the sick, raises the dead, feeds the multitudes. It's no wonder children become disillusioned when their prayers go unanswered. When expectations aren't met.

Two weeks ago, I sat with Arlene Dunn after Wilbert, her husband of sixty-three years, passed away. "I'm so grateful," she said, "for our happy life."

Arlene wasn't angry with God for taking Wilbert, or for the years of caregiving that had taken a toll on her own health. She was grateful for the love she'd shared with her husband.

It was after midnight when I walked outside. The night sky never fails to put me in my place, but it had been a while since I'd paid my respects to its Creator.

A perfectly split moon tilted toward a smattering of stars making up a constellation I couldn't name, and it came to me that even though our lives change, God is the same. Yesterday, today, and forever.

Last evening, I set up two folding chairs at the far end of the yard and took my daughter out to study the night sky. With the help of a library book (and a flashlight), we identified constellations and mapped the paths of planets. We talked about the wonder of creation and how, although God doesn't promise us a trouble-free world, his love is constant. We talked about how that's miracle enough.

Our days will continue to start with a hectic rush to the schoolhouse and most likely end with me trying to pretend cold chicken out of a bucket is a good, healthy dinner. But I'm going to be more particular about the expectations I set for myself. I can't protect my daughter from all of life's inevitable hurts or even answer all her questions, but I can guarantee steadfast love.

As I study the word of God and pray for forgiveness for my shortcomings, I am reminded of a favorite verse.

"Above all, keep loving one another earnestly, since love covers a multitude of sins." —1 Peter 4:8

Roy's loopy handwriting barely fit between the lines. Fern tried to make out words he'd crossed through and changed. She straightened the pages. *A multitude of sins*. Nothing would cover the multitude she carried. Her child struggled because of her. What kind of person could expect forgiveness for that, or ever forgive herself? Only a downright selfish one.

Roy had called her *a friend*, but she didn't have a thing to offer Roy Puckett but trouble.

Leona

"You have to be prepared, Leona," Clive Baker said. A patronizing smile stretched across his tanned face. They waited for Ned in the dark-paneled conference room. "You need to stay above this and keep Ned as far away from Steven as possible." He tapped his pen on the table. "There's going to be a lot of talk."

Leona sat across from Clive at the long, intimidating table. She imagined this room had been the site of many difficult conversations. She trusted Clive not to define "talk" but wondered what he knew about Steven Carter. Steven was ten years younger than Clive and Ned. She'd only seen him at annual holiday parties and had told Ned she couldn't believe Oak Park Orthopedics had hired the chatty, overly friendly boy.

Stay above it. Code for put on a good show. Leona imagined Clive knew she'd "stayed above it" for years.

Clive glanced at his watch. Ned was late. Leona was about to ask how quickly they could extract him from the charges and put them where they belonged, in Steven Carter's lap, when the conference room door opened and Ned shuffled in. He was a rumpled mess in the worn navy sportscoat he refused to give up and a pair of baggy khakis. The hair he had left stood up in tufts around his head, giving him the appearance of a baby bird. As angry as Leona was, she still had the inclination to straighten his jacket and comb his hair.

He took a seat beside Clive. Before anyone could speak, Clive's blonde assistant rushed in with a mug of coffee and placed it in front of Ned. "Would anyone else care for coffee?"

"No, Kendra, thank you," Clive said politely. He waited for her to make her exit. "I've made copies of the charges. Let's take a minute and read them over together." He slid folders to Leona and Ned.

"Thanks for coming, Leona," said Ned, without looking her way. He sipped his coffee.

"Yes, thank you," Clive said. He shifted in his chair toward Ned. "I can't stress strongly enough how important it is for you to have family support through this. We need your personal life on an even keel. The investigators are watching for anything that points to your involvement."

Leona had expected this meeting to be about deflecting the charges. Clive's somber tone sounded like defeat, and she wasn't having it. "Ned, what are the partners saying? Ben? Gregory? The rest of them? We've known them for years. Surely, they're standing up for you."

Before Ned could answer, Clive spoke up. "They're under strict legal orders not to discuss the investigation. And trust me, everyone at Oak Park Orthopedic is staying as far away from this as possible."

She'd considered the newspaper headline an irritation that could be taken care of like other truths that existed but certainly didn't thrive in the light of day. "Surely our first course of action should be to sue the *News and Observer* for defamation of character. Have you even contacted Ralph Lewis at the paper?"

"Leona," Clive said, "we're dealing with the Federal Government, the FBI, not people we know."

"Damn it," Ned said, studying the evidence against him.

"Every fraudulent claim is linked to a procedure done by you that involved Steven," Clive said. "Meaning every time you sent a patient to radiology and he did the imaging, a discrepancy occurred. It points to collusion."

The conference room became quiet, but Leona heard a symphony of voices. Paige, Amanda, even the ghost of her mother-in-law, asking how she had ever let this happen.

"I wasn't going to bring it up until we'd gone through everything," Clive said, "but this morning I did get the impression they might deal."

"Deal?" Ned said.

Clive nodded. "I can't promise they'd keep you completely out of the grand jury hearing. The attorney general is none too happy. They believe close to a million dollars went into your pocket. But if you could prove otherwise, they'd be very appreciative of your help."

"That money's not in my pocket, and you know it," Ned said. "What kind of help are they talking about?"

"You'd have to wear a wire. Meet with Steven."

"No," Ned said before Clive could continue. "I won't."

"Well, of course you will," Leona said. "Are you out of your mind? He's a thief. Look what he's done to you."

Without turning away from Ned, Clive held up a flat palm in her direction. He spoke so softly Leona could barely hear. "Let's be honest, Ned. What do you think Steven's answer will be when they make him the same offer?" Ned stared at the claims spread before him as Clive spoke. "Do you think he'll turn them down if he sees a chance to reduce his role in this? I'm not speaking ill of Steven. I know how you feel about him." Clive looked at Leona. "Would you give us a moment alone?"

"No, I will not," she said.

Clive turned back to Ned. "I've got to ask you again. Did you know what he was doing?"

Ned straightened up in his chair. "Stop assuming he's guilty. This is bullshit. Just let me talk to him."

Clive shook his head. "It doesn't work that way. Ned. Look. Your signature is all over these claims."

"You think I have time to read everything I sign?" Ned took a deep breath and blew it out. "If he did this, he did it for us. He wanted us to leave Raleigh and set up a practice."

"What?" Leona said.

"Does anyone else know about this?" Clive said.

Ned shook his head.

"Testifying against him may be the only way I can keep you out of jail." Clive paused. "No matter what you didn't know, there's just too much evidence for me to keep you out of the investigation."

"I won't let him take the fall," Ned said. "We need to figure it out. Together."

Leona stood. She gripped the back of the chair for balance.

"Leona," Clive said. She raised her own palm, and he had sense enough not to speak.

"Together?" she said. "Your loyalty is admirable, Ned. I'm very impressed. But while you're here making it impossible for Clive to help you, I'll be at home figuring out how to tell our daughters that their father will never practice medicine again, unless you count volunteer hours in a prison infirmary." The stricken look on his face didn't stop her. "But I'll tell them you did it out of loyalty. Loyalty to a criminal who has destroyed everything we've worked for. Congratulations. You have finally made a complete, total—public—ass of yourself."

She was almost to the door when Ned spoke up. "Quit making out like I'm abandoning my family. This is not that, Leona, and you know it."

"I won't listen to this," she said.

The heels of her pumps sank into the navy carpet, making a hasty exit difficult. She made her way down the long hallway. Without speaking, she passed the receptionist and stood before the gold, mirrored elevators that blurred her reflection. By the time she found her car in the parking garage, she felt nauseous.

She found a Kleenex in the glove compartment and patted the perspiration from her face. Debussy hummed from the CD player. Classical music. Art collecting. Gourmet cooking. Master gardening. Interior design. Leona thought of all she'd done to create Mrs. Ned Thomas, doctor's wife.

She pulled out into the sunlight. When her friends claimed they were too frightened to drive in downtown traffic, she was tempted to tell them, "You'd be surprised what you can do if you have to."

She turned off Glenwood Avenue. The trees became more plentiful with each block. Stately homes designed by the city's most admired architects sat back from the road, pretending they didn't want to be seen.

Her own home sat behind a curved brick wall covered in ivy. She'd never taken this house for granted. Each brick made by hand. A towering copper roof. A house with a proud history. That's what the realtor had said years ago. *Be the owner of a proud history.*

Leona pushed the button of her garage door opener and eased the Lexus into its roomy slot. Another push and the door made its motorized descent. She slipped the gear into park. The garage door met the ground. She gripped the soft leather of the steering wheel. The car purred. She was eye-to-eye with herself in the rearview mirror when the light activated by the garage door blinked off, leaving her in semidarkness. Her heartbeat had only slightly slowed since she left Clive and Ned. Her hands fell to her lap. The car engine revved as if taking a deep breath. Leona had never been so tired.

Inside, the kitchen phone trilled. Paige or Amanda, she imagined, needing reassurance that life, as they knew it, would go on. She turned off the ignition.

Her daughters were loved and adored. Their childhoods had been as perfect as she and Ned could make them, but occasionally an undercurrent of resentment erupted in unexplained anger and confusion. The girls blamed their mother's sharp tongue. They felt sorry for their easy-going father. Leona told them they had separate bedrooms because he snored, but when the girls got older, she suspected they questioned the lie. *The Ice Queen*, she'd heard them say. What choice did she have but to freeze?

The phone stopped ringing. Leona heard the beep of the answering machine.

She shut her eyes and dropped her head back against the headrest. She'd done her very best to give Paige and Amanda wonderful lives. She'd taught them manners, morals. What was proper and respectable. She'd taught them how to fit in. *Fit in.*

Leona opened her eyes. That's how she'd survived. Growing up where any moment could turn into an unhinged brawl, she'd aligned herself with Ned's family, thinking if she followed his mother's rules, she'd be safe.

Mother, do something, Paige had said.

How had she failed her children so deeply?

Dean

Dean turned his jeep up through the sandy field. All his coming and going had flattened the weeds into a road. He hadn't moved back to the house, even after his aunt hightailed it to Raleigh a week ago. It worried him something terrible that his uncle was in trouble with the FBI. The FBI could make people disappear. Dean knew that because he'd watched *The FBI Story* with Jimmy Stewart. That was just one of the VHS movies he'd found in a cardboard box in his uncle's bedroom closet.

He liked being on his own down at the trailer, watching his emus strut and preen, watching movies he'd never seen or heard tell of. His favorite was *Easy Rider*, about a couple of drug-smoking hippies who rode motorcycles. He'd always wanted a motorcycle. And there was sex in the movie. Sex had him curious.

He was thinking maybe Brandi could bring a pizza and a two-liter Dr. Pepper to the trailer Friday night and they could watch *Easy Rider*. He was wondering what she'd say about drug-smoking hippies when he heard what sounded like a girl screaming her last.

The preacher's daughter was staying with his mama and Belle after school. She wasn't supposed to get around the emus without Dean, but Hannah didn't much care what she was supposed to do. She was inside the fence, and Bill and Hillary were trying to run her down.

Dean jumped out of his jeep, opened the gate, and waved his arms. "Over here," he hollered. He took off for the barn, and Bill and Hillary changed course and trotted after him, expecting feed in their trough. As soon as they went in the barn, Dean backed out and shut the door.

"What the hell were you doing?" he said, hurrying over to where Hannah stood.

A trickle of blood crept across her forehead and ran down her nose. She held an empty feed bag. "They pecked me," she said. She put a hand on her head and held out a palm wet with blood. She smiled like she'd found gold in her hair. "I took them some corn, and when the corn ran out, they pecked me, and I started running. Then they started running. They chased me around and around. They like me."

Dean got her in the jeep and drove to the house. Belle sat at the kitchen table peeling potatoes. His mama had just taken a skillet of cornbread out of the oven. Her mouth dropped open. "Lord help my time of day!"

"She was inside the fence and got her head pecked," Dean said.

"Bill and Hillary both pecked my head," Hannah claimed, like that would win her a prize.

"I thought you were outside with the cats," Fern said. Hannah had taken it upon herself to domesticate Belle's strays. "Oh, my Lord, climb up here on this stool and let me see if you need stitches. What is your daddy going to think?"

"Doris Whitlow says I don't have any business being over here," Hannah said, swinging her legs back and forth against the stool.

"How come her to say that?" Dean said. He reached in the refrigerator for a Coke.

"Beats me," said Hannah," but she told Daddy it didn't look right and that I didn't need to pick up any more bad habits."

Belle hovered around Hannah like she needed to be right up in her face to see. She scrunched up her nose. "They didn't get you too bad."

Fern pressed a wet washcloth against Hannah's forehead. "Dean, get me some gauze and Neosporin out of Belle's medicine cabinet."

When Dean came back, the scissors were on the table and bits of bloody hair lay on a paper towel. His mama rubbed Neosporin on the dots of broken skin and was fixing a bandage just as the preacher walked through the back door. "Hannah?"

"I thought she was out playing with the cats," Fern said, "but she was visiting with the emus. She got pecked right along the hairline, not deep. I don't believe there will be a scar. I had to cut her hair a little."

His mama lifted the bandage and the preacher bent down to look. "What were you doing out there?"

"I just wanted to give them some corn," Hannah said. "They'd been hollering."

"You're lucky they didn't crack your damn head open," Dean said.

Roy put his hands on Hannah's shoulders. "You know good and well you're not to go down there without Dean."

His mama carried the washcloth to the sink. "Dean, take Hannah and Belle in the front room, would you please."

Fern

*D*oris Whitlow. Stung by Hannah's account, Fern rinsed the bloody cloth under the faucet. Red splashed against the porcelain. "I should have been watching her," she said to Roy. "She could have gotten hurt if she'd fallen." A lump in Fern's throat blocked more apology. Hannah had only been staying with them after school for a week, and she was already bleeding in the kitchen.

"Hannah has a way of slipping watch," Roy said. "Don't blame yourself. Now, if she's too much to handle …"

"Doris Whitlow will be more than glad to take her back, right?" Fern wrung out the cloth and let it drop into the sink. "Hannah told us what Doris said." Fern reached for a paper towel to dry her shaky hands. "And she's right. I mean, look what happened."

Roy took Fern's hands, paper towel and all, into his own. "The women of the church feel obligated to help because I'm a widower. That's all."

She blinked back tears. "That's not all, and you know it." She'd been reluctant to trust Roy's friendship, but over time, his candor had worn her down. She not only trusted him, she liked him. A lot. And her hands felt good in his.

He shrugged. "Don't worry over this."

"It's you who ought to worry." She pulled away and crossed her arms. "I know how fickle those folks are."

"I let Doris know I didn't mean to change our arrangement."

"I knew it wouldn't be long before you got an earful," Fern said. Her heart raced imagining all Doris might have said.

Roy took a seat at the kitchen table, making himself at home like he always did. "Doris cornered me one Wednesday night, but I kindly reminded her before she could get going that there's no place for gossip in a church family. It's just because you're not married, I'm not married, and they know I spend right much time over here." He smiled, "Let me think, what was it you said the first day we met? 'You know how church people are.'" He fiddled with the salt and pepper shakers like they needed rearranging and gave her a careful glance. "Being here makes me happy, Fern. It feels good to laugh again. And to hear Hannah laugh. I'd say things are going rather well."

"Daddy," Hannah came to the kitchen door. "Miss Fern said we could come to lunch Sunday."

Roy pushed up out of the chair. "You might want to tell Miss Fern you're sorry you caused such a fuss and see if that invitation still stands."

"Sorry about the fuss," Hannah said. "Can we have biscuits?"

A fter dinner, Fern went out on the porch. She needed to call Leona and didn't want Belle to hear her asking about Ned.

Leona didn't answer right away, but when she finally did, she got testy when Fern asked about Steven Carter. "I can't discuss it," she said. Can't, or won't, Fern thought. But she changed the subject and told her about Hannah's emu adventure.

"That child is a hellion," Leona said. "Roy's lucky you'll keep her. But I believe he has an ulterior motive. I could tell the day he stopped by that he enjoys your company."

After they hung up, Fern thought about what her sister had said. Roy did enjoy her company. He'd said so. The preacher's shy confession had her feeling a little giddy. Not giddy like the old days with Mac, and he didn't give her the nervous shivers like Doyle, but what was it he said? *It feels good to laugh again.* Yes, it did. Standing in the kitchen, drying the dishes, laughing with Roy, she could almost imagine what it would feel like to be an old married woman. She envied the couples she saw in Food Lion filling up their cart with a loaf of bread and a quart of milk, not talking, just knowing what they needed. Fern knew better than to idealize marriage, but on lonely days, her daydreams got away from her. Roy had entered those dreams with his corny jokes and easy smile.

Dean came up on the porch, swinging a baseball bat. "Mr. Blue said this was Daddy's." He held it out to her. "Here."

Fern ran a hand over the worn wood, aged smooth as skin. *Mac*. The grimy tape around the grip had frayed. She pulled a string from the adhesive and wrapped it around her finger. She could see Mac clearly in her mind walking up the driveway after practice. The bat resting across his shoulders, his long arms draped around each end. She handed it back to Dean, not wanting to summon more memories.

"He gave me some pictures too." Dean reached in the pocket of his jean jacket and handed her a crinkled Kodak. "This is you."

Cherry Grove. The Blues' beach cottage. She wore a two-piece bathing suit and was kneeling beside Mac, his body covered in sand. He smiled up at her like he was just where he wanted to be. Trapped by her side. The girl in the picture, all bone and brawn, sure of herself, unafraid, stared straight into the camera proud to be seen.

Dean gripped the bat like a trophy. "He said Daddy could have gone pro if he'd had half a chance."

Fern heard pride in her son's voice. "Mac said he couldn't keep playing games while other boys fought and died," she said. "He wasn't one to shy away from a hard situation. He was a brave man."

Dean went down the steps and around the house, swinging at what only he could see.

Fern studied the picture of her younger self. Her selfish, arrogant self.

How dare she think about Roy Puckett. Roy had no idea who she was, but Doris Whitlow and that bunch would sure tell him if she didn't back off and leave their preacher alone. She was just daring folks to spill the secret that would catch fire and burn right back to Dean.

Fern tightened the string around her finger. She needed to remember the harm she was capable of. She'd been careless with Mac's heart. She couldn't risk being careless with Dean's or Roy's.

The Citizen-Times lay on the table when Fern came down the next morning, a sign that Dean had come to the house for breakfast and left for work. She made a cup of coffee and unfolded the paper.

Ned and Steven Carter. A picture two columns wide. Byline: Robert Yarborough.

Relationship Points to Collusion

A grand jury will determine whether Dr. Ned Thomas, formerly of Carthage, will be charged with conspiracy to commit Medicare fraud. According to records obtained from the Attorney General's office, Thomas, along with Steven Carter, a radiologist with Oak Park Orthopedics, have been under investigation since October of last year. A statement from Thomas's attorney denies any collusion between the two and insists that any illegal activity carried out by Carter was done without the knowledge of Dr. Thomas. However, sources say the personal connection between Thomas and Carter make that highly unlikely.

"There's more to it than a professional relationship," said an associate of Dr. Thomas's, who asked to remain anonymous.

"I don't see Steven doing anything without Doc knowing," said Brad Mahoney, owner of The Complex, a popular Hillsborough Street bar that caters to the gay community. "They've been coming in here together a couple a times a week for the past year."

Dr. Thomas is married to Carthage native, the former Leona Barrett.

The phone rang, but Fern didn't pick up until she heard Carol Ann's voice on the answering machine.

"Now, before you jump to any conclusions," Carol Ann said.

"Conclusions? Robert heard us talking about Ned and ran with it."

"If you've read it, you know he had more to go on. When he talked to me …"

"When did he talk to you?" Fern sank into a kitchen chair.

"The other night. We went over to the Fox and Hound for a drink."

"Oh for the love of God."

"It's not what you think."

"I'm sure."

"Listen to me. Robert had already been up to Raleigh and talked to someone who said it's no secret that Ned and Steven are a thing. Everybody knows, but I'll be over there after church so you can kick my ass if you still want to."

"It's my ass that needs kicking," Fern said. "Leona's going to be glad to oblige. I don't care what Robert says, there's no way this is true."

"Well, time will tell. It always does," Carol Ann said. "And I don't care if you are mad. I'm still coming to lunch."

Fern hung up the phone knowing full well she should call Leona and warn her about the article, but she called Robert instead.

"You weren't sick last week. You were in Raleigh digging up dirt."

"Just doing my job, Fern."

"This is trashy, Robert. It has nothing to do with your job. Did Jack Whitaker give you the go-ahead on this?"

"Yes. It's the motive. Don't you see? I have it from a very good source that your brother-in-law and his boyfriend were in this together all the way. She said, 'thick as thieves,' but Whitaker wouldn't let me put that in there. She—I mean, my source—was really pissed about it. Even quoted the Bible, or something. Anyway, it seems to be an open-and-shut case." While Robert spoke, Fern wrote on a notepad she used for grocery lists. *She. Pissed. Bible.*

"See, that's the problem, Mr. Reporter. I may not have a fancy degree, but I know one thing. What 'seems to be' is not what you put in a newspaper. What 'is' is what you put in a newspaper. And let me tell you right now, Ned wouldn't do such a thing."

"Fern. People do crazy things for love."

"That's pure-T bullshit. And who is this very good source?"

"You know I can't tell you that."

"Oh, now you have scruples. Now you have ethics."

"A friend from college set me up, okay? Hey, get me an interview with your sister."

"Are you out of your mind? She'll never talk to you."

"Carol Ann says she knows all about her husband's sexual persuasion."

"Carol Ann doesn't know a thing except what she conjures up in her head. What about all your high ideals about journalism I've had to listen to?"

"It's the times, Fern. I'm only giving the readers what they want. Look at the Clinton/Lewinsky thing. I've got to go. We'll talk in the morning."

"You won't talk to me in the morning. I quit," Fern said, surprising herself.

"What? Come on. You don't even like your sister."

Fern pushed the "off" button on the cordless phone and fought the urge to throw it against the kitchen wall.

Dean came in the back door. He nodded at the paper. "Is Uncle Ned a crook?"

"No, honey, I think it's just a big misunderstanding." She heard Belle coming down the hall and stuffed the newspaper in the potato bin. "Let's keep this to ourselves and not worry Belle." The phone rang again, and she let it ring, scared it might be Leona.

The machine kicked in. "Fern." She recognized the voice of one of her second cousins. "What this paper says about Ned is the craziest thing I ever heard tell of. You reckon it's true? I reckon it is if it's in the paper. Well, I guess you aren't going to pick up. I don't blame you." *BEEP.*

"Mama," Dean said, closing the refrigerator door. "I asked Doyle Blue to dinner. I didn't think you'd mind setting one more plate. He ain't had a home cooked meal in a while."

Dean opened a can of Dr. Pepper and went out the back door before Fern could even process what he'd said.

Carol Ann showed up around one o'clock with her signature "Yoo-hoo." She surveyed the cut-up chicken, flour, and buttermilk. "What in the world is going on in here?"

"Dean invited Doyle to dinner, and I'd already invited Roy and Hannah."

"Well, that's a tableful. And you're frying chicken, Lord help us." Carol Ann attended the Episcopal Church in Southern Pines because she claimed it was good for business. She shed her suit jacket and found an apron. "So, who's this for, Doyle or the preacher? A woman doesn't fry chicken unless she's a grandmother or after a man."

"Oh, for heaven's sake, don't be crazy. And the preacher has a name."

"Roy," Carol Ann said, smiling. She peeked into the pot of boiling potatoes. "Biscuits or cornbread?"

"Biscuits." Fern poured buttermilk over her bowl of chicken and set it aside.

"Oh, girl, you've got it bad."

Fern rinsed her hands in the sink. "I'm still mad at you."

"How pissed off is Leona?"

"I haven't talked to her."

"What are you waiting for? You don't want her calling you." Carol Ann drained the potatoes. A steam cloud rose. "She can't blame you for this."

"The hell she can't. Robert heard us talking, heard you talking, I should say. But whatever, it's because of us that Robert got on this trail to begin with, and Leona is going to figure that out pronto."

Carol Ann put the pot on the drain board. "Leona knows everything and always has. Robert made one call to Raleigh and knew more than I ever will. You're the only one with your head in the sand."

Fern pulled a chair from the table and stepped up on it to wrestle her electric skillet off the shelf above the stove. One wrong move and she'd bring every pot up there down on her head. "Ned's gay," she said, "and Leona knows it. That's bull." She handed the skillet down to Carol Ann.

"Listen. Pick up the phone and call her. Get it over with."

"You just want to hear what she has to say," Fern said.

"I know what she's going to say. She's going to deny it just like she has every day of her life. But you're about to jump out of your own skin, and I want you to calm down before you fire up a pan of grease. Call her."

"I've got to get through this lunch." Fern fell back against the counter. "Doyle Blue is coming. We're all going to be sitting in there at the table. Now, isn't that the craziest thing you ever heard tell of in your life?"

"One big happy family," Carol Ann said, popping a chunk of boiled potato in her mouth.

Leona

Pulsing beads from the shower head beat against the knot of nerves trapped at the nape of Leona's neck. What she would give to be on a massage table breathing in the soothing scent of lavender, but that would mean having to answer questions about Ned from whoever she might run into at the day spa.

Ned had at least moved home. Clive had gotten his attention with stories about doctors who spent years in prison for Medicare fraud. Tomorrow he and Clive were meeting with a high-powered defense attorney who had experience going up against federal prosecutors. "This is out of my area of expertise," Clive had told Ned and Leona. Leona had to bite her tongue to stop from asking what exactly his expertise entailed besides walking around the country club in pastel pants like some sort of overgrown child.

It had been a week since the *News and Observer* article. A week since Ned and Steven had been asked to take a leave of absence from Oak Park Orthopedic. Leona pleaded with Ned to consider the possibility that Steven had set him up and to cooperate with the FBI, but Ned wouldn't have it.

His self-pity infuriated her. He spent hours slumped in his recliner with a glass of bourbon watching old movies, only cheering up when Paige or Amanda visited with the children. Seeing him buoyed by their sympathy like some sort of martyr added to Leona's rage.

Nothing about being pathetic appealed to Leona. She believed if the world perceived weakness, it would take you down. Perception was reality, and as much as she loathed having to see people, she and Ned needed to be seen together at church this morning. They needed to act as if the investigation was nothing to be concerned about. "Happens all the time," she'd say to anyone with questions. "It's just one of those things."

She felt sure Reverend Parnell would keep his distance. He'd want no part of any unpleasantness that could sully the reputation of First Methodist or jeopardize the check Ned wrote every month. That suited her fine. It had been a hard week. The *News and Observer* report had been picked up by the local television stations and, of course, by the rumor-spreading apparatus that existed in the medical community.

She deflected inquiries from friends, what few she had, by saying, "We'll be glad when we can tell our side of the story." Deflecting scrutiny was second nature to Leona. It was how she'd grown up.

She never had girlfriends, never allowed herself to be close to other women. She'd never trusted another soul to understand her choice to stay with Ned. She didn't have to. Privilege came with a simple script. She had, from the beginning at Meredith College, implied that she came from wealth by telling anyone who asked that she was from Pinehurst, not Carthage. As Ned's practice grew and their circle tightened, it became easier and easier to belong without ever having to reveal another thing about herself. As long as she bought her clothes from the right boutiques, lived in the right neighborhood, and campaigned for Senator Jesse Helms, her place was secure.

Leona had distinguished herself in one way. She was the consummate volunteer. Her appreciation of rules, organization, and control—she had no qualms about telling people what to do—made her the perfect committee chairwoman. But even after all the money she'd raised, all the golf tournaments she'd overseen, all the galas she'd saved from disaster, phone calls had already come telling her not to worry about the symphony luncheon, or the botanical garden's spring tour. She'd expected the syrupy sweet callers feigning sympathy while dismissing her "until things calmed down." Leona thanked them and played her part. She wasn't surprised. When a friend's son was accused of rape, it was Leona who made the call to tell her she and her husband need not attend the medical auxiliary ball. No embarrassing fuss, just the polite, "We know you need your privacy during this difficult time."

She stepped out of the shower and wrapped herself in a terry robe.

"Leona?" Ned called to her from the doorway of the bedroom.

"What is it?" His breach of her domain signaled trouble. She peaked around the door.

"Clive called. He's in Pinehurst. He said the *Citizen-Times* has a front-page story about Steven and me."

Ned wore his paisley pajama bottoms and the faded Duke Blue Devils t-shirt she hated.

It took a minute for her to comprehend what he'd said.

"What kind of story?"

"Clive's faxing it. What have you told Fern?"

"Nothing. Don't be ridiculous." The phone rang. Ned stepped into the room to answer it while Leona dried her hair.

"Leona says she's never told her sister anything," she heard Ned say.

Her mind raced. Ned, still on the phone, lumbered out of the room. Leona followed him down the stairs. "I don't know any Yarboroughs down there," he said.

"Fern's boss. Is that Clive? Give me that phone," Leona said. "I'm calling her."

Ned held the phone away from his mouth, "He says not to talk to her. Don't even take her calls."

They went into the study. The fax machine groaned and spat out a jittery page. With a look, she dared Ned to touch it. "Let me call you back." He put the phone down and sat behind his desk. "Give it to me."

"You just wait," Leona said. The faint type was difficult to read. She grabbed a pair of Ned's reading glasses and sat in the leather wing chair by the window. *An anonymous source*. "We'll sue," she said. "For libel." She handed the page to Ned.

"Glasses," he said. She flung them at him and watched his face while he read. "The truth is not slander," he said.

She started to speak, but he stopped her. "You know what, Leona? I'm sick of you acting like I'm some sort of freak that needs to be kept under the porch. I'm glad this is happening." He waved the fax in the air. "I'm glad to have it out in the open."

Rage lifted her from the chair. She leaned over the desk and braced herself with both hands. "How can you say that?"

Her chest rose and fell. A damp heat coursed through her body. Ned leaned back in his chair. They hadn't looked straight at one another in a very long time, but they did now. "You don't understand," he said, his voice steady and resigned. "You don't know what it's like. I just want to be who I am. Maybe if you'd accepted who I was, if you'd let me go a long time ago, not made me feel so damn guilty, maybe this wouldn't be happening. Have you ever thought about that?"

He sounded different. Unwavering. Leona pushed away from the desk. "How dare you blame me."

"I'm just saying." He raised his arms in the air, "I am who I am, Leona. Sorry if that doesn't fit in your fairy tale, but I want to live how I want to live. Is that too much to ask?"

The floor beneath her bare feet, the walls around her, all seemed foreign, unfamiliar. She had to get her world spinning again. "We have to go to church."

Ned shook his head. "It's over, Leona. Don't you see?"

Leona turned and walked into the foyer. Sunlight coming through the octagon window over the front door reflected off the crystal chandelier. A rainbow of color speckled the marble floor. She gripped the banister and started up the stairs. "Paige and Amanda expect us at church."

Ned came out of the study. He stood in the dappled light. "Call them. Tell them to come here," he said. "We've got to tell them now, today."

"You can't be serious," Leona said.

"We can't keep lying. Denying everything. If you don't call them, I will. Clive thinks this *Citizen-Times* thing will be on the local news tonight. We've got to tell them."

"Tell them what?" Leona shouted. The echo of her question encircled them.

"The truth," he said.

The organ's prelude filled the sanctuary. Leona found her seat beside Paige and seven-year-old Tyler. Paige's youngest, Abby, was in the nursery, and her husband only came to church on holidays. Amanda, Eric, and their four-year-old, Katie, who refused to stay in the nursery but rarely made it through a whole service, sat in the pew in front of them.

"Where's Daddy?" Paige said.

"Getting ready for the appointment with the trial attorneys," Leona said. "They have experience with these kinds of things." She'd planned the excuse, even practiced the tone and slight smile. She passed her grandchildren the peppermints she always brought for them. Katie blew her a kiss from over her mother's shoulder.

She closed her eyes for prayer, but instead of Reverend Parnell's words, she heard Ned's. *I want to be who I am.* He should be here with these children, Leona thought. Being a father, a grandfather. That's who he is.

In the contemporary sanctuary, with its wood-beamed cathedral ceiling and geometrically cut lead glass windows, Leona didn't have to look left or right to know who sat where. Members had what might as well have been reserved seats. Leona suspected many of them believed God had chosen those seats for their families from the multitudes, chosen them for privileged lives.

A gold art deco cross hung high behind the choir loft. She'd served on the committee that selected the cross. She and Ned had recently returned from Italy, where she'd been moved by icons that didn't shy away from the anguish of Jesus on the cross. Naked, bloody Jesus. When she'd suggested to the committee that their cross include the beleaguered Jesus, a nervous conversation ensued about how the resurrection, not the crucifixion, should be emphasized in the sanctuary of First Methodist. She'd quickly agreed, embarrassed that she'd let her emotions get the best of her.

Reverend Parnell's sermons were almost always about how the righteous would reap divine rewards. Clean, bloodless sermons meant to bolster his well-heeled congregation. Leona understood that now.

"Take a moment to bid your neighbor peace," he said. Leona disliked this false familiarity, but Amanda spun around. Her bright brown eyes and sweet smile were all Ned's.

She reached for Leona's hands. "Go in peace, Mother."

Leona surprised them both with tears.

Before the choir began its final benediction, the assistant pastor spoke. "Don't forget Wednesday is the last day to contribute to the Good Works Fund Drive."

Paige led them out of the pew. "I'm secretary of the Good Works committee," she said. "You and Daddy haven't sent your check."

A check, Leona thought, looking inside her purse for a Kleenex. That's all anybody ever wanted. Why hadn't she thought of it before? She hugged the children and told the girls she'd call them later.

Fern

Doyle sat on Fern's left, Roy on her right. The platter of crispy chicken taunted her. She couldn't imagine enjoying one bite of her effort. She hadn't called Leona, and imagining her sister reading what Robert had written had taken her appetite.

Hannah picked at the crust of a biscuit. Fern knew she was impatient for Roy to say the blessing. Carol Ann, between Doyle and Dean, looked from one to the other, then at Fern as if signaling that the gathering was indeed odd.

Fern had told Belle about Doyle's threat to tell Dean he was his father. From her seat at the other end of the table, Belle glared at Doyle like she might, at any moment, throw a hex his way. He seemed oblivious. Those sky-blue eyes are only meant for pretty sights, Fern thought. He appeared not one bit concerned that he hadn't been welcomed with open arms. She even heard him tell Carol Ann, "This house was like a second home to me growing up. It feels good to be back."

Dean got his coloring from Doyle. Fair but easy to tan. She was thankful he didn't have those blue eyes. She studied their hands. Wide across the knuckles. Strong, stout fingers. Doyle seemed not one bit ill at ease with Dean. He let Dean be Dean without an ounce of pity or condescension. She was at least thankful for that.

Roy blessed the food, and the bowls and platters started around like no one had ever passed food before. Doyle tried to hand Fern the lima beans and she came close to dumping the biscuits in his lap.

"I was sorry to read about Ned's troubles in the paper this morning," said Doyle.

Fern shook her head and mouthed Belle doesn't know. She looked at Dean, afraid he might say something, but he was busy educating Carol Ann about the wonders of emu oil.

Doyle made a little "o" with his mouth and turned to Roy. "So, how do you like Carthage? A little smaller than what you're used to, isn't it?"

Roy buttered his biscuit in a way that made Fern glad she'd made them. "We were only in Charleston three years," he said. "Before that we'd been in towns about the same size as this. And I grew up in Cool Springs, South Carolina, population one thousand and ninety-eight. It sat in a low spot smack dab in the middle of the state and was often referred to as the screen door to Hades. Whoever named it Cool Springs had a sense of humor."

Doyle laughed. "Is that what made you a preacher? Living so close to Hades?"

"I learned to pray for a breeze at an early age," Roy said, smiling.

"You know, the Devil has a place up near Siler City," Carol Ann said. "The Devil's stomping ground. They say that's where he paces in a circle and makes his plans."

"Won't nothing grow on it," Dean said, talking through a mouthful of mashed potatoes. "They say a dog won't go near it."

Doyle gave Fern a sideways glance. "Some of us have seen it firsthand."

"Have you all been out there?" Carol Ann said. "Where was I?"

"You were dating that prissy boy from Pinehurst," Fern said. "We didn't see you for months."

"What happened?" Carol Ann said.

Doyle laughed, "It was Mac's idea."

"It was always Mac's idea if it was something crazy," Carol Ann said.

Dean's furrowed brow made Fern wish she could change the subject.

"How come you to say that?" Dean said.

"Mac was always up for an adventure," Doyle said, "and he'd wanted to go out there for the longest time, but I always came up with some excuse. I've never been one to poke the Devil with a stick. But one evening, we were out there on the porch enjoying a pitcher of Miss Belle's fine lemonade when Mac hopped up and said, 'Let's go for a ride.'"

"Which meant in Doyle's Camaro, I bet," Carol Ann said. "Because unless you all took Belle's old Mercury wagon, that was the only way of getting around." Carol Ann looked at Roy. "Doyle was the only one of us who had a car."

"Yeah, and I thought a ride sounded fine," Doyle said, "I thought we'd cruise over to Juniper Lake. But when Mac started giving directions, I said, 'Where are you taking us?' He said, 'Don't you worry about it, just drive.'"

Dean's grin prompted Fern to put in her two cents. "I didn't know where we were until we came up on that little dirt road."

Doyle laughed, "I remember, you said, 'If you're taking us to the Devil's stomping ground, we're turning around right now.'"

"It was late in the day," Fern said.

Doyle nodded. "It was, but Mac said we were practically there, so I kept going. Mac and I were in the front seat, Fern in the back." He looked at Fern. "I could see you in the rearview. If you hadn't been smiling, I would have turned around. Anyway, we went down this sandy road, the car swerved, and all I could think of was how I didn't want to get stuck or bust a tire. Mac said, 'Stop here.' Well, I didn't see anything but a bare spot through the brush. Mac said, 'This is where you park.' So, we parked and got out and started down this little thorny path through the pine thicket."

"I was scared to death," Fern said. "And, Lord, it was hot, and buggy."

"Well, it was July, as I recall," Doyle said. "Hot as a ditch of tar. Finally, we came up on a big old circle forty feet wide with nothing growing in it, not one weed, just a round bare spot of copper dirt and sand." He swung his arms around for emphasis. "By this time, the sun was about down, and the tree frogs were hollering. Mac didn't do a thing but jump right in the middle of that circle. He started dancing around calling, 'Hey Devil, come on out and show yourself. Show us what you got.'"

"And he shamed us into stepping in there with him," Fern said.

"That next week is when he got his letter saying to report to Camp Jackson," Doyle said.

Fern's heart rose in her chest. The taps and scrapes of silverware stopped. "We should have stopped him," she said, her voice faint. "We shouldn't have …" How was it that she'd never put this story together with all that came later?

Doyle started to speak, but his words stalled, and he only cleared his throat. His eyes glistened. He broke Fern's gaze.

"We gotta go out there," Hannah said, splintering the gloom.

"Honey," Fern said. Her voice shook. "This is just silly talk, something we did when we were kids." She looked at Roy. He wore his worry like a man who should never attempt poker.

"In my line of work, we know you don't have to drive all the way to Siler City to get the Devil riled up," he said. His effort to be lively fell short.

Belle glared at Doyle. "Amen," she said.

Carol Ann spoke up. "Doyle, how do you like being back in Carthage?"

Fern was grateful to her friend for changing the subject.

"It feels good," he said, giving Carol Ann his full attention.

"Charlotte has a lot going on," Carol Ann said, "Don't you miss the fast lane?"

"Not a bit. I was about to get run over," Doyle said with a crooked smile.

Dean put down his gnawed chicken bone. "Mr. Blue is an alcoholic. He told me all about it. Mama's an alcoholic, too. And both her mama and daddy were. We come from a long line of alcoholics."

"Is that how come none of y'all go to church?" Hannah said.

"Hannah," Roy said.

Carol Ann spoke up. "Fern, could I bother you for some more tea? All this talk about drinking has me thirsty."

Fern made her way into the kitchen. Her hands shook as she refilled Carol Ann's glass.

Roy came to the doorway.

"I haven't had a drink in twenty-five years," Fern said. "I have Belle to thank for pulling me through. Belle and Dean." She put the tea pitcher back on the counter and stared out the kitchen window, afraid to look at him.

"Quitting is hard work. You should be proud." He leaned against the counter beside her.

"We shouldn't have brought up the Devil's stomping ground in front of Hannah."

He smiled. "Charleston is one big ghost story. She's heard plenty." He tilted his head close to hers. "You worry too much. Since Hannah's been staying with you and Belle in the afternoons, I haven't been summoned to the schoolhouse one time."

Fern smiled. For a moment she remembered the girl she used to be, one worthy of kindness. What if Roy never learned her whole story? Could she stay innocent in his eyes? Doyle's voice coming from the dining room reminded her of all she stood to lose.

"Come on," Roy said. "You worked mighty hard on this lunch. I mean to enjoy it."

Back in the dining room, Doyle looked from Fern to Roy as if he'd caught her having a life she didn't deserve.

Leona

Leona found Ned in the den, showered and dressed. Hushed tones from an innocuous golf tournament droned from the television.

"Call Steven," she said. "Tell him we'll write him a check for any amount of money to say there's nothing between you. Tell him we'll pay all of his attorney's fees." Her new plan had her lightheaded with relief.

"For God's sake, Steven doesn't want a check." Ned picked up the remote and muted the television. "Didn't you hear a word I said this morning? I'm done with this. I called Paige and Amanda and left messages for them to come over. Clive said WRAL already called wanting a statement."

"We'll deny it," she said, "Don't you see?"

"No. We can't. I can't, and I won't."

Paige's voice called from the kitchen. "Hello, this needs to be quick. The children are with the neighbors."

Leona squeezed his arm. "Think about what you're doing."

He covered her hand with his. "I have. I trust our girls."

Paige came in the den still in the skirt, blouse and heels she'd worn to church. "What couldn't wait? Has that man confessed? Cleared Daddy?" She seemed oblivious to the tension between her parents.

The phone rang and Leona ignored it.

"Aren't you going to get that?" said Paige.

"No," Leona said.

The voice mail message clicked. Fern's voice filled the room. "Leona? Please pick up."

"What does she want?" said Paige.

"Who knows. I'll get us some tea." Leona left her daughter talking to Ned.

"Amanda is always late," she heard Paige say, "and I need to get out of here."

Leona brought back glasses of tea, and they pretended to watch the golf tournament while waiting for Amanda. Paige talked non-stop about her children, her in-laws, her committees, but Leona barely heard a word. She never, ever thought Ned would actually do this. If she was going to stop him, she needed to stop him now. "Ned, will you help me in the kitchen, please?"

"What do you need from the kitchen, Mom?" Paige asked. "Wouldn't you like a sandwich?"

"No, I'm fine." Paige, who had inherited her mother's fundraising prowess, started up about a committee she chaired for her children's private school, as if she sensed whatever her parents wanted to say needed to be deterred.

Leona checked the time. Half past one. Maybe Amanda wouldn't come. Her diamond-encircled watch had belonged to Ned's mother. It was impractical, archaic, and Leona had to squint to read the face. "You're not who I would have chosen for Ned," Mrs. Thomas had said to her the day of the wedding, when she gave Leona the watch. "But I believe you'll stick with him. Maybe even save him from himself." She knew, Leona thought. How had she never realized that? Leona wound the crown too tight. The tiny piece came off in her hand.

"Sorry I'm late." Amanda rushed in holding up a bakery bag. "I brought bagels. What have I missed? Is there news?" She put the bag on the coffee table and took a seat on the opposite end of the sofa from her sister. Amanda no longer wore the flowing dress she'd worn to church. She'd changed into jeans and a sweater.

Still believing she could steer Ned clear of his confession, Leona said, "We wanted to see how you both are holding up. I know there's a lot of talk."

"That's not…" Ned started to say.

Leona cut him off. "I'd think you'd care to hear how your daughters are doing."

Ned stared at the floor. Leona took his silence as a sign that he'd changed his mind. Then, he stared up at her. "Leona, I talk to my daughters just about every day. I know how they're doing." He looked to Paige and Amanda. "Evidence has come out that will hurt my case. There's a chance it will be on tonight's news or in the *News and Observer* tomorrow. I wanted to let you know what to expect."

"What kind of evidence?" said Paige.

"They're trying to link your father to Steven Carter," Leona said. She calmed her voice. "To make it appear …," she faltered. The girls glared at her. She recognized their warning not to disparage the father they loved so dearly.

Ned pulled the folded fax from the inside pocket of his corduroy jacket. "This is what came out in the *Citizen-Times* today."

Words she could not hide were within reach of her daughters' hands. Leona felt numb, like in a dream when danger was imminent. She wanted to intervene, but her arms, heavy and useless, stayed put. Ned handed the fax to Paige.

"Isn't that where Aunt Fern works?" Paige asked.

Leona nodded.

Birds bickered around a feeder outside the window. While Paige read, their indignant cries filled the silence.

"This is pure insinuation," Paige said. She tossed the fax on the sofa as if it might catch fire. "You have to sue."

Leona recognized the tactic. Paige had learned from the best how to refuse the truth. *Yes. Don't believe it.*

Amanda reached for the fax. Her thick auburn hair, pulled back from her face with combs, made her look like a perplexed angel.

"What's going on with newspapers?" Paige asked. She sat back with her arms crossed against her chest. "They've all become tabloids."

"Daddy, is this true?" Amanda said.

"Oh, for heaven's sake, Amanda," Paige said. "Don't be ridiculous."

"Girls," Ned stood. He buried his hands in the pockets of his khakis. Leona thought of the family gatherings they'd had in this room, all the happy announcements made. Surely he wouldn't ruin everything they'd created.

"When I married your mother," he said, "I had every intention of being a good husband."

"You're a very good husband," Paige said.

"Ned," Leona said. "Please. I won't have it."

"Let Daddy talk," Amanda said. Leona had never heard her youngest child speak with such force.

"Years ago, I realized something about myself that was difficult to understand." Ned's voice rose. "I'm sorry if this is confusing. I was confused for a good long while, too, but I've accepted myself, and I hope you will too."

"You're coming out to us," Amanda said.

Leona froze.

"Yes," Ned said.

The color drained from Paige's face. "Oh, my God."

"I hope you still love me." Ned's voice cracked.

Amanda went to him, and they embraced. "Of course we love you." Her words came with a sob. "We love you so much."

Paige stared at her mother, dry-eyed.

Fern

Fern and Carol Ann cleaned up the kitchen while Roy read the article about Ned in the *Citizen-Times*. Doyle, Dean, and Hannah had gone down to check on the emus, and Belle was taking a well-earned nap.

Carol Ann wasted no time filling Roy in on her version of Ned's relationship with Steven Carter. Fern couldn't believe what Carol Ann didn't mind saying to a preacher. "I always knew Ned was funny," she told him.

A plate nearly slipped from Fern's hands. "That's the craziest thing I've ever heard," she said. "Are you going to dry these dishes, or am I?"

"Testy I reckon," Carol Ann said. "Trust me. I know about these things." She pulled a drying towel from the drawer and shook it at Fern.

"Ned and Leona have been married for nearly thirty years," Fern said.

"People stay married for all kinds of reasons," Roy said from behind the newspaper.

"See," Carol Ann said. "Roy knows."

Fern shook her own towel back at her friend. The last thing she wanted Roy to hear in her kitchen was a lecture on the world according to Carol Ann Kelley.

"Now," Carol Ann said. "I admit, I've said 'I do' to a few bank accounts myself, but you know as well as I do, Leona married Ned because he was going to be a doctor. She had her sights set on him from the get-go, and as long as she can be Mrs. Ned Thomas, I assure you, she couldn't care less about sex."

"Roy, are we the most sinful bunch you've ever come across?" Fern said. "You're going to leave here and not look back, afraid you'll turn into a pillar of salt."

Roy set the paper aside, and Fern feared he had finally realized that Barrett House was no place for a man of the cloth. Carol Ann must have anticipated a sermon. She stepped in front of him with her hands on her hips. "You can't tell me it's a sin to be a homosexual," she said. "That's like saying it's a sin to be blue-eyed or blond headed. Trust me, I have experience in this department, and if I can't make a man go hetro, no one can. It's all in the DNA."

Roy reared back. He clasped his big hands together and rested them on the top of his head. "I agree."

Carol Ann pushed. "So, you don't think Ned will burn in hell?"

"No," he said. "People love who they love. I don't believe there's any sin in that. And, I have friends who couldn't anymore change their nature than they could change any other God-given part of themselves. So, no. I don't think Ned is going to burn in hell." He put the newspaper on the table. "One of the finest Christian men I've ever known died of AIDS. He was married. He and his family belonged to my church in Charleston, and I worked with his nonprofit to feed the hungry. After he died, I vowed to do what I could to move my congregations away from homophobic beliefs. It's slow going, though."

"You'd better not talk that way over at New Hope," Fern said. It seemed like every time she was with Roy, he did or said something that not only surprised her but chipped away at the armor protecting her wary heart.

"Fern's right," Carol Ann said. "They hear that, they'll toss you over to that bunch of belly dancing Unitarians in Southern Pines." Carol Ann commenced her tale of the time she took belly dancing lessons at the Unitarian Church. "That was a peculiar bunch, and believe me, belly dancing is harder than it looks."

Roy and Carol Ann traded stories while Fern scrubbed tiny bits of fried chicken off the electric skillet. She thought about what Roy had said. People love who they love.

"Fern," Roy said. "You want us to get out of here so you can call Leona?"

"I'll call when I'm ready," she said, unable to hide her irritation.

"Leona and Fern have a history," Carol Ann said.

"Most sisters do," Roy said. He smiled, proud of his joke.

"Do you preach funny sermons?" Carol Ann asked.

"I try to add a little humor when it's appropriate."

"What did you preach about today?"

"I dressed it up a little, but basically the message was pride goeth before the fall." He turned to Fern. "An oldie but a goodie."

As if her own guilty conscious wasn't bad enough, she thought. Now she had her own private preacher doling out guilt in her kitchen.

"What is it—two hours to Raleigh?" Roy said. "Why don't you go up there?"

"Heaven's no," Fern said. "I don't even remember how to get to her house."

"I can help you with that," Carol Ann said. "I rode by there the last time I went to the state realtor convention."

"What did you do that for?" Fern asked.

"Just curious. Roy's right. Go. I can stay with Belle."

"Trust me, Leona will do fine cussing me out over the telephone." Fern reached around Roy for the canister of flour to take into the pantry. It slipped from her hands onto the floor. The thick glass cracked, and Martha White's finest carpeted the linoleum.

"Lord God Almighty," Fern said.

"Oh, honey," Carol Ann said, "I'll get the broom."

Roy ignored the mess she'd made. He stood with her amid the spilled flour and broken glass. "Go, Fern. Go to her. Sometimes during the week when the sanctuary's empty, I sit in different pews and think about the folks I see every Sunday. Being in their seats helps me feel what it's like to be them. I see what they see. Understand what they need. It might help you to go sit in Leona's seat."

"I don't know about going up there, Roy," she said. "Hand me the phone."

"Move," Carol Ann nudged her with the broom. "But be careful where you step. Don't track that flour everywhere."

Fern took the phone out on the back porch and dialed Leona's number. She got the answering machine. "Leona? Ned? Please pick up." She heard a beep. Her time was up. Back in the kitchen, Roy and Carol Ann were still cleaning up flour. Fern picked up the front page of the newspaper and studied the picture of Ned and Steven. Ned looked smitten. Her mind opened to what she'd known all morning. The newspaper story wasn't only embarrassing, it might be true and extremely harmful to Ned's case.

"If I'm going to Raleigh, I'd better get on the road."

Everyone had settled on the front porch when Fern came out with her overnight bag. "I'll be back in the morning," she said, leaning down to hug Belle.

Belle reached beside her rocker and handed Fern a paper sack. "Take these quilt pieces to Leona and tell her I've found many an answer in a quilt block."

Fern held the bag to her chest. "She and Ned are having a little trouble. I'm going to see if there's anything I can do."

Belle gave Fern's arm a squeeze. "You think I don't know you hide the newspapers you don't want me to see in the potato bin? I know about the trouble. Go help your sister. Tell Leona and Ned I love them. Don't worry. Carol Ann and I will have a big time."

Carol Ann rocked beside her, "If you call and can't find us, we might be over at the Elks Club."

"The Elks Club," Hannah said. "What's an Elks Club?"

"It's where men go to get drunk and dance with near-naked women," Dean said.

"Dean, some of your answers aren't fit for a twelve-year-old," Fern said, hugging her son.

"Not to worry," Roy said, pushing himself up from the swing. He carried Fern's bag to the car. "It's always good to have a jumping-off place for family discussions."

He opened the car door for her but didn't move out of the way. "What?" Fern said. "I know you've got something to say."

"You've got me figured out." He scratched the back of his neck. "If I'm overstepping, you can tell me to mind my own business."

"And if I did, I doubt you'd back down one iota, so you might as well go ahead and say what's on your mind."

He took a breath. "Don't go up there asking questions or pushing for answers. The best thing for you to do is listen. Whatever's going on, whatever the truth of the matter is, let your sister talk."

"She's not going to tell me anything," Fern said. "She'll bless me out for being a gossip, paint a pretty picture, and I'll be back before breakfast."

"South of Heaven nobody gets by without trouble," Roy said, "and trouble changes people." He stepped closer to her. "I've been there. I think you have too. We get it in our heads that we can make it through with no problems, no heartaches, if we follow one rule or the other, but that's not the way it is. For anyone. Not even that strong-willed sister of yours. She needs to know she's not alone. That someone cares."

Not only his words, but the way he looked at her when he said them caused Fern to want to say three simple ones back to him, but she only mumbled her thanks and stumbled into the car.

He's a preacher, she reminded herself all the way to Raleigh. That's how preachers talk. Stop trying to make more of it.

Fern drove up and down Leona's street four times before spotting the house number on an ivy-covered mailbox. Carol Ann's directions, written large on one of Roy's legal pads, had been a lifesaver, but a wavy brick wall hid the house from the street. It seemed odd to Fern that Leona would hide her beautiful home.

Fern parked and crept up the driveway like a thief. It was close to seven o'clock. White dogwoods glowed in the twilight and red azaleas flamed against a canvas of emerald grass. Fern thought of home. Of the bamboo threatening to overtake the yard. The jumbled jasmine vines creeping up the porch steps. Messy flower beds amid sparse grass. Belle's only criterion for planting being whether a flower or shrub needed sun or shade. No wonder Leona called their yard a disaster. Damn that smooth-talking Roy Puckett for making this seem like a good idea. A light came on in an upstairs window. It was now or never. She made her way up the walk. The door flew open.

"How dare you." Leona's words came in a spit-out whisper.

"How did you know I was here?"

"I saw you from upstairs," Leona said, blocking the door.

"Please. Let me explain," Fern said. "I swear to you, I had nothing to do with that article in the paper."

"Keep your voice down," Leona said, stepping aside to let her in. "Upstairs," she whispered. She led Fern up the curved staircase and down a narrow hall lined with elegantly framed portraits of the girls and their children.

"It was a very difficult afternoon," Leona said. "Thanks to you."

"Where's Ned?"

"In the den with his bourbon."

Leona's blue-and-white bedroom looked like something out of the magazines Carol Ann kept stacked on her coffee table. Leona shut the door and faced her. "What made you do it, Fern? Jealousy? Or just pure, unadulterated hatred? And to think you had me believing you'd changed."

"I didn't do a damn thing," Fern said, feeling the impulse to defend herself rise.

"Your boss had to have something to go on," Leona said. "Don't play the innocent with me."

Fern reminded herself she was the sinner come to confess. Leona had every reason to be mad. "I swear to you, I had no idea what Robert was up to. I mean, I knew he was curious. He about worried me to death after that first story came out in the *Observer*." She took a breath. "Robert overhead Carol Ann and I talking, and Carol Ann said some things that were just ridiculous. I told him it was a bunch of hooey."

Leona motioned for Fern to follow her through French doors into a sitting room. Built-in bookcases packed tight with hardbacks and photographs stretched across the back wall. An ice bucket and a bottle of vodka sat on a glass-top table between two deep-blue velvet chairs.

"I thought you didn't drink the hard stuff," Fern said.

"I decided to give it a try. It doesn't change anything, does it?"

"As I recall, it makes everything worse."

Leona collapsed into a chair and nodded to the other. "Sit." Her voice came out soft and low, almost hospitable. "What made you say Carol Ann's talk was hooey?"

Fern adjusted herself in the small chair not made for comfort. She felt like a giant in a dollhouse. "Ned's not a criminal. And it's not like you all need money."

Leona's tired eyes shifted, as if trying to focus. "What about the article your boss wrote? Do you think that's hooey too?"

Something deep inside Fern flipped. "Carol Ann has said some things through the years about Ned. But I know she gets carried away."

"Ned's gay," Leona said.

How come the truth always came as a surprise when a lie sounded just about right, Fern thought.

Leona held up a finger as if checking the direction of the wind. "But he didn't take the money. I believe Steven Carter did that all on his own. Clive may still be able to prove Ned wasn't involved, but ..." Her voice trailed off and she folded her hands in her lap. "Fraud. Isn't that perfect?" She gave Fern a small smile. "Surely you believed your old friend, Carol Ann."

"I did not," Fern said. "I did not believe her."

"Well for once, you should have."

Fern had so many questions, but remembered what Roy said. Let her talk.

"I've known since right after Amanda was born," Leona said. "I thought about leaving. Threatened. But we had our family." She fluttered a hand toward the bookshelves crowded with photographs. "I had more than myself to think about."

"Didn't you ever want the real thing?" Fern said.

"Oh, Fern, what do either one of us know about that? You had it and look what you did."

"Well," Fern said, "you're right about that."

"I wanted what I wanted," Leona said. "I wanted our girls to have a family. And, at that time in his career, Ned needed us. So we stayed together. I told myself it was a crazy phase he was going through. I know how naive that sounds, but I was young, and things weren't like they are now. Then the world began to change. Ned got braver, so I made him talk to therapists, ministers. I even threatened to tell his mother. As time went on, I read everything I could get my hands on, and I finally had to admit to myself that Ned was homosexual. Nothing was going to change him." Leona picked up her glass and took a sip of what Fern hoped was mostly melted ice. "Even then, when he tried to leave, I wouldn't let him. I held on. I told myself that I was not going to let anything happen that would upset Paige or Amanda. I couldn't stand the thought of them growing up like we did, with all the gossip. I know this all sounds ridiculous."

"No," Fern said. "The easiest lies you ever tell are the ones you tell yourself. I know all about that. You know I do."

Fern slipped off her shoes and put her feet up on the ottoman next to Leona's. Leona's feet were slim and smooth, but that didn't mean her walk to get where she was had been any easier than Fern's.

"Are you shocked?" Leona said. The sharp edge had left her voice. Her face was open, without contempt.

Fern didn't hear any challenge, any trap. "What don't I know about doing everything in your power to keep your children from getting hurt?"

"That's what came to me in the kitchen that day. When you told me about wanting to protect Dean. You said exactly what I've always felt." Leona brought her legs to her chest and curled into the chair. "I found Ned and Steven together at Heron Point. Ned said he wanted a divorce. That he was done pretending. That's why I came to Carthage. I thought I could buy time. Come up with a way to keep him from leaving."

When all else fails, we tell each other the truth, Fern thought.

"We told Amanda and Paige today. Ned said we had to before they read what was in the paper. They looked at us like we were strangers." Leona's breath caught in her throat. "Amanda took it pretty well. I think she may have suspected.

Paige was shocked. And very angry. She left in a huff. Her husband is an ambitious man. His family isn't going to like their son's father-in-law in jail."

Fern's eyes welled up. "I quit over this. I told Robert this morning. I'm sorry. I'm so sorry."

"Nobody has said that."

"What?"

"That they were sorry," Leona wiped away her own tears.

"What about your friends?"

She laughed. "A woman I've known for years hid behind the produce in the grocery store to avoid having to speak."

Fern knew what that was like. When she was pregnant with Dean and the whole town was talking, Leona kept her distance, but she wouldn't remind her sister of that. "How have you and Ned lived together? I mean, didn't the girls wonder?"

"Years ago, we told them Ned snored and that's why he stayed downstairs. They never questioned. No child wants to think about their parents' sex life," she said.

"Leona?" Ned's voice came through the closed bedroom door. "Clive's on his way over to talk about tomorrow."

Leona put two fingers to her lips signaling Fern to be quiet. "I'll be down," she said.

"What happens tomorrow?" Fern whispered.

"He and Clive are meeting with a high-powered defense attorney who has experience with medical fraud. Stay here. I'll bring dinner up."

Left alone while Leona met with Clive and Ned, Fern remembered what Roy had said about putting herself in her sister's place. She studied the books on Leona's shelves, surprised to see many of the same authors she liked. A silver frame held a black-and-white photograph of Leona's family gathered on a beach. Paige and Amanda, their husbands and children, all wearing crisp white shirts, sun-streaked hair blowing in the wind. The picture looked like an advertisement for guaranteed happiness.

In a sepia-toned photograph, Grandma and Grandpa Barrett sat in wicker chairs on the majestic porch of Pinehurst

Country Club, young, newly married, with no hint of the ruin to come.

Leona surrounded herself with how she wanted the world to be, Fern thought. Like we all do. But Fern knew the high price of pretending. No ease. No comfort. No faith in second chances.

L eona brought back turkey sandwiches on a tray.
"I know Ned's upset with me," Fern said. "But I really want to tell him I'm not a spy for the *Citizen-Times*."

Leona set their plates on the cushioned ottoman and handed Fern a linen napkin. "He's too emotional right now." She spread her own napkin across her lap. "I've been so angry, but he doesn't deserve to lose his license." She took a bite of sandwich. "What have I missed back home?"

Fern was glad to hear her call Carthage home. She gave her sister an edited, slightly humorous rundown of Sunday lunch with Doyle and Roy.

"I'm glad you have Roy around," Leona said. "You smile when you talk about him."

"I do not," said Fern.

"You're smiling now," Leona said. She checked her watch. "I need sleep."

"I'll get my overnight bag," Fern said. "And Belle sent you a sack of quilt pieces."

"I've missed our time together," Leona said. "Give me your keys. I'll get your things."

When Leona came back, she said, "You can stay in Amanda's room."

"Could I stay in here? Your bed looks big enough for ten people." Fern said. "And I'm so tired, I don't think I'll move."

Fern went into the bathroom that was almost as big as her bedroom back home. A well-lit mirror stretched across the wall. "Good God."

Leona came to the door. "Are you okay? What's the matter?"

"Look at my hair," Fern said. "I didn't know it was this gray. And these wrinkles." The medicine cabinet mirror back home hadn't kept her aging face a complete secret, but it had made it possible to ignore the worst. Her eyebrows looked like briar patches.

"The mirrors back home make it difficult to get a clear picture," Leona said.

"Why didn't you tell me?"

"Oh, that would have gone over well."

Fern leaned in closer to the mirror. "Carol Ann has been trying to get me to her hairdresser. Now I know why. Should I cut it?"

"Maybe a trim. I've always envied your hair. And your height," Leona said, standing beside her. "Look at us. Mutt and Jeff."

"Beauty and the Beast," Fern said, glad to see her sister smile. "It's going to be okay, Leona. I saw the pictures of you with your grandchildren. There's a lot of love there. I sure would like to meet them."

"You will," Leona said.

The sisters got into bed and Leona turned off the light. "Remember how you and James used to show up in my bed when Mama and Daddy fought?" she said.

"God, they were a mess," Fern said. "Mama waking us up in the middle of the night. Coming in your room with that old brown suitcase, saying she was going back to Red Springs. I'd cry and beg her to stay."

"She wanted Daddy to beg her," Leona said. "And he always did."

"Did you know she was going to leave the day of the funeral?"

"I heard her and Belle arguing. But no, I didn't know she was leaving. I remember Belle saying something about Daddy's debts."

"I believe the store was practically bankrupt by the time he sold it. After you went away to school, Belle was always meeting with old Mr. Tyson at the bank. She'd tell Bernice 'I'm robbing Peter to pay Paul.'"

"Probably trying to keep my tuition paid. I was so determined to go."

"She wanted you to go," Fern said. "She wanted all of us to."

"You and James took to Belle so fast," Leona said. "I was jealous. It had been the three of us for so long."

"How could I have not seen that?" Fern sat up in the bed. "What a little shit I was."

"You were a child."

"You took care of us," Fern said. "I don't think I've ever thanked you for that."

"We took care of each other," Leona said.

The sisters got quiet.

"Leona. Thank you for believing me," Fern said. "For letting me in the house."

"Thank you for not believing Carol Ann," she said, "for giving me the benefit of the doubt." Leona rolled on her side and faced her sister. "That day in the kitchen you said we were the perfect family. Did you really think so?"

"Yes. And you still are. You and Ned are such good parents and grandparents. Families can look all kinds of ways."

"That's what Belle has tried to tell us all along," Leona said. "Hush now. I can't keep my eyes open."

Fern woke from a dream, something about Roy, but the scene faded as her mind tried to sort out her surroundings. The scent of lavender reminded her. Leona's bed. But Leona wasn't there.

She tip-toed down the carpeted hallway to the top of the stairs and heard low voices. Ned and Leona. She couldn't make out their words but didn't detect the pitch of trouble. Footsteps on the marble foyer made her jump back. "I'm taking my breakfast upstairs," she heard Leona say.

Fern trotted down the hall, not wanting Leona to know she'd been snooping. She ducked into the bathroom, and when she came out, a coffee pot, toast and boiled eggs sat on the wicker tray in the sitting room.

"You snore," Leona said, motioning for her to take a seat.

"I hope I didn't keep you awake."

"I was awake anyway," Leona said. Her face looked drawn.

"I'm sorry I have to keep you hidden, but Ned's a nervous wreck."

Fern poured coffee into a sturdy white mug. She took a sip and somehow managed to slurp. "I keep thinking about something Robert said. About his anonymous source."

Leona put her coffee down. "Did he tell you who it was?"

"No. But he let it slip that it was a woman. Someone who worked at Oak Park Orthopedic. He said she was very upset about Steven and Ned."

"I imagine everyone is furious," Leona said, looking away.

"No. About them. Their relationship. And, he said the woman had details about the false insurance claims. The strangest thing, though, is he said she'd quoted the Bible."

"Someone angry because they're gay." Leona sat up in her chair. "I've been so upset and focused on Steven, I never even thought about who else might be involved."

"You think they were set up?" Fern said.

Leona remembered what Ned said in Clive's office. *Do you think I have time to read everything I sign?* "Come with me downstairs."

Ned sat at the breakfast room table in his pajamas with the newspaper spread out around him and the television on. "Fern?"

"Hello, Ned," Fern said. She was still wearing the sweatpants and t-shirt she'd slept in.

"She came last night," Leona said, sounding all business. "She has information you need to hear."

"I'm sorry about what came out in the *Citizen-Times*," Fern said. "I had no idea Robert was writing that story."

"Tell him what Robert told you," Leona said.

They sat at the table with more coffee, and Fern repeated everything Robert had said about the person he talked to at Oak Park.

Ned groaned. "A woman in the business office sent a letter to human resources about us a few months ago. But I don't know how she could have falsified all those claims."

"That's for the FBI to figure out," Leona said, standing up. She pushed her chair back beneath the table. "I'm going with you this morning."

"You don't want to do that," Ned said, glancing at Fern.

"You can say what you need to," Leona said. "Fern knows everything."

"The defense attorney we're meeting with said it would be good if Steven and I fought this together," Ned said. "He's meeting us there."

Fern gathered the breakfast dishes and carried them to the sink. If Leona was going to have a fit, she wanted to give her room.

"What time do we leave?" Leona asked.

After they'd pulled out of the driveway in Ned's Escalade, Fern called Carol Ann, who fished for news, but Fern was careful not to betray her sister. Leona's life wasn't hers to tell.

Fern peeked into the formal living room. Beige walls. White trim. Tufted sofas with curved arms faced each other. The only color in the room came from an oil painting above the fireplace—Paige and Amanda when they were little girls picking daisies in a grassy field. Blue-smocked dresses. Matching hair bows. What would it be like to see yourself so adored?

Fern remembered the silhouette portraits Grandma Barrett had done of Leona, James, and her when they were children. Their soft profiles captured in black and white. Days after their daddy's funeral, Fern noticed the silhouettes were gone from the front room. Only discolored ovals remained on the wall where they'd hung one above the other. She knew her mother had taken them. That was the only message she'd left to say she loved them a little.

In the kitchen, Fern smiled, seeing colorful drawings covering the stainless-steel doors of the refrigerator, gifts to Leona from her grandchildren. An oversized coffeemaker that looked like something out of a restaurant took up one corner of the otherwise sparce countertops. Where did Leona keep her can opener? The toaster? Her cannisters?

From the television in the breakfast room, a newswoman said, "Severe weather moved through Tennessee overnight and is expected here by mid-morning. These storms could bring heavy rain and possible tornado activity. Meteorologist Chris Hohman will be with us in the next hour with the latest forecast."

Fern finished washing the breakfast dishes before heading home.

Leona

Rolling clouds reflected off the mirrored glass of the law firm's impressive office tower. This is going to cost us, Leona thought, walking to the entrance with Ned and Clive.

As the elevator rose to the top floor, Leona swore to herself that she'd concentrate on what she needed to do to help Ned, that she'd put her anger aside. When the doors slid open, she saw that would not be possible.

Steven Carter, standing in a tight circle of men, stopped talking when he saw her. To his credit, he didn't try to hide his wide-eyed shock. Leona was pleased to see his discomfort. Even though she knew it was illogical, the more she forgave Ned, the more liable Steven became in her mind. Blame, like a bullet fired straight up, had to land somewhere.

The prominent attorney they'd come to see, Brad Preston, broke from the group. He took giant steps to the elevator to give Leona a firm handshake. "Mrs. Thomas, I didn't know you were coming." She wasn't surprised that he'd done his research and recognized her. She recognized him from his relentless television commercials, but he was much taller than she'd realized. She couldn't help but stare at his thick black hair combed back to extenuate a perfect widow's peak. His leering smile told her he knew he had her attention.

The conference room was as shiny as the building, with chrome furniture and an abstract alabaster sculpture on a pedestal artfully lit. Leona was the only woman in a room of men, and they seated her at the far end of the table. Steven Carter's bald baby-faced attorney shuffled papers as if he hoped that would make everyone take him seriously. Clive in his horn-rimmed glasses, doing his best to look bored, seemed like a relic compared to Preston, who reminded Leona of the sculpture, pretentious and difficult to read.

Their presentation set out to prove that if they weren't hired immediately, Ned and Steven would not only go to jail, they would lose everything. Medical licenses. Homes. Investments.

Interwoven with their dire predictions, they made clear the difficulty in proving innocence in fraud cases. "There's just so much evidence, and frankly, your personal relationship complicates the case a great deal."

Leona remembered how Clive had at least shown her some consideration in their meeting. Not Brad Preston. And through it all, she had to deal with the pining glances exchanged between Ned and Steven.

"So, what don't we know?" Preston asked, bracing his elbows on the table and clasping his hands together. "I can't have any surprises."

Steven Carter's attorney raised his hand like a schoolboy. "These e-mails might come up." He passed printouts to Preston, who began reading aloud. Leona stiffened. She expected love letters, but the e-mails were worse. Steven had been corresponding with a real estate agent in Costa Rica. "My partner and I plan to open an orthopedic clinic in Playa Herradura and we're looking for a secluded home with an ocean view," Preston read.

Clive, Preston, and Ned all talked at once.

Leona concentrated on the rain hitting the windows. How the drops shuddered and resisted before the wind slurred them across the glass. Rain. Wind. All you could see of the sky was a foggy blur. She sat up as tall as she could and took a deep breath to propel her voice. "May we please discuss the possibility that they were set up?"

Everyone turned to her.

"Brad, I know Clive shared the news we learned this morning about the woman at Oak Park Orthopedics angry about Steven's and Ned's relationship. The quote from the newspaper article uses the exact same language used in a letter sent to the human resource director some time ago."

"And you said she works in the business office?" Preston asked Clive. "Okay. Yes. A setup is an absolute possibility. But I warn you. The Feds don't like to change course once they get going, unless, of course, it can be proven without a doubt."

Leona shifted in the chair. "I believe that's why we're here," she said with a tight smile. "That's why, as they say, you make the big bucks."

As soon as they stepped out of the building, a reporter from the *News and Observer* ambushed Ned and Leona, a woman clearly tipped off by Brad Preston, who would benefit from having his name associated with a case causing so much talk. Leona could only imagine future headlines that would make Robert Yarbrough's article in the *Citizen-Times* sound like a puff-piece.

"Dr. Thomas, is it true you stole thousands from Medicare?"

"Mrs. Thomas, did you know? Are you divorcing?"

Leona instinctively locked arms with Ned. The rain and awkward umbrellas helped them avoid the trap. How many conversations had she had about Hillary Clinton? *Is their marriage a sham? How can she stay with him?* Leona suspected she knew exactly what kept Hillary Clinton by her husband's side. Their daughter. Maybe he was a good father, too. Maybe Hillary Clinton was also determined to keep her family together.

Ned pulled the Escalade into the garage, barely missing the side wall. Leona assumed he was expecting her to start an argument, but without a word, she went in and walked straight upstairs. She threw her suit jacket across a chair, stepped out of her skirt, and pulled her blouse over her head without undoing the buttons. In the muted light of the stormy afternoon, she wrapped herself in her robe and fell across the bed.

"Leona?" Ned yelled from the bottom of the stairs. "Amanda's here with Katie."

Rambunctious footsteps hit the stairs. "Gran, where are you?" Katie, four, burst into the room.

Jumping trampoline-style on the king-sized bed was one of Katie's favorite things, and Leona sat on the side trying to catch her for a hug. "Be careful. Don't fall." Katie's squeals drowned out her warnings.

Leona changed into slacks and a sweater and corralled Katie back down the stairs. Ned leaned against the kitchen counter with a beer. Amanda chatted, busy with groceries. It could have been any ordinary day.

"I thought you all would need some lunch," Amanda said.

"Gran, look," Katie said. "Figs."

Whatever their family was or wasn't, Leona was Gran. Ned was Pop. Amanda and Katie were in the kitchen. And there was laughter.

When Paige and Amanda were growing up, Leona kept her house pristine, but grandchildren changed her. Messes were allowed. Leona loved nothing more than the lively sound of their voices and finding the toys they'd leave behind.

"Have you talked to your sister?" Leona asked. She spread peanut butter on graham crackers and arranged them on a plate for Katie.

"I tried to get her to come, but she wouldn't."

"Call and tell her we have news," Leona said. "We may have figured out who falsified those claims."

"Really? Not Steven? That's great news," Amanda said, helping herself to a graham cracker.

The way she said Steven's name made Leona wonder if she'd met him. She put the thought out of her mind.

Paige agreed to come, and to Leona's surprise and delight, she brought Tyler and Abby. Ned herded all the children into the den for an old-fashioned game of Clue. He fought a one-man battle against Nintendo and all the other electronic games the children talked about constantly. Leona had told him a year ago he should get more computer savvy. Maybe if he'd listened to her, he would have known what was going on with the billing in his office.

Paige poured a glass of tea. "So, what's the news?"

"Fern came yesterday," Leona said.

"Was she looking for more nonsense to put in her paper?"

"She didn't have anything to do with that," Leona said. "But her boss at the bureau did, and he told her about his source. A woman in the business office. Someone who resents Steven and your father. Probably the same person who tried to cause them trouble a while back."

"What kind of trouble?" Paige said.

"She wrote a letter to the human resources director," Leona said.

"Saying what?"

"Think about it, Paige," Amanda said. "She's probably some homophobic zealot."

Ned came in the kitchen. "The kids are watching Aladdin. They've requested popcorn."

"I was telling them we think we know who falsified the claims," Leona said, reaching for the microwave popcorn in an upper cabinet.

"Yes," Ned said. "Clive and Preston are meeting with the federal investigator this afternoon. You would have been proud of your mom today, girls." He slipped a piece of turkey from the platter of cold cuts. "She put Brad Preston on notice to get this case solved."

Amanda draped herself across Ned's back and kissed his temple. "Thank you, Mom."

"We need to thank Fern," Leona said. "She brought us the information."

"Surely there's a bottle of champagne in this house," Paige said. "I could use a mimosa."

She went into the den and came back with a bottle of Veuve Clicquot from the wet bar's wine fridge. "Let's think positive."

Ned grimaced. "Honey, we're not out of the woods yet."

Paige quickly twisted the wire cage and popped the cork. "We need to control what's being said."

Rain beat against the window. The storm had darkened the day, and Leona turned on the overhead light.

"This doesn't change anything," Ned said. Amanda kept an arm around her father. "We, your mother and I ..."

Paige stopped pouring champagne. "The mother and father who raised me would never do this to our family."

"How can you be so selfish?" Amanda said.

"Don't you dare start with your liberal bullshit." Paige put a hand to her mouth. "We can get past this. Mother tell them."

"We are past it," Ned said, "There's no going back. It would be unfair—"

"Unfair? To whom? I can't listen to this." Paige grabbed her purse off the counter and called into the den. "Tyler. Abby. We've got to go. Get your things. Now."

"I'll bring them home," Amanda said. "Let them finish watching the movie."

Paige didn't argue. She walked out through the garage into the wind and rain. Leona followed, pleading for her to come back, but to no avail.

Back in the kitchen, Amanda sat at the kitchen table with Ned. The look on her face revealed complete solidarity with her father. It was as if she blamed her mother for the entire situation, but Leona was at a loss for what Amanda expected her to do. Go back in time? Change every decision that led them to this moment? Anger at Ned rose inside Leona but found no place to land.

"I'm going to watch *Aladdin*," Leona said. "A genie granting wishes sounds really good to me right now."

After Amanda and the children left, Leona went upstairs and lay on her bed. She stared at the ceiling and recalled all the times in the past she and Ned had come close to separating. But regardless of who pushed or pulled, they'd always found a reason to stay together. Not just Paige and Amanda, or Ned's mother, or Ned's career. Since their first high school date, they'd been bound by what they thought ought to be and had tried to make the impossible work.

She'd spent so many years being angry. But their life was not all about anger. Ned understood her, he knew her. She couldn't imagine a better father, even though she criticized him for spoiling the girls, for being too lenient. He was their constant defender. Their biggest fan. As a family they'd shared many more happy times than bad. Vacations. Birthday parties. Weddings. Late nights at the hospital waiting for the births of their grandchildren. They'd shared worries and relief. Sadness and joy. Had it been conventional? More so than not.

She and Ned had come as close to keeping their wedding vows as most ever did. Take the sex out of it, she thought, and they were like any other married couple. From what she had deduced from listening to women her age, the sex fled regardless.

Even now, she couldn't claim not to feel love for Ned. How could you not love the man who cared as deeply about your children's well-being as you? Who cried over a grandchild's smile? Ned was the heart of their family, and she was the muscle. It was too late to go back, to remake their lives, but what now? Paige was furious that Leona had allowed the truth to come to light, and Amanda seemed ready to condemn her for not being forthright sooner.

"Leona?" Ned tapped on the door.

She sat up and turned on the bedside lamp.

"I thought you could use this." He held out a glass of wine. "Some day, huh?"

"Has it only been a day? Seems like two lifetimes." She took a sip of the merlot.

"So, where do we go from here?" He sat on the edge of the bed.

"That's what I've been trying to figure out," she said, adjusting a pillow behind her head. She patted the space beside her. "Lean back. It's been a day."

Ned settled beside her and crossed his sock feet.

"Did you tell Steven you'd go away with him? To Costa Rica?"

"No. I told him I wouldn't. But he's young. Estranged from his family. I'm sorry about what I said yesterday. I know you were trying to help us."

"We're going to be here a while if we start apologizing for everything said for the past thirty years."

"Well, I'm sorry you had to sit there today and listen to everything."

"I mean it, Ned. I'm not in the mood for all this confession." Leona spoke more severely than she'd meant to. "What's important now is how we handle the consequences, and I don't mind telling you, I'm at a loss." Thunder rattled the house.

"I told Clive to get the divorce going. He reminded me North Carolina law requires us to live apart for a year. Would it be okay if I moved to Heron Point?"

"Won't you be going back to work?"

"No," Ned said. "They were pretty quick to throw me under the bus. Listen, I'm not trying to claim the house. I just need to establish a new address. I told Clive to give you whatever you want."

The room felt like a refuge, as if they'd left their weapons outside the door and met as two old enemies exhausted from the fight. "What I want," Leona said, "is what I've always wanted. Our family. Intact." She turned to Ned. "I know now that may not look like what I've always thought it would. You said something the day you left about the example we'd set for Paige and Amanda. How it was wrong. I didn't understand what you meant, but I do now. I want our girls to be themselves, not what society thinks they should be. Fern and Belle and Dean have never looked or acted like I wanted them to, like my idea. But I'm learning we miss a lot when we narrow our lives to what we think should be true."

Ned reached over and took her hand. "I told Amanda to give you a break, to think about what it's been like for you all these years."

"Thank you," Leona said. "Now I need to have that same conversation with Paige."

"Look at us," Ned said. "Parenting is forever, huh?"

Tears filled his eyes. His unabashed emotion had always embarrassed her, even angered her at times. But she was beginning to understand that her anger came from fear, fear of what she'd seen uninhibited emotions lead to. She squeezed his hand and wondered if it was possible to learn how to be less afraid.

Dean

D ean stood at the door of Frank's Garage. Low, dense clouds hovered over the courthouse, and rain, pushed by the wind, blew sideways. Mr. Frank poked his head out of his office door. "A tornado warning just came across the TV, boys. Get in here."

Dean remembered how back in '91 a tornado touched down in Pine Bluff and killed five people. He took off out the door. Mr. Frank hollered after him, "Dean!"

"I gotta go," he yelled. His mama was still in Raleigh, and Hannah, off from school because of a teacher's workday, was at the house with Belle.

The jeep's plastic windows flapped in the wind, and Dean was soaked to the bone by the time he got to the house. Hannah lay scrunched up in a quilt on the floor watching a movie. Belle dozed in her chair.

"What are you doing home?" Hannah asked.

Dean picked up the remote and changed the channel. The skinny weatherman on channel 11 pointed to a map lit up with red. "… tornado activity … moving rapidly to the east … Moore County in under thirty minutes … take cover now."

Hannah scrambled up.

Dean shook Belle's shoulder to wake her. "A storm's coming," he said. His head began to hum. He hurried to the closet under the stairs and pulled out the vacuum cleaner. He wrapped his arms around the thick row of coats, lifted the hangers off the rod, and threw them on the hallway floor.

"What about Bill and Hillary, and the cats?" Hannah asked.

"Ain't got time." Dean went to the kitchen for a chair. "Get Belle."

The chair barely fit in the closet. Hannah led Belle to the hall. "Get in here," Dean said.

Belle gave Dean a peculiar look but didn't argue. She clutched her macramé bag to her chest and settled in the chair. Dean yanked the chain that hung from the bare bulb overhead. "Hannah, get in here, you hear me?"

She backed away from him. "Bill and Hillary. We gotta get them, Dean, we gotta."

The tapping of the rain became hard knocks.

"Hail," said Belle.

Bees. Dean heard what sounded like a swarm of giant bees banging against the roof. He grabbed Hannah's arm, pulled her into the closet, and shut the door.

The lightbulb flickered on and off and on again. Hannah squatted beside Belle and held on to her legs. "I have you, Miss Belle." Dean braced himself against the door with his arms stretched across the frame. The boards quivered as if an electric current was loose, running amuck inside the walls.

"What's happening?" Hannah yelled.

"Tornado," Dean said. "Gotta be." A crash, then a thump shook the house. It felt to Dean like God himself had rammed a giant fist through the roof. The lightbulb popped.

Dean's head hummed. Whatever had come through the upstairs could be about to mash them flat. Thunder cracked, but in seconds his ears stopped ringing. The buzz of giant bees faded. Belle prayed out loud to sweet Jesus. The house rocked, creaked like a cradle, and became still.

Dean pushed the door open against broken glass and splintered wood. The front door stood wide open. The coats and jackets he'd thrown from the closet had crawled up the stairs as if to outrun the wind. The windowpanes in the front room were picked clean, and the drapes hung soaked and solemn like they were stunned by what they'd seen. Belle's chair, where she'd been dozing not thirty minutes past, lay upside down against the hearth. No piece of furniture sat upright. Belle and Hannah made their way out of the closet.

"Lord help my time of day," Belle said.

Fern

The rain started only a few miles outside Raleigh, just as the Honda's gas gauge dropped to empty. Fern found an Exxon, stepped out of the car into a puddle, and hurried through the downpour. A bell rang when the door closed behind her, startling the wide-eyed boy with tattoos up his arms. He fiddled with a too-loud radio behind the counter.

"They're saying tornados could come out of this storm," he said. "You'd best not go south."

She laid a ten-dollar bill on the counter. "I don't have a choice."

She left him yammering about dangerous wind and rain and ran back through both to pump her gas and get to Carthage. There was no way to heat the car without fogging the windows. Her cotton blouse stuck to her wet skin. She leaned forward and gripped the steering wheel, barely able to see the road through the deluge of rain. The wipers scraped and cranked but hardly touched the windshield. Every mile or so the car felt lifted by the wind. The voice on her radio gave way to static. Cars lined both sides of the road, their red hazard lights flashing. Fern drove blind until she couldn't. Surely Roy would check on Hannah and Belle. Dean was at the garage. She pulled over, leaned her head against the steering wheel, closed her eyes and prayed the only way she knew how. *Please. Please. Please.*

The Welcome to Carthage sign lay in a heap of pine. The rain had let up, but limbs and leaves carpeted the road. The tattered green-and-white striped awning of Sunny's Scoops clung to a silver pole waving in the wind as if in surrender. Stoplights dangled from wires. Not that it mattered. Fern didn't see another soul out and about. She turned on

McReynolds Road. A downed sweetgum blocked her way. Its massive tangle of roots looked like an ogre's face. She didn't think twice before bumping off the pavement to make her own path. Her tires spun in the wet sandy dirt, and she came close to sliding into a ditch, but made it back onto the road slick with pine needles. She drove over a silver trash can top and watched for drooping power lines, but knew she'd stop for nothing. By the time she turned up the drive, her hands shook against the steering wheel. Gray shingles littered the yard. A towering longleaf pine rested against the roof. The house appeared lopsided, like the air had gone out of one side. The right end of the porch, parted from the house, rested on top of Dean's overturned jeep.

Fern stumbled, weak kneed, through scattered camellia blossoms and shattered glass. The air smelled of upturned earth. Roy's car was out front, still running with the door open. The swing drooped from one chain, and a rocking chair straddled what was left of the porch railing as if it had tried to follow the others that lay upside down in the azaleas. The door stood wide open.

She followed Hannah's voice. "Then Dean grabbed me and put me in the closet with Miss Belle, and just as he shut the door, we heard a great big swoosh."

In the foyer, Roy, down on his knees, held Hannah. Belle leaned against Dean.

"It was like a monster came in the house!" Hannah said.

Without letting go of his daughter, Roy stood and reached for Fern. She pressed herself against his chest. "Dean saved the day," Roy said. He hugged her to him like they might still blow away. "I was at the nursing home at the other end of the county when I heard the warning."

Belle staggered. Fern broke free of Roy and helped her to the chair that sat half-in, half-out of the closet.

A screech startled her. An emu stuck a pointy beak through a broken windowpane of the front room's French doors. "What in the world?" Fern said.

"Bill and Hillary's fence blew over and they were in the yard." Hannah said. "But remember when they chased me that time? They chased me again right in the house. And the cats are fine too. I already found them in the shed."

Fern put her arm around Dean. He had yet to speak, his eyes a blank stare. She led him to the kitchen. Water pooled on the table from an overturned vase of forsythia, but last night's dishes sat upright in the drying rack. The afternoon light, dulled by an opaque sky, cast gray shadows around the room. Fern flipped the light switch but the electricity was out. She found Dean's pills in the cabinet and shook two from the bottle. "Sit down here," she said, putting the pills in his shaky hand.

Another voice came from the foyer. "Everybody okay?" Doyle stepped into the kitchen.

"Dean came home just in time," Fern said. "He got Hannah and Belle into the closet." She choked up and couldn't say more.

Doyle swung a chair out and sat knee to knee with Dean. He bent forward and put a hand on Dean's shoulder. "You did good, son," he said.

Son. Fern's chest tightened.

Dean blinked. "That was the damnedest thing I've ever seen."

Fern released a sigh of relief.

Hannah came to the kitchen door. "Miss Belle needs you."

Belle was halfway up the stairs. Roy stood behind her ready to catch her if she fell. She batted him away. "I've got to find the children," she said.

Fern stepped around Roy, and Belle shook her cane at her. "Matilda, what did you do with the children? I told you to stay away from here."

"Belle, it's me. It's Fern."

"I gave you the money, now go," she said.

"Miss Belle," Roy said, guiding her. "Let's go back downstairs."

"You were the ruin of my brother, but you won't harm the children. I'll see to that," Belle said to Fern while trying to shake loose from Roy.

They made it down the stairs just as Carol Ann came in the door. Belle pulled away and grabbed on to her arm. "I've got to find the children. Just look what she's done."

"She thinks I'm Mama," Fern whispered. "She called me Matilda."

Doyle and Dean came from the kitchen. "What's wrong with Belle?" Dean said.

"She's confused," Fern said.

Belle began to shake. Roy caught her before she collapsed. He went down on his knees and cradled her on the floor.

"Call an ambulance," Carol Ann said.

"Phones aren't working," Doyle said. "Not even my mobile."

"Let's get her to Southern Pines," Fern said. "To the emergency room."

With Dean's help, Roy carried Belle to Carol Ann's car and laid her across Fern's lap in the backseat. "We'll follow you," Roy said.

"No," Fern said. "Stay here. Take care of Hannah. She's upset."

Carol Ann eased the car back out on the road covered in downed limbs.

Fern buried her face in Belle's soft white hair. Abnormal tangles. That's how Dr. McManus described Alzheimer's. Little knots of confusion that, up until now, had been quick to undo. Fern recalled how Belle would wiggle and knead a gnarled thread on a quilt. "Just cut it," Fern would say. "No," Belle would answer. "You've got to be patient. It'll come."

But what if this tangle, this knot, stayed tight and everlasting?

They passed utility trucks and came up on a crew that waved them around a downed power line. Halfway to Southern Pines, Belle opened her eyes and tried to pull away from Fern, but she didn't have the strength.

"Belle," Fern said. "You fainted. We're taking you to the hospital." Fern helped her sit up. "Let's go to Dr. McManus's office," she said to Carol Ann.

"That wind came up quick," Belle said.

Relieved to hear her speak, Fern squeezed her hand and Belle didn't pull away. "You remember the wind?"

"I sure do," Belle said. She stared out the window.

With the help of two nurses and a wheelchair, they got Belle to an examining room.

"Let's take your blood pressure," the nurse said. "So, you were right in the middle of it, huh? It must have hopped over Southern Pines, thank the Lord. You were right to come here. My daughter works at the hospital, and she said the emergency room is full of folks." Air swooshed from the blood pressure cuff. "It's high. 165 over 80. I need to get an oxygen level."

Dr. McManus, a man Fern had never seen the least bit ruffled, came in and she recounted the storm. "Mmm," he said, like Fern had just told him Belle went to the fair and rode the rides. He lifted Belle's eyelids and shined his penlight in each.

"She didn't recognize me," Fern said in a whisper, not wanting Belle to hear. "She was talking out of her head."

"Who is this," Dr. McManus asked nodding toward Fern.

"That's Fern," Belle said.

Dr. McManus flipped through his notes. "Miss Belle, have you been drinking your Ensure, staying hydrated?"

"Yes," Belle said.

"No," Fern said. A wash of guilt came over her.

"Her oxygen level is low. I'm going to admit her and get her stabilized."

The nurse stretched a clear mask around Belle's nose and mouth. "Take some deep breaths for me, Miss Barrett."

Fern backed away. "I haven't been paying attention like I should."

"Now, Fern," Dr. McManus said. He held a clipboard against his round belly and peered at her over half-glasses that rested on the end of his nose. "This isn't unusual. I believe we'll see a change for the better in the morning." He lowered his voice. "I've told you to expect progressive deterioration, and it sounds like what she witnessed at the house was no small thing. I'll call over for an ambulance to speed up admission."

Fern went back to Belle's side. "I'm sorry, honey. I'll do better."

Belle struggled to lift the oxygen mask. Fern helped her. "Is Leona with you?"

"No. She's in Raleigh."

Belle gazed at the ceiling. "And James. I thought he was home."

Like other times, she'd returned to the present trying to make sense of her mind's detour.

Carol Ann came in. "The phones are working, and everybody's looking for you. Roy and Doyle want to know what's going on. Go call them back. I'll stay with Belle."

Fern called Doyle first to make sure Dean knew Belle was okay, then she called Roy.

His house had made it fine, with only limbs in the yard and a downed mailbox. He and Hannah were on their way to the church to open a shelter for folks without power, or worse.

When she called Leona, her sister said, "I'm coming home."

Fern didn't argue. "How did things go with the attorney?"

"Good. Thanks to you, I believe we'll get the FBI headed in the right direction."

It was almost six o'clock before Belle got into a hospital room, its blue walls faded and scuffed. A privacy curtain drooped to the ground where two hooks had come loose from the slider bar on the ceiling. A cheerful nurse brought Belle a supper tray. "I hear that tornado hit your house. Go downstairs and get some dinner," she said to Fern and Carol Ann. "I'll stay here until Miss Barrett eats every bite."

In the crowded cafeteria, Carol Ann ordered for them. "Two cheeseburgers, two orders of fries, one piece of lemon meringue pie, one chocolate cream, and two coffees."

"What about your diet?" Fern asked.

"It's not that kind of day," Carol Ann said.

Fern found a table. "Leona was right to be worried about Belle."

"Leona was running from her own problems when she came to Carthage," Carol Ann reminded her.

"I haven't been paying attention."

"You? I had Belle for one night, and she about got blown to smithereens. I might not ever get over it. I didn't even hear anything about a tornado until it was over."

Fern shook her head, "Storms come out of nowhere."

Carol Ann took a long breath, "Don't they, though." She wrestled with an ornery bottle of ketchup until ketchup splattered all over her plate. "There," she said like that was what she'd meant to do. "So, what happened with Leona?"

"It's a long story," Fern said, "but turns out what I got out of Robert about his anonymous source might lead to the real culprit."

"So, Robert ended up helping," Carol Ann said.

"I wouldn't go that far." Before Fern could say more, Carol Ann held up her hand and waved. "We have company."

Fern's mind pictured Roy, but she turned to see Dean and Doyle. She reached for Dean, but he ignored her. "Belle don't look good," he said.

"She'll be fine. The storm rattled her."

He sat down. "She didn't get hit in the head or nothing, I swear."

Fern took hold of his hand, "You did great, honey. This is just her mind wandering. Dr. McManus said she'll be back to her old self tomorrow."

Doyle stood behind Dean with his hands in his pockets. "I thought it would be best if we came right over. Dean's been worried."

Fern nodded. She knew how persistent Dean could be when he got nervous. "Have you all had anything to eat?"

"No," Doyle said. "We just got done putting plastic on the windows. Freddie Harris from State Farm came by. Said he'll come back tomorrow at noon, but it doesn't sound like it's going to be any trouble getting your insurance. You would have thought it was his house. I called a friend in Charlotte. He's bringing a crew up tomorrow to get that tree off your roof. It went all the way through the attic. The porch and the front rooms took the brunt of it. There's right much mess, but we wiped the furniture off as good as we could."

Fern knew she ought to tell him how grateful she was for his help, but she couldn't stand the thought of being beholden. "Are Bill and Hillary back at the barn?"

Doyle smiled. "Yep."

"What about upstairs?" Carol Ann said.

"The spare room got soaked pretty bad, but the other rooms are fine."

Fern's cheeks flushed. Doyle had been in her bedroom. He'd seen how she lived.

"Mama, a woman from WTVD came to ask me about the tornado," Dean said.

Fern sat up in the chair. "You all were on TV?"

"Just me," Dean said.

"Those burgers look good," Doyle said. "Dean? Does a burger suit you?"

Dean nodded, and Doyle headed for the grill.

Carol Ann sighed. "I love to see a man take charge."

Fern gathered up her pie and coffee. "Dean, come on up to Belle's room after you eat."

"Well, Fern," Carol Ann said, "can't we finish our dinner?"

"Bring it with you. We need to get back upstairs."

Once they were in the elevator alone, Carol Ann said, "What was that about?"

"He's taking over," Fern said. "He's been all over the house, in my room."

"Well, you know what? It's about time he stepped up."

Fern shook her head. "My Lord, what if they'd been on television together."

"So what," Carol Ann said.

"Think of the talk. I worry somebody's going to say something to Dean."

"Nobody would do that. People love Dean too much to hurt him."

There'd been a shift change, and a new nurse met them at Belle's door. "Her pocketbook was just sitting out," she said, sounding as if she'd like to make an arrest. "I put it in the cabinet. You can't leave things lying about around here. They'll get took."

"Thank you," Fern said. "I forgot all about it. She likes to keep it close."

Carol Ann motioned for Fern to follow her out to the hall. "Come spend the night at the house."

"And leave Belle with that hateful old thing? No way. I'll be fine."

The surly nurse wheeled her cart out the door without stopping. "There's a blanket in the closet, and that chair folds out. By the way, my name is Mrs. Fuller, and I'll be with you until seven in the morning."

"She heard us," Fern said when Nurse Fuller was a safe distance down the hall.

"No doubt."

Fern

Belle slept. The oxygen mask was gone, but a small tube rested above her lip. Her mouth opened and closed like a baby bird, and the fluorescent light above the bed heightened the shadows of her sunken eyes and cheeks. Fern stroked her thinning hair. At home, their routine made it easy to overlook how fragile Belle had become. The heart monitor's squiggly green lines made Fern's own heart race. She had worried so about Belle's mind, she'd overlooked her frail body.

Carol Ann sat in the recliner with an old *People* magazine she'd lifted from the visitors' lounge. Fern pulled a chair up beside Belle's bed. "Lord, what a day," she whispered.

"So, did Leona believe you didn't have anything to do with that article?" Carol Ann said.

"Yes. Thank God."

"But what I said is true, isn't it? And it's going to come out?"

"I believe so. She'll be here tomorrow. Don't be asking her a million questions."

"Like, how's your sex life?"

Fern couldn't help but smile. "Yes, like that."

Doyle pushed open the door and Dean followed him in, chin tucked, hands in his pockets. Fern moved her chair so he could get beside the bed.

"She's still asleep?" Dean said.

"Yes, honey," Fern said. "It's the medicine. They want her to rest."

"Dean's going home with me tonight," Doyle said. "We'll get to work in the morning clearing up the yard."

"How'd the trailer make out?" Fern hoped to hear it had blown to bits.

"Not a scratch," Dean said, "but the power's still out."

"Leona's coming in the morning," Fern said. "Dean, is it okay if she talks to the insurance man? She knows more about the house than I do."

"Yeah," he said, not taking his eyes off Belle. "What's that they're putting in her?"

"Fluids. To get her strength up."

"I swear that tornado didn't touch a hair on her head."

"I know honey. You did so good."

Doyle patted Dean on the shoulder. "Let's get on home. Fern, my phone's working at the house. Call if you need us. We'll check with you in the morning."

It sounded to Fern like he'd won, like Dean was his to take. She faced Doyle in hopes he'd hear what she could not say. "When we get our power back on, Dean will want to be home. We don't want to put you out."

He shook his head. "It's no problem, and you know it."

"Doyle," Carol Ann said, not looking up from her magazine, "I'm sure if Fern was in her right mind and not so awfully tired, she'd thank you for everything you're doing."

Doyle smiled. "I'm sure she would."

Fern hugged Dean. "Don't forget to watch me on the news," he said. "That girl said I'd be on tonight."

"Come on partner," Doyle said. "We'll pop some popcorn for your big debut."

Fern barely waited for Dean and Doyle to get out of earshot. "Partner? Did you hear that?"

"Doyle seems to really care about him," Carol Ann said.

"That can change," Fern said. "Doyle cares right up until caring no longer suits him. I imagine all Martha would have to do is wave a handful of cash and he'd be back in Charlotte so fast we wouldn't even see his shadow."

After Carol Ann left, Fern pulled a blanket and pillow out of the closet and made an awkward nest in the recliner. Just as she found a comfortable position that wouldn't bend her neck backward, Nurse Fuller flipped on the overhead light. "They said at the desk her house was hit by that tornado. That's what they're calling it now. A tornado." She checked Belle's IV bag.

"Yes," Fern said, struggling to straighten up in the worn-out recliner. "I believe it just addled her, seeing the mess and all."

"She's Alzheimer's, isn't she? That's what her chart says." Nurse Fuller wrapped the blood pressure cuff around Belle's limp arm.

"She has more good days than bad," Fern said.

The air released from the cuff with a swoosh. "Something like this can push them over and they never get right again. I've seen it." Belle slept through the nurse's less than careful care.

"How's her blood pressure?" Fern asked, fighting the urge to tell Nurse Fuller to go straight to hell.

"Better than it was. 155 over 60."

"Well, good. I'm sure we'll see the old Belle in the morning asking for a cup of coffee and a *News and Observer*."

Nurse Fuller folded her blood pressure cuff. "If you want any ice, it's down the hall on the right."

"I'm fine," Fern said, glad to see her go. She was tempted to ask about the nearest smoking porch, despite the promise she and Hannah had made to each other not to smoke.

She repositioned the recliner so she could see the television that sat high on a metal rack and found the remote. The eleven o'clock news had started. "We begin with team coverage of today's storm in Moore County where Susan Andrews is standing by live." A pretty blonde appeared in front of the Carthage courthouse wearing a bright yellow rain slicker although the rain was long gone. "Thanks Larry. It's calm in Carthage now, but that wasn't the case this afternoon when an F1 tornado with eighty-mile-per-hour winds uprooted trees, took down power lines, and caused major damage to a home on McReynolds Road." Barrett House appeared on the screen. "As you can see, a tree went all the way through the roof. We talked to the owner, Dean McQueen."

Fern turned up the volume. "It sounded like a bunch of bees, is what it sounded like. Then there was a lot of crashing. Me and Belle and Hannah, the preacher's girl, was in the hall closet, and it kind of felt like we lifted plumb off the ground."

A sweeping shot of video from inside the front room showed upended furniture and shattered glass. Our mess for all the world to see, Fern thought.

Susan Andrews came back on the television screen. "This tornado was only on the ground for a matter of minutes, but as you can tell, it was quite an experience for Carthage residents. Many are still waiting for their electricity to be restored. Back to you, Larry."

"Thank you, Susan. The community of Carthage is coming together tonight. The Ladies Auxiliary at New Hope Methodist provided dinner for those without power." Fern smiled to see Roy handing out bowls of chili with Hannah by his side. "Duke Energy officials expect all electricity in the area to be restored by tomorrow morning."

Belle had slept through Dean's television debut. She muttered in her dream and lifted her frail hands into the air, seeming to arrange imaginary quilt blocks. Fern recalled all the hours she'd sat with Belle while she stitched her creations. It hurt to see her empty hands.

Fern turned off the television. As weary as she was, she couldn't sleep. She kept thinking about what Belle said in the foyer. *My Lord, what a mess*. Weren't those her words all those years ago? The day Fern's daddy died? Did seeing the house in shambles throw her mind back to that day? And what did she mean about giving her mother money?

Fern craved a cigarette, despite her promise to Hannah. Surely she could find a smoking porch. She struggled out of the recliner. In the metal cabinet, she found Belle's macramé bag. Like a thief, she rummaged through it—Salem-Lights, a Bic lighter, a baby blue handkerchief, and Belle's old red leather checkbook from a defunct account. An intercom beeped from the hallway, and Fern jumped like a pickpocket caught. Out of curiosity, she opened the checkbook. *Matilda Barrett*. Check after check written to Matilda Barrett. Some for fifty dollars, others for one hundred. The dates skipped back and forth between 1965 and 1970, but the handwriting looked recent. Belle's ageing scrawl.

I gave you the money, now go.

Fern put the checkbook back in the bag and stuffed it in the cabinet, no longer caring about a cigarette.

From the hospital bed, Belle moaned and tried to rise. "What is it, honey?" Fern went to her and gently massaged her boney shoulder. Belle's fingers turned this way and that as if making a whip stich to mend a ghostly remnant. Fern studied her beloved aunt's face. "What don't we know, Belle? What secrets do you keep?"

D r. McManus came in a little before seven a.m. "How's she doing?"

"I believe she quilted all night long," Fern said. She'd been awake off and on all night. When the nurse came in to check on Belle at six a.m., she'd given up on sleep.

He bent down. "Good morning." Belle opened her eyes.

Fern carefully placed Belle's glasses on her face and looped the hearing aids around her ears. Belle patted them down. "Now," she said, blinking. "Good morning." Her voice shook but she sounded stronger. Fern stepped back.

"How are you feeling?" Dr. McManus said. "Do you know my name?"

"You're my doctor," Belle said. "McManus."

"And who's this?" he asked, pointing to Fern.

"Fern," Belle said.

"That's right," he glanced at his chart. "You seem better this morning and your blood pressure's good, but we'll keep you one more day." He ambled to the door, still talking. "We'll do some more bloodwork, make sure your electrolytes are in line. So, have a rest and I'll see you in the morning." Fern followed him out.

"What about you? You have any relief coming?" he asked, as if he'd expected the conversation to continue in the hallway.

"Leona's on her way."

Dr. McManus stuck his pen in his coat pocket. "Been reading about Ned."

"He didn't steal that money," Fern said.

Dr. McManus bopped her on the shoulder with his clipboard and wandered down the hall. "Crazy world out there, huh?"

When Fern went back into the room, a new nurse, younger, with a kind, open face, had Belle propped up against fluffed pillows. "I'm going to get you some breakfast, then give you a nice bath," she said in a sweet singsong. "We'll change that old gown, and you'll feel better." She raised the blinds. "Look out there, the sun's just a shining. No reason we can't all have a blessed day."

"I'm going in search of coffee," Fern said. "Belle, would you like a fresh cup?"

"I sure would," she said.

Fern's worries from the night before eased. Even the oppressive hospital hallway seemed less glum. When Roy and Hannah stepped out of the elevator, Fern choked up with relief. "She's better," she said before they could ask. Roy hugged her in a move so natural, parting felt awkward.

"Where is she?" Hannah asked.

"Right down there. Room 412." Hannah left them, and Fern pulled away from Roy. She was embarrassed, but he didn't seem the least bit uncomfortable with his overfamiliarity.

"Hannah insisted we come first thing," he said. "Doyle and Dean were pulling up to your house when we left."

The chrome elevator door offered a blurry reflection of Fern's wild hair. She could only imagine how she must look in sharp focus. "Go see Belle. I'm going after coffee."

She ducked into the ladies' room. The mirror revealed a haggard sight. She looked closer. Was there nothing about her face that said only Fern? Belle spoke her name this morning, but would she leave the world calling Fern *Matilda*?

She got back from the cafeteria to find Roy consoling a shaken Hannah in the visitor's lounge across from the elevators. Had something happened? She hurried to Belle's room and found her spry and happy for the coffee. "Be right back," she told her, heading to the lounge.

"Mama was in a bed just like that and she died," Hannah said to Roy.

Hannah grabbed Fern's arm. "You tell me. Tell me Miss Belle won't die."

Hannah's anguish stopped Fern from offering the simple reassurance so tempting to give a child. She took Hannah's hands into hers.

"Honey, I truly believe Belle will come home, and you all will finish your quilt and watch those awful westerns you both love and eat Little Debbie cakes for breakfast, lunch, and dinner. But we're not made to last forever. That's why every day it's important to be good to one another. Now, get back in there, give her one of your big smiles, and kiss her goodbye."

"You'll stay with her?" Hannah asked.

"Yes, and Leona's on her way."

"Okay," Hannah said. She slid from the plastic chair and walked back to Belle's room.

"Thank you," Roy said. He looked pale. "I didn't think about what being back in a hospital would be like for her. That's the first time I've seen her break down in a while. Sorry. I came to comfort you." Roy's happiness and sorrow always settled around his eyes.

"It's a comfort knowing you and Hannah care so much for Belle," Fern said.

Hannah came back, and Roy gave Fern's shoulders a goodbye squeeze. "I need to check on some church members who have storm damage," he said, "but I'll get to your house with a broom and a bucket directly."

When she went back into Belle's room, Fern thought her aunt was asleep, but Belle opened her eyes and smiled. "I feel like I've been ironing over a hot stove with a briar in my foot. Hand me that coffee."

Fern laughed at the old saying she'd heard for years. "Well, you did right much quilting last night." She raised the head of the bed and helped Belle take a sip of coffee. "Your hands stayed busy all night long."

The fast clip-clop of hard soles foretold Leona's arrival. She came in talking. "How did they manage to make such a small hospital so confusing?" She nudged Fern aside and spoke to Belle. "How are you this morning?"

"Better," Belle said. "You look pretty. I've still got my gown on."

Leona squeezed Belle's hand. "I'm glad to see you smiling."

"Dr. McManus says she can probably go home tomorrow, if we have a home," Fern said. "I need a shower and a change of clothes, but I want you to talk to Freddie Harris. Insurance people always run all over me." She kissed Belle. "I'm going over to the house." She motioned for Leona to follow her into the hall.

"How was your meeting with the new attorney?" Fern asked.

Leona leaned a shoulder against the wall. "Humiliating. But thanks to your information, Ned has a much better chance of being cleared."

Fern wanted to tell her sister not to worry, but optimism seemed quaint.

"We should have faced this a long time ago," Leona said, surprising Fern with her candor. "But God knows, I thought we were doing the right thing."

"The right thing," Fern said. "I don't pretend to know what that is anymore." She took a breath. "Leona, right after the storm, Belle started talking out of her head. She called me Matilda, and said, 'Stay away from the children.' Then she went on and on about how she wasn't giving Mama any more money. I looked at her old checkbook last night. It's full of checks written to Matilda Barrett. They're dated between the year Mama left and the year she died. Belle must write them when her mind wanders."

"When she drifts to the past," Leona said. The sisters stood amid the bustle of the hospital hallway. "Does that mean those checks are a memory?"

"I think she paid Mama to stay away from us," Fern said.

"Yes. And Mama did."

Fern

The biggest yellow bucket truck Fern had ever seen blocked the drive, so she parked down by the road. They'd lifted the tree off the house, and a large blue tarp marked where it had plunged through the roof. Two men with chain saws labored over the felled pine. Heavy plastic hung over the blown-out downstairs windows. Fern started up the hill, her legs heavy and her mind dull from the sleepless night. Dean, pushing a wobbly wheelbarrow full of limbs and shingles, came to meet her. "How's Belle?"

"Ready to come home," she said. "I saw you on TV last night."

He blushed. A shadow of stubble on his chin made him look older. "That Robert fellow came this morning. Him and another man took pictures for the paper." He pointed to the side of the house. "Guess we got hit worse than anybody."

"I'm sorry about your jeep. Maybe we can find another one like it."

"Mr. Frank came and hauled it off. He said it was a damn good thing I left the garage when I did, and Mr. Blue, I mean Doyle, gave me one his trucks to drive until I can get something else."

Dean's new familiarity with Doyle and imagining him driving around town in a truck with a Blue Construction logo on the door worried Fern. She changed the subject. "What's the house like inside?"

"Your room is pretty much okay. The porch and the front rooms are torn up." Dean picked up a limb and threw it in his wheel barrel. "Mr. Blue, I mean, Doyle's up there now."

"He asked you to call him Doyle?"

"Yeah," Dean said. "I'm trying to remember."

Fern walked on. The azaleas looked as if they'd been beaten to the ground with a stick. Blood-red camellia blossoms littered the porch steps. Inside, broken glass still covered the foyer floor. In the dining room, Belle's quilt pieces were scattered hither and yon, making the room a kaleidoscope. Grandma Barrett's chandelier dangled from a cord dangerously close to the mahogany table mottled by rain.

In the front room, Belle's prize crazy quilt lay in a twist beside her gooseneck rocker. Soggy drapes rested in a heap. Only one end of the thick wooden rod that held them was still attached to the wall. The velvet settee sat sideways in the room. The Magnavox stereo that hadn't worked in years had been upended, and Fern imagined her parents' albums that had never been moved from the stereo's cabinet, ruined. Fragments of magazines and newspaper made a collage across Grandma Barrett's Oriental rug. No lamp sat upright. The shelves beside the fireplace had been wiped clean and the Britannica encyclopedias she'd loved as a child lay sprawled across the room. The rose-patterned vase that had been atop the mantle for as long as Fern could remember was now a pile of jagged chips on the hearth. But Grandma's portrait hung perfectly level. Untouched. Her sour expression seemed to imply that Fern alone was to blame for the earthly chaos. "Why don't you go screw yourself," Fern said.

"Fern?" Doyle stood at the door. Glass crackled beneath his work boots. He took off his baseball cap.

"Talking to Grandma," Fern said. "I can't believe that portrait's still hanging.

"Me either. But you all were pretty lucky." He waved his hand around the room. "This is the worst of it. I mean the thing must have cut right through here," he moved his hand in an arc, "then knocked that tree over and headed straight back up. You can almost track its path. It's strange. The kitchen's fine."

Doyle's blasé manner reminded Fern of his lifelong habit of sidestepping trouble. "You're telling me I'm lucky?"

He nodded. "Well, yeah, I'd say so. You didn't get a direct hit. More of a swipe."

Fern moved carefully around the room gathering ruined photographs freed from their tarnished five-and-dime frames, mostly outdated school pictures of Leona's children and grandchildren sent in Christmas cards that Belle treasured.

"You know," she said, "I got to thinking on the way over here from the hospital how you can be going along, minding your own business, doing the best you can, and out of nowhere, all hell can break loose." She stacked the frames on a shelf. "Those straight-line winds made a beeline to this house, gave it a good swipe, as you say, then hightailed it back to the heavens. Now, doesn't that strike you as odd?" She stood before him in the blouse and slacks she'd slept in with her hands on her hips.

"Odd, yes, but odd's not unusual when you're talking about natural disasters."

"Really. Just luck of the draw? Well, I don't think so. I have to tell you, I feel chosen, especially chosen. Possibly cursed."

Doyle shrugged, "That sounds like something you need to talk to your preacher about."

"My preacher?"

"Yes. Roy. You two are good friends, right? He's over here all the time."

"He's our neighbor, and we keep Hannah after school." She stopped. Why should she explain anything to Doyle Blue?

He threw up his hands. "None of my business."

"Speaking of," she said, "Dean will not be driving all over town in one of your trucks."

"Oh, come on," Doyle said. "Why not?"

Fern shook her head. "People talk." She wrestled Belle's beloved crazy quilt, heavy with water, off the floor.

Doyle helped her take it out to the front porch. "What if it's a truck with no logo?"

Together, they draped it over a stretch of railing still in place. "Fine," she said, rubbing her hand across the velvet. "I hope this isn't ruined."

"It ought to be okay," Doyle said. "Funny how old things hold up better than new."

A lump rose in her throat. She took in a breath of air that had no business being so clear and fresh after yesterday's fury. The sun warmed her face like a sincere apology. "I've got to get back to the hospital so Leona can come meet with Freddie Harris." They went back inside.

"I didn't clean up much," Doyle said. "Freddie ought to see the worst."

Fern started up the stairs. Each step a hard win for her weary body.

"I didn't mean to imply anything about the preacher," Doyle said. "He seems like a good guy."

She turned around. "He is."

"So, what you said about a curse. Is my coming back here a curse, you think? That bad?"

Fern came back down two steps, her nerves frayed just enough to give him a no-frills answer. "Right now, today, you seem like a blessing with your big trucks and men with chain saws and kindness to Dean. But I worry your kindness comes with a price." She dropped down one more step, until she was eye-to-eye with Doyle. "Dean is my greatest gift. If God showed up right this minute and said, "You can change everything," I wouldn't because that would mean losing Dean. But I know you. You do as you please, use pretty talk to wrap it all up like Christmas, and make everybody smile and go along."

"Come on, Fern, are you saying all that happened between us was only me *doing as I pleased?*" He shook his head. "I'm no saint, but by God, you've known me all my life. I'm not the Devil." He turned around to leave.

Roy stood at the door. "I'll come back," he said.

"No, no. Go on in," Doyle said. "But good luck." He went down the porch steps in a hurry, got in his truck, and slammed the door.

Roy stayed put. He wore a faded red t-shirt, baggy khaki shorts and sneakers. He held a push broom in one hand and a bucket in the other. Fern couldn't help but be distracted by his muscular legs.

"Everything all right?"

"Not exactly, Roy." His stricken face caused her to settle herself. "Sorry. I didn't mean to snap at you."

"That's okay. It was a stupid question. Listen, thank you for what you said to Hannah. We had a good talk on the way home. The best in a long time."

"I'm glad. Her visit did Belle good too." Fern swept shards of glass out of her way with her loafer. "As bad as I hate for her to be in the hospital, I'm glad she's away from this mess."

"Folks at the church want to help," Roy said. He set the bucket down. "Aside from trees down and wind damage, your house got hit the hardest. Doris called this morning asking what she and the auxiliary could do."

"They can kiss my ass."

Roy's stunned expression almost made Fern regret her words, but she recovered. "One minute they're telling you to keep Hannah away from here, and the next they're acting like my best friends."

Roy forced a grin. "I'd call that progress."

Fern unfurled her arms as if asking him to consider the circumstances. "Why, pray tell, is everyone so damn happy this morning?"

"All things considered, I'm feeling pretty blessed," Roy said. He leaned the broom against the wall and laid the palm of his hand against the hall closet door. "Our family was in here"—then he pointed to the front room—"when they could have been in there."

Fern crossed her arms. "I'm sorry," she said. She sat down on a stairstep. His words *our family* rang a sweet note in her head.

He tried to fit himself on the step below her. "I didn't mean to preach." He sat so close her knees touched his shoulder.

"You just don't know Doris and that bunch," she said.

"I know how they are," he said. "But they know Belle's in the hospital and that you've got a mess in here. Sometimes letting folks do something for you is the first step to mending whatever has come between you."

"They just want in my business, is all," Fern said.

"Well, your business could use some help." He reached into his pocket for a handkerchief and wiped his face. "Doyle wants Freddie Harris to see all the damage, but I'm going to at least get this glass in a pile," he said. "And, however you feel about Doris, she makes a mean pound cake."

Fern wanted to protest but found the good sense to smile. "Thank you. Tell her I'd just love a piece of pound cake."

Roy squeezed her knee. It was an innocent squeeze, but they both stood too fast, almost losing their balance on the stairs. "I better get to it," he said.

He went out the door. Fern lingered trying to remember why she was going upstairs.

Back at the hospital, Fern found Carol Ann curled up in the recliner wearing an emerald green pantsuit and enough gold jewelry to start her own signature line. Leona sat stiff and upright in the chair by Belle's bed, apparently not one bit happy with Carol Ann's company. Belle's eyes were closed, and she made little puffing breaths that meant she was sound asleep. "The house is torn up," Fern said, not in a full whisper, but low. "The dining room table took on a lot of water, but Grandma's portrait made it through, wouldn't you know. How's Belle?"

"She doesn't seem confused one bit," Carol Ann said. "I told Leona she seemed weak yesterday, but she's been up to the bathroom, and she ate a good lunch."

"Sounds like Dean saved the day." Leona said.

"He did." Fern recalled Roy's hand against the closet door and gently smoothed Belle's tousled hair. "We need to get her home, but I don't know when that can be."

"You all are coming home with me," Carol Ann said. "I've already told Leona I won't have it any other way."

Fern didn't give Leona time to protest. "Well, there is no way in the world Belle can be around all that mess at the house. But I warn you, there's no telling how long it's going to take before we have glass in the windows and a front door we can shut."

Carol Ann straightened up in the chair. "You do know you have one of the best historic home renovators in the state over there right now, don't you?"

"What do you mean?" Leona said with a rude edge that didn't faze Carol Ann.

"Doyle." She pulled a magazine from her leather bag and carried it to Leona.

Leona read from the cover, "Myers Park Turns to Blue." She flipped to the inside. "Doyle Blue, The Queen City's King for Restoration."

"Oh, and I offered your sister a job," Carol Ann said to Fern.

"Is that so?" Fern sat lightly on the foot of Belle's bed.

"Yes, indeed. I need somebody to decorate my new spec houses, and I told her I can get her all the work she'd ever want down here."

Leona stayed fixated on the magazine. "That's not possible at the moment."

"I don't know why not," Carol Ann said.

Leona glared at Fern, letting her know she suspected Fern had told Carol Ann everything. "I need to be incorporated, for one thing, in order to buy wholesale."

Fern recognized Leona's I-know-and-you-don't mode.

"So, incorporate," Carol Ann said, with her own I-fail-to-see-the-problem attitude.

"It's not that easy," Leona said. "It would take quite an investment." She fiddled with the solitary diamond that hung from a gold chain around her pale neck.

Carol Ann plumped her hair with manicured fingers and popped her gum. "Honey, I've got money."

Fern dreaded Leona's reaction to Carol Ann's frank declaration.

"There's a lot to consider," Leona said, shutting down the conversation. "I need to go meet Freddie Harris." She handed Fern the magazine. "It makes sense to hire Doyle. Okay if I talk to him about it?"

Fern studied the glossy cover. Doyle's cool smile mocked her. "Might as well."

Leona

Leaving the hospital, Leona made one wrong turn after another. She drove around the traffic circle in Southern Pines twice before finally getting on the road to Carthage.

Carol Ann Kelley and her big ideas. Spec houses? Leona couldn't imagine leaving Raleigh. Moving away from the girls and her grandchildren. And working for Carol Ann? Never.

She prided herself on always having a plan, but when she tried to envision the future it was like trying to piece together a dream. Nothing made sense.

Yet Carol Ann believed she knew exactly what Leona ought to do? Ridiculous.

After getting her degree, Leona had meant to use it, but Ned and the girls needed her at home. Designing Heron Point had revived her passion. But Carthage? Going into business with Carol Ann? Unthinkable. Totally absurd.

Leona drove into Carthage. Bent trees, sagging power lines, and people raking up piles of debris in their yards shook her thoughts from the uncertain future to the upended present. When she turned up the driveway to Barrett House, the sun shone directly into her eyes, causing her to see only a glowing silhouette of the house on the hill, a shrine to her grandmother's noble intentions and high hopes. Anytime his Virginia-born wife got too haughty, her grandfather would throw out the adage calling North Carolina a *vale of humility between two mountains of conceit*. But for Leona, stories about Richmond's elegant parties and refined manners took the place of fairy tales.

She shaded her eyes against the glaring sun. Even before the storm, the house needed a fresh coat of white paint. Now the cracked and peeling chips had been all but erased, leaving a dilapidated grey. Fern had warned her, but seeing the fallen porch, the blue tarp stretched across the roof, and plastic covering the shattered windows caused Leona to wonder if her grandmother's home might finally be done for.

She stepped out of the car just as Dean came around a battered camellia with a ladder balanced on his shoulder. He'd startled her but she hoped he hadn't noticed. She wanted to be more at ease with him. "Is Freddie Harris here?"

"He's in there with Doyle and the preacher."

"It's hard seeing the house like this," she said. "Dean, thank you for all you did yesterday."

He nodded, and she walked past him, but the intensity of his stare stopped her. "What?"

"Just because my name's on the deed don't mean it ain't your home place." He shrugged, causing the ladder to rattle. "If you want to come home to live, you can. Family's family. I mean, you're not half as bad as I thought you'd be."

In a world fraught with duality, Dean's truth telling was refreshing. Humility might not be in her DNA, but Leona found herself in the vale now. Her view had changed.

"I'll take that as a compliment," she said. She stepped toward him, meaning to give him a hug, but managed to scare them both. Dean backed his ladder into the camellia, and Leona stumbled away, embarrassed by her awkward attempt. "I'd better get inside," she said.

The front door stood open. An oversized box fan, turned on high, blocked the doorway to the front room, but it didn't relieve the stench of soaked wood and the musty beginnings of mildew.

"Hello." Roy came from the back of the house. He held a push broom. An impressive pile of broken glass sat in the middle of the hallway. Leona had never seen him dressed in anything other than a Sunday suit. He looked younger in shorts and a t-shirt. "Wouldn't you know we'd have a heat wave today?" He yelled above the roar of the fan.

"You're good to help us," Leona said.

"Glad to. Doyle and the insurance man are in the attic looking at where the tree came through."

Leona made her way around the fan, and Roy followed. "This is the worst," he said. "A strong wind caught the front of the house, but the back was spared. I better get this glass to the dumpster." He stopped before going out the door. "Leona. We don't know each other well, and forgive me if I'm overstepping, but if you ever need to talk, I'm here."

"Thank you, Roy," Leona said. She appreciated Roy's sincerity like she'd appreciated Dean's, but after spending so many years suppressing her feeling she had no idea how to react. She left him and went into the front room, not wanting to say more.

Sunlight, usually kept at bay by thick drapes, revealed elegant molding. Shelves cleared of Fern's and Belle's bric-a-brac had restored dignity. With the furniture helter-skelter, the room seemed full of possibility. It occurred to her that even though there was nothing she could do to stop the chaos that had taken over her life, she could restore this house, one room at a time.

If Leona were the sort to believe in such things, she'd say their grandmother's unscathed portrait was a sign.

"Leona?" Doyle caught her staring at Grandma Barrett. "Funny. Fern went straight to your grandmother earlier today. She must have been a tough old bird."

"She was tough," Leona said. "And determined to live life on her own terms. Unfortunately, her family made that very difficult."

"Well. Life slips in plenty of curveballs, huh?"

Leona had no intention of discussing curveballs with Doyle Blue and was glad when Freddie Harris wandered in. She hadn't seen him since high school, but nothing had changed about his pigeon-toed walk.

"Hey, Leona," he said. "It's been a long time."

"Yes, it has. Thank you for getting to us so quickly."

Freddie still wore his pants belted too high above his waist. "Oh, this is quite a job. I hate seeing the old places get run down, you know?" He clutched his clipboard. "This used to be a showplace."

"With your help we'll get it back in showplace shape," Doyle said.

"This being a historic home means the repairs must be done in concurrence with preservation code," Leona said. "I hope you'll take that into consideration."

Freddie flipped through his paperwork. "The policy does indicate that this is a historic property, and seeing how we've all known one another all our lives, I say get me some estimates and we'll get going. I'll need a list of your damaged inventory." He handed Leona a folder. "So, how's Ned doing? I haven't seen him in years."

"He's fine." Leona managed a smile. Was it possible Freddie was the only person on Earth not to read the paper or watch the news?

After Freddie left, Doyle said, "That was probably the easiest adjustment meeting I've ever been involved with. From what he said upstairs, you'll get a check to cover the tree removal and the insulation repair right away."

"It's disconcerting to be doing business with little Freddie Harris."

Doyle laughed. "Yeah, I know what you mean. I keep running into people I haven't seen in thirty years, and it's hard not to get tickled when they act like adults." He grinned. "That said, it sure is nice to not have to go through a bunch of rigmarole." Doyle opened the leather portfolio he'd held under his arm. "Leona, I have experience renovating homes in Charlotte." He pulled out an envelope. "I brought some references. I'd like to do the work here."

"Carol Ann already shared your credentials," she said. "You're hired."

"Thank you." He laughed. "I should've known Carol Ann would do a background check. You know, I can relate to what Freddie said about this place. Being here brings back good memories."

"Really? I'm surprised." Leona didn't hide her sarcasm.

"You were in college by the time Fern and Mac started courting. I was the third wheel." He pointed to the porch. "We spent many a night out there drinking Miss Belle's fine lemonade, planning bright futures."

The fan blades whirled. Warm, damp air rushed around them like ghosts. Leona was surprised how easily he spoke about Mac.

Doyle gazed out the window as if spying on the boy he once was. "Nothing turned out like I thought. Not one single thing."

"Why is that, I wonder?" Leona said, not really meaning to sound impolite.

"Oh, when you're young, you imagine your best self out in the world, not the sorry son of a bitch you're likely to become. And you never imagine this business of living will be as cruel as it invariably is." They stood quietly for a moment. Doyle laughed. "Or, as my life coach likes to remind me, we make bad choices."

"What's next?" Leona said, uncomfortable with the personal turn in the conversation. From Doyle's expression, she realized she'd asked a loaded question. "I mean, with the house."

He nodded as if rearranging his thoughts. "I'll get a crew to pull that insulation out of the attic and carry the drapes and the rug out of here. Do you want us to try to save the rug?"

"Yes. It's original to the house. Brought from Richmond from Grandma's family home." Doyle helped Leona tilt Belle's chair upright. "I'd like to get rid of this, but maybe Carol Ann knows a good upholstery person. Fern and Belle will be staying with her, which is very kind, but not a perfect solution. How long do you think it will be before the house is livable?"

Doyle shrugged. "Hard to say. It's going to take a while with these windows. I know a Raleigh company that specializes in antique sashes and jambs, but they'll have to come down here and look at what we've got." He rubbed a hand over the window frame. "We might as well get some weather stripping on here. Do it right. They'll need to be stripped and squared."

Doyle's attention to detail impressed Leona. "What about the glass?" she asked. "Wasn't it glimmer glass?"

He smiled. "Yes. How'd you know?"

"I took historic preservation classes as part of my interior design degree at NC State."

He tilted his head in surprise. "I didn't know you did that."

"How would you?" She bent and lifted a corner of the damp rug. "These floors have needed to be refinished for ages."

Doyle pulled a notebook and pencil out of his portfolio. "Let me put something together for Freddie. With half the porch ripped off, we're good to go on a full paint and repair job outside."

Leona nudged the mound of ruined draperies with her shoe. "Good riddance to these old things." She studied the ceiling, "I can imagine giving Barrett House a whole new start."

"Can you now," Doyle said. "I can too."

"So," she said, not sure how far she wanted to go with her question, "in your opinion, since you've just come back, do you believe there's room for one more interior designer?"

"There's always room for a good one. It's amazing how much construction's going on around here, and of course, people have complained about it since the Tufts came to Pinehurst, but retirees keep coming with money to spend. I expect business to be good for a while." He paused and put his hands on his hips, "And I'll tell you something, Leona. I never thought I'd be back here, but it feels good. Being home reminds me of a time when I thought anything was possible." He laughed. "Laying off the bourbon has a lot to do with that, too."

She ignored his confession and turned to the kitchen.

"To remodel, we'd have to gut it," he said, following her.

Leona mentally emptied the room. "The floor used to be black and white tile."

"That's what I'm putting down in the kitchen at my old place," Doyle said. "And I'm going with open shelving. I'd love for you to see it."

"Carol Ann said you were renovating your parents' home."

"Yes, it needed serious updating, and one thing has led to another. I enjoy it, though. There's something invigorating about getting a place just right." He laughed. "What am I saying? You know all about that. You're a designer."

She stared at him. Something about the conversation made her uneasy. "I need to see the dining room."

She ran her hand over the rain-damaged table.

"I'll talk to a guy I know who might be able to refinish it," Doyle said, "but the wind really wrecked the chandelier."

Leona gathered a handful of loose crystals from the floor. "Take it down," she said. "I'll work on it when I come back. We might be able to salvage it." Leona wished she hadn't said we.

The windows had blown out in the upstairs spare room where Fern kept Belle's quilt blocks. Leona peeled pieces of damp cloth from the floor and gathered bits of ribbon and scattered spools of thread. As a girl, she'd hated how Belle's quilting scraps covered every tabletop. Now it broke her heart to see her aunt's creations ruined. "Leave this," she said. "There might be some things I can dry out. I need to get back to the hospital."

Doyle walked her out. In the side yard, Roy emptied a bucket of glass in a dumpster. "I told Roy my guys could do that, but he's pretty adamant about helping."

"He's a good man. Good for Fern." Leona hoped Doyle got her full meaning.

Doyle leaned against the car, blocking her from the door. "I upset your sister this morning. You might want to ask if she's okay with me working over here."

"We talked about it," Leona said. "She gave the okay."

"Good. Hey, I hope everything turns out all right for Ned."

Leona reached around him for the door handle, forcing him to move. "Let me know when you get your estimate together." Why did everyone insist on talking about Ned? *Because this is home. Because they care.* She turned to Doyle. "Thank you," she said.

On the way back to the hospital, Leona's mind wandered to the potential of empty rooms with high ceilings. To black-and-white tile floors and open shelves. To Doyle Blue's blue, blue eyes. "Oh, for God's sake," she said to herself.

Fern

After a month at Carol Ann's pristine mini-mansion, Fern and Belle were more than happy to be back at Barrett House, despite the heavy plastic still covering the front windows and stale air pouring from an overworked air conditioning system that couldn't compete with Mother Nature's hot breath.

In the Carolina Sandhills, no official calendar cued the heat. The motley collection of fans Fern pulled from the attic only stirred up endless dust from the refinished floors. White sheets protected clumps of furniture Leona hadn't hauled to Goodwill, making the house appear to be in mourning.

Leona drove back and forth from Raleigh to oversee the work. It hadn't taken much for the FBI to coerce a confession from the woman who'd set Ned and Steven up or to trace the thousands of dollars she'd given to a megachurch in Charlotte.

Ned was moving to Heron Point. She was surprised when her sister casually mentioned that Steven Carter would be going with him. Leona seemed at peace, but Fern knew from all Leona didn't say that she and Paige were still on the outs.

She'd expected Leona and Doyle to be at each other's throats, but their mutual admiration for beadboard and period molding kept them more than civil. When Fern suggested they go to Lowes Hardware for porch spindles, they'd been appalled, and she'd gotten a lecture on authenticity. Even Dean chimed in to remind her that Barrett House was on the North Carolina Historic Register. What Doyle spent on authenticity, they saved on salary. He seemed dead set to do his part for nothing. Fern suspected his generosity had everything to do with his self-imposed penance.

Barrett House sported a new roof, a new porch, and refinished floors. Fern's head reeled with all that had been rewired and re-piped. Carol Ann and Leona's mutual obsession with redecorating had reinvented the two of them into best buddies.

Leona, Carol Ann, Doyle and even Dean—who'd gone part-time at the garage to be Doyle's right-hand man—strutted around delighted with every exposed wire and bare board. In Fern's opinion, the renovation had upset more than the tornado had. Every time Doyle called Dean "partner," her own barometric pressure rose. But aside from all that was upended, Belle's mind had adjusted to the coming and going. She still had moments when one decade overlapped another, but she hadn't mistaken Fern for Matilda again.

Men on ladders surrounded the house like princes out to save damsels in distress, and even Fern couldn't help but be impressed by the miracle of new paint on old wood. She avoided Doyle as much as she could avoid someone constantly in front of her face, but his devotion to the house made her feel guilty for being ungrateful.

The temperature rose past eighty degrees the day they moved back into Barrett House. Fern noticed Doyle taking a break on the re-hung, repainted porch swing and decided to carry him a peace offering.

He gave her a wary glance when she walked out with a ham sandwich and a glass of iced tea. A light breeze lifted his thinning hair from his forehead. She was surprised. Even with him right before her day in, day out, he stayed a boy in her mind.

"You look like you could use some lunch," she said.

"Well, thank you. That's exactly what I need. Paint looks good, huh?"

"Yes, it does."

Fern handed him the tray and sat down on the steps. "Sure is good to be back home," she said.

"The window glass should be here Thursday."

She swatted at a fly. "No complaints. I don't know anything about all this, but I know we'd have been up the creek without you."

"Well," he said. "I'm glad to do it." He bit into the sandwich.

Not a single cloud eased the sun, but the breeze carried relief along with the smell of fresh-cut lumber from the new porch floor. Fern noticed Doyle's cotton shirts somehow never seemed work-worn or wrinkled, and while she'd made an effort by pulling her hair back and putting on a clean white shirt and a decent pair of shorts, she still felt shoddy beside him. "Listen," she said. "I didn't mean to sound so ugly that day after the storm."

He swallowed. "You had every reason to be upset. The house was in shambles, and besides, what have I ever done to make you think I wasn't a pure jackass?"

Fern tried to steer the conversation onto another path. "I read those articles about your work over in Charlotte. You have a fine reputation."

"I'm not talking about restoring homes, Fern. I'm talking about me as a person."

"It wasn't all you, Doyle. Like you said, I was there, too." Bitterness slipped into her voice. "Thank you for loaning Dean a truck."

"So, you noticed it's one without my name on the door," he said.

Sweat trickled down the sides of her face, down her back, between her shoulder blades.

He let out a sigh. "Fern, don't you think it's time we sat him down and told him the truth?" He raised an arm in the air. "Even this old house is getting a fresh start. Why can't we do the same?"

"This old house is not a boy whose heart would break."

"He's not a boy anymore," Doyle said. "I'm not so sure he'd be unhappy. We've really bonded."

"Bonded. Is that another word from your life coach? Good Lord, this isn't some made-for-TV movie."

"You don't want to tell him because you don't want your preacher to know," Doyle said.

She stood and put her hands on her hips. "Why do you keep calling Roy my preacher?"

"It's okay. I'm glad for you and Roy. We aren't getting any younger." He put his plate down beside him on the swing and crossed his arms.

"There is no me and Roy."

Fern hadn't heard the school bus squeal to a stop, but she turned to find Hannah behind her.

"Hey, honey. Let me get that book bag off your shoulder before it falls."

"I got it," Hannah said, giving Doyle what Fern had heard her call the "stink-eye." Fern followed her into the house, where Belle sat transfixed by *As the World Turns*. Fern couldn't help but think whatever was happening in Oakdale between Bob and Nancy made about as much sense as what had just transpired on the porch. It's like a damn soap-opera around here, she thought.

In the dining room, Leona and Carol Ann chatted like two Martha Stewarts, surrounded by decorator magazines, fabric samples, and wallpaper books.

Neither of them looked up when Fern pulled out a chair and joined them at the table, still scratched and speckled from the storm. She wanted to tell them what Doyle had said, but they were too engrossed in their conversation to even glance her way.

"How about this one," Carol Ann said. She handed Leona a block of cloth. "Could that be the valance? The underside of the leaves picks up the sage."

Leona lifted the swatch up to the window. "I like the way the pattern takes on the light."

"But wouldn't a solid make more sense?" Carol Ann asked. "I mean, can't you have too many patterns?"

"Certainly," said Leona, "but something subtle like this takes on the appearance of a solid. You won't even notice the leaves, but the texture makes the room more interesting. It's subliminal."

Carol Ann slapped the table. "Leona, I am not taking no for an answer," she said. "We're going into business and that's that. You need to be making money as an interior designer."

Leona stroked the fabric. Her polished nails glowed red. "That's what I meant to do after I got my degree."

"Like I told you, with my connections, I can get you all the work you can handle. I've got spec houses right now that need flooring, lighting, the works. You can start tomorrow."

Leona shook her head. "We've got our hands full here."

If Leona had other homes to redo, Fern thought, maybe she'd leave this one alone. "You ought to do it," she said.

"We need new blood around here," Carol Ann said. "People come from all over, buy high-priced homes and condos, and then turn around and go to Charlotte and Raleigh for interior design. Or worse, they paint everything green and hang old golf clubs and polo mallets on the wall. You speak their language. Know what they're looking for. What do you need to start?"

The tone of Carol Ann's sale's pitch reminded Fern of one of those old-fashioned cash registers dinging and ringing.

"A space, for one thing," Leona said. "I'd need a place set up where clients could choose fabrics, go through accessory and furniture books."

Carol Ann flung her arms into the air, her bracelets jangled. "It's all right here. A genuine historic home would add credibility." She let out a whoop and fingered imaginary dollar bills.

Fern thought her expression was downright scary and had second thoughts about a Carol Ann-Leona enterprise. "Leona might not want to do anything full-time, especially in Carthage," Fern said, offering her sister an out.

"She sure as hell can't stay in Raleigh," Carol Ann said, like Leona wasn't sitting right beside her.

"Paige is already keeping the children away. If I leave Raleigh, I could lose them."

"I know you, sister," Fern said. "No one, not even Paige, is going to keep you from those grandbabies."

"Barrett House of Interior Design," Carol Ann said. "We'll transform this place into a decorator show house, set you up an office, and sell you like Moore County's own empress of good taste from one of our oldest families."

"Carol Ann," Fern said. "Fannie Frye comes from one of Moore County's oldest families, and I know good and well nobody wants her decorating their house."

"I do like the idea of paying tribute to Grandma Barrett," Leona said.

Fern forced herself not to sound altogether hateful. "Guess that means her smug mug stays over the mantel, but I would advise against putting it on a business card."

"We'd have to remodel the kitchen," Leona said, ignoring her. "And fix up a powder room. We couldn't very well call ourselves interior decorators with this house in disarray."

"You all are talking big money," Fern said. "That insurance check is spent."

"How many times do I have to tell you, money is not a problem," Carol Ann said, like it was the most natural thing in the world to say out loud. Fern couldn't help but think Carol Ann and Leona looked like two models on the same catalog page.

"Ned's had several calls from realtors wanting to know if our house is for sale," Leona said. "When I think of what could have happened if that woman hadn't confessed, it takes my breath away. We could have lost everything."

"How generous is Ned being?" Carol Ann said.

Fern leaned back and crossed her arms. "Oh, now you're giving divorce advice on property law."

Carol Ann ignored her and focused on Leona. "If we're going to be business partners, what you get out of this divorce matters to all of us, so listen up. You need to do this right. Fern, do you remember Hal?"

Fern nodded, "That's what I was talking about."

"I didn't leave a half roll of toilet paper in that condo," Carol Ann said.

"I got the only phone call Carol Ann could make from the jail after she got hauled in for grand theft," Fern said.

"They never even put me in a cell. I sat over there in Sheriff Digby's office and drank coffee all afternoon. I did, however, learn that it helps to have the law on your side. Even though you and Ned are cordial now, I'm here to tell you, even the most pleasant divorce can get ugly when it gets down to who-gets-the-chest-of-drawers. But that's not stopping us from putting together a business plan."

"Business plan?" Fern said. "So, are you thinking of moving the rest of us out on the street?" She directed her question to Carol Ann.

"No," she said. "There's plenty of room for everybody."

"Doyle and I were talking about how nice it would be to extend Belle's room and include the back porch," Leona said. "We could make a den and open up the kitchen."

"Oh, were you now," Fern said. "Well, how nice." She let the sarcasm drip.

Leona gave her the indignant look that usually preceded a full-blown huff. "We were only discussing possibilities."

"Aren't you forgetting one small detail?" Fern said.

"Dean," Leona said.

"He'll be a partner," Carol Ann said. "Have you noticed how he's taken to helping Doyle? He's just as persnickety. A perfect installation man." Carol Ann took Fern's and Leona's hands into hers. "A family business. What's not to love? And, Fern, let's face it, you need a job."

Leona left for Raleigh, but Carol Ann stayed for supper. Fern knew she was waiting for her to bring up Barrett House of Design. They cleaned up the dishes while Hannah and Belle played Candyland, or their version of it, at the kitchen table. The old board game was one of many things that had bubbled up from the attic before the new insulation was installed. Boxes of grimy nostalgia still lined the upstairs hall. A bundle of Fern's daddy's bamboo fishing poles leaned precariously against the wall by her bedroom door. The snarled lines with little red-and-white bobbers made her curious about the man. Had he ever been anything but trouble?

Dean said he'd clean the rods, maybe try one out. He'd moved all his clothes to the trailer. This evening, he hadn't even shown up for dinner. That meant he was off somewhere with Brandi. Or Doyle.

"Wonder where Dean is tonight," Carol Ann said, as if reading her mind. They'd carried their peach cobbler dessert to the porch. The much-anticipated spindles had yet to arrive, and with the railing down it felt more like a dock. A lazy sun hovered above the pines in an orangey-pink sky. Mourning doves called to one another. After a day of hammering, hollering men, the tranquil evening felt like a blessing.

"Are you implying that since he's hardly home anymore, it's okay to kick him out of his own house?" Fern asked, taking a seat in one of the freshly painted, bright white rocking chairs.

"I'm saying I believe he enjoys his independence." Carol Ann sat in the swing, hanging from new rust-free chains. When Leona had suggested they replace the old swing, Fern wouldn't hear of it. Doyle had backed Fern up, telling Leona the swing had a history.

"Listen," Carol Ann said, "I'm sorry this whole thing with Leona has you riled up."

"I'm not riled," Fern said, sounding completely riled. She moved the rocking chair so she could ignore the paint cans stacked at the end of the porch and the dumpster in the side yard chock-full of rotten wood.

"I know it's strange that Leona and I have, you know, found common interest."

"You mean bonded? That's what Doyle said today about him and Dean. He said they'd bonded." Fern took a large bite of cobbler.

Carol Ann picked at the peaches. She and Leona were on the Atkins diet. That might be why Fern had decided to tempt her with a favorite.

"Leona's calmed down a lot," Carol Ann said. "She seems happier, don't you think?"

Fern ignored the question. "I'm glad you've found somebody you can drink wine with. You all can go get manicures and massages and start a bridge club for all I care."

"Now, whoa here." Carol Ann put her barely touched bowl beside her on the swing. "The two of you have made peace, and you ought to be glad I'm not pissing her off like I used to. She's damn good at what she does, and I would think you'd be a little bit glad she's getting her life together, not to mention fixing up this house."

"I was fine with things the way they were," Fern said. She pushed herself back and forth in the rocker.

"Honey, you were not fine," Carol Ann said, then hurried on before Fern could argue. "You know Leona and I can talk all day long about crown molding, but you and I get down to the sheetrock. Now, tell me what's happening with Roy."

"Doyle keeps calling him 'my preacher,'" Fern said.

Carol Ann laughed. "It's pretty obvious Roy's smitten. Now that you're back home, you two can get back to circling one another until one of you has sense enough to make a move. Speaking of, have you noticed your sister and Doyle?"

"What?"

"You and Roy aren't the only ones circling. It's like mating season down here, and for once, I am not involved." Carol Ann picked up her bowl of cobbler and took a big bite of puffy crust. "It would be good for Leona to get her bell rung. I doubt she ever has."

"What in God's name are you talking about?" Fern said, unable to hide a smile.

"You know what I'm talking about, and it wouldn't hurt you either. I can see the headline in the *Citizen-Times* now: Barrett Sisters Get Their Bells Rung."

"Lord have mercy." Leona and Doyle? Was she jealous? No. "Do you trust him? Doyle, I mean. What do you think he's up to?"

"He's up to liking your sister. A lot. And she gets very un-Leona-like around him. Don't think I've gone Holy Roller, but maybe things do happen for a reason. That storm shook things up, and both of you have needed shaking up for a long time. You know what they say, the Lord works in mysterious ways."

Across the road, Roy's porch light flicked on.

Fern smiled. "The Lord has a hell of a sense of humor."

Leona

Paige was the only person Leona knew who was more punctual than herself. Regina's Café doubled as a gallery for local artists. A skinny hostess dressed in black pants and a crisp white shirt led Leona to the table where her daughter waited. Leona scanned the room, grateful not to see anyone she knew.

It had been over a month since Paige left the house in a huff. She'd taken advantage of Leona's hectic schedule at Barrett House to avoid her. Leona finally coerced Paige into meeting for lunch.

Leona pressed her cheek against her daughter's flushed face and wondered if the glass of chardonnay on the table was her first.

"Am I late?"

"Of course not," Paige said. "I finished shopping earlier than expected." Leona envied her daughter's smooth blonde blunt cut. Her own hair had too much curl to pull off the chic style.

Paige lifted a shopping bag from a chair. "I can't come this way without going in Little Bo Peep. You know that." She pulled out a pink gingham smocked dress.

"Oh, that's perfect," Leona said, imagining her granddaughter.

Paige's demeanor signaled to Leona that she expected them to act as if their last time together hadn't ended with her storming out of the house. As if there would be no more talk of FBI investigations. Homosexuality. Divorce.

"I couldn't resist," Paige said, carefully placing the dress back in the bag.

"I loved buying clothes for you and Amanda. I still do, although I don't think you ever wear what I give you."

Paige sipped her wine, "Amanda wears those awful bohemian dresses to cover her weight, but they just make her look bigger."

Leona held her tongue. She wouldn't exactly describe Amanda's look as bohemian, but she wasn't about to get into a disagreement about semantics or discuss Amanda's weight. Not today. Today, Leona needed to mend their rift, while somehow making Paige understand there would be no going back to the life they'd known. *Curveballs.* That's what Doyle Blue said. Why was she thinking about Doyle Blue?

"How's everything in Carthage?" Paige asked.

"Okay. Thanks to Dean's quick thinking, Belle and the preacher's daughter weren't hurt. I'm beginning to believe the tornado was a blessing in disguise. The house is getting a much-needed makeover."

"I can't picture you living down there with that oddball."

"Dean's doing much better." Leona wanted to tell Paige more, but now was not the time.

They both ordered the chicken salad Regina's was known for and Leona asked for a glass of chardonnay. She never drank at lunch but wanted so much to reconnect with Paige. Listening to Fern and Carol Ann's easy banter had made Leona realize her oldest daughter was also her closest friend. "I saw your sister yesterday," Leona said. "I kept Katie while she ran errands."

"I always regret snapping at Amanda," Paige said. "But she's so unrealistic."

Leona's wine came, and she took a sip. *Define unrealistic*, she wanted to say, but didn't. Instead, she focused on the paintings, mostly watercolors—her favorite. Soft colors swirled as if chosen at random, although the overall effect left nothing to chance.

"When's Daddy going back to work?"

"He's not going back," Leona said. "They offered him a buyout, and he took it."

"But the woman confessed. It's over."

"His partners didn't stand by him. He doesn't feel comfortable staying."

"Oh, God," Paige said. "Laurel Elliot and Katherine Lane just walked in. I'm sure they saw me, but they did a look-through."

Leona had never heard the term but understood the meaning. In high school she'd experienced plenty of look-throughs thanks to her parents' escapades.

Their salads came. As the waiter walked away, Paige readjusted the scarf that kept slipping off her shoulder. "When is the newspaper going to write a retraction? They owe our family a public apology. I'm sure I don't have to tell you how upset Jim is about this whole situation. And thank God, I didn't tell him what Daddy told us." Paige straightened up in her chair, and reached for her wine. "We need to let everyone know it's time to move on. I'm thinking of a dinner party. Something small. Only six or so couples."

Paige's confidence was like a salve. Leona hadn't felt confident in anything since the day she drove to Heron Point and found Ned with Steven. How tempting to twist their lives back into the knot that had held them for so long. She'd done it before. Paige was talking about caterers, dates, whether the party should be indoors or out. Leona's half-glass of chardonnay had her light-headed. She imagined silver trays of hors d'oeuvres. Women in summer dresses. Ned making gin and tonics on the patio. Ned.

"Ask Daddy if I should invite Clive," Paige said. "I know you're not crazy about him, but he did stick by Daddy."

"We're getting a divorce," Leona said to break the spell she was falling under. Going along with Paige, avoiding what needed to be said, would solve nothing, and only bring about more hurt for her daughter.

Paige's eyes narrowed. "What about everything you always taught us about how family comes first." The rebuke sounded rehearsed.

"We can't." Leona said. "Paige, we can't go back to the way it was. We've told you that. Your father's been staying at Heron Point. He's home now getting more of his things and he'll go back tomorrow to stay until he figures out where he wants to be." Leona stopped short of telling Paige that Steven Carter would be going with him.

Paige feigned interest in her salad. "Jim said if you and Daddy divorce, it will be admitting the rumors are true and you should both leave Raleigh."

Leona let the words sink in. Paige's husband wanted his disgraced in-laws out of sight. Her first thought was how dare he—how dare she—give them their walking papers. Leona remembered how thrilled she'd been when Paige married into the Whitney family. *She'll be set for life.* How right and wrong she'd been.

"I'm starting my own interior design business. In Carthage," Leona said.

"What?" Paige reacted as if Leona had made a joke. "You hate it there."

"There's opportunity. Carol Ann Kelley has offered to be a partner." Stating the plan outright made Leona realize how badly she wanted it.

Paige looked amused. "Aunt Fern's trashy friend? You've got to be kidding." She held up her wine glass, signaling the waiter for another.

"Don't you think you've had enough?" Leona said.

"Mother, please."

Leona wished she hadn't said anything about the wine.

"So, what makes you think you can do it?"

"What? Divorce?"

"No. Run your own design business. Aside from your degree, what credentials do you have? Who's going to hire you? You don't even have a portfolio."

The challenge was unmistakable. Leona had heard her daughter be brutal to others, especially to Amanda. She knew what Paige was capable of. Leona was capable of it herself. "Don't," she said. "Don't do this."

"Do what? I'm just asking. It's not like you to be so impulsive. I don't want you to embarrass yourself any more than you already have." Paige looked away. "You need to know, if Daddy moves in with that man, we won't see him. Ever."

Leona remembered what she'd said to Ned the day he moved out. *Do you honestly think you'll see your grandchildren again?* Hearing the same threat from Paige was like looking in a mirror. She saw spite. Cruelty. It was one thing for Paige to disparage her. But Ned? She wouldn't have it.

"So, just like that, you're going to abandon him," Leona said. Her voice shook.

"He abandoned us." Paige leaned toward her mother and whispered, "He was unfaithful to you. With a man. How can you sit there and defend him?"

"It's taken me a long time to understand … everything." Leona reached for her water glass. She needed to clear her head. "It's unfair to expect you to quickly accept what's taken me years to even acknowledge. But please, for your own sake, don't punish your father. Don't push him away. He loves you so much and, frankly, he deserves to be true to himself. We all do."

"Try telling that to Jim's mother," Paige said, slurring her words. "She wants me to take the children to the beach when school's out. Stay out of sight for the summer. She's right, of course."

Paige was turning away from her own family. Looking elsewhere for her worth. Just like I did, Leona thought.

Leona got the waiter's attention and paid the check. She stood and gathered Paige's shopping bags. "I'm driving you home. You've had too much to drink."

"Mother. Lower your voice. People are looking."

"Let them." She wove through the tables with her head held high, making a point to speak to the women who'd snubbed them.

Leona had a lifetime of stories to tell Paige and Amanda. Stories she'd intentionally kept from her daughters so not to burden them with her miserable childhood. But as a result, she'd burdened them with her fear. She wanted to tell Paige she'd been wrong to try to be so right. "You have to rise above it," her grandmother used to say. Leona had always thought rising above meant taking control, but what Grandma Barrett meant was looking the other way if the view didn't suit. To navigate the real world meant finding the courage to give the unexpected turns a chance, not grind to a stubborn halt.

Making peace with Fern and Belle had shown Leona how much time she'd wasted on resentment and blame.

"If you're taking me home, you're going the wrong way," Paige said when her mother turned the car out of the parking lot.

"We're going to see your father and talk this out. He misses you terribly." Traffic was heavy, and they came to a stop at a busy intersection.

"I don't want to see him."

"Well, you're going to," Leona said. She felt like her old self. Determined. Resolute. And there was something new. Resilience. Waiting at the light, she said, "I've spent my whole life wishing for things to be different, Paige. I won't have you wasting your life trying to change what can't be changed. And I don't want my grandchildren to grow up thinking going away to the beach for the summer will magically solve all their problems. This whole charade stops here and now." The light turned green, but Leona turned and looked at her daughter, ignoring the people blowing their horns behind her. "Family does come first. That means accepting each other. For once, learn from my mistakes." Leona saw her future. One where she showed her daughters a new way to be. "Always remember," she said easing the Lexus through the intersection, "no one loves you like your family."

"Mother, you need to call Dr. Shelley. Something is very wrong."

Dean

D ean only worked part-time at the garage now that he was helping Doyle Blue put the house back together. But Cora Wallace didn't trust another soul, and it had taken until nearly dark to tune up her Impala. By the time he turned on the dirt track toward the barn, Bill and Hillary were hollering something fierce.

He got them fed and then he walked through the pines to the house, expecting to see his own supper warming on the stove. But he didn't see any supper. A man's voice carried from the front room. "After we found the crash site, it took another ten years to get permission from the Vietnamese government to excavate." Dean stepped into the room. Two Army men were sitting on the divan, stiff hats on their knees and medals on their chests. Belle rocked, shredding a Kleenex. Leona stood behind his mama's chair like she meant to keep it steady. No one spoke to Dean for a few long minutes. His mama's face was red and wet from crying. Dean's breath caught in his throat. He studied the men. One looked old enough to be his daddy.

His mama looked up. "This is my son, Dean," she said to the men. "Honey, they found your daddy. His remains."

His remains. Crash site.

"Where was he at?" Dean asked.

Dean had asked Mac's ghost a million times, *Are you still over there? Did you ever come home? Was that you I saw yesterday?*

"Laos," the older man said. His jaw reminded Dean of a wrestler he'd seen on TV. It seemed to Dean like it would be hard to talk with so much bone in your face. Both men stood like they meant to shake Dean's hand. When he didn't move toward them, they sat back down.

"We recently got access to the crash site in Ban Kahn. It's a village just across the border from South Vietnam," said the pale man with wire-rimmed glasses. "Your father's unit was in Laos for a mission. One of the very last."

"Looks like you could have found him before now," Belle said, clear as anything. "Why'd it take you so long?"

"It's a difficult area," the jawbone said. "If it hadn't been for a man who came forward to lead us to the site, we might not have ever found it. It's a very complicated terrain."

"Dean, come sit with your mother," Leona said. She pulled a side chair close to his mama's, and then led him to it.

"Mrs. McQueen," said the younger man, "our records show you haven't taken advantage of our family advisors. I hope you will. They'll put you in touch with other families who have gone through the wait that your family has." He nodded at Dean. "You and your son are eligible. A counselor will contact you in a day or two, and I suggest you take advantage of their professional support."

His mama shook her head. "That's not necessary."

"Listen to him, Fern," Leona said. "They know about these things."

The older man pulled a folder from a black bag. "We need to know where you would like the remains sent." The man stood up with a handful of papers. "Here's information on having the burial at Arlington National Cemetery."

Leona stepped around. "I'll take that. Why don't you gentlemen come with me? Let's give Fern and Dean some time." She put her hand on Fern's shoulder. "I'll get the information, Fern. You don't have to decide anything right now."

Leona helped Belle up. "I didn't want him to go over there," Belle said, turning to the men in uniform. "I tried every way I could to talk him out of it, but he said he had to do it."

When they were alone, his mama pressed Dean's hand to her cheek. She wore the thin gold band Dean had never seen off her finger. "Did you think he was alive?" she said.

"Yes," he said. "No. I don't know." He eased down on the footstool in front of her. When she pulled him to her, he fell to his knees. He couldn't remember the last time they'd held one another so tight. She smelled like he remembered. Like rose soap. His mama had him so tight around the neck he could hardly talk.

"When I was playing little league ball, I used to think I saw him with you in the stands."

"You still talk to him up there, at the bench, don't you?"

"Yeah." Dean spoke into her trembling shoulder. "I tell him things, you know, about what's going on. I reckon I've told him everything that's ever happened in my life."

Dean wanted to stay in his mama's arms. He wanted her to talk to him about his daddy. He wanted them to cry together for what was forever lost and for what they'd never had.

Out in the hall, Leona said goodbye to the Army men, but Doyle Blue's voice came from the porch. Dean pulled away from his mama.

His mama staggered up. The French doors were closed, but Dean saw Doyle talking to Leona. Then he pushed opened the door and went right past Dean.

"Fern?" Doyle said, and he grabbed his mama up and held her like Dean had never seen anybody do. He put his head in her neck where Dean's had been. Holding onto one another, Doyle and his mama didn't look like who they ought to be.

Dean left them that way. He didn't want to see or hear any more.

Fern

At eight o'clock the next morning, Fern told herself it was too early to call Mac's sister, but after she'd cleaned out the refrigerator and taken out the trash, she couldn't summon one more good excuse.

She got comfortable at the kitchen table and found Geraldine's number in the ratty red address book she'd used all her life. Her young, careful handwriting looked nothing like the scrawl it had become. Geraldine and Wilson McLeod, 593 Summer Lane, Matthews, North Carolina. She half hoped there wouldn't be an answer. But the phone clicked, and she recognized Geraldine's drawl.

"Geraldine, it's Fern."

"Well, Lord help my time of day. Fern?"

"Geraldine, the Army came yesterday. They found Mac. His remains."

"Oh, God! Wilson!" Geraldine called out away from the phone.

"Fern?" Wilson came on the line. "What did you say? Geraldine's crying so hard I can't understand her."

"The Army found Mac's remains." Remains. She hated the word, but how else to say it? Bones. Teeth. Words the man had said last night.

"Well, I'll be darn." She heard Wilson talking to Geraldine, "Calm down now. Here, sit down." He came back on the line. "What do we do now, Fern?"

"They can send," Fern paused, "the body here, to the funeral home. We need to talk about a service. He should be buried with his mama and daddy, Wilson. He needs to be buried in Carthage, not up there in Arlington. Lieutenant Robbins said they'll send an honor guard, do the whole thing up like they do."

"I need to call you back. Is the number still the same?"

"Yes."

She clicked the phone off and reached for a pack of Salems hidden in the junk drawer, ignoring the no-smoking jar of shame where she'd drop a quarter later. Her hands shook. Only in the pitch dark of night after dreams so real she expected to find Mac stretched out beside her had she ever imagined him alive.

The back door creaked. Dean looked like he hadn't slept at all. After Doyle left, she'd walked down to the trailer to take him a grilled cheese. He'd eaten the sandwich but said he didn't want to talk.

She pulled herself up and went to the coffee pot, not bothering to hide her cigarette. "I'm behind this morning," she said.

Dean disappeared in the pantry and came out with a box of Special K.

"Let me fix you a real breakfast," Fern said. "We only had those sandwiches for dinner."

"Nah." He got a bowl out of the cabinet and milk from the refrigerator. He wouldn't look her in the face.

The phone rang and Fern answered. It was Wilson.

"Geraldine agrees the funeral ought to be down there," he said. "There's a plot for him with her mama and daddy." He paused, then said, "Fern, I don't know a good way to ask this, so I'm just going to have to come out and ask. Does your boy still think of Mac as his daddy?"

She moved to the far side of the kitchen, afraid Dean might somehow hear. If Dean hadn't been there, she would tell Wilson McLeod to go straight to hell. "Dean is very proud of his daddy," she said. "We want to do everything we can to honor Mac's memory. I hope Geraldine feels the same."

Dean stared into his bowl. Fern didn't believe he'd taken a bite. Fern said a nervous goodbye to Wilson.

"That was your uncle. Is it all right with you if we do the burial here and not up at Arlington?"

Dean shrugged.

She poured another cup of coffee and sat down. "I believe he ought to be home. The Army's had him long enough."

"Doyle Blue told me Daddy could have been a big-name ball player if he hadn't gone over there. How come you never talk about him, Mama? How come nobody ever talks about him?"

"It was a long time ago."

"But he was my daddy. And how come Aunt Geraldine or nobody from Daddy's side ever comes around?"

"You knew your Granny and Grandpa. When they died, Geraldine quit coming home."

Fern treated Dean like a child. She felt a shudder of guilt. Would he be different if she hadn't needed him to stay forever innocent? It was easier to fool a child, but Dean wasn't a child anymore.

"I gotta go," he said.

"Honey, why don't you stay home today?"

"No, I gotta go." Dean left his half-eaten bowl of cereal on the table. She tried to hug him before he left, but he pulled away. He hadn't been gone long when a van pulled up behind the house.

Sandhills Plumbing. Fern met two men at the back door. "You all can't be in here today," she said.

"What's Mrs. Thomas going to say to that?" The man with *Earl* embroidered above the pocket of his navy jumpsuit grinned. "She said if we didn't get here today, she was going to find somebody else for the job."

Fern had the urge to kick the man right off the porch steps and to keep kicking him until nobody would dare darken her door again. "Come in, then." Only a fool would have taken her words as welcome. She grabbed Dean's cereal bowl and carried it to the kitchen sink.

"We'll need to cut the water off," Earl said. "Might be off all day."

Fern didn't even turn around. "Let me go find *Mrs. Thomas*."

She met Leona in the foyer. "Your men are here," Fern said.

Fern followed Leona back to the kitchen. "This way," Leona said. Earl gave Fern a satisfied nod before traipsing past and scuffing the floor with his dirty boots. What did that matter, Fern thought. In a few days, the linoleum would be pulled up and replaced with something else Leona had picked out and Carol Ann had paid for. *It shouldn't be any of my concern what happens to the floor, or the walls or the ceilings or anything else in this house where I've spent my entire life.* Fern threw a dishrag across the room. It landed in the doorway at Roy's feet.

"Leona called and told me your news," he said. He picked up the rag and carried it to the sink.

Fern busied herself with the dishes.

He put his hands on her shoulders. The weight and warmth of his touch stilled her, held her in place.

"The storm, this house, Belle out of her head, now this," Fern said. "I swear, all I've tried to do for the longest time is keep my head down so people would leave me the hell alone."

Roy pulled her to him. "You're not alone, Fern," he said into her hair. "Even if that's really what you want."

Leona walked in and Roy stepped back, but only slightly.

"I need some time." Fern dried her hands, brushed past her sister and hurried up the stairs to her room. She crawled under her old quilt. Warm morning air rippled through the yellowed lace curtains. She defied Leona's mandate that the windows be kept shut. Fresh air soothed Fern, and she took deep breaths infused by the fresh green branches that brushed the screen. The storm had spared the pecan tree and she was grateful. As a girl, Fern could see over it, past the pines and into the tobacco field, but little by little the world had grown up around her. *And I let it,* she thought. She had pulled what was hers close and kept it tight. She'd daydreamed about other lives, but after seeing how wrong so much could go, she hadn't dared risk a wider world of choice and chance.

She traced the uneven patches of her quilt, a wedding present from Belle, and remembered the night long ago when the men came to tell them Mac was missing. That night, she lay in this same bed believing her affair with Doyle was to blame. She'd let go of Mac in her heart when that had been the only thing holding him to the world. She'd let him go, and he was gone, so gone the United States Army couldn't find even a small piece of him.

Mac had always kidded Fern about her Indian blood from her mother's side, said she had powers. That night she'd tried to conjure those powers to bring him to life, she'd pleaded with him to show himself, to send her a sign. She'd made promises to heaven and hell, to Mac and to herself that she would never touch Doyle Blue again.

By the time the sun came up, she was grief-stricken with regret. What if Mac's spirit had come to her to say a last goodbye and found her on that skinny cot at the hunting lodge with Doyle Blue?

That same afternoon Mac's mama and daddy had sat in the front room. They couldn't imagine their only son would be lost for long. Family and friends drifted in and out, not knowing what to say or do. The mood shifted between hope and despair.

"Anything is possible," people said over and over. And Mac's legend grew. "Why, he's just hid somewhere, waiting for the dust to settle. You can't keep Mac down. Remember that game we played against Sanford?"

Doyle came from Raleigh. He brought Martha. She carried ham biscuits carefully arranged on a silver platter. Mac's best friend and his wife. It was only natural for them to be there. Fern accepted his hug with stiff arms, their bodies not daring to touch.

Mrs. McQueen told Doyle stories about Mac while Martha sat beside Fern and talked on and on about nothing in that polite way that left no room for unpleasant words.

"Doyle was heartbroken Mac couldn't be here for the wedding," Martha said.

Why she doesn't know a thing, Fern thought. She doesn't know a thing in this world and never will. Fern had wanted to take Martha's delicate face between her hands and tell her all the horrible things that might be happening to Mac. How he could be in a bamboo cage with rats the size of house cats eating at his flesh. How he could be dying a slow, dreadful death or be blown to bloody bits so small not one of them would ever be recognized. How he might have burned up alive, and how she'd been naked as a jaybird beneath Doyle's long, smooth body just yesterday afternoon. How he'd held her so tight he cut off her breath and moaned her name with every thrust.

Fern wanted Martha to see the raw truth. She wanted to say words that would make Martha run and jump off the porch like she was on fire. Instead, the two sat side by side, Fern's heart pounding in her chest.

Martha took her hand. "Now might not be the time to tell you, but Doyle and I are expecting. And if it's a boy, we'd like to name him after Mac."

Fern felt the weight in her own bloated belly. Understood the tenderness of her swollen breasts. She and Doyle had made only half attempts at being cautious. Being more careful would have been an admission of planned deceit.

She stood, stumbled through the crowded room and up the stairs. Belle followed and knelt beside her on the cold bathroom tile while she heaved and spit.

When a soldier returned to Carthage, there was a hero's homecoming. When a soldier died, there was a hero's funeral. No one knew what to do with a soldier missing—MIA—but Mac's mother insisted on a prayer service. Preacher Perry walked a fine line, praying for Mac's safe return as well as for his soul. Fern had sat, her back straight against the pew, and felt the mid-day queasiness she could set a clock by. She barely made it to the church's restroom after the service.

"Fern?"

Carol Ann had followed her. Fern came out of the stall. Before her affair with Doyle, there was nothing Fern knew that Carol Ann didn't. Fern knew more about Carol Ann's first time having sex than Buddy Wallace did, and he'd been right there with her in the backseat of his Ford Fairlane.

The two friends told each other everything they knew or thought they knew, but that was when they thought they had life all figured out. Fern couldn't bring herself to admit she'd fallen in with the liars and cheats.

"What do you think is making you so sick?" Carol Ann said.

"Just nerves," Fern said.

That next week Fern waited to hear from Doyle. When she didn't, she called and asked him to meet her at Verlie's Diner in Pittsboro that coming Saturday. He fumbled through a hundred reasons why he couldn't until Fern put it to him plain. "I have to see you."

He was waiting in a back booth. "Have you heard anything?" he said.

Fern recognized the hurt in his voice and was grateful for the bit of solid ground he put them on by going first to Mac. She shook her head. "Do you think he's alive?" she asked. As crazy as it was, Doyle was the only person Fern knew who would tell her the truth.

"No."

She didn't say anything. "Do you?" he asked.

"Anything's possible," she answered, repeating the Army's line.

"Mac wouldn't let them take him," Doyle said. "Not alive. I don't trust the Army, Fern. They don't have a body, so they say he's missing because how do they explain a death without a body?" After a moment, he said, "It's bad over there and getting worse. But if Mac was alive, he'd have by God found somebody to tell by now."

"Maybe he doesn't want to be found," Fern said.

Doyle sat up straighter. "How come you to say that?"

She shrugged. She couldn't stand to think about the halfhearted letters she'd written him since California. Had Mac noticed her declarations of love were scarce? She'd been so angry about him reenlisting. Mad like a schoolgirl when a boy wouldn't do as she pleased. She'd used those childish feelings to justify being with Doyle. Now she was trying to make sense of the full-grown consequence.

A waitress brought their coffee.

"How long have you known you were going to be a father?" Fern said.

"I didn't know how to tell you." He looked away.

"Well, you're the only one having trouble with that," she said. Everyone who came in the drugstore had something to say about Doyle and Martha's news, testing Fern's reaction.

What they got was a mix. Shame could mimic sorrow, and she suffered from both. It was like she'd come awake after being hypnotized and been told she'd done a ridiculous thing. She'd kept her sin tucked down deep, telling herself that maybe, just maybe her nausea was caused by nerves and liquor. Sleep would only come after Fern drank what she pretended was a medicinal amount of Four Roses bourbon. But beneath her denial, she knew the truth.

Doyle had shifted in the booth. "What are you going to do?"

That was the question she asked herself in the dark before the bourbon took hold. Hearing it from him caught her off guard. For a moment she imagined he somehow knew she was carrying his child, that he had pulled her darkest thought out into the daylight.

"What do you mean?" she said.

"Will you stay in Carthage?"

His question carried the lilt of an acquaintance pretending to be concerned. His jaw was set, his eyes dull. She knew he was as frightened as she was by what they'd become. Both split in two, the loyal wife and the loyal friend. They'd betrayed a man they both loved.

"Where else would I go?"

He shook his head and poured more cream in his coffee. Fern always kidded Doyle about how light he liked his coffee.

"I don't know," he said. "I got to thinking that you might move off somewhere. Get a new start. I could help you with that."

Fern hadn't come knowing what she was going to say. She didn't even know what she expected of Doyle. No two thoughts led to a logical third, but she had come ready to tell him she believed she was pregnant. Keeping it to herself had her petrified, but there was no way to tell him now. Doyle was treating her like those girls he used to two-time in high school.

He looked around the diner, avoiding her eyes. "I hate to see you waiting for something that's not going to happen."

Her face grew hot. She was just somebody he needed out of the way, and he didn't know the half of it. A bolt of pride struck her. "Are you trying to say you hate to see me sitting around Carthage waiting for someone who might never come home, or are you saying you don't want me waiting around for you?"

Doyle shifted to see who might have heard her question. Fern slid out of the booth and stood. He looked at her with more relief than regret.

"I'm sorry," he said. Even those two words sounded rehearsed.

"You sure are," she said. "You're the sorriest thing I ever saw in my life." She bent down to where only he could hear. "Don't you and Martha dare name your child after Mac."

Fern hadn't wanted to name Dean after Mac, but his mother and father expected it. Michael Dean McQueen was born on September 6. A ten-month baby, said those who wanted to believe Fern had gotten pregnant when she met Mac in San Diego. A miracle, Mac's mother said. A bastard, said the rest. Belle did everything she could to pull Fern through, to rescue hope from despair.

Doyle and Martha sent Dean a silver monogrammed cup that Fern threw in the bamboo. Doyle disappeared into his life at North Carolina State. When Fern ran into his mother at the grocery store shortly after Dean was born, they'd exchanged nervous "hellos" but nothing more. She didn't even ask Fern about her baby.

Mac's mother embraced Dean as her grandson. Mrs. McQueen had needed to believe for her own sake that Mac lived on. Fern needed to believe she could bury her lie.

Now, in her upstairs bedroom that had turned stifling hot, she tossed the quilt aside and closed the window. What she knew now that she didn't know then was that lies didn't die. There was more life in a lie than the truth ever hoped for.

Leona

It sounded as if the men from Sandhills Plumbing were using sledgehammers to tear out the bathroom. Their knocking and yelling, and the fact that there wasn't a working bathroom downstairs, had prompted Leona to send Belle home with Roy, where she and Hannah could keep each other company.

After they left, Leona took the crusty spice rack off the kitchen wall and cleared the broken toaster and rusty can opener from the counter. She threw out the spindly spider plant cuttings drooping from jars on the windowsill and scrubbed the wall behind the stove with a heavy hand.

Seeing Doyle and Fern embrace the night before had done something to her. She wasn't sure what. Or she was sure, but even with her new resolve to stop kidding herself and face truth head-on, she wasn't ready to think about how much she looked forward to seeing Doyle Blue every day.

A car door slammed. Leona scrubbed harder. Doyle. Each morning they went over the day's work schedule, but lately they'd spent time drinking coffee and talking about what Leona wanted to bring to Carthage. The Raleigh house had sold after being on the market for only a week. Doyle had offered a truck and crew to pick up furniture, and said he'd be happy to go along.

"Good morning," he said, coming in the back door. He eyed the rusty appliances lying on the table.

"Thought I'd do some cleaning," she said. "The Mr. Coffee made the cut, need a cup?" She wore slacks and a crisp blouse.

"Sure, I'll get it," he said. "How's Fern this morning?"

"Touchy." She folded her arms and faced him. "I called Roy thinking she'd want to talk to him, but that didn't go well, then Carol Ann came. She just left. Evidently, Fern wants to be alone."

Doyle sat at the table with his coffee. "I've always known Mac died over there, but now his loss is more real somehow. Fern said he volunteered for that last mission. That's just like him. I see why she's so against me telling Dean the truth. He deserves a dad who was a hero, and that sure as hell isn't me."

They'd never discussed Doyle's desire to claim Dean as his son. "Heroes are rare," Leona said. "I wish we'd all been braver a long time ago. I've been thinking a lot about how things could have been different, but it's human nature to think we can zig and zag and outsmart the consequences." She rinsed and dried her hands. "But we never do." She joined Doyle at the table. "It's not a good idea for you to come with me to Raleigh. Carol Ann's going and the girls are meeting me at the house. It could get contentious, especially with Paige. She isn't handling any of this well."

"Yeah, no problem. I understand," Doyle said. "You can tell the guys what needs to be moved." A loud crash shook the room, causing the cat clock to fall to the floor. "I better go check on the bathroom before they knock the house down." He picked up the clock and put it on the table.

Leona went back to her scrubbing. She couldn't pretend not to be disappointed. She'd looked forward to showing Doyle the house.

He stuck his head around the door. "You know we'll be tearing out this kitchen soon, right? I mean, you're working awfully hard in here."

"Just need to stay busy," she said, barely glancing his way.

He nodded and left.

Her scrubbing was getting her nowhere. She couldn't erase years of grease and grime from the wall behind the stove. Doyle and Fern had had an affair. They had a child together. She couldn't erase that either.

She dropped the can opener and the toaster in the trash, then went into the pantry and threw out all the mysterious jars of dark jellies and decomposing pickles, okra, corn, and tomatoes. There was a limit to how long something could be preserved even when tightly sealed. She inspected the cat clock, hoping the silly thing was done for, but the second hand ticked away.

She poured a new cup of coffee. Her old way of seeing the world in black and white had been easier, but now that she'd seen the gray, it was impossible to unsee, no matter how complicated. Being brave enough to admit the truth was one thing. Being brave enough to live the truth was proving much more difficult.

Fern

Fern heard Doyle talking to the workmen downstairs. She was embarrassed about the night before. Embarrassed and confused about how it felt to be in his arms, crying over Mac like all those years ago.

Doyle. Geraldine's hysterics. All of it hurled her back to a time she'd tried to forget. But with all that was about to be brought forth, she could no longer escape the question that haunted her. What did Mac know?

She believed the answer lay between the lines of one of his letters buried deep in her closet.

She always thought she'd go through the letters, share them with Dean. Mac's own words would mean so much to him, but she'd never been willing to add to her deceit. Five shoeboxes of letters that she hadn't touched in years sat one atop the other. She wiped dust from the lids and carried the boxes to the bed. In the third one, she found the letter she was looking for, dated February 14, 1972.

Dear Fern,

Happy Valentine's Day, Valentine. I wish I could have a piece of that red velvet cake I know you made for Belle. Tell her happy birthday, okay? I hope she'll forgive me one of these days for enlisting. I'll tell you, Fern. Belle isn't wrong to do all the protesting she does against this war. Tell her I said so, okay?

We're waiting for choppers to take us God knows where. Maybe I could get one to bring me home. Wouldn't Belle have a fit over a big old Huey landing in her garden? Lord, the sand would scatter. I saw one of the prettiest sunsets I believe I've ever seen last evening. The sky was pink as a cherry blossom and from where we were, you could see forever into the valley green with crops. I'd give anything to have a picture to send you. Not a one of us out here has a camera. You'll get a kick out of this. A little boy came through here yesterday trying to sell us Bamboo soup. Tell Belle I know now what we can do with all that bamboo.

Fern, I know I screwed up. I should have talked to you before re-enlisting. I don't blame you for being mad. But it's like I said, I'm doing something important over here. I don't mean that like you think, I'm not even sure how come we're over here, but we are, and I don't want to brag, but there've been times when I've kept some of these fellows from getting their heads blown off. You asked me if I've ever killed anybody, and the answer is yes. I've killed strangers to save friends. That's just the way it is. I know you don't want to hear about that. I know you think I belong at home with you, but I've got to see this thing through 'til we're all out of here.

It won't last much longer. This is the tail-end. When I get home, I want us to make a new start. I've been thinking about kids. We'll need eight for a good ball team. Boys and girls, don't matter to me. I guess that kid that came through here got to me. He was a cute little fellow and not a bit afraid.

Geraldine said Doyle was making it back in Carthage pretty often, keeping you company. I imagine Raleigh's not much fun with that Chapman bunch. But didn't we try to tell him? I guess he gets lonely over there with Martha. Tell him to write his old buddy a letter. You might want to call Geraldine and go to a movie or something. You know how she gets.

They're yelling for us to come on, so I better go.

I love you, Fern, you know I do. Don't give up on me. A lot of fellows get those Dear John letters. Promise you'll never send me one. Okay? Be sweet.

Your husband in training,
Mac

Leaning back against the headboard of the four-poster-bed, she closed her eyes and pictured Mac, innocent and brave, running to that chopper that would soon be the death of his pure, bright heart while a million miles from war, she plotted her next rendezvous with Doyle. How could she have been so cruel? Had she loved Doyle? No. Even then being with him felt like playing a part.

She remembered how she'd left him all those years ago at the diner, knowing she was on her own. Pregnant the wrong amount of time. Mac's furlough had been in November. She'd started seeing Doyle the end of December. What had been the hazy idea of a baby became real that day. Surrounded by loss and humiliation, she had felt the weight in the pit of her stomach. She'd driven back to Carthage but not before stopping at the liquor store.

Carol Ann had come home from Elon for spring break. Fern drove straight to her house. "We need to go for a drive," she told Carol Ann.

They'd stopped for Cokes at the Sinclair station, and Fern spiked the cold, sweating bottles with bourbon while Carol Ann fussed with the radio. They were almost to Hope Mills before the bourbon got Fern talking. With the wind whistling in the open windows, and nervous static coming from the radio, Fern had to say it loud. "I'm pregnant."

"Pull over," Carol Ann said, like Fern had just told her the car was on fire.

Fern bumped the Mercury station wagon off the side of the road. There was nothing for miles but scrub pine. A buggy chorus came from the woods. Carol Ann took off her sunglasses and stared at Fern's flat belly. "Are you sure?"

"Pretty sure," she said, pulling the bottle out from under the car seat and pouring bourbon into the remains of her Coke. "I haven't had a period in months. Three, coming up on four."

"But you met Mac in November," Carol Ann said. "That was," she counted on her fingers, "five months ago."

Fern only had to wait for her friend to figure out the rest.

Carol Ann hit the dashboard. "Damn it to hell. Doyle Blue. I should have known that slick son-of-a-bitch would jump at the chance."

"It takes two," Fern said, sounding pathetic, even to herself.

"It only takes one to think it up, and I know good and damn well that wasn't you. Are you sure?"

"I had my period when I came back from California. Doyle and I started seeing each other after that. I haven't had one since."

"What are you going to do?"

"I don't know," Fern said, silently hoping Carol Ann would answer her own question.

"You need to know for sure," Carol Ann said. "We need to know how far along you are. It matters."

Taking charge came naturally to Carol Ann, and Fern felt relief.

"Come with me back to school. There's a doctor up there. A woman. One who doesn't know you from Adam's house cat. She's the one who gave me my birth control pills."

Fern dropped her forehead against the steering wheel, her body heavy from the heat and all she'd had to drink. "Please don't hate me."

"Honey, I don't hate you. I could kick myself for not paying attention. You've always given Doyle the value of the doubt, but I've seen the way he looks at you. Oh, my Lord. And Martha's pregnant, too."

The radio came to life with Carole King singing "So Far Away." Fern reached over and turned it off. The lyrics said everything she felt about Mac being in Vietnam, but since her betrayal, she couldn't stand to hear words of love and longing.

"Does Doyle know?" Carol Ann asked.

"I met him in Pittsboro to tell him, but I couldn't. He started talking about how I might want to move off somewhere. He doesn't want anything to do with me. Leona got all up in my face when she was here. She said Mrs. Thomas told her there were rumors about me slipping around with Doyle."

"What did you say?"

"What do you think I said? I lied." Fern lit a cigarette and blew smoke out the window. "I can't give Belle something else to worry about. She's so upset about Mac, and about to lose her mind with James still over there."

Carol Ann bit her lip. "Listen. A girl on my hall got in trouble. She went somewhere in Raleigh, missed two days of class. A doctor did it."

"Girls die," Fern said. "I've heard people talk about it at the drug store."

They went back and forth, with Carol Ann saying rich girls had abortions all the time, and Fern claiming she couldn't live with herself. Then they'd switch sides. Carol Ann argued that Fern ought to have the baby, that it wasn't anybody's damn business, and Fern saying that she believed Mac would be found soon. He'd come home and know the child wasn't his.

Carol Ann tried to get Fern to spend the night at her house so they could talk more, but Fern said she'd been gone too long with Belle's car and needed to get home.

Belle waited for her on the porch wearing a wide-brimmed straw hat, baggy shirt, Bermuda shorts, and worn-out Keds. She'd been cleaning out the front flower beds, and piles of weeds lined the driveway. She stilled her rocking chair, took off her hat and fanned her face. Her freckled cheeks were flushed from the sun. "I was getting worried about you. Did you find anything?"

Fern had told Belle she was going to look for comfortable shoes to wear to work. "No," she said. "Nothing fit."

Belle rocked back in the chair and shook her raggedy Keds at Fern. "You're like me. Hard on shoes. You look a little peaked. Is your stomach still upset?"

"Just nerves." Fern started for the door. "I believe I'll get a Coke, want one?"

"Honey," Belle reached up and took Fern's arm. "I may be a dried-up old maid, but I know that nausea you've been having is more than nerves." She pulled the other rocker closer to hers. "Have a seat."

An hour later, Fern called Carol Ann. "I'm having a baby. Belle knows."

"You told her about Doyle?"

"Yes. She said we can handle it."

"Can you?" Carol Ann said. "Are you sure?"

"I'm not sure about anything, but I'm too far along, Carol Ann. I can't do that other."

Dr. Franklin confirmed that Fern was most likely four months pregnant, but when she and Belle went to tell Mac's family, Belle let her keep up the charade that she was carrying Mac's child. Geraldine cornered her when they were leaving. "Everybody knows you've been sneaking around with Doyle Blue," she whispered. "I don't believe for a minute that's my brother's baby."

Fern read Mac's last letter one more time. Geraldine had told him Doyle was *keeping her company*. She imagined that wasn't all she'd told him. There was no reason to believe Geraldine wouldn't tell Dean the truth the first chance she got.

Dean

D ean lay on his back, his head and shoulders beneath the front end of a Honda. Cars made sense to him in a way nothing else did. He'd had the car up on the rack but wanted to check one more thing around the right front with the wheels on the ground. He was working more at the garage now that the house was full of plumbers and heating and air conditioning men. He slid out from underneath the car to find a toothy black-headed woman smiling at him like he ought to know who she was, but he didn't. "You need to see Frank to get on the schedule."

"Oh, no," she said. "I came to see you."

Dean caught her Yankee accent.

"I'm Elaine Pettigrew. I work at the *Citizen-Times*. I took your mother's job, or actually, it's a different position. I'm more of an assistant reporter. Anyway, I want to talk to you about your father. The whole town is so proud to be honoring a real war hero." She grinned, showing a mouthful of teeth.

Whitey made his way over to where they stood. He couldn't stay out of other people's business to save his life.

"I can't talk to you right now," Dean said to the woman. "I got to get these wheels aligned."

"How about lunch tomorrow?" she said. "My treat. I'll meet you at the Burger Shack at noon?"

"All right," Dean said just to get rid of her.

Whitey shook his head when she got out of sight. "You're just a damn celebrity," he said. "Saving the preacher's girl during that tornado. Now you got something else to crow about. Your daddy the war hero. Did that woman say she was from the paper?"

Dean was not in the mood for Whitey. The boys had given Dean a hard time about being on the television after the tornado, and now all anybody talked about was his daddy coming home to be buried.

Whitey put a hand on the hood of the Honda. "You better get your facts straight before you do anymore talking to the newspaper." He leaned in. "Everybody knows that soldier coming back in a box ain't your daddy. Your real daddy's walking around town big as life. Think about it, pinhead, think about who's been sniffing around your mama, throwing money your way. Giving you that truck to drive. You think Doyle Blue just took a liking to you?"

"Whitey." Mr. Frank came up behind them. Dean's head roared, but all he could think was how he was going to knock the snot out of Whitey. He put up his fist, but Mr. Frank grabbed him around the waist and pulled him back.

"Whitey," Mr. Frank said, "get the hell out of here."

Whitey lifted his arms in the air. "What? What'd I do? I was just trying to help him out with these tires. You know how he gets."

Dean tried to jerk away from Mr. Frank. The more Whitey lied, the more he wanted to stomp him.

"Get out, Whitey. Get your things and get out. I mean it, you're fired." Mr. Frank put an arm around Dean's shoulders and walked him toward his office. Another boy working beside him got back to his truck tires in a hurry. Mr. Frank maneuvered Dean through the door and kicked it shut. Dean saw Whitey through the glass, cussing and kicking at the floor.

"Sit down," Mr. Frank said. He gave Dean a push.

Dean stumbled and fell down onto the old ripped up vinyl couch. Mr. Frank handed him a Styrofoam cup of lukewarm coffee that was usually just for customers. Dean's hands shook so bad he spilled coffee in his lap.

Mr. Frank motioned with his head for Tiffany, his secretary, to leave. He leaned back against his desk with his arms crossed over his belly. A pile of papers fell on the floor, but he didn't reach to pick them up. Tiffany shut the door behind her.

"What did that dumb fuck say?"

Dean didn't look up. The boys never told Mr. Frank all that Whitey said.

"Okay," Mr. Frank said. "I heard what he said, and I want you to forget it. I should have fired his ass a long time ago. Let's get out of here."

Dean followed him out and they got in Frank's Ford pick-up and drove to the Burger Shack. Mr. Frank ordered two burger baskets and two Dr. Peppers. They found a picnic table under a shade tree. Mr. Frank nodded to folks he knew, but Dean couldn't get his head straight enough to tell who all was there.

"You know," Mr. Frank said, "I went to school with your daddy. Your mama too. Mac was a hell of a ball player. Everybody thought he'd go pro."

That's what Doyle had told Dean, but Dean didn't want to think about Doyle Blue.

"They were sweethearts all the way through school. A lot of couples, they'd break up and mess around on each other. Not Mac and Fern. Nope, they never did any of that."

Mr. Frank took a second packet of catsup from a pile, twisted it open, and dabbed it on his fries. "I want you to forget what Whitey said. Whitey ain't nothing but an asshole."

Dean nodded. The knot that had been in his throat since Whitey said what he did started to loosen. He took a bite of hamburger and swallowed it. He and Mr. Frank sat quiet. "How come you never told me you knew him?" Dean asked after both their baskets were empty except for the hard ends of French fries.

"I don't know. I guess I thought with him missing and all it was better just not to say anything. I don't know what all you know, but boys coming home from Vietnam didn't have an easy time of it. By the time that war was over, wasn't nobody too sure we should have ever been over there in the first place, and there were a lot of stories about things that went on that made the soldiers look bad."

"I know some of that," Dean said.

"Well, Mac did what he had to do, did what the army asked him to, and he got killed doing it. There's honor in that."

"Were you over there?"

Mr. Frank looked over toward the road. "Nah, I had a bad back."

Dean had never heard him say anything about a bad back.

"Okay, the truth was I acted like I had a bad back. I was too damn scared to go over there. I've never told a soul, but that's the truth. And I wasn't the only one. I can name a long list of people you know who didn't go because they were scared, who found a way to get out of it. But your Uncle James went. And Mac went. He could have gone on to college and played ball on a scholarship and never gone over there."

Mr. Frank stopped talking. He put his big grease-stained hands flat on the table. "Shouldn't nobody disrespect the memory of Mac McQueen."

Mr. Frank had never talked like this to Dean. He usually just grunted at him or told him to hurry up the job he was working on. But now, Mr. Frank looked at Dean for the longest time. "You all right?"

"Yeah," he said.

They drove back around the courthouse to the garage, past the memorial bench.

Mr. Frank never did say Whitey lied, Dean thought. He never did.

They pulled back up to the garage. Brandi's old Dodge sat half-on, half-off the curb. "Come here," she hollered at Dean.

"Take the rest of the day," Frank said. "Go on."

Dean knew there was no sense in arguing with Mr. Frank or Brandi.

Brandi tore around the courthouse, not even looking at the road. She had one arm flung out the window of the Dodge like she was fixing to give a signal.

"You'd better watch where you're going," Dean said. He rolled down his window. Brandi cared more about saving gas than running her air conditioner.

"I'm not going anywhere but around this circle. A monkey could do that. Whitey come in the Stop'n Go," she said. "He said Frank fired him. He said it was because you and him had words."

"He had words with himself."

Brandi took 15-501 South. The Statler Brothers were belting out a Jesus song on the radio.

"What do you think about what he said?"

"I'm going to kill him, is what I think."

"Hang on here," she said. "I'd just go on and not think nothing of it."

Brandi picked up speed and Dean hollered over the wind and the radio and the uneasy grumble of the Dodge's engine. "The hell you say. If somebody told you your daddy wasn't your daddy, you'd have a damn fit." She didn't say anything to that, and he went on. "How come you think Doyle Blue gave me money to build that fence?"

"He likes you I guess."

"You know I hate a lie," Dean said.

"If you ain't going to forget about it, you might as well ask your mama, because I got to tell you, Whitey's going all over town yabbering his pie hole. You know what I'm saying?"

Dean didn't say yes or no.

"It ain't going to change nothing," she said. "Ain't going to change who you are."

"It changes everything I know," he said.

"Well. You might just have to know something else."

Fern

It had only been a week since the news came about Mac, but after Dean told Brandi, the word spread to everyone who came in the Stop 'n Go. The whole town was talking about Mac McQueen. When Robert called saying he'd gotten a press release from the Army and wanted a quote for a story, Fern hung up on him. At Leona's insistence, a date three weeks away had been set for Mac's funeral. She and Carol Ann were coordinating with the Survivor Assistance office at Fort Bragg as well as organizing a reception at the house after the service.

The reception had spurred the restoration process into overdrive. Doyle was on his way to Raleigh to pick up a vanity for the downstairs bathroom now being referred to as the powder room, and black-and-white tile waited to be laid in the cleared-out kitchen.

Leona had badgered Fern until she agreed to update her bedroom. "The wallpaper is falling down around you," she said. "And how long has it been since you cleaned out your closet?" Never was the answer, but Fern hadn't said it aloud.

Leona and Belle left to rent glass plates for the funeral gathering, leaving Fern to get her room cleared for the painters. Fern suspected Leona was only trying to keep her distracted.

She pulled dresses and pants and blouses not worn in decades off swayed wire rods and pitched them on the bed, piled high with what was Goodwill bound. On the closet's top shelf, she found the jewelry box Belle had given her for her thirteenth birthday. Black lacquer with a delicate Japanese pagoda painted on the top. Inside, a tiny ballerina still twirled to the twinkly tune, "Around the World in Eighty Days." Tucked in a red velvet drawer she found the ruby stud earrings Mac had given her the first Christmas they were married. She sat on the corner of the bed and remembered opening the small black

box. He'd been so proud, he made her open the little package
before they even got out of bed Christmas morning. Fern had
never gotten a gift so fine. She'd worn them every day for years
and stopped only when any memory of Mac came wrapped in
guilt.

The front door slammed, and even with all the commotion
in the kitchen, Fern heard the newly installed glass rattle.
Imagining one of the burly construction crew, she cursed
under her breath and went to the top of the stairs, ready to tell
the culprit to be more careful.

Dean stood in the foyer. With the kitchen torn up, she
wasn't expecting him home for lunch. "You okay?" she said,
going down the stairs.

She followed him into the front room. Dean paced, his chin
pressed into his chest. He slapped a fist into his open palm.
The furniture, covered with sheets to keep the dust at bay,
gave the room an eerie feel.

"Honey? What's wrong?"

"Whitey said Doyle Blue's my daddy." His chest rose and
fell with shallow breaths. "Any truth to it?" He spoke as if he'd
been running a race, breathless and spent.

Fern felt light-headed.

*Any truth to it? Yes. No. Doyle Blue is your father, but you're
Mac's son.*

"Come sit with me, honey," Fern said, lowering herself
onto the covered settee. To her relief, he sat down beside her.
When she reached for his hands, he didn't pull away. Since
he was a child, she'd held his hands to calm his mind when
trying to explain wrongs that mystified his pure heart. The
smoothness of his palms, although worked hard, were still the
hands of a boy. She held them tight.

"Dean, when your daddy, when Mac, was gone, I lost my
way. I gave up thinking things would ever be right."

He looked up at her and blinked. She saw he'd expected
a denial, and for a split second she wondered if she could get
away with one more lie. But with Mac coming home, hiding
the truth no longer seemed possible.

"We'd been friends all of our lives. The three of us. Mac,
Doyle, and me. We missed Mac. We were lonely for him, but

everything got twisted. That happens sometimes with people. What we did was wrong."

She watched him take in her confession. She knew he was trying hard to make sense of something that made no sense. He pulled his hands away and stood. "How come you to lie?"

"I had to." As soon as the words were said, Fern realized they weren't true. "I didn't want you to think bad of me." Dean narrowed his eyes as if trying to decipher small print.

How do you explain sin to an innocent boy who doesn't understand guile and guilt, lying and cheating? How do you explain acting one way and being another?

"I was so ashamed," Fern said.

"Whitey said everybody knows. Everybody but me." Dean hit his chest with his fist. Sweat trickled across his brow. "That ain't right, Mama. That ain't right."

He picked up Belle's rocker like he meant to throw it but pounded it back down on the floor. The sheet covering it slid away and Dean stomped and kicked it until the sheet was wound around his feet.

"It wasn't right." Fern went to his side. "I never meant to hurt you. I was trying to protect you." She heard her lie. "I was trying to protect myself." What she saw come over him was worse than any fit. Hurt. Confusion. Disbelief and fear. He was lost in her hell now, and both were burning.

"How come he never told me?" he said. "Up there at the bench. How come?"

Fern put her arms around him, and he didn't pull away. Their bodies shook, his from pain, hers from fear that he would throw her off and be gone. She held her boy and thanked God for every second he let her. She made promises. *Lord if you'll take this hurt from him, I'll never lie again. I'll never tell another lie as long as I live. Please, take his hurt.*

Dean broke away like he couldn't stand the sight of her.

She reached for him but stopped herself. "Can you forgive me?" She asked the question knowing full well she didn't deserve an answer.

He studied her like he'd forgotten who she was. Like he had never known her a day in his life. And in the half-second it took him to look away and back, he was no longer a boy. He was a man with a man's disappointment in a world good for nothing. He looked at her the way a mother never ever even wants to imagine a child can look, then walked out the door.

"Dean, come back here. Where are you going?"

Dean jumped in the truck and took off. Fern ran down the driveway calling his name.

Fern

Leona found Fern curled among the refuse of old clothes piled on her bed.

"A boy Dean works with told him Doyle was his father," Fern said without raising her head.

Leona sat beside her. "What did you tell him?"

"The truth." Fern rolled over and looked up at her sister. "The world has stopped keeping our secrets."

Leona rested a hand on her sister's arm.

Fern choked out the words. "I always knew it could happen, but not in any kind of real way. Not outside my head. What should I do?" Fern had never asked her sister for one bit of advice, never taken any she'd given. But she was more than ready for Leona's help now.

"You need to let Doyle know in case Dean confronts him."

Doyle. What if Dean had gone straight to him?

Leona brought Fern the phone and dialed Doyle's number.

Fern's voice shook as she told him what happened. She waited for the "I told you so" she believed she might be owed.

"I need to find him," he said.

"But what will you say?"

"That I love him," Doyle said. "That I'm proud to be his father."

Dean didn't come home that night. Frank called Tuesday morning to say he hadn't shown up for work, and Fern found a note on the trailer door: *Don't come looking.* The police chief claimed he couldn't treat it like a missing person because of the note and because Dean was an adult who hadn't even been gone two full days. But Fern knew what could happen when a boy went missing.

Friday evening, five days after Dean had disappeared, she sat on the porch in the dark. With every passing car, she willed headlights to shine up the drive.

Belle asked a hundred times a day, "Is Dean home?" Doyle kept the emus fed and watered and checked in with Fern for news. Hannah waited at the trailer until dinner every night, and then she made Roy ride around town to look for Dean. Fern knew Roy would have done that anyway. She believed that's what he did most of the day.

Brandi promised she'd look out for him.

Carol Ann had pestered every law enforcement officer she knew—and she knew plenty—to unofficially be on the lookout for Dean. Leona was doing all she could by reminding Fern of every logical reason why Dean would soon return. "He's never liked being away from home, am I right?"

Mac's remains were scheduled to arrive at the Charlotte airport Wednesday. Geraldine and Wilson expected Fern and Dean to be there with them to meet the plane. Leona would have to come up with some excuse. There was no way Fern would go without Dean.

Once again, her secrets wove a web of lies.

Leona stayed on the porch until Fern told her to go on up. "I'm right behind you," she said, but she lit a cigarette. Tossing and turning in the bed only churned up Fern's darkest what-if's.

She wanted the world to stop, to wait for Dean to come home. Mac's funeral, two weeks away, had the town in a frenzy. Even though Fern still refused to talk to them, the newspaper had practically turned into the *Mac McQueen Times*. Leona had finally sent Robert a statement "from the family." Every edition of the *Citizen-Times* carried another photograph of Mac from his baseball days. Everyone he'd ever played ball with had a story. The phone rang and rang and rang. Wives whose husbands were still MIA, local television reporters in search of a story about a lost soldier found, the Pineview Garden Club wanting to release doves at the service. "It's a military funeral with a rifle volley," Leona told them. "No doves."

The mayor wanted them to delay the service and have it a week later as part of the town's July fourth celebration. He said the Carthage High School band could lead the processional. Fern had never been so appreciative of Leona's no-nonsense ability to deliver a firm no.

When Roy had called that afternoon to talk about the eulogy, Fern hung up on him. She was sorry, but not sorry enough to call him back. She couldn't think about burying Mac with Dean missing.

A full moon lit the night. Roy's porch light came on, and he walked out his front door. His shadow followed him as he crossed the road and came up the steps like it was natural for the two of them to meet in the dark.

"Good evening," he said, a little breathless.

"Good evening to you," Fern said.

The rhythmic chatter of night bugs and tree frogs made it seem as if they weren't entirely alone. Roy glanced up at the moon like he wished he could turn it off. His shirt collar lay open, a round-neck t-shirt peeked from underneath. His shirttail was half in, half out, and his hair a tumble of curls.

"Nice night for porch sitting," he said.

"It's cooled off a bit," Fern said.

"Mind if I join you?"

"Suit yourself."

He pulled one of the rockers away from the wall and positioned it across from where she sat on the swing, leaving a safe distance.

"Sorry about the call," he said. "I thought maybe talking about the service would help get your mind off Dean."

"Sorry I hung up like I did."

"What can I do?"

"There's nothing." Fern shrugged. She shifted her weight and the swing chains creaked as if coming undone. "Roy, you don't understand."

"Tell me."

She pushed the swing back with one foot and let it rock forward. "Tell you what?"

He leaned toward her. "What's Dean running from?"

She shook her head. "You wouldn't understand."

"You think I'm just some backwoods preacher too naive to understand real problems? You know better." His words sounded like a feather pillow.

"You didn't bring your problems on yourself," she said.

"Your husband was killed in Vietnam. You're only now getting ready to bury him. You didn't bring that on yourself. The world did that and I'd think there would be relief in knowing, in finally laying the past to rest."

"When has the past ever taken a rest?" Fern said. "As for Mac, more has been upturned than will ever be buried."

He pressed his hands together like he was praying or begging. Praying, begging, Fern thought, it was all the same. "What's happening that I can't see?" Roy said. "Why did Dean run away?"

"Do you know this is none of your business?" She put her bare feet flat on the floor and pushed the swing away from him. "What is it about preachers? How come you think you have to know everything?"

"I'm not here as a preacher, Fern," he said, cutting her off. He dropped his head. "That's wrong. Wherever I am, I'm a preacher." He looked up, "But that's not the only reason I couldn't let you sit over here by yourself in the dark."

Fern breathed in the sweetness of his words, but her cautious heart sounded warning. "You need to stay away from me," she spoke in a near whisper.

"Let's not rehash that."

"No, I mean it. You're going to hear things, I can't believe you haven't already, and I don't want you to be sorry."

A cloud passed over the moon. Fern imagined she and Roy as two ghosts, two souls long dead worrying over the living. If we were able, she thought, that's what we'd do. Even after death. None of us would ever shut up or let go or quit aggravating a thing to pieces. Maybe that's why God put such a high fence between Heaven and Earth.

"Geraldine McLeod and her husband are driving up here tomorrow," Roy's ghost face said. "She wants to meet with me about the service."

Geraldine will tell Roy all she knows. Fern pulled her knees to her chest.

"What is it?" he said. "What are you afraid she'll tell me that you won't?" The moon, now unencumbered by clouds, colored Roy's face soft blue. He sounded like a father persuading a child to claim the dent in the bumper of the family car. He sounded like whatever it was she'd broken, he could fix.

She lifted her hair away from her damp neck. The swing rocked like it was a part of her—and wasn't it? This swing where she'd taken refuge when her mama and daddy fought, where she and Mac spent days and nights swaying to new love, her whole life had passed on this porch. Her place in the world, shade and shelter.

She imagined the girl who'd walked up the hill that snowy afternoon sitting here on the porch with Roy. For so long she'd kept that girl separate from herself, but she felt a merging, a coming together of herself, then and now. Sweat turned to chills. Tremors from deep down ran through her, breaking up secrets held in stone.

"Mac is not Dean's father." The words came out high-pitched and feeble like how a mummy might talk after a thousand years dead. She'd told him and not told him, both. Still buying time, she thought. That's what liars do.

Roy stayed very still. "Fern," he whispered. He reached a hand over and held her arm, not gripping, but holding. He did not say it couldn't be true. He pulled her hands from her face and held them. "It's okay."

The tremors eased, not all the way, but a little. "Dean found out Monday. One of the boys up at Frank's told him. See, everybody in town has always known. It was a big old scandal back in the day. The only thing that saved me was I'd met Mac for an R&R a month before. He'd told me he was coming home soon." She stopped. Roy pulled himself toward her until their knees touched. Fern kept her eyes closed, her head down.

"Go on," he said.

"When I came home, I found out he'd reenlisted. He'd lied to me." She stopped, not wanting to make excuses. "I worked up at the drugstore. Doyle was in school in Raleigh. He and Martha were married. They came to Pinehurst all the time to see her parents." She opened her wet eyes. "He and Mac were best friends." Roy nodded. "He was the only one I could talk to about Mac. Then, well …" Roy quit rubbing her hands and tilted his head like he was trying to hear what had not been said.

"Then you met someone?" he said.

"No. Doyle and I got involved."

"Doyle?" Roy blinked like he'd just woken up unsure of where he was. He dropped her hands.

Fern sat back. She'd spoken the truth, and no flame had lit the sky, no giant hole in the earth had swallowed her up. She was still on the porch, breathing. She could only nod. Down the road, a dog barked like it didn't know what else to do on a night so full of shadows.

Roy stood. The rocker pitched back. Fern wanted him where he'd been, across from her. He gazed out at the yard with his hands in his pockets.

"When Mac turned up missing, we came to our senses," Fern said, wanting to finish what she'd started.

"Has Doyle always known?" Roy asked.

"Yes." She wanted to tell it now, to get it out. "I started drinking. Bad drinking. Back then, nobody said anything about how dangerous it was. Belle did everything she could to make me stop for my own good, but I couldn't stop. It hurt Dean. That's why he has trouble." The clouds moved back and forth across the moon, changing the light, changing the dark. "Doyle's back home because he wants to tell Dean," Fern said. "I believe it's part of his rehab thing, you know. He wants to make amends."

Roy bowed his head. He held his eyes shut with his thumb and forefinger. His shoulders rose and fell. "Are the two of you still involved?"

"What are you talking about?" Fern said.

Roy started to pace. "Well, he's here all the time."

"He's working on the house."

"He's a successful man. He has a lot to offer."

"Oh, Roy, for heaven's sake," Fern said.

"Have I been a fool all this time?"

"What do you mean a fool?"

He stopped his pacing. "I've told you everything," he said. "It's okay, Fern. I don't know what got into me." He started down the stairs. "I need to go check on Hannah." He turned slightly but kept his eyes to the ground. "I'll keep you in my prayers."

She felt tricked somehow. "You'll what?" She stood and went to the edge of the porch. "You'll pray for old sinful Fern? You think you know about sin?" Her words trembled. "Let me tell you something. All you know is what you've read in books or gotten secondhand from fools like me stupid enough to fall for that angel face of yours and spill our guts."

"Fern."

She heard pity. For her or for him, she couldn't tell. She wanted to get in the house, away from him. The newly replaced glass shook in the frame when she slammed the door. She moved further into the dark hall. Her heartbeat marked the minutes. He came back up on the porch and reached for the door but dropped his hand and turned away. She stepped to the door. He was halfway down the drive. At the road, he stopped and looked back, but went on. She watched until his yellow porch light flicked off and then waited still, for what she did not know.

Leona

Leona had been up for so long she brewed a second pot of coffee. She turned the frail pages of the family Bible in search of a verse. She was meeting with Roy and Geraldine at the church to finalize plans for Mac's service and wanted to make sure nothing was left to Geraldine's bad taste. Fern straggled in wearing a t-shirt and a pair of blue-and-yellow plaid Bermuda shorts Leona was quite sure had once belonged to James. With her bushy hair pulled back in a ponytail, her sister looked like a fifteen-year-old who had tragically aged thirty years overnight.

Fern glanced at the Bible. "Oh, Lord, don't preach to me this morning."

"Are you sure you don't have anything you want read at the service?"

Fern shook her head and poured a cup of coffee. "I told Roy everything last night and he hightailed it off the porch quicker than you can say amen. So, I expect he and Geraldine will be talking about Fern the harlot up there at the church today."

"What do you mean *everything*?"

"Mac. Doyle. Dean. Everything." Fern rested against the counter.

"To be honest," Leona said, "I'm surprised he hadn't heard all about it."

"Well, me too, but Carol Ann swears I'm old news." She pushed off the counter like the motion took all the energy she could muster. "I need to see if Dean's back at the trailer."

"I'll go with you," Leona said.

They walked past the scuppernong vine brimming with the tiny grapes holding their promise. "Fern, did Mac have a favorite hymn?" Leona was determined to get some guidance.

"I don't remember. I just want this over. Can't Roy just do what he does every Sunday?"

"Well, he could," Leona said, being careful on the slippery pine needles. "But the service needs to honor Mac." She felt ridiculous stating the obvious and wanted to say more, but her sister looked too pitiful to push.

Doyle was going toward the barn carrying a feed bucket just as the sisters came through the pines. The emus threw back their heads and stepped anxiously about, both making an unsettling drumming sound that came from deep inside their chests. Leona thought it was as if they, too, were nervous about Dean's absence.

"No sign?" Fern called out.

"Nope," he said.

Leona had been avoiding Doyle, hoping to quell the feelings she had for him, but she couldn't help but think how even in jeans, he looked distinguished.

"Doyle," she said, "I'm meeting with Roy this afternoon about Mac's service. He needs something to go on—stories, anecdotes, anything. I could use help."

"Oh, for heaven's sake, don't drag him into this," Fern said low enough so only Leona could hear.

Doyle stuck his head out the barn door. "I'll help if I can."

Back at the house, Doyle and Fern squirmed in the kitchen chairs like two outlaws brought in for questioning.

"How can we go through with this funeral without Dean?" Fern said.

"It's too late to postpone," Leona said, taking a seat across from them with her notebook. "It's in the paper. Now, talk to me about Mac."

Doyle took off his ball cap. He ran a hand through his thick gray hair and fiddled with the cap. "Mac liked to stir things up." He laughed. "We called it raising hell back then, but it was all pretty tame."

"Tame," Fern said, like the word set off an alarm. She straightened up. "What did you and Mac McQueen ever do that was tame?"

"Oh, we weren't that bad." Doyle scratched his ear. He gave her a shy glance. "You were with us half the time."

"I was with you all the time. We're lucky we survived your hotrod driving." She buried her head in her hands, closed her eyes, and propped her elbows on the table. "Or, I guess we are." She talked through her fingers.

Doyle cleared his throat. "Leona, tell the preacher that Mac was a natural athlete. That he could have played pro ball."

"But he volunteered to serve his country," Leona said, glad to have something to write down.

Fern threw her head back, "His daddy volunteered him. Mac didn't have a choice."

"He had a choice," Doyle said, not shying from Fern. "He signed up."

"You think he wanted to go?" She challenged him. "From the beginning?"

"I think he didn't want not to go," Doyle said. "Mac wanted to prove something to his old man, maybe even to himself. He always said playing ball came too easy." Doyle shrugged, "He wanted to see what he could do. You know all this, Fernie. Good God Almighty. We talked about it a million times."

Leona had wondered about Fern's true feelings for Doyle after seeing them embrace the night the men came with the news about Mac. She'd thought there might still be a romantic spark between them. But here they sat. Two ornery old friends who bickered like siblings. Their thoughts flowing from the same stream. Leona could imagine Mac with them. He was with them now. Perhaps they'd been reaching for him when they found each other all those years ago.

"Doyle, do you know if Mac had a favorite hymn?" Leona asked.

"Anything by Johnny Cash," Doyle said.

"Ha," Fern said. "Yeah, tell Roy that."

"This is Mac's memorial service," Leona said, suddenly worried that neither of them was going to be any help at all. "I know you both are worn out and worried about Dean. So am I. But Mac deserves consideration. He deserves to be honored."

"I read some of Mac's letters the other day," Fern said, looking down at her hands.

"Remember the one he wrote you about that old farmer he saw over there?" Doyle said. "He said the guy reminded him of his daddy?"

Fern nodded.

"I have some letters." Doyle reached over and shook the back of Fern's chair. "One he wrote me about you."

She turned to him. "About what?"

"I'll bring it by." Doyle grabbed his cap. He stepped to the door but stopped short of leaving. "Leona, tell the preacher Mac fought and died for what he believed in. I'm not talking about *our* side or *their* side. I'm saying he fought for his men and the people caught in the middle. His letters were full of stories about the guys in his platoon who shouldn't have been over there, and the farmers, and the mothers and the children trying to live in a warzone. He fought to keep them alive, out of harm's way. That was his war, and it broke his heart. He lost everything for it." He looked at Fern. "Everything."

Across topped the steeple of New Hope Methodist. Leona admired the white clapboard church and the unpretentious elongated stained-glass windows. Longleaf pines filtered heat from the afternoon sun. Slick rusty-brown pine needles and cones littered the churchyard. She walked along the low rail fence bordering the graveyard. The family plot where Grandma and Grandpa Barrett, her father, and her brother were buried was overgrown and neglected. She opened up her notebook and wrote herself a reminder to get flowers for their graves.

Inside the church she followed a hallway to the preacher's office. The drab walls and dull lighting seemed inhospitable compared to the lovely exterior. The clip-clop of her footsteps on the linoleum squares sounded quarrelsome and out of place. The office door stood open. "Roy?"

"You're early." He came in behind her.

"Well, I thought we'd talk before Geraldine and Wilson got here."

Roy appeared more rumpled than usual, but his office was neat even with moving boxes lining the walls. "How long have you been in Carthage?"

He dropped into the worn brown leather swivel chair behind the scarred cherry desk. "Almost six months."

Leona smiled. "You'll be the first nonprofit project for Barrett House of Design, how about that?"

"Thank you," he said. "I accept your benevolence."

Two framed photographs sat catty-corner to one another on the bookshelf. Hannah as a toddler, and a wedding photograph of a slim-faced Roy and a wide-eyed bride with a Farah Fawcett hairdo. Leona picked up the wedding photograph for a closer look. "She's beautiful," she said.

"Yes, she was," he said. "Inside and out."

"How long have you been a widower?"

"Two years."

Leona put the photograph back. "Not that long."

"Sometimes it seems longer, sometimes not," he said.

She sat across from him in a dingy yellow chair in need of reupholstering.

"Roy, we don't have much time, so I'll get right to it. Fern told me she gave you the background behind her feud with Geraldine. I don't blame Geraldine for her anger. No one was more upset with Fern than I was, but we've got to stick to the matter at hand. Mac deserves to be buried with dignity and honor, without Geraldine's drama. She was always a silly girl, and I have no doubt she's grown into a silly woman. The fact is: Fern was Mac's wife. She is up front and center here, and Dean too, regardless of what we all know."

Roy sat up, "Is Dean back?"

"No, but we don't want Geraldine to know he's missing. We'll present her with our plan. I am open to small changes, but nothing monumental, and I will not tolerate her," she paused, "or anyone, disparaging my sister."

Leona's words had barely left her mouth when Geraldine and Wilson appeared at the door. The girl Geraldine used to be had aged into a puffy, wrinkled woman, but the dark beady eyes were unmistakable.

"I wanted this to be a private meeting, Reverend Puckett," Geraldine said, turning her head away from Leona and lowering herself into a chair on the far side of the desk. Wilson hesitated, but finally sat in the middle chair.

"Mrs. McLeod, you know Leona is working with me on the service. I thought it made sense for her to be here," Roy said.

"I was telling Reverend Puckett that our goal here is to give Mac the respectful burial he deserves," Leona said.

"I'm tired of you trying to take over this whole thing," Geraldine said. "And if you want to respect Mac, then you and yours would do right and stay away."

Wilson sighed but stayed quiet.

Hostility cued Leona's composure, another survival skill she'd mastered as a child of volatile parents. "If you are trying to shock Reverend Puckett, please know that he is aware of the cause of your animosity toward my sister and, because he is a true Christian man, he will not tolerate your attempt to turn this into a circus fit for the tabloids."

Geraldine glared. "Aren't you one to talk. You think we don't know about Ned? It's been all over the papers. And let me tell you something. I will not sit back and pretend that Fern Barrett is anything other than a …"

"Let us pray," Roy's booming voice startled them into silence. He rose, knocking his chair back against the credenza. Books fell like dominos. He lifted his arms into the air and closed his eyes. "Remind us, dear Lord, that we are all sinners and strengthen our hearts to hold our sorrows. Take our pride out of play and calm the storms that cloud our view. Let us remember our holy duty to honor Mac McQueen, your brave son. In Jesus's name, we pray, Amen."

"Amen," said Wilson.

Roy opened his eyes but avoided Leona's stare.

"Okay. Now," he said. His preacher voice defied interruption. "We have a soul to celebrate. We must honor this man. *That* is my mission." He turned to Geraldine. His voice softened. "I know you're hurting, but we've got to put earthly slights aside and do right by your brother."

Geraldine's lips quivered. Her heavy mascara and red rouge only brought attention to early wrinkles. "Fern ought to do right by him and not show her face."

"Do you doubt your brother's love for his wife?" Roy asked, sitting back down.

Geraldine looked down at her lap. "No."

"Neither do I," Roy said.

Roy's face flashed bright red. Leona couldn't help but smile. Roy loves Fern. She opened her notebook and began to explain the protocol for the military burial—the honor guard, pallbearers, and the twenty-one-gun salute. She told them that Nita Cox would lead the congregation in singing "Amazing Grace," and a bagpiper from Sandhill's Community College would play as they moved from the church to the gravesite, where taps would be performed by a bugler from Fort Bragg.

"I wonder if he knows 'Danny Boy' on the bagpipes," Geraldine said. "Daddy used to sing that."

"I imagine so," said Leona. "I'll ask."

"Tell me about your brother," Roy said. His gentle voice soothed the room.

"He wanted to be somebody," Geraldine said. "He wanted to be the best. The best ball player, the best brother, son. Husband. Mac wanted to do it all, see it all. When the Army told me how he always volunteered to go on those missions, I wasn't one bit surprised. There's a man coming Sunday from New York who was in Mac's platoon. He said Mac would chase a helicopter down if it tried to lift off without him."

She began to cry. "I gave up years ago thinking he was still alive. A lot of people think we still have men over there, but I knew Mac would have found a way home. There's just something so final about this. And, Leona, I'll be honest. I don't know how Fern can show her face. I had a cousin tell me that Doyle Blue is back in town." She leaned toward Roy. "Do you know what she did?"

"Geraldine, the preacher doesn't want to hear all that," Wilson said.

Roy rubbed his right ear like he wanted to turn the sound down. "The sins of others are always a great mystery while our own missteps seem like little accidents." Roy patted the top of the closed Bible in front of him, "And we are told time and time again that forgiveness is not just for the good of the sinner, but that it heals the heart of the accuser as well."

Roy cleared his throat. He went on to tell them his suggested Bible readings for the service. When all that needed to be decided had been agreed upon, Roy walked with them to the parking lot. Geraldine and Wilson made a hasty retreat.

"I suspect Fern's confession wasn't easy for you to hear," Leona said.

Roy stared up at the pines. Their fragile limbs, as if surprised by a strong breeze, shivered against the pure blue sky. "I'm afraid I didn't handle it very well."

"It's okay to be human, Roy, take it from one who's just learning."

He smiled. "That prayer in there was more for me than Geraldine. I have conflicting emotions. I think that's what you call it."

"Really?" Leona opened her car door. "My guess is you're not conflicted at all."

Fern

Carol Ann swore Fern would come to love her bedroom's new pale-blue walls, but even with her furniture back in place, Fern felt like a squatter. Dean had been missing for nine days. Nothing in the world seemed right. Fern's mind served up a carousel of worst-case scenarios. She was in no mood for blue walls or the heap of mess that still needed sorting from drawers and trunks. Bell-bottom jeans and flimsy peasant blouses were just more proof of the ridiculous girl she'd been. She was still ridiculous. What made her think she could be honest with a preacher?

Leona was with him now, talking about Mac's service. And Geraldine. She imagined the clucking of tongues.

"Miss Fern?"

She was relieved to hear Hannah hopping up the stairs. After last night, she'd worried Roy would find someone else to keep her.

The girl stuck her head in the door. "Is Dean back?" she asked.

"Not yet, sweetheart."

Hannah picked up a blue bottle of perfume from Fern's dresser.

"That was my mama's," Fern said. "She died when I was your age."

"Was she sick?"

"She was," Fern said. "For a long time."

Hannah undid the bottle and brought it to her nose, then walked it over to Fern. "Did she smell like this?"

"Yes," Fern said, surprised that what remained of her mother's ancient Evening in Paris perfume could bring back so much.

"My mama smelled like peaches," Hannah said. "I don't know why, but she did."

"Do you have many of your mother's things?"

"There are some boxes in the extra room. But I don't know what's in them."

Fern hugged her. "I know you miss her, honey. It hurts to remember, sometimes, but it's good, too. Remembering will keep your mama close. We'll ask your daddy if we can go through those boxes sometime. Would you like that?"

Hannah nodded, and pulled away. Fern knew to give her time to talk about her mother, not to push. She only hoped Roy wouldn't shut her out of his daughter's life, even if he was done with her.

Hannah went back to Fern's pile of castaways. She was fascinated by the old-timey clothes, and about half of all Fern discarded ended up going home with her.

"What's this?" She held up a shriveled piece of stretched elastic with little silver clasps hanging off the legs.

"That's a girdle, honey. Believe it or not, I used to fit into that old thing." Fern pulled a pair of nylons from the bottom of a drawer, "It was before panty hose, so you put your hose on and hooked them to it, and it held your belly in."

Hannah wiggled the girdle over her shorts. "Miss Brandi ought to get one."

"I wouldn't suggest that to her if I was you," Fern said. "You don't want to hurt Brandi's feelings."

Fern sat on her vanity bench with a stack of ratty t-shirts in her lap. Hannah waddled over, stiff legged in the tight Lycra. "Miss Fern, you know the other afternoon when we went to the Stop 'n Go, and you asked Miss Brandi if she'd heard from Dean? I believe she might have had her fingers crossed behind her back when she told you no."

Fern dumped the t-shirts from her lap onto the floor. "Come on. I need a slushie." They got halfway down the steps before she made Hannah take off the girdle.

Fern detected guilt on Brandi's pretty, round face when she and Hannah walked in the door. Fern wondered how she'd missed that look before.

"Hey," Fern said. "We need two slushies. Coke for one ..."

"And cherry for me," said Hannah.

Brandi sauntered over to the machine. "How are you all today? It's hot, ain't it? I heard it's supposed to rain later this afternoon. Did you get the roof back on your house?" She glanced over her shoulder at Fern.

"Yeah, they're working on the inside now. I've made them stay away from Dean's room."

"He wouldn't like it if people messed with his stuff," Hannah said.

Brandi handed Hannah her cherry slushie and started to fix Fern's. "Is Mr. Blue still feeding them birds?"

"Twice a day," Fern said.

"Hillary's sick," Hannah said.

Fern looked down at Hannah, who had her own fingers crossed behind her back. Brandi put Fern's slushie on the counter. "What's wrong with her?"

Hannah shrugged. "I think she misses Dean." The gas bell rang, and Brandi started the pump. Fern pulled out her wallet and gave Brandi her last five-dollar bill. "Brandi. Dean needs to come home," she said.

Two teenage boys came in the door, and Fern waited for them to go back to the drink cooler. Brandi handed her the change.

"I believe he's stayed gone long enough, don't you?" Fern said.

Brandi sighed. "If you went down to my house, you might see him."

"Thank you." With her hand on Hannah's shoulder, she guided her out the door. Hannah raised her hand to show Brandi her crossed fingers.

"Hillary's not really sick."

I wanna go." Hannah bounced on the car seat when Fern pulled into the driveway.

"Honey, you need to stay here with Belle. Dean and I need to have a grown-up talk."

"But I helped you find him, I ought to get to go."

"You did, and I promise you a big prize for that, but right now you need to go in the house, wake up Belle and tell her where I am. Leona will be home soon, tell her, too. Okay?" She took Hannah's hands in hers. "Thank you, my angel."

Fern drove to Brandi's brick rancher in West End. She could have kicked herself for not looking there before, but she never in her life imagined Brandi capable of keeping a secret. She spotted a shed in the woods behind the house. A closer look showed the white truck, barely visible through thick vines. Fern went to the front door. "Dean?" she called. "I know you're in there."

He opened the door. His eyes looked like he hadn't seen daylight in a while. "She ought not to have told you."

The drapes were pulled tight, and the only light came from the TV. Andy and Opie were down by the fishing hole. Fern wished she had Andy Griffith with her now. He always knew what to say to Opie. Of course, Fern didn't recall him ever having to talk to Opie about infidelity. Dean flopped onto the couch and stretched out. He stared at the TV like she was not in the room, like Andy and Opie were saying all he needed to hear.

Fern sat on the ottoman. A commercial came on. "Honey, can you turn that off and talk to me, please?"

He reached for the remote that lay on top of a stack of *National Enquirers* on the coffee table and turned off the television.

"Listen," she said. "I can't change what I did, and I wouldn't, because it would mean not having you. And I don't expect you to understand."

He stared at her. "Why, because there's something wrong with me?"

"No," she said. "Because what I did was not right, and I can barely understand it myself. But we've got to get through this. I want you home. I need you home. I'm not talking about you forgiving me. I just want you home."

"How am I going to show my face with people knowing what they know?"

In the past, Fern had used Mac's memory to encourage Dean, to remind him he came from brave stock. What would she do now? "Nobody blames you for what I did. You're a hardworking man who people know they can trust. Surely Brandi told you how worried people are. The whole town is looking for you. There's always going to be bullies like Whitey. But there are more good people than bad. And all the good people of this town love you."

"Have you talked to Mr. Frank?"

"Yes. He wants you back at work."

"Are Bill and Hillary all right?"

"They're fine. Doyle's been feeding them, looking in on them."

"Does he know I know?"

"Yes. He's been looking for you, too. Doyle came back to Carthage because of you." Tears pooled in Dean's eyes, and it was all she could do to keep her seat. "He's wanted to tell you the truth, but I wouldn't let him. I'm sorry. I was wrong about that, too. Please come home, honey."

His head fell back against the sofa. There was something different about him that Fern couldn't name.

"I believe I'll be staying here."

"Why would you do that?"

His eyes shifted and she followed his glaze. The bedroom door stood ajar. Rumpled sheets. "Lord God Almighty," Fern said softly.

"Will you come see Belle and Hannah? Please?" she stuttered.

He turned the TV back on. Andy grinned at Opie and tussled his hair. "I'll be over there after while," Dean said.

Fern wanted more. She wanted him to say *yes ma'am* and follow her out to the car. She wanted her child to act like a child. But the world had never much cared what she wanted. The world always had something else in mind altogether.

Dean

F rank put the fear of God in the rest of the boys. When Dean went back to work full time at the garage, nobody said one word about Whitey Whitehead.

Despite his mama begging him to move home, Dean stayed with Brandi. He liked what he'd found there. For the first time in his life, he was not agitated by all he didn't know. He was more than okay with the mystery, the wonder, the miracle of what had always, from the distance of hearsay, seemed mighty peculiar. Questions he wasn't certain had answers had come and gone without pause. If not for his mother's lie, Dean would be on top of the world. As it was, he spent his days with his head in an engine, where every part made sense, and his nights with Brandi, where every part remained a curiosity. Thoughts of his mama were pushed aside by recollections of what he'd done the night before and what he'd do again just as soon as he and Brandi got back to her house in the pines.

He missed the renovation work at Barrett House, but that was just the way it had to be. He didn't want anything to do with Doyle Blue, couldn't even stand the sight of the truck Doyle had all but said was his to keep. He drove an old car Mr. Frank loaned him.

He didn't want anything to do with Mac McQueen, either. When he went past the bench, he kept his eyes on the road. He'd told his mama and Brandi he was not going to the service. What was left of Mac McQueen would soon be buried six feet deep, and that suited Dean just fine. Mac had lied to him, too. Pretended to be his daddy. He had no use for liars.

At noon, he stepped outside the garage to clear his head of fumes. The town was done up for the Fourth of July. Red, white, and blue bunting hung from storefronts, and a banner stretched across the road inviting everyone to the parade.

American flags, stuck in the ground around the courthouse, hung limp in the summer heat. A white hearse came down McNeil Street where Dean stood. The sun hit the long side window and Dean made out the casket inside. The funeral for Mac McQueen was tomorrow. The hearse was headed toward the church. Dean knew from what the paper said that there wouldn't be any visitation at the funeral home, only a gathering at Barrett House after the service.

He planned to be as far from all the hoopla as he could get, but for the rest of the afternoon he couldn't shake the site of the coffin. The more he tried, the stronger the vision came, until he dropped his wrench to the ground and walked out of the garage.

He parked next to the preacher's car and ran up the front steps of the church. He wanted a word with the ghost who raised him. Just a word. The thick wood door creaked, and even when he tried to shut it easy, it closed hard and sent an echo up into the rafters.

Sun came through the stained glass behind the vestibule, lighting up Jesus. He reached out to the little children and looked like he might keep on reaching until he touched the flag-draped casket in front of the pulpit. Dean walked down the aisle and slipped into a pew.

He'd read the Army's report. He knew what the casket held. Femur. Rib. A handful of teeth. A skeletal hand. This was as close as he'd ever been to any solid part of the man. If Whitey hadn't of said nothing, Dean thought, I'd be sitting here right now thinking it was my daddy's bones in that box. Mac McQueen. Michael Dean McQueen. Mac McQueen's boy. He'd tried to join the Army because he wanted to be like him. Played ball. Wore his cap. Had his initials tattooed on the bulk of his right arm. He'd tried to do like he thought Mac would want him to. All his life, that's what he'd done. Any time he had ever been scared he'd told himself, "Daddy wasn't scared of nothing." All that time he didn't even know who his daddy was. Dean's hands trembled. He squeezed them into fists. He'd come this far, and he meant to say what he'd come to say.

"How come you didn't tell me the truth?" The church walls took in his question. "How come you to talk to me like you were my daddy?"

"Dean?"

Dean's heart about jumped out of his chest. He looked around and saw the preacher.

Roy, his shirtsleeves rolled up to his elbows and a thin black necktie hanging loose around his neck, came down the aisle and took a seat beside him. Dean remembered what Hannah had said about how her daddy knew stuff nobody else did because he talked right to God, and God talked back. Hannah claimed he'd read the Bible front to back. Dean wondered about what might be in the Bible, what God might have told the preacher. What all a preacher might know.

"I've thought wrong my whole life," Dean said, not knowing what else to say.

He didn't want to bawl in front of Preacher Roy, but he was about to. He tried to stand but the preacher grabbed his arm. His hand was big, but his grip stayed soft.

"Sit down, son." Roy swiveled the best he could and leaned into the pew in front of them causing the wood to squeal. He dropped his head. "Your mama told me about the situation. Dean, in a perfect world, Mac McQueen would be your father."

Dean looked away, ashamed of his wet face. "She run around on him while he was over there fighting in a war and she's going to burn in hell. Ain't that what the Bible says?" He started to shake.

"The Bible says," Roy put an arm around Dean's shoulder, "all have sinned and fallen short of the glory of God." The preacher let out a breath, one it seemed like he'd been holding for a long time. "Heaven's full of repented sinners and hell's overrun by a pious crowd ignorant of their evil ways."

Dean shook his head. "She lied. And she'd a kept on lying if Whitey hadn't told me the truth. A preacher ain't supposed to say it's all right for somebody to lie."

Preacher Roy loosened his grip. They leaned back against the pew, shoulder to shoulder. "Your mama was trying to get back to the right road. That lie was a shortcut. But lies never get you where you mean to go. You just get more and more lost."

"Well, she can stay lost."

"If that's the way it worked, son, I'd be out of a job." Preacher Roy lifted his head like he was talking to Jesus and the little children. "When we sin, we feel ashamed. We push away. That's what hell is, being out of God's light. But God doesn't want us in hell. He wants us near, no matter what."

"What if Hannah was to tell you a lie?" Dean said. "Wouldn't you be mad?"

The preacher clasped his hands together, made a little steeple with his fingers and held it against his chin. "I've told Hannah she never has to lie to me. Because when you love somebody, I mean really love somebody, no matter what they do, you still love them. You may not like what they've done, but you still love them." Tears welled up in Roy's eyes and he had trouble getting his words out. "A lie puts a burden on the heart of the one who tells it. We need to comfort, not condemn." He blinked as if he was coming awake. "You find out the truth about something and feel like a fool, but the truly foolish thing is to let pride overcome your own good sense." The preacher pursed his lips, grabbed the pew in front of them and shook it.

"Did you learn that reading the Bible?"

"It's all in there." Roy wrangled a handkerchief from his pocket and wiped his face. "But sometimes God has to knock you in the head to make you remember."

Dean pointed to the coffin. "He's been talking to me my whole life." He waited to see how the preacher took this news.

"Mac McQueen has been with you," Roy patted his chest, "in your heart."

"In my head," Dean said. "I've heard him in my head just as good as I'm hearing you right now." Preacher Roy nodded and smiled, not like he was laughing at him, but like he got what he was saying.

"He talked to you and you talked to him."

"Yes." Dean said. "Since I was a kid."

"He's always been there for you," Roy said. "Dean, has Hannah ever told you she's adopted?"

"Yeah. She said she never knew her other mama and daddy, the real ones, never even seen a picture of them, and if they walked in the door, she wouldn't know them."

"That's right," Roy said.

"But, even if this other fellow did come walking in the door, it's you who raised her, helped her along, listened to what she had to say. Even if he came back, you'd still be her real daddy, wouldn't you?"

"Yes," Roy said. "I'd still be her daddy. I'll always be her daddy."

Dean sat with the preacher's words, then nodded toward the coffin. "He'll always be mine. I reckon he adopted me."

Preacher Roy smiled. "I reckon he did."

It was mid-afternoon by the time Dean left the church. He pulled over at the courthouse and got out. A breeze came up and rustled the American flag that had been put beside the bench.

Dean didn't know how come he was at the bench. If Mac McQueen had wanted to talk, it looked like he would've talked at the church where what was left of him lay, but before Dean even took a seat, Mac spoke, loud and clear.

When did you start listening to Whitey Whitehead? Everybody knows he don't know his ass from third base.

Fern

Fern fried bacon for BLT's. Mac's funeral was tomorrow, and she didn't have the energy for a more complicated supper. She'd spent the day vacuuming, dusting, polishing, and doing anything else Leona and Carol Ann needed to get the house ready for the reception. There'd been a last-minute trip to Belk's in Southern Pines to find just the right frame for a picture of Mac to sit beside a vase of Belle's white peonies.

The long fold-out table Carol Ann commandeered from the church sat in the front room ready for the funeral essentials. Fried chicken. Ham biscuits. Banana pudding. Leona had ironed the tablecloth multiple times to get the creases out.

The kitchen's new spotless white cabinets and fancy countertops made Fern antsy, and she wiped up bacon grease as fast as it popped from the pan. Their mismatched dishes had been replaced with Leona's white ones with blue rims. Thankfully, the oak table had made the cut, and Fern had saved her favorite mugs from the Goodwill box. She'd also drawn the line at the cat clock. "It stays," she'd said.

Leona sat at the table with her list and a slim gold pen she gripped like a wand. Carol Ann, wearing one of Belle's aprons over her paisley blouse, tossed up a salad Fern wouldn't touch with a ten-foot pole—a can of tuna fish, barely cooked green beans, and two boiled eggs atop a bed of lettuce. "Are you still thinking we'll have around a hundred people?" Carol Ann asked Leona.

"Could be. Thank heavens the women from the church offered to help."

"I still can't believe you said yes," Fern said.

"These are people who knew Mac, Fern. Friends," Leona said.

"And it's good for business," Carol Ann said. "They can see what we've done in here." She wiped her hands on the towel slung over her shoulder and reached into her oversized Coach bag that took up considerable space on the kitchen table. She pulled out a small white box. "I got business cards, just something simple. I thought we might set them around."

Fern leaned over Leona's shoulder to study the raised script on heavy white stock.

Barrett House of Design, Leona Barrett Thomas, A.S.I.D.

"What in the world is A.S.I.D.?" Fern asked.

"American Society of Interior Design," Carol Ann said. "These are just something to get us started. We can do more later."

Leona cradled the card in her palm like something precious. "I don't know about putting them out, but …" She cleared her throat. "Thank you. This is something I never thought I'd see."

"You're welcome," Carol Ann said. "And, Fern, we're going to put you to work. You'll be earning your keep in no time."

"Well, you know I'm thrilled about that." Fern's sarcasm passed unnoticed. She arranged sandwiches and potato chips on three plates and then headed to Belle's new den, where she and Hannah were watching John Wayne's *True Grit* for about the hundredth time. The front room had become too fancy for a television, so Doyle enclosed the back porch for a TV room. When he showed up with a small greenhouse to sit beside the shed, Belle had even managed a weak Thank you.

Hannah and Belle hardly noticed when Fern put the plates on their trays. She carried hers out to the porch swing. Roy's living room light was on. She wondered if he would come after Hannah or just call for her to come home like he'd been doing. Balancing her anger at Roy with how badly she missed him kept her too confused to think clearly, not that she wanted to. Clear thought led to panic over Dean. He only came around for dinner when Brandi worked late. Fern planned to have a talk with Brandi. She didn't approve of them playing house. As soon as tomorrow got over with, Fern intended to get hold of all that had gotten away from her. First off, she would tell Leona and Carol Ann that she'd sling hash at the Waffle House before she'd work for the two of them, and second on the list was telling Doyle what he could do with his pathetic hangdog looks.

As if summoned by her thoughts, his Ford Explorer bumped up the driveway. Who she talked to on her front porch wasn't any of Roy Puckett's business, yet she stood and motioned for Doyle to drive around back.

She met him as he climbed out of the cab. "Have you talked to Dean?"

"No," he said. "He told Frank to tell me to leave him alone."

Doyle followed her to the glider. The old metal creaked with their weight but held. It came to Fern that she was past caring about Doyle seeing her barefoot in her brother's old clothes.

"Has he changed his mind about coming to the service?" Doyle asked.

"You'll have to ask Brandi," Fern said. "He talks to her, not me. I don't know what in the world he's doing down there."

Doyle bent forward and rested his elbows on his knees. He gave Fern a side-eyed glance and chuckled, "You don't?"

Fern got his meaning and shook her head. "Stop it. I can't handle that right now."

"He's grown, Fern."

Fern let out a sigh and swatted at a mosquito on her arm. It was early evening. The sky had turned silver blue.

"Listen," he said. "About tomorrow. I'd like to be there if it's okay with you."

His pitiful look made Fern want to shake him. "Now that Dean knows, I don't give a damn what anybody thinks." Roy's face came to her mind.

"Have you seen Geraldine?"

"No. Leona met with her and Roy at the church to go over the service. God only knows what she'll do tomorrow. But if she wants to have one of her fits, she'll just have at it. Doyle, I read one of Mac's last letters. I feel sure Geraldine told him about us."

Doyle got up and headed for his truck. The glider slid sideways. He came back and held out a letter addressed to him in Mac's bold scrawl. "This is the last letter I got. A month after he went missing."

"I can't," Fern said.

He sat down and took the pages out of the wrinkled airmail envelope. There was just enough light left to see Mac's words.

"Hey pal," Doyle read. "Did you fall into a sand trap over there and break your writing hand or what? Man, you'd hate it over here, no golf courses, no tennis courts. Haven't even seen one polo field or a porterhouse steak."

Fern wanted him to stop and not stop. Doyle knew Mac's cadence, and with her eyes shut, she could fully imagine the words coming from her husband's mouth.

"Listen, this is kind of tough, so I'll just say it. If Fern is done with me, if I'm out of the picture, I don't blame anybody but myself. But you've got to promise you'll take care of her. I can maybe stand it if you promise me that. If you make her happy, I'll put hard feelings away. I know it hurt her when I re-enlisted, but I didn't have a choice. I'd never forgive myself if I didn't see this through.

You know as well as I do, she deserves more than she's ever had, not that I think I'm some kind of prize. Maybe I should have stepped to the side way back when you said you liked her first, but I'm not that nice of a guy. (I see you nodding.) Doyle, just do right by her, will you? I may be talking crazy. I love my wife, and I always will, and don't you ever doubt that she loves me, but it's hell on earth over here and looking more and more like I'm the devil in charge. It's hard to keep my head straight. I've seen men blown to pieces without a second's warning. There's no time for bullshit. I don't see how anybody leaves here and goes back home and takes up where they left off. I don't expect I will.

Okay, they're yelling for me, got to drop this in the box. Don't let me down, buddy."

Fern took the letter from him. Her throat constricted and she could hardly speak. "He killed himself. He knew and he killed himself."

Doyle shook his head. "No."

"Oh, my God." Fern pitched forward, thinking she might be sick. Doyle's hand came to rest flat on her back, not pushing, but there.

"Listen," he said. "Whatever he knew, whatever he thought, he didn't blame you. He's talking to me. He knew it was me."

"He killed himself," Fern said. "I've always known I killed him."

"No, Fern," Doyle said. "The chopper went down. They got shot down. He died fighting."

Fern's whole life reshuffled. What was, what could have been.

"When did you get this?" She searched for a date.

"After I met you in Pittsboro."

"Why didn't you tell me?"

Doyle dropped his head into his hands. "I was too ashamed. God Almighty, remember that day at the diner? I was a damn coward. Somebody had told old man Chapman about us, could have been Geraldine, I don't know. But he let me know right quick that all he had to do was make one telephone call and I'd be A-1, on the next plane to Vietnam. He said even if the war was about over, he'd make sure I was in the thick of it."

Doyle wiped his face on his sleeve. "Mac spoke to me from the grave with this letter. He asked me to do right by you, and I ran off to save my own ass. Even after Mama called and told me you were pregnant. I let Mac down, let you down, Dean, everybody. Oh, Lord," he said. "I haven't lived easy, Fern. I regret the biggest parts of my life."

Fern broke out in a sweat.

Doyle pointed to the letter she held in her shaky hand. "I dream about him, you know. It's always the same thing. He's dying and I don't save him. Don't get to him in time. Or in one dream, he's drowning in a black-water pond, and I don't reach out far enough, too afraid of slipping in myself. I've watched him die a hundred times."

"I dream he catches us together," Fern said. "When I come awake, I'm always relieved it's a dream until I remember that if it wasn't, he'd be alive."

"When Mama told me you were having a baby, I knew good and well it was mine. Were you going to tell me? At the diner?"

"Yes."

"That day, if I'd said …"

"Doyle, don't …"

"Would you have come away with me?"

"I was scared. So, yes. Maybe. But who would we have become? Martha and your child wouldn't have just vanished off the face of the earth." She stopped herself from saying *like Mac*. "We wouldn't have had any kind of life together."

"And what kind have we had apart?"

The last bit of daylight faded. The yellow tails of fireflies blinked and disappeared like nervous questions searching for answers.

"I've thought so much about that first day," Fern said. "The day it snowed. Maybe we were trying to put our world back together, back to when it made sense, when it wasn't so hard and sad."

"That's how it felt," Doyle said. "I hate you went through all you did. Like Mac said, you deserved better."

"I never wanted the same as you," Fern said, crossing her arms, looking up at the faint stars. She ground a foot into the sandy dirt. "I would have never been happy leaving Belle, or this crazy old house. I've taken one step right, two steps wrong, but Dean has given me everything to live for. I stopped drinking because he needed me. I wouldn't have made it without him. I thank you for that."

Doyle looked up at the dark sky as if he wanted to see what Fern saw. "Dean reminds me of Mac, the way he goes after a thing with his whole heart."

"Mac would love those crazy birds."

Doyle laughed. "He would. One day Dean and I were down there watching them, and I realized I was talking to him like Mac used to talk to me. You know, telling him he could do anything he set his mind to. Remember, we used to call him 'Coach' when he got like that. He'd be awfully proud of how you've kept this place going, how you looked after James, now Belle. You rose, Fern. I just wish …"

"If wishes were ponies, all beggars would ride."

Doyle leaned back. "Don't we wish we had a nickel for every time Mac said that."

He pushed up from the glider like the visit had aged him. "I'd appreciate it if you could forgive me a little," he said with his back to her.

Fern reached out and took his hand. "I do. Now we need to start forgiving ourselves." She let go, and he left her in the full dark, glad, she imagined, to be rid of all he'd carried for so long.

L eona and Carol Ann sat at the kitchen table with a bottle of chardonnay.

"What did Doyle want?" Leona asked. Fern couldn't help but notice her suspicious tone.

"He's nervous about coming to the service tomorrow," Fern said, not ready to share the letter heavy in her pocket. The new stainless-steel refrigerator looked like something that ought to be in a restaurant, in Fern's opinion, but the roomy shelves made it easy for her to spot the chocolate milk. She poured herself a glass.

"Has he talked to Dean?" Carol Ann asked.

"He tried, but Dean won't have it," Fern said. "I hope eventually he'll give Doyle a chance. Lord knows what he'll do now that Brandi has a hold of him."

Leona and Carol Ann exchanged a glance.

"What?" Fern said.

"Well," Carol Ann said, "you didn't want him talking to Doyle, now you don't like Brandi."

"I know," Fern said. "I won't know what I want until tomorrow gets over with."

"Listen," Leona said, putting down her wine glass. "I think we should go up to the church. You need to see everything before there's a crowd."

By everything Fern knew she meant Mac's coffin.

"Roy gave me a key to the church."

"No. We'll go early tomorrow," she said, putting them off. She rinsed out her glass. "I'll see you all in the morning." She left Leona and Carol Ann with their chardonnay.

Thankfully, all the renovation hadn't changed the creaks in the stairs. Carol Ann claimed people wanted their homes to reflect the lives they wish they had. She said people believed if they lived in a certain kind of house, they'd be a certain kind of person. Fern wondered what it said about her that she preferred the house like it had been, without fresh paint and polished floors.

She crawled into bed and scrunched up in her quilt. She thought about Doyle's question. Would she have gone away with him? Thank God, he hadn't given her the chance.

Because of all she'd been through, the woman she was wasn't the girl she'd been. She'd had to face the truth about what she was capable of, good and bad. As hard as it had been to raise Dean alone, to live with what she'd done, she had become more of herself. With Doyle, she would have become less.

She took Mac's letter out of her pocket and held it to her chest.

If Mac had made it home, they would have raised Dean, had more children, been a family. Mac loved her. She was his, and he was hers. They would have lived with his ghosts, her sin, not as two innocents in an evergreen paradise, but as husband and wife in an imperfect world. Wasn't that the real lesson of Adam and Eve?

Fern sat up in bed, raised her window, and looked out at the dark night. "Mac, I believe you do talk to Dean. I believe you're out there. Help him, please. He needs you more than ever."

She rested her arms on the windowsill. If Dean would only forgive her, she'd never pine for Eden again.

Carol Ann and Leona had chosen a black crepe suit for Fern to wear to the service. While Leona wrapped Fern's hair into a chignon, Fern remembered the ruby studs and rummaged through her newly organized vanity drawer to find the little black box. She slipped the gold posts through her pierced ears.

Fern teared up off and on all morning. When Carol Ann said, "I know you're sad," Fern said, "It's not that." When Leona said, "I know you're nervous," Fern said, "It's not that."

There were no words for the muddle of emotions surging through her, head to heart.

They left the house with no time to spare in the old white limousine sent from the funeral home. "Thank the Lord it didn't rain," Carol Ann said on the way to the church.

"Maybe rain would keep the gawkers away," Fern said.

"Fern," Leona said. "Mac was loved and respected in this town. Today is about him." She patted Fern's knee as if to make up for the admonishment.

Belle commented on every rose bush and every clematis vine they passed like she was on a garden tour. It made Fern wonder if she remembered where they were going and why. They circled the courthouse. The flags meant to commemorate the Fourth of July on the courthouse lawn felt like a reprimand for how unpatriotic Fern felt on this day of remembrance for Mac.

The driver wove the limousine between tightly parked cars that filled the church parking lot. In the cramped vestibule Fern exchanged a nervous hello with Roy. He led the family in prayer, then down the aisle. Geraldine and Wilson kept their distance. She was glad to see Ned and Amanda. The pews were overflowing, but Fern looked past the leering faces to the bouquets of hydrangea, Queen Anne's lace, and spring-green bells of Ireland that sat on each sill of the arched stained-glass windows. Flowers ordered from Raleigh by Leona. Matching sprays in white wicker baskets sat at each end of the flag-draped coffin. Fern hadn't thought all white flowers with greenery sounded right when Leona described what she'd chosen, but of course they were perfect. Natural like Mac.

Geraldine's red, white and blue carnation wreath with a navy ribbon draped across it—*To My Loving Brother* in sparkly silver letters—had been pushed back and turned at an angle to lend the least damage.

Roy stepped behind the oak pulpit. He thumbed through his Bible and stumbled through a prayer. Fern wondered if the soldiers standing at attention along the back wall made him nervous or if he just couldn't stand being in the same space with her.

Geraldine had insisted on "The Battle Hymn of the
Republic." *His truth is marching on.* Truth. None of what Fern
saw around her felt the least bit true. It was like they were all
pretending there was a body in that coffin. Pretending she was
a faithful widow who deserved the town's pity. If Mac were
here, she thought, he'd say, "Get real."

Geraldine sat across the aisle with Wilson and a slew of
McQueen cousins stealing glances at Belle, Leona, and Fern,
who made a sparse display on the front pew on their side.
Behind them, Carol Ann sat with Hannah. Carol Ann squeezed
Fern's shoulder, letting her know she was near, but Fern's
mind was on who wasn't there and should be.

"Fern," Leona whispered. She nodded for Fern to turn
around. Dean, head hung and tilted to the side, hands in his
pockets, walked down the aisle. Sunlight streamed through the
windows, lighting his way. He wore the suit Fern had bought
him for James's funeral. His hair was slicked back, wet from a
shower and freshly combed. Leona motioned for him to sit by
her. Fern fought the urge to reach or speak, afraid of what he
might do. She heard whispering. Pews creaked.

He stepped around the flag draped coffin. Roy held out an
open hand, directing him to sit in one of the oversized chairs
beside the pulpit. Dean looked tired but steady.

Wilson hovered over Geraldine, who appeared to be having
a fit. Fern wondered if Doyle was there but didn't dare look
around to see. Roy closed his Bible and let the congregation
settle.

"Dean has some words he'd like to share with you," he
said.

Fern's heart pushed against her chest. She grabbed Belle's
frail hand and saw Leona take the other.

Behind the imposing pulpit, Dean seemed small. He cleared
his throat and glanced back at Roy, who nodded, urging him
to go on. Dean took in the congregation.

"Most of you all out there know your daddies. Some of
ya'll like 'em and some of you don't. I've known some daddies
I wouldn't want nothing to do with. But there are some good
ones, like Paul Williams sitting over there. I see him around
with his kids. And Preacher Roy, he's a good daddy."

Dean clutched the sides of the podium and leaned in. "Coming up, I made do with the daddy I had. I know you all see me up at the courthouse. I don't know when that bench was put up there because I was a baby and babies don't remember stuff like that, but I remember Mama showing it to me back when I was a little kid." Dean looked down, then raised his head. "See, I was scared about having to go to school and I told Mama I wasn't going. That's when she took me up to the courthouse and showed me the name carved in stone. Michael Dean McQueen. My name. She told me that bench was made for my daddy because of how brave he was. Well, I got to thinking I had some brave in me. I took a hold of that and went on, thinking when Daddy got back home, he'd be proud."

Dean stopped and turned his back to the congregation. Fern started to stand, to go to him, but Carol Ann put a hand on her shoulder. Dean turned back around.

"I've spent many an hour at that bench. And I know a lot of you here today think I'm half crazy, so what I'm about to say won't surprise you one damn bit." He nodded at Roy. "Sorry, preacher." He faced the congregation and cleared his throat. "I'm here to tell you that me and my daddy talk. I've sat on that bench and told him everything that's ever happened in my life, the good and the bad. I tell him about people making fun of me 'cause I'm different. I don't think like everybody else. He says ain't nothing wrong with different, and not to worry about what people say."

"There's nothing I can't say to him, and there's nothing he can't say to me. I'm here to tell you there are a lot of you out there who've never had the daddy I've had, somebody who listens, and helps you along."

Dean stared down at the coffin. "I've asked him where he's at." His voice broke. "I reckon he just didn't have the heart to tell me he was gone for good."

The church was so still Dean could whisper and be heard.

"Some of you out there think this is just me being crazy. That there's no way I've been talking to somebody killed in a war, but I'm telling you what I know, and I'll tell you something else. A daddy is somebody who talks to you like he's talked to me. I know that for a fact, so you all can say what you want to, but I know what I know."

Dean stepped down from behind the pulpit and rested his hands on the flag-draped coffin. "This is my daddy and that's the damn truth and that's all I've got to say about it. Amen."

Nita Cox's pure voice rose in "Amazing Grace" and the choir joined in. Fern thought she might burst. There was too much inside her for one body to hold—sorrow, remorse, pride, relief, acceptance—all she'd tried to name for so long. She stumbled, weak-kneed, past the coffin to where Roy held Dean in a tight hug. Roy guided her to her son. Fern kissed Dean's cheek and tasted salty tears.

When they broke apart, the congregation was well into the second verse of "Amazing Grace." Roy handed Fern his handkerchief. Doyle, standing in the back row, nodded to her before slipping out a side door. She studied the congregation. Row after row of people she'd known all her life, their faces lifted in a song of grace. She shifted her sight to the ground, but the voices coaxed her to raise her head high. Doris Whitlow, Eva Dunn, Ruby Frye, Mary and Fred Cameron, Polly Pruitt, Abe Flinchum. Everyone she'd ever known. Fern couldn't help but think how much they'd aged. How long had it been since she'd looked any one of them in the face? Yet she knew every verse of their lives by heart, and they knew hers. Together they were one song. One hymn.

Leona and Belle held a hymnal between them. Carol Ann, her arm around Hannah, sang loud and off-key.

The song ended, but the congregation stayed on their feet. Roy moved to the dais.

The soldiers took their places alongside the coffin, lifted it, and walked Mac solemnly down the center aisle. Roy led Dean and Fern to Belle and Leona. Geraldine stepped up to Dean. "Mac would be so proud to have a son like you," she whispered through her tears.

Dean mumbled his thanks and followed the procession. Geraldine motioned for Fern to go ahead of her. Hands reached out and Fern took them like she'd been away a long, long time and this was her welcome home. In the vestibule, she paused before following the coffin out into the bright sun.

"You all right with what I said in there?" Dean asked.

"Oh, honey, it was beautiful," Fern said. She took his arm. Roy walked behind them.

"Preacher Roy says it's not our place to judge. God forgives people and we're no better than God. I ain't mad no more."

She turned back to Roy, who acted as if he wasn't listening. She gave his arm a squeeze of thanks before going through the wooden gate to the cemetery.

The heels of Fern's new black pumps sank into the sandy soil. The bagpiper's "Danny Boy" drifted through the pines. She moved toward the green funeral home tent. Roy took his place behind the coffin, a Bible in his hands. Carol Ann, Hannah, and Leona helped Belle along. Leona had made baskets of flowers for the family graves. Belle bent to straighten forsythia branches that rested against her brother's tombstone. No one rushed her. Fern motioned for Brandi, Ned, and Amanda to join the family in the folding chairs that wobbled on the uneven ground.

It seemed everyone who came stayed for the burial. The air smelled of upturned earth and hothouse flowers. They gathered around, making the tent a solemn chamber. Fern reached a shy hand beneath the draped flag and was surprised by the coffin's warmth. Mac, encased in wood and steel.

A bugle sounded taps. The heavy notes pulsed through her, down her arm and into the wood, then back into her breaking heart. Fern's chest became so heavy she couldn't sit up. Leona braced her. "It's okay, Fern. It's okay," she whispered. "Let it out. I'll hold you." When the last of the bugle's notes faded, her hand dropped from the coffin. Leona pulled Fern gently back. Guns fired three shots, and Fern wanted them to stop. Mac wouldn't want such a showy display. She knew this because he'd come back to her fully alive and whole. His smell, his touch, his voice, his heart. His love. "Thank you," she whispered.

She looked up and met Roy's gaze. He nodded, bowed his head and began to pray.

Roy talked to God with ease. Like an old friend.

After his prayer, two solders lifted the flag and began their folding ceremony. *Boys, just boys. Mac's age back then.* When the pale, brown-eyed soldier with furrowed brow stood before her with the folded flag, she hesitated, but slowly accepted the thick triangle. Once it was hers alone, she pressed the flag, heavy and warm, to her chest.

Roy came up beside Fern, signaling it was time to leave. She stood and slid her hand over the warm wood one more time before walking back to the limousine. The ground no longer threatened to swallow her whole.

Inside the car, Belle patted Dean's knee. "You'd make a good preacher."

"I'm proud of you, Dean," Leona said.

Dean stared out the window. Fern wondered what he was thinking, and for the first time in a long time, she was not afraid to know.

"Are you okay?" Leona asked Fern.

She nodded. "I thought I'd settled Mac in my mind years ago, but I'd only hid from him." She wanted to say more, about how she hadn't let herself mourn her husband, how she'd never felt like she deserved to mourn him, how her fear of Dean knowing the truth made her put all truth away. She wanted to say these things, but learning to speak from an open heart not stilled by lies or remorse would take time.

The limousine made a slow loop around the courthouse. "We do the best we can," said Belle. She stared out the dusty window lit by a too-bright sun. "Matilda should be buried over there with Spencer," she said. "He loved her, I know he did, but I couldn't have her upsetting you children. I gave her what she wanted and told her if she didn't stay away, I'd have her put in jail for back taxes."

Belle turned from the window. "I should have told you all the truth," she said. "But you'd been through so much."

Dean, sprawled out on the dingy white leather seat across from them, shook his head. "Y'all got to quit lying all the time."

Leona had been right to accept help from New Hope's Ladies Auxiliary. By the time they got back to the house, platters of fried chicken, ham biscuits, and casseroles of every kind covered the table in the front room. Women Fern hadn't talked to in years worked in Leona's new kitchen like it was their own. She moved from one room to another as the house filled with people. She met the eyes of old friends, felt their touch, and heard over and over, "You should be so proud of Dean." Words she translated into, "We'll move on from here."

Roy and Ned were deep in conversation. Smiling, nodding. Fern felt Roy watching her. Belle had Amanda beside her on the settee. She held Amanda's arm with both hands like she might never let her go. Fern was sorry Paige hadn't come, but more than anyone, she understood how some things took time.

On her way to the kitchen, she ran into Geraldine. "I wonder if we might have a word," Geraldine said. "In private." Her eyes were wide and tired and circled with flakes of mascara.

Geraldine followed Fern through the kitchen where Agnes Muse piled another platter with ham biscuits. The curiosity on Agnes's face reminded Fern that anytime she thought she wasn't showing her true feelings she needed to find a mirror.

They made their way outside. Geraldine's black polyester pantsuit looked as if it might break out in a sweat. Fern led her to the glider, where the pecan tree offered a little shade.

"Dean is a good boy, and how he loves Mac means everything to me. It's like he really is Mac's flesh and blood, so I want you to know that I'm going to try as hard as I can to forgive you." Geraldine spoke in the high-pitched whimper she'd had ever since she was a child. She clasped her hands to her chest. "I get so sad sometimes thinking about Mac. I guess being mad at you gave me something to do with all that hurt."

Geraldine saying something that made sense shocked Fern. "I've been angry, too," Fern said, "with myself. Angry enough to forget what I lost. What we lost."

"You all were the most in love people I've ever known," Geraldine said. "And I realized listening to Dean, you were just a little more than children when you married."

"I was lucky," Fern said. "He was such a sweet boy, wasn't he?"

"Yes," Geraldine said, nodding. "And I see that in Dean. What he said up there today, why, it sounded just like Mac talking."

Fern was tempted to confront Geraldine. To let her know she knew about the letter she wrote Mac, but the fight had left her. "You know I loved him," Fern said. "You were there from the first days. Why, you were hiding in the bushes the first time we kissed."

Geraldine smiled. "I followed you all around like a puppy dog." She reached out and squeezed Fern's arm. "Dean said for us to come back. He said he'd take me to the bench, show me how he talks to Mac."

Making peace with Geraldine was one thing, spending more time with her quite another. Maybe that was penance. Fern stood and she and Geraldine made their way back to the house.

"I believe I'll stay out here for a few minutes," Fern said when they got to the back porch. Geraldine left her sitting on the steps.

Fern's insides churned and she imagined every new thing trying to find a rightful place. Mac laid to rest. Dean speaking his truth. Forgiveness at the church. Geraldine. Was it real? Would it last? Crows quarreled in the trees as if debating her questions. One of Belle's tabby cats stretched out in the shade, paying them no mind.

She heard somebody coming. A shadow showed itself. Roy.

"Hey," she said.

"I thought I'd find you out here," he said.

"I appreciate what you did for Dean."

A nervous smile spread across his face. "I only provided the pulpit." He buried his hands in his pockets, "I hope you were all right with it, I mean, maybe I ought to have spoken to you before."

Fern shook her head. "It was good for Dean to do it on his own. He sounded like a man up there today."

"He is, Fern. He's a good man. You raised him right."

"Do you believe what Dean says? That he hears Mac?"

Roy leaned against the stair railing. "I do. I've always been drawn to the mystery." Sun coming through the branches lit up his curls. "Faith and trust go hand in hand. Dean reminded me there's no room for foolish pride. We have to accept what we don't know and what we do know." He put a hand to his heart. "Here."

The crows gave up their quarrel and lifted from the trees in a rush. "I'm sorry I let you down the other night," he said.

"You're a preacher, Roy," Fern said, repeating the blunt words he'd said to her. "I don't expect you to see me the way you did before, but please know I'll do whatever it takes to keep you and Hannah in my life. Come to church. Sit on the front row. Whatever."

"Fern, you don't have to change a thing. Yes, I'm a preacher, but that night on the front porch I was nothing but a jealous man."

A new relief broke inside her. "That's not all bad."

He laughed. "You think not?"

"Yeah." They kept still, as if the moment might flee like that flock of crows. A hum of voices came from inside the house.

"This isn't the time," Roy said, "but there's more I'd like to say, if you're willing to hear me out."

It felt natural to stand and step to him. "I'm willing," she said. He put his arms around her and kissed the top of her head. If she lifted her face, they'd do more, but she wanted their first real kiss to be on the front porch, not the back.

"Hannah's telling anybody who'll listen about the tornado," Roy said. "It's sounding more and more like a movie of the week. I need you to help me make her understand she doesn't need to embellish quite so much."

She looked up at him. "You want me to teach your child to tell the truth?"

"Yes," he said. "That and anything else you think might help. I believe it's going to take us both, full time, to get her raised."

A slow heat consumed Fern, one that had nothing to do with the weather or middle age. This heat sprang from an untangled heart.

Dean

Evening came and the house stayed full. Folks who hadn't set foot inside Barrett House in years made themselves right at home.

Dean walked through the kitchen where his mama, Aunt Leona, Carol Ann and a passel of women stood slack-jawed as Brandi described how she made her famous Stop 'n Go biscuits. Seemed to Dean like the women should be tired from of all their talking, but it appeared they still had a lot to say. "Who needs more coffee?" his mama asked.

It was past time to feed Bill and Hillary. Dean eased out the back door. Doyle Blue's truck sat parked by the trailer. He came out of the barn with his eyes to the ground carrying an empty feed bucket. Dean met him at the fence gate.

Without looking up, Doyle said, "I liked what you said today."

"Well," Dean said. "I didn't mean no disrespect."

"I know," Doyle said. He faced his son. "I'd like to, well, I wish we could get back to being friends."

"I reckon we can," Dean said. "I ain't mad no more. I was, but I ain't now." Dean kicked at the dirt. "You know, even if we have a flock, I believe we'll be more in the feather and egg business than the meat and oil. Hannah and Belle won't stand for much else."

The emus pecked at their trough. When there was nothing left, they pecked at the wood for the longest time, like there might be one last bit of corn to be had.

Doyle nodded. "Sometimes you start out one way and end up another. And that's all right. We might be able to work out a deal with Carol Ann and Leona about the feathers they're so crazy about. And, Dean, you don't have to say yea or nay right now, but I hope you'll consider coming to work at Blue

Construction. You did a heck of a job getting Barrett House back in shape. You'd be your own boss, handle your own projects. Think on it, would you?"

"Yeah, I'll think on it," Dean said. He remembered Zig Ziglar's advice. *Success comes when opportunity meets preparation.* He needed to make more than he did at the garage if he was going to make an honest woman out of Brandi.

"You had anything to eat?"

"No," Doyle said.

"Well, come on up to the house, there's plenty."

"I don't know. That might not look right."

Dean shrugged. "Getting hung up on all that just messes up your mind. You're hungry and we got food. Come on." Doyle came through the gate and shut it behind him. They walked together through the pines. It was near dark, but Dean's mama had the back porch light on.

Epilogue

The Citizen-Times, July 24, 1998

Emus Escape Moore County Farm

The search is on for two Australian emus. The five-foot-tall birds escaped their enclosure on McReynolds Road in Carthage after their fence was damaged by a falling tree.

"That pine must have got shook by the storm and took its time falling," said Dean McQueen, owner of the emus known as Bill and Hillary.

Emu meat is popular due to a low fat content, and many believe emu oil has healing qualities. McQueen had planned to raise emus for profit, but says he changed his mind after becoming attached to the two he bought from Peavy Farm in Pittsboro. "They're odd, but there's something about them that makes you want them around. They ain't like any other birds you know."

Emus can't fly but can run at a speed of up to thirty miles an hour. They could be in the Moore County area or beyond.

McQueen offers this advice. "If you see them, don't chase them. They can outrun you, I guarantee. But if you have some corn, they'll walk right up to you. They'll follow you wherever you want to go."

The End

Special thanks

To Galax, Virginia, Mrs. Randall, Judi Nelson, Susanne Porter, Patty Weatherman Jones, Debbie Weatherman Cure, Carly Simon, Linda Rondstadt, Carole King, Cindy Gay, Carl Johnson, David Smith, Mimi Smith, Tobie Pate, Donna Dean Pitts, WRCB, David Muscari, Bill Johnson, Betsy Fox, Lawson Fox, Molly Duffy, Drew Duffy, Dale Edgerton, Walter Bennett, Paul Mihas, Peggy Payne, Geri Siliman, Brenda Tapia, William Friday, Zona Norwood, Hindman Settlement School, Silas House, Jason Howard, Mike Croley, Lee Smith, Sheila Kay Adams, Pam Duncan, The Raycom Bus, Elizabeth Baucom, Denise McTear, Kathie Llewellyn, Kory Wells, Gloria Ballard, Karen Alea Ford, Chris Bailey, Peggy Grover, Paul Babb, Stephanie Babb, Kathy Gardner-Jones, Anjay Williamson, Michele Reap, Kelly Graham, Lisa Grimes, Jerry Brown, Joyce Brown, David Williams, Barb Williams, Lisa Cupola, Beverly Williams, R.A. Allen, Marjorie Rhem, Elizabeth Cox, Courtney Santos, Bailey Meredith, Cary Holladay, John Bensko, Richard Bausch, Sonja Livingston, Kristin Iverson, Tom Russell, Lee K. Abbott, Frye Galliard, Nancy Gaillard, Louisiana, Coco Wilder, Alice Wilder, Emerson Rhudy, Stanley Wilder, Jean Coco, Ava Haymon, Eleanor Canon, Mary Mikell, Patti Snyder, Christine Kooi, Jan Boydstun, Lori Tucker, Victoria Robertson, UPC, Table Rock Writers, Jennie Moore Ivey, Vicki Brumback, Ruth Petty Jones, Susan Gregg Gilmore, Abigail DeWitt, Judy Goldman, John Bemis, Virginia Crank, Matraca Berg, Dawn Shamp, Amy Blumenthal, Philip Shabazz, Joseph Bathanti, Eamon McLoughlin, Becky Guynn, Karin Carlson, Marjorie Hudson, Sherry Bader, Judy Lessler, Pam Van Dyk, Elizabeth Palmerton, Sarah Boone, Mary Hart, Eric Braun, Georgann Eubanks, Donna Campbell, Cindy Campbell, Janequia Evans, Jennifer Evans, Janequia Evans, Susan Campbell, Sue Weaver-Dunlap, Denton Loving, Kathryn Milam, Laurel Ferejohn, Meagan Smith Lucas, M. Scott Douglass, Maggie Meredith, William Brock, Darnell Arnoult, Bryson Brock, Violet Meredith, Elizabeth Meredith, Laurie Meredith, Carolyn Buchan, Mama Nell Flinchum, Alice Leon, Scott Frye, Douglas Williams, Telisha Williams, Laura Schneider, Becki Vasquez, Andres Vasquez, Lucas Vasquez, Gavin Vasquez, Doug Williams, Annelle Williams, Perry Frye, Nell Frye, and especially Lee Meredith.

Thank you for the life lessons. Encouragement. Patience. Challenge. Belief. Inspiration. Example. Most of all, thank you for the journey. Thank you for the love.